A Ballad of Severed Souls

A Ballad of Severed Souls

Soul Bound Book One

This book contains varying degrees of the following: bodily injury, descriptions of war, consensual sexual content, grief, and death. Please read safely and responsibly.

A BALLAD OF SEVERED SOULS

Copyright © 2025 by Jodie Angell

All rights reserved. This book or any portion thereof may not be reproduced, distributed, or transmitted in any form or by any means without the express written consent of the copyright holder, except in the case of brief quotations for the purpose of reviews and certain other noncommercial uses permitted by copyright law.

This is a work of fiction. Names, characters, places, and incidents are a product of the author's imagination or are used fictitiously. Any resemblance to actual people, living or dead, or to businesses, companies, events, institutions, or locales is completely coincidental.

ISBN: 978-1-0686881-4-0

Cover design: Artscandare
Map illustration: Conor Busuttil
Le Major Font: Copyright © 2018 by Calamar.

ABOUT THE AUTHOR

Jodie Angell is from the rainy valleys of South Wales, whose love (after coffee, of course) has always been fantasy, romance, and a touch of darkness. She lives with her fiancé, but regularly visits her parents and their scrumptious Frenchie, Harvey.

She loves to read, crochet, play cosy games, and keep her plants alive. When she's doing none of those things, she'll be deep in writing or planning her next fictional world.

For Abel. My greatest gift.
May you grow to love stories as much as I do.

The Realm of
Kirromund

Toichrist

Uldan Island

Saintlandsther

Temauten

Hastehill Isles

ONE

The Winter Solstice

Shivering in her fur coat, Adelina adjusted the stack of firewood clutched in her arms. Rolling hills and farms stretched ahead, and a bitter winter breeze whipped through the tallgrass.

She trudged along a beaten trail winding towards the village. Large pine trees dotted the fields and framed the small town, shielding the buildings from the harsh seasonal winds.

A hand clamped onto her shoulder. She leapt forward, almost losing her grip on the wood as a scream escaped her mouth. A hearty laugh filled the air as Damir, her best friend, hunched over, holding his stomach.

"That's not funny." She pouted and planted her gloved hand on her hip.

Damir smirked, then tucked his hand into the nook of her elbow. "Come on. We mustn't be late. Your ma's expecting us at noon."

"She's been preparing for this lunch all week—says it's important for me to remember where I come from and be grateful for what I have, especially right now." As they drew nearer to the village, Adelina's stomach rumbled. The scent of warm, fresh bread mixed with the woodsy aroma of rosemary wafted through the air. "Seems as if the whole town is getting ready for the solstice."

They hurried along the path towards an iron archway. A weathered stone wall marked the perimeter of the settlement. Snow blanketed the top, blemished by the small tracks of robins. Jutting out of the ground was a signpost with a quaint message etched into its rough surface. *Welcome to Aramoor. Home to Temauten's famous rosemary twist.*

"She's right. The winter solstice is a time for us to forget what lies beyond these walls." Damir scooped up a handful of snow, patted it into a tight ball, then launched it in Adelina's direction.

She ducked out of the way, her boots skidding on the ice. A boisterous laugh escaped her lips as she tumbled into the shrubs, sending snow and logs into the air.

"Ad! Are you okay?" Stifling a chuckle, he stuck his hand out. He hoisted her out of the bush, then brushed her down.

Adelina blew a strand of hair out of her face. "Ma is going to kill me. Lunch'll be ready and I won't have time to clean."

"I'll tell her it was me." He bent, gathered the logs, then led the way through the archway. Buildings lined either side of the path, and further into the town, laundry hung on rope between houses, from one window to another.

"It *was* you." She swatted him on the arm. "Do you think it'll be hard—the test? It's in three days, and I can't even begin to comprehend—"

"We ought not worry about it now, when a feast awaits us." He strode along the frosted cobbles in the direction of Adelina's home.

She sighed, thoughts of the impending test festering in her mind like a cloud that wouldn't pass. As she hurried after him, the question burrowed into her stomach, heavy and immovable. What if she was the person who Filip Tarasov was looking for?

An influential and wealthy nobleman who lived in Toichrist, north of Temauten, his name sent shivers down her spine. He possessed a strong, ancient power known as *nether*. The test was used to identify the long-lost other half of his power, one that shared an unbreakable, magnetic bond. They called it *astral*.

Rubbing her fingers up and down her arms, she wondered if astral flowed within her veins. She shook her head and dropped her hands to her sides. There was no history of magic in her family, nor anyone in the small village in which they lived.

When they reached the Orlov home, Damir opened the door for her, and they were greeted by warmth emanating from the large stove in the centre of the room. A layer of white-painted pebbles covered the brick frame of the oven, keeping the surface cool to the touch. Inside the opening, stood two pots, simmering.

"The bread smells fantastic, Ma," Adelina chimed as she kissed her mother's cheeks. Her gaze wandered to the fresh loaf resting on the wire rack on the table beside them.

Velinka held her daughter at arms-length and tutted. "Oh, look at you. Snow everywhere. Damir, are your parents joining us?"

He dropped the logs into a basket, removed his ushanka from his head, then shook her hand. "Yes, they'll be around any time now."

Velinka checked her leather-strap watch, then flattened her apron. "The stew will be ready in a few minutes." She took a towel, folded it several times, then gripped the pot's handle and pulled it out of the stove to inspect.

Adelina handed her mother a wooden spoon to stir the beef stew with.

"Be a dear and fetch the plates and cutlery." She gestured to her daughter. "Lay the table and grab a bottle of vodka from the cupboard."

When a knock sounded at the door, Velinka placed the pot back into the stove, then crossed the room to answer. Jasen and Mirelle Litvin, Damir's parents, stood in the entrance with bright smiles upon their faces.

"These are for you, Velinka." Jasen handed her a bouquet of pansies.

"Oh, there was no need to bring flowers."

"You have prepared a wonderful feast for us. Please, I insist."

"Very well." She took the bouquet as a warm smile spread across her lips, then rummaged in the cupboard for a vase. Once she'd filled it with water, she settled the pansies inside.

Velinka returned to Jasen, and offered her hand to him, which he shook. He and his wife removed their coats, ushankas, and gloves, hung them on the coat rack, then stepped into the living area.

"Please sit, everyone. Dinner will be served momentarily." Velinka gestured to the wooden chairs around the large oak table.

Mirelle kissed her on each cheek, then took a seat beside her husband.

Once she finished dressing the table, Adelina relaxed into her chair next to Damir. Her stomach groaned loudly, and her mouth watered in anticipation—her mother's rosemary twist was the finest in the village, although she was modest herself.

The door flung open, and Daro Orlov strode in with his younger daughter, Tihana, in tow. "Afternoon, everyone. Please excuse my tardiness. I've been busy at the workshop."

He crossed the room, embraced his wife, and planted a gentle kiss on her cheek.

Tihana removed her out-clothes, then scooted in next to her sister at the dinner table. Her hair was braided down the length of her back, and her cheeks were rosy from the chilly winter breeze.

"How's the business treating you?" Jasen asked.

"There's a steady flow of customers. Not only am I making new stoves, but I'm servicing now, too."

"You're quite the successful businessman. The whole town is talking about you." Mirelle smiled.

Velinka unscrewed the bottle of vodka, then poured a glass for everyone. "Today, we celebrate prosperity and the winter solstice. Please join me in a toast for another fruitful year. And let's not forget Adelina and Damir's test in a few days. I'm sure you'll both be fine."

A ripple of anxiety rose from the pit of Adelina's stomach at the thought of the test.

"I'll do the test, as is expected of me. It happens every year, and no one with astral magic is ever found." She injected as much confidence into her tone as she could. "And if they do find the person who has it—however small the possibility—they'll have a lot to deal with."

Her gaze focused on her mother, who shrunk a fraction in her chair.

"They'd be taken away from their family, everything they've ever known. If the test shows they have astral magic, how could they trust Filip's intensions? We all know he is a powerful man, and with an astral wielder by his side, he would be at his strongest. I pray it isn't you. A life of subservience is not what I envision for you." She narrowed her gaze on Adelina.

From the corner of her eye, Adelina spotted Damir lowering his head. In her case, she wouldn't just lose her family, but him too.

"Whoever is the wielder, I hope they would choose to find the light in the darkness, that they will do what they can to help people," she said, although her voice was small. She straightened her shoulders and lifted her chin. "If Filip wants power, he needs to be reminded of those below him—those who need wielders."

Silence hung over the table—the genial atmosphere from a few moments ago turned tense.

Velinka cleared her throat, plastered a large smile on her face, then clasped her cup between her hands and gulped a large mouthful. Clomping the cup beside her plate, she dished up the beef stew. Steam plumed from the bowls of food as she set them in front of each guest.

The two families waited as she turned to carve the fresh rosemary twist into thick slices. She stacked them onto a plate and placed it in the centre of the table.

"Tuck in," she said—her forehead furrowing.

Adelina stretched across the table, then clasped her mother's hand. "It'll be fine. Don't worry."

Nodding, Velinka brought a spoonful of food to her mouth.

Adelina grabbed her bread and dunked it into the hearty stew. She took a large bite, savouring the sweetness of the caramelised onions, the earthiness of bay leaves, and the smoky heat of paprika, which all complimented the lean beef. She moaned approval as her tastebuds buzzed. "This is wonderful."

Velinka blushed, and her shoulders relaxed. "Thank you, dear. Daro, my love, have you received word from Pyotr? Are he and the wife all right since their stove broke down a few weeks ago?"

Daro paused with his spoon halfway to his mouth. A silence fell over the dinner table.

He placed his cutlery in the bowl and cleared his throat. "There was a crack in the flue's brickwork, which is dangerous. They're under strict instruction not to use it until it's replaced."

Jasen scratched his chin and leaned back in his chair. "I've seen him stumbling out of the tavern at *all* hours of the evening. I feel for his wife—"

"Darling, we shouldn't speak ill of the neighbours." Mirelle placed her dainty hand on top of her husband's and raised her brows.

"No, it's quite all right," Velinka said. "Daro agreed to repair the stove if Pyotr could agree to pay in partial sums."

Jasen tutted. "Good luck, but I wouldn't hold him to it."

While the guests finished the meals and vodka, Adelina wriggled in her chair, eager to be excused. Damir cocked an eyebrow at her, which she returned with a playful glare.

Tihana hopped up from her chair and took the empty bowls to the kitchen sink while the chatter continued at the table.

Daro leaned closer to his wife and kissed her warmly. "Lunch was splendid as always."

She patted his arm, then rose, took off her apron, and hung it on a hook by the kitchen door. "How about another drink?"

As quickly as the words left her mouth, the glasses were filled with vodka. The adults remained in conversation, Tihana disappeared into her bedroom, and Adelina escorted Damir to the chairs on the porch.

Her stomach was warm, and her head fuzzy from the second helping of vodka. The alcohol dulled the bitterness of the winter breeze nipping at her cheeks, and alongside it, muted her inhibitions.

She drew a knitted blanket over their laps and cradled the glass to her chest. Damir swigged the last of his drink, then placed the cup on the wooden table beside them.

He turned to face her and hoisted the covering up to his chin. "Are you looking forward to the celebrations this evening?"

A Ballad of Severed Souls

"The villagers dance around a giant tree, light a bonfire, eat loads of food, and drink their body weight in alcohol." She laughed. "What's not to like?"

"I'm glad I get to spend it with you." His gaze deepened.

Heat rising in her face, she nestled into him. They'd known each other for most of their lives, but of late, their friendship was turning into something more. She wasn't sure, but she liked it. As the alcohol warmed her body, she admitted she was glad for the evolving feelings. He draped his arm around her, holding her close to his chest as they watched the snow fall over Aramoor.

As the sun set, melodic tunes of carollers echoed through the village. A group of people dressed in animal skins, horns, and straw masks strolled down the streets, rapped on doors, and recited poetry.

Songs of prosperity were sung, well-wishing the neighbours and bountiful harvest to the men and their wives. Good husbands were wished for young girls, and good wives for boys. Some tunes carried promises of health to the ailing, and cheery folk danced through the streets. Musicians played their flutes and fiddles, creating a lilting, bright medley.

Adelina tucked her hand into the crook of Damir's elbow as he escorted her towards the bonfire. They passed other families who'd set up market stalls, selling candy, toys, and housewares as the dancers' costumes came into sight.

"This has to be one of my favourite parts of the solstice!" Tihana skipped ahead, always keeping within sight. She joined the goat, bear, and wolf-costumed performers in their ritualistic dance in front of the oak tree in the centre of the village.

Adelina smiled warmly as she watched her little sister. Damir led her to a cluster of wooden stools dotted around a stack of logs and twigs.

They sat beside each other and were joined by their parents.

Velinka rested her hand on her daughter's knee. "Did you know a lot of marriages are arranged at the winter solstice?" She winked.

"Mother." Adelina's cheeks burned.

Damir would've heard, but kept a straight face, and flattened his coat with the palms of his hands.

An elderly member of the community, Radek, stood in front of the unlit bonfire and turned to face the gathering crowd. The music dwindled.

"Thank you all for contributing to another fine winter solstice." His eyes twinkled and crow's feet sprouted from the outer corners. "It is the time of year in which friends, family, and neighbours gather to celebrate a prosperous year, but to also banish negative influences we do not wish to carry with us into the next one. Together, we must get rid of things no longer serving us, no matter how big or small—a job no longer fruitful, an oven no longer warming the home, sins keeping us from the light. As a community, we invite a new season into our lives. A new sun will be born with the New Year."

The crowd cheered as the performers stepped into a line beside Radek.

A Ballad of Severed Souls

"Today, we look upon the goat and see Thor's personal chariot goats. They're eaten at night and resurrected each morning—let this symbolise prosperity and fertility within Aramoor." Radek gestured to the performer wearing grey canvas clothing, and goat horns upon his head.

The performer picked up a lit, staked torch and tossed it onto the bonfire, creating sparks of orange flames. The gathered villagers clapped in applause.

"However, we must not forget the dangers forever present. Evil forces may attempt to steer us from our path of righteousness. May our wit and courage continue to overcome this in the New Year." Radek gestured to the performer wearing a necklace of sharp teeth, and a thick wolf's pelt draped over his shoulders. The performer bent, grabbed the next torch, then threw it into the crackling fire.

The final actor, draped in brown bear fur, danced goofily in front of the children, who squealed and applauded with approval.

"Look upon the bear and banish your fears and forces of evil!"

His last word boomed across the village square. The crowd rose to their feet, threw their arms into the air, and shouted with joy.

Velinka hugged her children, then kissed her husband on the cheek.

Damir turned to Adelina and pulled her into a gentle embrace. Her heart swelled with fondness.

Sweets were offered to the children while adults gathered around the fire, sipping glasses of vodka and trading resolutions and promises for the future.

Adelina took Damir by the arm and steered him towards a line of three food stalls. "Where shall we start?"

"Dessert first." He grinned, then turned to face the woman manning the first stand. "Two rogaliki, please."

The woman nodded and plopped the flaky, horn-shaped pastry onto paper plates. Damir paid her, took the plates, then handed one to Adelina.

She placed the sweet treat into her mouth, then moaned with delight. "My favourite part of the festival is the food!"

"Wait until you have the baranki." He steered her towards the next stall as she wiped her mouth with the back of her hand.

"I'll pay for these." Her gaze fell upon the freshly cooked bagels stacked on trays. Beside them were large pots of jam and soured cream.

The stall owner leaned forward and beamed. "My bread 'as caught ye eye, 'as it?"

"How much for two?" Adelina stood on her tiptoes and sniffed the yeasty, warm aroma.

"Tha'll be three ruble, miss." The woman served the bread wrapped in paper, then spooned a dollop of jam and sour cream into small paper pots for them to take.

Adelina handed her the coins, picked up the food, and sat on a nearby stool beside Damir.

Tearing the bagel in half, she dunked one end into the jam, then bit off a large chunk. "I wish we could have this every day."

"We have the spring equinox in March." Damir eyed her and scoffed down the last of his bagel.

A Ballad of Severed Souls

"There'll be flowers to buy, but not as much food." She shrugged. Her stomach grew fuller, but from the corners of her eyes, the final stall beckoned her.

"Got room for one more?" He nudged her gently. "The last one's the best. A giant round pie filled with beef."

"Maybe we should've started there first." She laughed.

"I'll be right back." He jumped to his feet and dashed to the far-right stall.

Moments later, he returned with two thick slices of pie and handed one to Adelina.

He pulled a wooden fork from his pocket and gave it to her. "What's the bet I'll clear my plate, and you won't?"

He tucked into his meal, wolfing down each forkful, while Adelina savoured every bite, relishing the rich taste.

"The pie represents a cow—a mother figure and provider," Velinka whispered over her shoulder as she appeared behind her. Adelina smiled, then offered some of the pie to her mother.

They shared the meal until the plate was clear.

"Where are the others?" Adelina asked.

"They're sitting around the bonfire, telling stories no doubt," her mother said. "Although I've made your father promise not to speak about work until the festivities are over."

She tugged Adelina to her chest and hugged her. Her gaze travelled to Damir as she stood. "Take care of my daughter this evening."

"Of course." He bowed his head.

The celebrations continued into the night. The fire raged, illuminating the small village, and the melodies from flutes and fiddles carried on the breeze.

When the festival ended, the families parted. After a long hug, Adelina waved to Damir as she turned towards home. Her cheeks burned and a smile spread across her mouth. She loved his gentleness, patience, and playfulness. Now all she had to do was pass the test.

Candles were lit and positioned on top of the dresser in Adelina's bedroom. A silver stream of moonlight cascaded through the gap between the drawn, grey turin curtains.

She rubbed her hands in front of the lit fire in the hearth, then pulled the clips out of her hair and unravelled the bun. When her curls tumbled loosely down the length of her back, she set the clips on the dresser.

She slipped out of her poppy embroidered poneva skirt, set it on the back of the wooden chair beside the fire, then hoisted the cotton under-dress over her head. Standing stark naked in her bedroom, she warmed from the gentle heat flickering in front of her.

A cream nightdress, washed by her mother, lay on her bed. She poked her head through the garment and let the fabric slide down her body. The sleeves were tied into bows at the wrists, and the material was ruched beneath her breasts. She traced the detailed hemmed neckline.

A Ballad of Severed Souls

Her parents made every effort to buy them good quality clothes, since the family business was doing well.

She ran her fingers down her arms, wondering again if astral flowed within her veins. She shook her head and dropped her hands to her sides.

A tired sigh escaped her lips as she pulled back the duvet on her wooden-framed bed, then slid onto the mattress. With the covers drawn to her chin, and the fire warming her cheeks, she closed her eyes and welcomed sleep.

When the moon was at its highest and the hearth light dwindled, Adelina's mind sank into dreams.

Fog hung low as she wandered through a meadow. The wildflowers wilted, and frost crunched beneath her feet. She hugged herself for warmth as she followed the winding path. A crow squawked in the distance, then landed on a nearby tree stump.

Where was she and where'd the crow come from?

Soon after, the field transitioned into a water-slicked corridor. Torches, affixed in brackets on the wall, provided a dim light against the shadows of her new surroundings. She tiptoed through the passageway as a cold shiver ran down her spine. Her heart hammered as she neared an intricately carved stone altar. A pair of candles flickered, casting yellow pools onto the dark surface to where a leather-bound book lay open.

Her gaze fell upon the revealed page, but her vision blurred, and she couldn't make out the symbols or text. A tightening sensation gripped her throat.

Something wasn't right.

She needed to leave; she shouldn't be here.

Jodie Angell

But a compulsion inside urged her to stay, find out what the book contained.

She edged closer and wrapped her fingers around the side of the stone altar. As she pressed onto the tips of her toes, a crow flew through the corridor and squawked. Startled, she waited until the bird landed on an age-worn statue nearby. Its beady gaze met hers. With it, an intense burning coursed through her body, then pulsed behind her left shoulder.

Pulling back her collar, she glanced into the rusted mirror beside the altar. A gasp escaped her lips as a searing heat rose from the area where her birthmark was. The circular shape morphed into the symbol for the new sun, scorching her skin and raising blood to the surface.

She lifted her shaky fingers and traced the swollen surface. The sun's rays splayed out from the centre. She stumbled backwards, hit her head on the water-slicked floor, and the crow soared towards her.

Adelina bolted upright. Her night dress clung to her body, sodden with sweat. She wiped her forehead with her hand and sucked in ragged breaths.

Throwing back the covers, she darted across the room to the mirror hanging above the dresser. She tugged off her nightgown, turned, then peered over her shoulder.

The sun mark. Clear as day, and red raw.

How could something in a dream happen in reality? What did it mean?

TWO

Up in Flames

The following morning, Damir rapped on the door.

Velinka opened it and welcomed him into the living room. She set an iron key on the table and returned to her armchair.

"These are for you, as promised." He nodded to the stack of pine wood in his arms.

"Oh, thank you, dear." She gestured to a dark brown wicker basket at the base of the stairwell. "Set them in there for now. Daro left for work an hour ago, and I've been mending some of the girls' poneva skirts. They should be down any moment now, but while you wait, you can keep me company. Take a seat."

As she brought a piece of thread through the eye of a needle, he removed his coat, hung it on the stand, then reclined into the wooden chair closest to the stove. Once he'd slipped off his gloves, he rubbed his hands together for warmth. He frowned—why in the realm wasn't Adelina downstairs? It was well past dawn.

"Where's Adelina?" he asked.

"She didn't sleep well. I heard her pacing throughout the night—the walls are thin." Velinka brought the red thread through the fabric, setting about her work of mending a poppy petal. "I went to check on her and she assured me she was fine."

Pursing his lips, he nodded once. If something was bothering Adelina, she'd confide in him. Right?

Someone came clomping down the staircase beside Damir.

"Ah. That'd be the girls," Velinka said.

Tihana hopped off the bottom step, cradling a tattered bunny in her arms. She climbed onto her seat at the dining table, then positioned the toy in her father's vacant chair. "Where's Pa?"

"Work, dear. He's taken breakfast with him."

Damir resisted the urge to crane his neck to get a glance up the stairwell. Instead, he tapped his foot. The rapid beat of his heart slowed as soft footsteps echoed through the floorboards above his head.

Moments later, Adelina emerged in her nightdress, rubbing her eyes.

Her mother gasped. "Darling, we have a guest!"

Damir clamped his palms over his eyes. "I saw nothing." But the corners of his lips twitched.

"Sorry, Ma. I tossed and turned all night. Bad dream."

"Go and change at once." Velinka tutted.

When she padded back up the staircase, Damir opened his eyes. Although he'd said otherwise, he'd

A Ballad of Severed Souls

glimpsed the ruched fabric beneath her breasts, the delicate lace hem around the neckline, and her bare collarbones peeking over the top. He cleared his throat and reverted his attention to the pile of skirts. His cheeks cooled.

"Adelina is twenty years of age. You'd think she'd know by now to dress before leaving her room. If Tihana can manage, so can she." Velinka gestured to her youngest daughter, who sat patiently beside him. Her clothes were neatly pressed, and her hair plaited down the length of her back.

"It's no problem at all," he said. "Is there anything I can help you with while we wait for Adelina?"

"In fact, there is. We are out of water. It is usually Tihana's chore to take the pail to the well and fill it. Can you accompany her, please?" Velinka asked.

"Of course," Damir said as Tihana shoved her feet into her boots, then wrestled with her bulky overcoat.

"Thank you." Velinka smiled, turning her attention back to her work.

Damir slid into his coat, then took Tihana's from her and held it out. "Here."

Grinning, she slipped her arms into the holes. "Thanks."

He opened the door and guided her out. It clicked shut behind them.

Adelina entered the sitting room as her mother placed a tin of loose tea leaves on the dining table.

"I've sent the others to fetch some water for tea," her mother said.

"Sorry for earlier, Ma. I wasn't expecting Damir so early." She yawned.

"Dear, you look dreadful." Velinka patted her arm.

"Didn't sleep well." The images from her vivid dream taunted her, and the scar tingled on her left shoulder. She needed to tell Damir—he'd reassure her. Most importantly, he'd believe her when she told him she thought it was connected to the test somehow.

"A good mug of tea will make you feel better." Velinka slipped onto a seat at the dining table as Damir and Tihana hurried in through the door, pail of water in hand.

As her mother poured the tea, she dragged a hand over her face. Gods, she was tired.

"I have a list of items I'll need you to fetch me from the market, dear. Perhaps Damir can accompany you." Velinka wiggled her eyebrows, setting a steaming mug in front of her.

Adelina's cheeks warmed. "*Ma.*"

"What was that?" Damir asked, although Adelina was positive he'd heard. Afterall, he was only a few feet away. Perhaps he was pretending he hadn't to be polite.

"Would you escort my daughter to the market, please?" Velinka scooted past Adelina, picked up an old newsletter from the sideboard, and handed it to him. "I've run out of parchment, so I've written the items at the top."

"Of course." Damir smiled.

By the front door, Adelina dressed in her coat and gloves, then threw her satchel over her shoulder. Her mother waved goodbye from the porch as the pair strolled along the cobbles into town.

"Damir, there's something I have to tell you." She gave him a sideways glance. "It feels like I've been holding my breath all morning."

"What's wrong?" He stopped in front of her and placed a hand on her arm as his brows knitted into a frown.

"Maybe we should go somewhere more private." She surveyed her surroundings. The market ahead bustled with locals. What would people think if they overheard her talking about a dream that affected her in real life, mere days before the test?

He nodded and placed her hand in the nook of his elbow. On their way to the market, they passed a group of locals clearing away the remnants of the previous night's festivities. Further down, the street was lined with stalls selling fabrics, herbs and spices, fruit and vegetables, and chickens clucking in their coops. Fresh bales of hay were stacked outside the barn, and Adelina glimpsed the owner brushing a horse's tan coat.

On the other end of the market, past the town's famous bakery, was a trail leading to a scenic route along the stream flowing straight through Aramoor. Snow-covered pines dotted the flat ground, and a bench was positioned next to the body of water.

Damir wiped the snow away with his gloved hand, then took a seat. A heavy sigh escaped Adelina's lips as she relaxed beside him. She shook her head and rubbed her eyes.

"You're starting to worry me, Ad." He leaned closer, pulling her hands away from her face. "What's happened?"

She hastily told him about the dream, then tilted her head back and looked up at the thick white clouds. "I'd show you the mark if it wasn't so cold out here."

"I believe you," he said. "But what does it mean?"

"I have no idea." She swallowed. A dull headache crept into her temples.

He pressed two fingers to his chin. "Why the mark of the new sun? Is the mark connected to the test itself or to astral magic?"

She knew what it would mean if she possessed the magic Filip Tarasov had spent the last decade searching for. He'd want her with him to reunite the divided people of Temauten, Toichrist, and Saintlandsther. "I don't know the answers to those questions. What I *do* know is the people have been separated for so long over money, land, and power. What if I can help? Filip says his desire is to bring peace. If I *do* have astral magic, I couldn't walk away from that."

Damir drew her close and stroked her hair. "I know, but to live here without you…well, it's not a fate I wish to explore. When I imagine the future, one thing is constant. You. You're always there."

"If Filip took me with him, he would never let me leave." She pulled away. A curl tumbled loose from her bun.

A moment passed as a thick crease wedged itself between his eyebrows. He opened his mouth, then closed it again.

"What is it?" Her chest tightened.

"We've known each other forever, right?" He swallowed. "We could leave. Live somewhere. You and me. I've spent so much time with the carpenters—I'm sure I could find an apprenticeship, and you're good at needlework—you could work for a seamstress."

Adelina's lips parted as she digested his rambled words. Whatever she *thought* he was going to say, it wasn't that.

"You know we can't leave. They would find us wherever we go. Filip and his men have a register of every person in every town," she said.

He tilted his head to the sky and sighed. "I just...I can't risk losing you."

"What are you not telling me?" She clasped his hand, willing him to utter whatever weighed on his mind.

His cheeks reddened as he lowered his gaze back to her. "The thought of you leaving me is crippling. If you told me you wanted to run away to escape Filip—if you feel this mark has sealed your fate—then I would go with you."

Sucking in a deep breath, she blinked slowly. Her heart soared.

"Damir, I..." She shook her head. "I don't want to be apart from you either, but whatever is in store for me, I won't run from it. But I'm glad I have you to help me through it."

A slight smile tilted the corner of his lips, but it wavered. "Come on. Let's get your Ma's things. Maybe a walk through the market will clear your mind."

He rose, then stuck out his hand.

She clasped his palm with hers, and he hoisted her from the bench. With his arm draped around her shoulder, they followed the trail towards the busy stalls.

Jodie Angell

Daro dabbed his sweat lined forehead with a rag, then tossed the scrap of material onto his workbench. In the two hours since opening, he'd already received three orders for refurbishment and a further two for services. As a good stove maker, he held a positive reputation amongst the villagers, and often he would receive tips or small gifts in gratitude.

Although, this particular morning was proving stressful for him—one order required a complete makeover. The property owner, Zsuzsanna, rifled through her satchel, then withdrew her coin purse. She placed the money on the counter, which Daro took with a warm smile.

"Thank you. From what you've told me, the original stove was built poorly. Especially if it's baking unevenly, and smoke's pluming out of it." He put the down-payment into a pouch, wrote a receipt on a piece of parchment, then handed it to her. "Can be mighty hard to fix too."

"Do whatever it takes," she said. "Rip it out and start again if you must. Take care, Daro." She bowed her head and left the workshop.

He swivelled around to study the makeshift calendar and accounting system he'd created, which hung behind his bench. Each workday was marked with a customer's details—some blocked out several days if the job warranted. Even during the winter festivities, he maintained a steady flow of customers. Once he'd scrawled Zsuzsanna's onto the following week's availability, he tapped his fingers against his lips. A singular name stuck out. Pyotr Lebedev, an ex-employee of Filip Tarasov and an alcoholic, was written at the bottom of the calendar. Two strikes followed his name, representing each month gone by without payment.

Shaking his head, he wondered what to do. Everyone in the town knew of Pyotr's predicament—battling with alcoholism, spending his earnings in the tavern. Daro considered Pyotr's wife, Inessa. She was raising two small children at home, like his own wife had. Did he have it in him to go round and demand his overdue payments? He shook his head. He'd deal with it another time, as he quite often told himself.

Tools were scattered along the shelves next to tins of white paint. Baskets filled with pebbles lined the walls, collected to create the cool layer over the stoves. Bricks were stacked, and small iron doors sat neatly in the corner. Daro also sold accessories, such as cast iron and enamel pots and pans. Rarely, he'd get his hands on copper kettles which would sell to higher class clientele around the time of the test each year, when Filip Tarasov entered the village with his wealthy men.

On the right-hand side of the workshop, Daro's own stove stood. Poppies were painted on the white-washed brickwork, which impressed interested customers when using the stove during demonstrations.

He grabbed a cloth from within his workbench drawer, then used it to wipe away the light dust gathering on the rim above the stove opening. Taking a couple of steps back, he admired his handiwork. "Best one I've ever made."

The bell rang above the main door as another customer entered. Daro turned around as Pyotr stumbled in through the entrance, and with him, a waft of stale beer.

Daro wrinkled his nose, wiped his hands on his overalls, then walked towards his visitor. "Morning Pyotr. Wife and kids okay?"

"They're fine." He waved his hand dismissively. "I've come to speak to you."

Pressing his lips into a thin line, Daro positioned himself behind the bench. "To discuss the payments?"

He ignored the sickly scent of alcohol clinging to his neighbour's clothes. It was either a case of early morning drinking or he was yet to go home from the night before.

Pyotr shrugged his right shoulder. "The thing is, it's little Anya's fourth birthday on the weekend. We could do with the money for her celebrations. Money's been a bit tight this month, what with the winter solstice. My darling wife needed to replace the pans as they were scorched by the broken stove. You know how it is."

Daro narrowed his gaze at him. His blood boiled. How could he use his wife and daughter as excuses for his failings?

"I understand your circumstances—I really do. However, I have my own family to support. Adelina, although she is now a grown woman, she still lives under my roof. Tihana is a child, and my dear wife, too. I have responsibilities, and a reputation to uphold. You have until the end of the week to pay the remaining balance." He placed his hands on his hips and kept his gaze locked on Pyotr.

"It must be nice to buy your family gifts when the cash comes flowing in." Pyotr edged closer. "We wouldn't want anything to happen."

"Are you threatening me?" Daro curled his fingers around the edge of the workbench until his knuckles turned white.

"We both know accidents happen. Here at your shop, you have so many flammable things. Valuable things. I could guard the shop for you while you're not here, make sure nothing bad happens—if you write off my debt of course."

"Consider your next words carefully."

"Come on, we were friends for ten years, Daro— that can't be easily forgotten. We could help each other out."

Daro gritted his teeth. "Ten years is a long time. People move on. Leave my shop before I throw you out."

"Suit yourself." He shrugged his shoulder, then left, letting the door slam shut behind him.

Alone and surrounded by silence, Daro puffed out a deep breath.

He stretched his arms, then turned his attention to the outstanding stove orders. An alcoholic's threat was empty, like his purse.

Bustling through the front door, Adelina clutched brown paper bags filled with groceries. She stacked them onto the dining table as Velinka dusted and organised the bookshelf opposite the stove and seating area.

"Thank you, dear," she said. "Would you mind putting the things away? I'm making sure I'm ready for when home education resumes for Tihana next week. Perhaps in the New Year, you could think of getting a job."

Adelina halted. "I haven't considered such things, what with the celebrations and the test in two days."

"As you said, you'll be fine. I've put my fears to rest." Velinka waved her hand, as if dismissing the likelihood she could be the person Filip was looking for. If only she knew about the dream. "Salma, down the road, is a well-established seamstress. You're skilled with a needle—you could ask for a part-time job to start with."

Adelina stared at her mother.

"Damir is a fine young man, too. I'm sure he will take care of you."

"What does he have to do with this?" Adelina frowned.

"Your father and I missed the opportunity to arrange a marriage for you at the winter solstice, but we both know he'd support you and any children you may have—"

"Whoa, hold on, Ma. Where is this coming from?" She raised her hands.

Velinka kept her gaze on the table between them. She blinked several times, then glanced up to meet her daughter's stare. "Sit down, dear. We ought to talk."

As they eased into their chairs, Adelina's pulse pumped in her ears.

A Ballad of Severed Souls

She reached across the table and clutched Velinka's trembling hand. "What is it?"

"While you were at the market, you father popped home for ten minutes." She shook her head. "He shared some troubling information about Pyotr."

"The alcoholic you mentioned at dinner?"

"Yes, dear. He's requested your father write off his debt." Her eyes darkened. "And insinuated something bad would happen if he refused."

"Something bad—like what?"

"Pyotr mentioned the contents of your father's shop are flammable and valuable." Velinka grimaced. "At best, he could steal a few things, and at worst...well, I dread to think."

Adelina sat back in her chair, letting go of her mother's hand. "Pa would never concede to threats. His business is his livelihood."

"I know, dear." Velinka rubbed her temples, closing her eyes.

While Adelina didn't wish to make her mother worry more than she probably was, her secret weighed on her.

"There's something I need to show you." She peeled back her collar and revealed her morphed birthmark.

Her mother gasped, then clamped a hand over her mouth. "How did you get that?"

"It happened in a dream. I woke up and it was still there."

"You should leave. Now." Velinka rose, darted into the kitchen, then pulled bread, cheese, and nuts from the pantry. She shoved them into a bag as Adelina hurried after her.

"What? I can't!" Adelina gripped her mother's hand and stopped her. "Listen, Ma. This mark isn't going away. I don't know what it means, but I'm sure it's connected to the test. It's got to be."

Velinka was silent for a moment. "The symbol is an ancient rune."

"And?"

"I've witnessed tests happening for the past ten years, dear. The magic has never been found because no one has ever been marked." Velinka's face paled.

"How do you know this? Why has no one said anything about a mark?" Adelina's heart pounded.

"Filip is careful to make sure no one finds out about it. Pyotr and your father used to be close friends some years ago, before he had a drinking problem. He told your father about the mark—not long after he left Filip's employ—information he shouldn't have shared. We've kept it a secret because if anyone found out...well, we'd be imprisoned or worse."

"This doesn't make sense. If Filip has spent the last ten years looking for astral magic, why wouldn't he want people to know about the mark?" Adelina kept her unwavering gaze locked on her mother as she gripped the kitchen counter.

"Filip is a person who likes power and control. If he is the only one with certain information, then he is at an advantage. If someone bore the sun mark *and* knew what it meant, they may be scared and try to flee, which is precisely what Filip doesn't want. You must leave Aramoor while you still can. We'll take you to your father—he can go see the stableman and arrange for a reliable, sturdy horse. You should ride tonight until you're far away from here. You can find a job—Damir will go with you."

A Ballad of Severed Souls

Adelina grabbed her mother by the shoulders. "I'm not going anywhere."

"Darling, I know you want to help, but you *must* leave."

"Why would you have me leave? I will go with Filip if I need to."

Her mother glanced away. "You are my daughter—how am I to trust your welfare with Filip—a stranger, *and* a powerful one?"

"I'm sorry, Ma, but I'm staying to do the test."

Velinka sighed and dragged a hand over her face. "Make sure your scar is covered at all times. Keep your bedroom door shut when you undress. Don't show anyone, not even Tihana or Pa. Do you hear me?"

"Yes, Ma," she replied in a thin voice. "But don't you think Pa should know?"

She shook her head. "He has enough to worry about after the threat Pyotr made against his livelihood and his shop. Let's not add to it."

Adelina flattened her shaking fingers against her poneva skirt, counted to three, then scooped up the grocery bags from the table. She emptied the rolls of cheese, potatoes, carrots, and onions into the pantry, then placed a fresh jar of honey beside them.

Fighting a rising panic, she left the room. Grabbing her coat, she flung it over her shoulders, then went out on to the porch. Her stomach twisted and her lungs tightened. Placing a hand on her breast, she fought for breath.

"Ad? What's wrong?" Damir jogged towards her. "I only left you for ten minutes. Has something happened?"

She glanced from one end of the street to the other. When she was sure they were alone, she gripped his arm. "I don't think I'm going to pass this test."

That evening, when Tihana was tucked in bed, Velinka boiled water on the stove while Adelina sat forward in her chair. She tapped her fingers against her knee and bit her lip.

"For heaven's sake, dear. Stop with the tapping. You'll be fine. The bathhouse will help ease your nerves," her mother said.

Adelina leaned back in her chair and let out a deep breath. "There's no history of magic in our bloodline, nor anyone we know. Why would I be marked? Why would it choose me? How can I be sure I'll truly be able to help?"

Her mother crossed the space between them and cupped her cheek in the palm of her hand. "You, my daughter, are an incredibly special person. This magic chose you for a reason. You were born to help."

"You won't be saying that when I'm taken away from you."

"I've had some time to think about this. If that happens, you know how to be strong, how to defend yourself. If Filip wants you, then I must believe he will treat you well. How else will I let you go?"

"How are you calm? After all, you wanted me to run away."

Velinka shook her head. "You're doing the right thing, my dear. I wanted to protect you. It is all I will ever do for my children."

Adelina kissed her mother's cheek. "I know, Ma."

Adelina was jolted awake in the early hours by a commotion downstairs. Loud sobs and clatters of furniture echoed through the house. She flung back the covers, darted out of the room. "Ma?"

"Oh, my darling!" Her mother drew her into a tight embrace.

"What's wrong?" She pulled away, and her gaze fell upon her mother's tear-streaked cheeks.

Daro sat at the dining table, face and clothes covered in soot. Little Tihana cowered in the corner, blubbering profusely. Candles flickered, and the final remnants of moonlight shone through the window.

"Pa?" Adelina hurried to her father and dropped to her knees in front of him. She took his hands in hers.

"There's…been a fire at the workshop," Daro said through gritted teeth. "Thankfully, a lot of people turned up to help put it out before it spread. Who knows the damage it could've caused otherwise?"

"How?" Her gaze darted from her father to her mother, then back again.

"Tihana, she—"

"She what?" Adelina pressed.

Her sister bolted from the room in a flood of tears.

Velinka patted her eyes with a handkerchief. "I ought to go see to her. Darling, are you all right to tell Adelina alone?"

Daro nodded to his wife who hurried after her youngest child.

"Your sister—she came to bring me supper last night at the workshop, although I wasn't there. Another customer needed my help with an emergency. As she was looking around for me, someone shattered the window. She hid inside the cooled stove, the clever girl." He shook his head.

"Who was it?" She gripped his hands tighter.

"From Tihana's description...Pyotr."

Adelina covered her mouth to stifle a gasp.

"He did threaten my livelihood, my shop, but I didn't think—I guess I was wrong." He rested his face in his hands. "My whole business. Gone as quick as a breath."

"Is Tihana hurt?" She glanced over her shoulder at the door to her sister's bedroom next to the staircase. Adelina had retired to bed early in the hopes of getting enough sleep for the looming test. Her stomach knotted—if only she'd stayed awake. Maybe she could've gone in her sister's place.

"Not badly. She followed Pyotr out of the broken window as the fire picked up momentum and a wooden beam had collapsed and blocked the door. She's got a small nick on her thigh from the glass, but nothing serious. Your ma's bandaged it up."

"Oh, Pa. I'm sorry." Adelina took the cup of tea from the table and placed it in her father's hand. "Drink this."

He offered a half-smile, then sipped the tea.

"Is there anything I can do to help?"

"Afraid not. The building is completely destroyed. I've savings from the stoves I've already completed, but all my materials were inside. I'll have to source new supplies before I can fulfil my other orders." He sat the cup aside and leaned his head back. "Leave me to myself, child. Tend to your sister."

Adelina planted a gentle kiss on her father's cheek, then slid into Tihana's room.

Her younger sister lay wrapped in blankets on her bed. She blinked, large water-filled eyes as she turned to face Adelina.

She rushed to Tihana's side. "I'm here now. Everything is going to be fine."

Adelina's gaze travelled to her trembling mother who sat in the chair on the opposite side of the bed. She held her hands to her mouth and shook her head.

Reverting her gaze back to her sister, Adelina stroked Tihana's hair and sung her softly to sleep.

THREE

The Test

The wooden frame of the workshop stood charred—the strong scent of burned wood lingering on the morning breeze. Broken glass from the fire littered the cobbles nearby. Adelina took a broom and swept the shards off the main trail.

She wiped her forehead with the back of her hand, then glanced at the wreckage. Large planks of wood from the original structure buried all of her father's belongings and supplies.

"Damir, give me a hand with this, would you?" Daro hoisted one end of a plank.

He nodded, then gripped the other side. Together, they threw the wood to the edge of the ruins.

"My materials were stacked over here." Daro gestured to the spot in front of them.

"Pa." Adelina climbed over the wood, then placed a hand on his arm. "Even if you find any bricks or paint, they will be burned and of no use to you. Your customers will understand. Why don't you go to the bathhouse, and we'll meet you at home? You must be starving and exhausted."

Tears sparkled in Daro's eyes. He rifled in his pocket, then pulled out a gold chain. Along it, slid a tarnished locket. He carried it with him always, for it contained tiny portraits of his family. "You're right."

"Here, let me help you." Adelina smiled warmly as she took the necklace and fastened it around her father's neck. She tucked it under his shirt. "There. It'll make you feel better. We're always with you."

Daro cleared his throat, kissed his daughter on the forehead, then left the wreckage behind without another word.

"Come on. We should get out of here too. The test is tomorrow, and we mustn't stay out all day in the cold." Damir took her by the arm and steered her away from what remained of the workshop.

He walked beside her down the cobbles. The streets bustled with activity as daily life resumed, irrespective of Daro's disaster. Smoke plumed into the air above the blacksmiths, and the stench of manure wafted from the stables and barns. Chickens clucked and skittered across the hay. Cows mooed deeply, and a horse whinnied in the distance.

Leaning into his embrace, she breathed in the lingering scent of charred wood and smoke clinging to his clothes.

"Morning, my precious daughter. It's time to wake." Velinka swept back a brown curl hanging over Adelina's face.

Adelina stirred. She wiped her eyes with her hand. "What time is it?"

"Just after seven. You ought to hurry to the bathhouse before it gets busy. I'll prepare breakfast. Your test is at ten." Her mother drew the covers back. "A fresh towel and felt hat are waiting for you downstairs."

As she sat up in bed, she scooped her hair and pulled it to one side. "Will you pin this for me?"

"Of course, dear. I've pressed your clothes too. Now hurry. I must tend to your sister's wounds." Velinka gestured to the neatly folded clothes positioned at the foot of the bed, then left the room.

Once Adelina was dressed, she rushed downstairs. She ignored the tingling sensation bubbling on the surface of her scar.

Damir awaited her in the living room. "I got here a few moments ago, and I'm yet to go to the bathhouse, so I'll accompany you."

A warmth washed over her. "I appreciate it. Honestly, I do. But you don't have to."

"I'm going to be with you every step of the way, and you can't change my mind." He nudged her. "Come on. Let's go enjoy the steam while we can."

She flung the towel and hat over her shoulder, heading out of the Orlov home with Damir in tow.

Half an hour later, once they were bathed and dressed, they left the bathhouse as locals crowded the cobbled street. People swarmed inside, hurrying to use the hut before it would require refuelling with firewood. She was glad she'd heeded her mother's words and went early to avoid the crowds.

The market was bustling with villagers. Shop owners laid out copper or porcelain kitchenware which would likely be purchased by the noblemen who accompanied Filip for the test.

Past the stalls was the open field where the winter solstice was held, and beyond was a round wooden structure which was utilised for the test. A potent waft of burning sage was carried on the breeze. The Sage Seer's hut.

Adelina wrinkled her nose. "They must be testing a batch in preparation."

"Do you know what will happen to us?" Damir asked.

She shrugged. "No idea. No one says—I don't think they're allowed to. All I know is we need to mark the register with a sample of our blood. It's so they have proof they've tested everyone in the village."

"Filip comes every year. He's visited every town for the last ten years. I wonder why he's never given up."

"I'm sure I'll find out." A chill ran down her spine. The test would solidify their suspicions.

He gave her hand a squeeze, and when they returned to the Orlov home, Velinka dished up cooked sausages and buttered rye bread. She served brewed tea into enamel mugs, then placed a dollop of honey into each. "Please sit and eat."

Tihana poked her head around her bedroom door, wearing her nightgown and clutching her bunny to her chest. "Ma? Can I have some?"

"Oh, darling. I know your leg hurts, but you cannot come out here dressed like that. I'll come in and help you change." Velinka hurried after her youngest daughter and closed the door shut behind them.

Silence enveloped Damir and Adelina. She glanced at the clock in the kitchen. An hour and a half before the test. The hands ticked each second slowly. Her heart thrummed as she tapped her fingers against the wooden table.

Damir placed his hand over hers. "I'm right beside you."

She rested her head on his shoulder, sucked in a breath, held it for a few moments, then let it out. "Are you scared we'll be separated? I'm so nervous I can't even stomach my food."

He swivelled in his chair, then studied her face. His gaze fell to her lips, slightly chapped from the harsh winter weather. "Of course, I'm scared. We spend every day together. Can you imagine what I'd be like without you?"

She giggled. "Look at all the food you scoffed at the winter solstice. There'd be no stopping you from eating everything in the village."

He cupped her cheek in the palm of his hand, and she leaned into it, keeping her gaze locked on him. The space between them shrank as he inched towards her. Their lips brushed gently.

Velinka entered the living room and closed Tihana's bedroom door behind her. The sound of her footsteps jolted Adelina. Her heart leapt into her throat.

Damir straightened and ran his hand through his hair.

Velinka smiled, collected the dishes from the table, then carried them into the kitchen to be cleaned.

Luckily, she hadn't seen their intimate moment. Although she rooted for them to be together, what was the point in giving her false hope when Adelina knew what lay ahead of her? She didn't think her parents would take kindly to their physical connection before a marriage took place. She cast her gaze onto the table, hiding her burning cheeks.

An eerie silence hung over the village as each twenty-year-old queued in single file. Ahead, was a wooden table positioned outside the Sage Seer's hut. The people in front of Damir and Adelina shuffled forwards. One at a time, the villagers were taken into the hut. Each test took about five minutes.

As the line shortened, Adelina caught sight of a tall, slender man outside the hut's entrance. His black hair was swept back from his angled face, and his dark gaze inspected the individuals before him. His large fur coat was draped over a black buttoned shirt, accompanied by fitted trousers, and knee-high leather boots.

Although his gaze briefly landed on Adelina, his expression remained blank. He turned, then entered the structure—his cape flapping behind him as he disappeared inside. Her heart sank into her boots.

After each test, he returned outside, glanced at the registers, then scanned the shortening queues ahead of him.

"For someone who's been searching for astral magic for the last ten years, he seems calm." Adelina nudged Damir, then gestured to Filip.

"We're up next." Damir stepped up to the wooden table. Behind it sat a man wearing spectacles.

"Name?" he asked.

"Damir Litvin, and this is Adelina Orlova."

She positioned herself beside him and glanced down at the large, leather-bound book lying open in front of the man. Across the parchment was a grid. Down the right side, were a list of names and a thumb print of blood pressed next to each.

The man scribed their names, then drew a pin from its case. "Fingers."

Damir winced as his blood was drawn. The man held his finger, pressed it against the paper, then gestured to the hut. "Stand over there."

Adelina eyed the needle, trying to ignore the tight knots in her stomach before stretching out her hand. She sucked in a sharp breath as the quick stab of a needle brought a bead of crimson liquid to the surface. Once her print was taken, she moved out of the way for the next person.

She fidgeted her weight from one foot to the other as she waited to be summoned inside.

The Sage Seer emerged from the hut.

"You." She pointed to Damir, and the pair of them entered the structure, leaving her alone outside.

A Ballad of Severed Souls

As she flattened her sweating palms against her thighs, she kept her gaze fixed on the remaining queue. The woodsy, astringent scent of burning sage wafted through the air, and so did the lilting tune of a song.

A few minutes later, Damir exited the testing facility—his gaze cast to the heavens, shoulders relaxed—and before she could say anything to him, the Sage Seer beckoned her inside.

The door closed behind her, and it took a moment for her eyes to adjust in the smoke-filled room. Candles were dotted across the wooden cabinets, providing the space with a warm glow. The Sage Seer grabbed a fresh bunch of herbs, then lit the ends.

Adelina coughed and rubbed her stinging eyes.

"Sit." The old woman gestured to the wooden chair beside her.

She glanced at the crooked seat, then obeyed. Her shoulders were stiff as she cautiously kept her gaze locked on the elderly woman.

Filip flung open the door and strode in. He positioned himself opposite them and crossed his arms.

The sun mark burned like wildfire on Adelina's shoulder.

"Begin," he instructed.

The Sage Seer nodded, then danced around the cabin. She waved the burning sage through the air as she hummed and circled the chair. Her tune developed into a melodic chant.

The song seemed distant as Adelina grew faint. Her eyesight blurred, and every ounce of her body was compelled to sleep. As her limbs slackened in the chair, her eyes closed, and the Seer's words dwindled.

The heady aroma of burning sage sent her plummeting into a trance. A vision materialised, somewhere deep in the recesses of her mind. An outstretched hand guided her through the darkness into another plane. Plumes of smoke circled her feet. As if she were no longer hindered by inhibitions or fears, she followed the faceless figure through the void.

The being faded away, and in its place, a golden spark emerged against the endless blackness.

Adelina frowned. She edged closer as her interest piqued. The light expanded—its form manifesting. She shielded her eyes from its brightness. When she grew accustomed to the blazing, magnificent golden light piercing through the darkness, she dropped her hands.

Before her stood a winged dragon. Fire blazed from its skin, and bright red scales lined the beast's stomach, face, neck, and limbs. Its tail curled around its body, and the fire calmed.

"What...are you?" Her voice was hollow and distant, as if detached from her body.

"Ssssvarog, God and Creator of the Ssssun." The fire serpent's forked tongue flicked out the corner of his mouth.

Her sun mark tingled—not the ferocious burning she felt in Filip's presence, but something about the dragon soothed her. "How can I see you?"

"You are in the sssspirit world, of courssssse. Ah, it'ssss been many a century ssssince I've sssseen sssssomeone with your power." He stalked towards her, his talon-like claws piercing the smoke surrounding them.

"Power?" She frowned.

"An ancient power livessss within you, *Adelina*." He flapped his fiery wings, sending orange sparks into the air.

"How do you know my name?" She took a step back.

"I am a God. I ssssee all, and I've waited a long time to meet you. Sssshow me your mark." He circled her, closing the distance between him.

She glanced down at her body. She no longer wore her fur coat, poneva skirt, and cotton shirt. Instead, an ethereal, sun-coloured gown hung from her shoulders and fitted her well.

Peeling back the sleeve, she revealed the mark to the dragon.

"Marveloussss," he hissed. "Assstral magic. Heed my warning. There are two ssssides. Day and night. Remember who you are."

Before she could ask him to explain, the vision dissipated, and a tingling sensation rose in Adelina's arms and legs as an energy pulled her back to the Sage Seer's hut.

She opened her eyes, then peered at her arms. Bright, yellow sunlight streamed from her skin, illuminated the hut, and pierced through the thick cloud of smoke. A gasp escaped her lips.

"A wonder…" is all Filip could manage as he stepped closer to her, then placed his fingers on her arm. His lips parted. "Magnificent."

An airy sensation filled Adelina as the magic poured from her body. Nothing hindered or frightened her. A strange power coursed through her veins, setting every nerve ending alight. *Astral magic?* She was alive, and more so than she'd ever been.

She tried to stand, then stumbled. Filip caught her in his arms.

"Steady, my sun." A smiled reached his bright and glossy eyes.

"I don't feel...so good." Her body turned to jelly.

"Seer, help her." He ordered the women as he assisted Adelina back into the chair.

"I'll give her some herbs to counteract the dizziness, but she must regain her strength."

"Rest, my sweet one," he whispered to Adelina, then faced the Sage Seer. "Ensure no one enters. No harm will come to her."

His footsteps echoed as he left the hut.

Adelina's head hung back against the chair as the room swirled. Her arms were heavy in her lap.

The Seer plucked several orpin rose flowers from a jar, then ground them with her pestle and mortar. Taking a pot of boiled water from the stove at the other side of the hut, she steeped the crushed petals in a mug. Steam spiralled into the air.

Its fragrant aroma filled Adelina's nostrils, encouraging her to hold on to consciousness.

She brought the mug to her. "Drink this."

Taking it between her fingers, Adelina sighed. The light pouring from her skin slowly diminished. She drank the medicinal tea, then shuffled over to a small cot. Once her head lay against the pillow, she succumbed to sleep.

"Wake up, dear."

Adelina stirred, and a grumble escaped her lips. "Ma?"

"I'm right here, my darling." Velinka knelt beside her daughter and stroked her arm. "Filip has allowed us all a moment with you before you leave."

She frowned, wondering what in the realm her mother was referring to. Then her memories returned.

Astral magic flowed within her. Word would've spread quickly—the whole village would know, and Filip would take her far away from here.

Pushing up on to her elbows, she blinked and looked around. Her father and sister stood in front of her, hugging one another as if by the side of a gravesite. Damir sat hunched over at the foot of the cot.

Tears sparkled in her mother's eyes. "Come on, dear. Sit up. Give me a hug."

It took a few seconds for the fogginess to leave Adelina's head, but as soon as she was certain the room wouldn't spin, she embraced her mother. She didn't want to abandon her family, but what choice did she have?

When she let go, she turned to her sister. "Oh, look at you—out of bed! You're so brave and strong."

Tihana pouted and tears fell from her eyes. She clutched her rabbit to her chest. "I don't want you to go."

"I know, Sis, but I'm going to help Filip bring peace to the divided countries." She choked on her words, but she needed to set an example. "Aren't you proud?" She squeezed Tihana's hands, and the girl nodded timidly.

Daro rested his hand on her shoulder. "My beautiful daughter, there's something I ought to tell you."

"What is it?" Her gaze darted from her mother, then back to her father.

"Filip has promised to rebuild my workshop and provide me with a year's worth of supplies," he said. "I suppose it's his way of ensuring your family are cared for in your absence."

Her mouth fell open. "Wow—how generous. I can't believe this has happened. I'll be leaving."

"I've arranged for Salma Abramova to escort you as a chaperone. Filip vows your virtue will not be besmirched."

As her father's last word left his mouth, Filip entered the hut, and with him, a stern presence.

He held his shoulders back and kept his gaze fixed on Adelina. "How are you feeling?"

She eyed him. "A little nauseous from the sage, but I'll be fine."

"Fear not. You'll be looked after at the palace."

"Palace?" her voice croaked.

"Of course. We will travel north to Toichrist. Beyond the border is a village known as Kirovo. There you'll be welcomed to Kirovo Palace—my home. Now if you accept my gesture of goodwill," he nodded to Daro, "then it is time to bid your farewells, Adelina Orlova. We have a long journey ahead."

He bowed his head graciously, then strode towards the door. "Miss Abramova and I'll meet you outside in ten minutes. A carriage awaits us."

She managed a nod, the lump in her throat thick as he left the hut.

"We've packed your things, dear." Her ma pointed to the leather trunk positioned beside her.

This is happening. I'm going away to an unknown land to do a stranger's bidding.

Adelina gripped her mother's hand and squeezed, refusing to show her how terrified she was. "I'm sorry to be leaving you."

Velinka patted her daughter's knee with her other hand. "You've nothing to apologise for. Filip has promised to fund the restorations, and more. He's also vowed to protect you—provide for you in ways we can't. He has a palace with servants and chefs. There's a lady who can train you to use your magic, and people who have access to other forms of magic."

"What else has he said?" Adelina asked as she rose. Curiosity was a welcome respite from her nerves.

"You'll learn how to master your magic. Filip says he needs your help. The rift between the people is far deeper than you know, and your abilities are needed. Why don't you talk to him about it? You'll make friends, Filip assured me. You won't be alone." Her words tumbled from her mouth.

Who is she trying to convince? I'll be far away from anyone I've ever loved.

"Here, take this." Daro unhooked his locket, then fastened it around his daughter's neck. "So, you know we'll always be with you."

Adelina's fingers brushed the locket, and her eyes watered. Her father drew her into a tight embrace and smoothed her hair. The tears fell freely now as her sister hugged her round the waist. Tihana pulled away, then darted out of the hut, crying loudly.

Once they were separated, Velinka embraced her daughter. She pulled back—her eyes glassy—and stroked her cheek. "We will write to you. I promise. Maybe we'll come to visit as soon as the restorations are complete." Velinka planted a kiss on her head, then took Daro's hand. "We love you, my darling."

"I love you too," she choked.

They left the tent, leaving Adelina alone with Damir.

His face paled as he stood. "We should've fled when we had the chance."

"Come with me?" she blurted. "I could ask—perhaps Filip would accommodate."

"I don't think so." He shook his head. "He's taking you to a facility for you to learn how to use your magic. There's no place for me there."

He closed the gap between them and cupped her cheek in his palm. She held her breath as their gazes locked.

A sigh escaped his lips. He dropped his hand and stepped back. Adelina frowned. While she understood he wouldn't be thrilled by their separation, she anticipated something, anything, that would give her hope he'd be there for her if she was able to return.

"I'm sorry…this is harder than I thought it would be. I can't watch you leave." His facial muscles twisted and his eyes glistened. Without a second's

A Ballad of Severed Souls

delay, he fled the hut, leaving her alone and surrounded by silence.

She swatted the fresh tears rolling down her cheeks. Perhaps she assumed herself impervious to heartbreak. After all, she couldn't say for certain she loved him but watching him leave made her chest tighten and each breath laborious. Her vision blurred, and she gripped the nearest cabinet.

"Adelina?" Filip's deep voice asked.

She flung around.

"Are you all right?"

Of course, I'm not all right!

"Uh, yes. Sorry...I just..." She cleared the tightening force in her throat and flattened her poneva skirt.

"Saying goodbye can be difficult, but I assure you, once you understand why I need you, you'll find peace, and maybe happiness." A kind smile spread across his lips as he picked up the trunk. "Come on. I'll escort you."

He supported her arm as they left the Sage Seer's hut, propelling her to a life she didn't want. She'd begun to picture a life with Damir, but the image shattered. She was leaving, perhaps for good, to learn magic and play a part in the future of the Realm of Kirromund. Her chest caved in with the weight of it.

Outside, Salma greeted her with a polite smile. "I've agreed to accompany you to the palace. You'll train to use your magic during the day, and in the evening, we can practise needlepoint, painting—anything you like."

"Thank you." Adelina said thinly.

The three of them followed the trail through Aramoor towards its snow-covered perimeter. Locals looked on in silence.

Once she reached the first of three horse-drawn carriages, Filip opened the door. Salma climbed inside, then beckoned to her.

Adelina cast a glance over her shoulder, hoping to see Damir one final time before her departure. Instead, her mother hurried along the cobbles, snow crunching underfoot, and tears tumbling down her face.

"We ought to leave now," Filip said firmly. "I'll be in the carriage in front and my guards will follow us."

"Not yet," Adelina whispered.

Her mother threw her arms around her, and gasped, "Oh, my sweet one. I had to see you one more time before you left. Here, take this."

She pulled away and placed a pocket watch in her daughter's hand. "This was your grandfather's."

Filip cleared his throat and fixed his gaze on Velinka. She withdrew and watched from the sideline as her daughter climbed into the carriage and the door closed behind her.

Adelina peered through the small window as the coachman whipped the horses. With a sharp jolt, the journey to Toichrist begun.

Once her mother and Aramoor were out of sight, she turned the pocket watch over in her hands. A frown knitted her brows. She'd never seen it before. Why was now the first time?

FOUR

Kirovo Palace

Alone in his bedroom, Damir pressed his back against the door and a deep sigh escaped his mouth. He rubbed his forehead, then dragged his hand over his face. What if marriage to Adelina *had* been arranged at the winter solstice? Would it have had any weight in keeping her in Aramoor, or potentially allowing him to escort her to Kirovo Palace?

He tugged the collar of his cotton shirt and paced the wooden floorboards. How could he let his best friend, someone he loved in perhaps more than a friendly way, walk away so easily?

Unspoken words danced on his tongue, and his stomach knotted. Full of regret at the missed opportunity, he frowned. How could he express his unshakable feelings for her when she was no longer down the cobble path from him?

With his hands on his hips, he pondered. His gaze travelled to the stack of parchment on the dresser. Striding across the room, he pulled out his chair, then collapsed onto it. Perhaps writing a letter to Adelina would ease his mind. After all, they'd shared a brief, unchaperoned kiss that had affirmed his affection for her, yet he'd fled without confirming his love for her.

He flattened his hands on the wooden surface, flexed his fingers, then placed a piece of empty parchment in front of him. With the quill in his hand, he dipped it into the inkpot and stared at the blank paper. Drawing his bottom lip between his teeth, he searched for the right words—ones to provide her with comfort in her new accommodation.

Dear Adelina, he scrawled at the top of the page.

Shaking his head, he screwed the paper into a ball and tossed it to the floor. Laying a fresh piece in front of him, he steadied his hand, and wrote in cursive:

My dearest Adelina,

Please accept my deepest apologies for leaving you so brashly. You deserved my solace, as you bring such light to my life.

I must disclose to you the warm feelings which my heart holds for you. A regret stirs within me now that you're gone. I wonder how this day may have ended differently if our marriage were arranged by our fathers, and what a splendid celebration it would have been.

When you're ready, and if the affection is returned, I will reveal my feelings to your father, and ask for his permission to wed you upon your return. I hold onto the hope you will find your way back to me. For now, I promise to write to you in the hope it brings you comfort during your training.

Ever yours,
Damir.

He sat back in his chair and stared at the parchment. The corners of his lips turned upwards into a smile, and his shoulders relaxed, free from the burden.

Once the letter was sealed in the envelope, he stuck a green stamp on the front and scribed the Kirovo Palace address. Gripping it, he hurried downstairs, flung on his fur coat, then stuffed his feet into his boots. As the door opened, a bitter wind nipped at his cheeks.

He followed the cobbles towards the only mailbox in the whole village. With great effort, he stuffed the envelope inside the already cramped enclosure. All he could do was wait for the coach to arrive the following morning to collect and distribute the mail. If the courier experienced no delays, Adelina would receive his letter within two weeks. He'd wait and hope she'd reply.

Leaning his head back, he watched the shifting clouds. White tufts dissipated and reformed, stretching across the sky. The snow had stopped, and soon, the weather would warm. An image of him and Adelina celebrating the spring equinox came to mind. He'd buy her a bunch of fresh peonies from the merchant, and perhaps a gift alongside it. Instead, he wondered if such an experience would happen. After all, the carriage took her farther and farther away from him, and into another man's palace.

He shook his shoulders, then headed towards the carpenter's workshop.

As he pushed the door open, a small bell dinged, alerting the shop owner of his arrival.

Alexei smiled from behind his workbench and rested his elbows on the rough, wooden surface. "Ah, nice to see a friendly face around here."

"Morning." Damir bowed his head, then checked his watch. "Ah, it's been a long day already."

"Test wiped it out of you, boy?"

"Something like that." He waved his hand flippantly.

"I heard all about it. They took that lovely lass of yours away from you." Alexei grabbed a rag and wiped his dirty hands with it. "Come on, let's take you to the tavern. I'll get you a pint on me, lad."

"Are you sure? I was supposed to help with your orders." He frowned.

"Course—they can wait."

With a grin on his face, Alexei guided his apprentice out into the chilly afternoon. Together, they strolled along the frosted cobbles, taking care over the icy stones.

The carriage trundled along the trodden dirt path. Harsh winds beat against the sides, but when Adelina peered out the window, her gaze fell upon the thinning clouds. The New Year was a few days away, and from there, spring awaited.

She sat back in her seat and flipped the pocket watch over in her hands. The surface gold was worn but still glinted under the daylight streaming through the window. Tracing her finger over the hinged metal lid, she pondered its significance.

"What do you have there, miss?" Salma, sitting opposite her, leaned forward to get a closer look.

"My grandfather's pocket watch." Adelina frowned. "Trouble is, I've never seen it before."

"What's the worry? You have a fine piece of eighteen-hundreds gold there. It'll be worth something."

However right she may be, Adelina would never consider selling such an item. Her mother gave it to her for a reason, and she was going to uncover it.

She opened the lid and stared at the unmoving hands. "It doesn't work."

"Are you surprised? It's an heirloom, so it will be decades old." Salma shifted her gaze to the landscape whizzing past.

"I'll search for a clockmaker in Toichrist, and have it fixed," Adelina decided.

A week of travelling through the lanes and vast countryside passed before they reached the border of Toichrist. Each night was spent in taverns along the way, and Filip ensured she was well-fed and washed before their journey continued. Another four days later, in the late afternoon, they arrived in the bustling village of Kirovo in the south of Toichrist.

Large stone buildings stood beside a wide river. The horses pulled the carriages over the bridge to join several other black carriages beating along the cobble paths.

Adelina gripped the round window frame and gasped at the bell tower. The clock chimed as the hands struck 9:00 a.m.

"Wait until you see the palace." Salma chuckled.

"You've been here?" She cast a glance over her shoulder at her chaperone.

"When I was a little girl—many years ago."

Adelina's lips parted as her gaze fell upon a grand building as they rode past. Its four white towers were adorned with golden, round roofs. Their peaks kissed the thin clouds above.

They journeyed through vast, open markets—the smell of rich spices wafting through the gap in the carriage door. Bakeries lined the streets alongside seamstresses and fabric shops, shoemakers, woodworkers, and taverns, to name a few.

"We're almost there." Salma looked over the top of her round spectacles.

A giddiness filled Adelina as they approached the tall iron gates of Kirovo Palace. Although her heart ached for her family and friends, the beautiful surroundings soothed her discomfort.

Two guards hauled open the gates, and the carriages rolled around a pond, then halted at the entrance of the palace.

Moments after stopping, Filip opened the door and smiled at her. "Welcome home."

Her gaze lingered on the stone palace in front of her. The walls were painted a sea foam green, which stood out against the white window frames and pillars. Each pillar's capital gleamed a brilliant gold. An oval shaped plaque hung above the entrance, welcoming guests to Kirovo Palace.

"Here." He lifted his hand for her to hold.

She bowed her head a fraction, then rested her fingers on top of his knuckles. He guided her to the stone steps running parallel to the building. A male and female servant awaited them.

"Fetch Ms. Orlova and Ms. Abramova's luggage and have it sent to their respective rooms," Filip said.

The female servant bowed and obeyed.

The man positioned outside the front door opened it, revealing an open foyer and marble flooring, which led to a grand staircase embellished with gilded frescoes and ornamentation, granite columns, and sweeping balustrades of marble.

The archway on the ground floor directly ahead led to the kitchens, pantry, and scullery—the scent of baking bread wafted through the open doors—and several doors indicated a variety of other rooms on the ground floor, ones she'd explore later.

Adelina pressed her palm to her breast. "It's beautiful."

Filip smiled. "I'm sure your chambers will please you both. Follow me."

He led them up the curving staircase and down a long corridor branching right from the main landing. Thick red carpet crushed underfoot, and golden framed portraits graced the walls.

"This one is yours, Salma." He pointed to the second door on the right. "The servants will show you around the palace. This evening, a feast will be served with our finest wine, seeing as we were unable to celebrate the New Year on our travels."

"Thank you, sir." She curtsied, then disappeared into her room.

"I've saved the best for you, of course." He smiled and cast Adelina a playful look from the corner of his eyes.

At the end of the corridor was a large, undressed window, and beside it, the door to her chamber. She glanced at him before entering the room.

Against the left wall was a mahogany four-poster bed dressed in blue covers and white drapes. An ornate coving connected the tall walls to the high ceilings, and a sprawling, cream rug spread across the wooden floorboards. Beautiful, framed portraits graced the walls, and a golden candelabra chandelier hung from the ceiling.

She gasped, spinning around to face a smiling Filip. "I'll be honest with you; I wasn't expecting a room so lavish."

"You must understand your value, Adelina. Perhaps you won't yet, but once your training commences, you will know and realise why I treat you so. I want you to be comfortable here."

"It's a remarkable home you have." She rested her hands on the wide windowsill, and glanced out at the rippling, circular pond, and the stretching, groomed gardens to either side.

"There will be plenty of time to explore the grounds, Adelina. Make yourself at home. The wardrobe is stocked with newly made gowns but alert me if you require fabric from town. You'll meet your maiden shortly—she'll take you to the bathrooms and help you dress. This evening, we will celebrate the prospects of a New Year."

"Thank you," she said.

When she was alone in her room, she traced her fingers lightly over the thin, white drapes hanging from the posters on her bed. She plonked onto the mattress, then flung back and stretched her arms out on the wide surface. A grin spread across her lips. Although she was grateful for everything her parents had done for her, she'd never experienced luxury like this before.

Within a split second, a wave of loneliness hit her, and she furrowed her brows. Her pleasure dissipated.

A Ballad of Severed Souls

The fineries surrounding her wouldn't dull the ache in her heart and its longing for Damir and her family. The following morning, she'd have her grandfather's pocket watch fixed in the hopes it would bring her comfort.

Moments later, someone rapped on the door. She hopped to her feet, composed herself, then opened it.

"Miss Adelina." A pale-faced woman in an apron curtsied. "My name is Natasha, and I'll be your maiden for the duration of your stay. You may call on me at any time—day or night. My chamber is at the back of the building with the rest of the household workers. May I escort you to the bathing room?"

"Of course." She smiled, skirting around her luggage stowed to the side of the doorway.

She followed Natasha along the ruby red carpet, across the landing overlooking the grand entrance, then through a corridor leading to the back of the palace. They passed a multitude of doors, curving steps, and winding corridors until they reached a steamy room.

"The bathtub has been filled for you, miss." Natasha opened the door and guided her inside.

Adelina removed her shoes, then dipped behind the wooden divider opposite the steaming granite tub. Thin voiles dressed the window, but from their height, no one would catch a glimpse.

She slipped out of her clothes, placing them on a small dresser in front of her. Cautiously, she tiptoed across the wooden flooring, eyed the servant, and climbed into the tub. A delighted sigh escaped her lips as she sank into the hot water.

Natasha unravelled her hair by freeing the curls from their pins. She placed them in a dish on a counter beneath an oval mirror, then returned with a glass jug. "Sit forward, miss."

Adelina scooted into the centre of the tub.

"There it is," Natasha said, a note of surprise in her airy tone.

"What?" Adelina glanced over her shoulder. "Oh, the sun mark."

Lifting her fingers, Natasha traced it. "It's one thing hearing about it, and another to see it." She smiled. "It's so great to have you here. Filip will be proud."

Adelina crossed her arms over her chest, unable to ignore the anxiety the sun mark gave her. How could she live up to what Filip expected of her?

Natasha filled the jug to the brim, then tilted Adelina's head back, keeping her forehead shielded by her left palm. The warm water poured onto her long, brown hair. Being bathed in this way reminded her of when her mother used to wash her tenderly as a child, and her heart ached.

Once her hair was washed and her body scrubbed, she stepped out of the bath, and Natasha wrapped a large cotton towel around her shoulders.

"Dry yourself behind the divider, and I will fetch you a gown suitable for this evening's festivities." Natasha curtsied before leaving the room.

A few moments later, she returned.

Wrapped in her towel and her wet hair sticking to her back, Adelina peered around the partition. Natasha placed several dress components and undergarments on top of a dresser, then placed the shoes on the floor.

Clasping her hand over her mouth, Adelina gazed at the white silk caftan and the embroidered velvet sarafan. The sleeves were long and open, while the skirts were ruched and gathered at the waist, held together by a golden cord.

"Now, while it may look pretty to the eye, I must warn you, miss—the garment will be heavy and the bodices will be tightly boned, but soon enough, you'll grow used to the customary fashion." She smiled.

Natasha helped her into her silk underdress, then pulled the thick layers of the sarafan over her head. At the waist, the dress puffed out into a bell-like shape. Next, Adelina was fitted into the corseted bodice, and the sleeves at the shoulders mirrored the style of the skirt.

Once fastened in place, she peered over her shoulder and gazed at the gold-embroidered train. "While beautiful, I feel as if I am wearing armour."

Natasha chuckled light-heartedly. "Fear not, you won't be the only lady dressed as such. Ms. Salma and the other ladies will be dressed in a similar fashion."

Adelina turned to face Natasha, then eyed her simple white dress. "I mean not to offend you, but I must say there are some differences between our garments."

"Well, of course." Natasha nodded. "When Mr. Tarasov greets you, you'll notice his clothing will be stitched with golden fabric, much like yours—to show your rank."

Her cheeks warmed. Ranks? How could a rural village girl be thrust into the life of luxury and status when she held no claim to such things?

"Forgive my lack of understanding, but I've come from Aramoor. If you know the place, then you will know I'm not used to all this finery."

"So, it may be, but you are of a great deal of importance now. Come, slip into your shoes, and let me escort you back to your chambers. I will fix your hair."

Adelina's heart leapt into her throat as she approached the grand stairwell. Guests gathered in the foyer, with glasses of wine in their hands. Their bustling chatter hushed as Filip turned his head upwards to catch a glance of her standing on the top step.

She gazed down at him, caught his reassuring smile, then glided down the stairs, using the rail for balance, and taking care not to trip in her heeled shoes. Salma awaited her at the bottom, and Filip, dressed in a gold embroidered shirt and trousers, made his way towards them.

"You look radiant." He took Adelina's hand in his and kissed it. "Now that you have joined us, I will assemble the guests in the reception room. The feast will be ready shortly."

A nearby servant carried a silver platter, with glasses filled halfway with a deep red wine. Filip took two, then handed one to her and Salma. "Enjoy."

He slipped away into the crowd.

Adelina placed her hand in the crook of Salma's elbow. "There are so many people, I'm not too sure where to start. Are they his friends? Benefactors? Perhaps some have magic. He mentioned there were others with abilities."

A Ballad of Severed Souls

"Don't fret, child. I am sure he will make introductions." Salma patted her hand.

Her greying hair was tied at the top of her head, and several loose strands curled around either side of her spectacles. She carried herself with grace and composure that Adelina hoped to one day mimic.

Once inside the reception, Filip returned to Adelina's side, then ushered her forwards, positioning her in front of the crowd. A fire crackling in the hearth behind them provided warmth, and the lit candelabra chandeliers filled the room with a radiant glow. Silverware was laid on each of the round, wooden tables, with flower arrangements in the centre.

"Ladies and gentlemen, may I introduce you to Ms. Adelina Orlova. She is the light I have been in search of for the past ten years. Finally, my prayers have been answered. I would like to thank you all for your continued support. Tomorrow, we will make a public appearance, but tonight, you have the honour of meeting my missing half—it is *she* who possesses astral magic."

The room filled with gasps and murmurs. Adelina stared into the crowd, her heart thrumming, her fingers trembling.

"I will advise you to treat Adelina with the utmost respect and, more importantly, join us both in this grand celebration, for a new age is upon us. The age of union, the three countries together, has begun!" He thrust his glass into the air, and the guests cheered, meeting his toast.

Adelina took a large gulp of wine, curtsied, then shimmied out of centre stage.

Filip caught her by the elbow and met her with a warm smile. "Fear not, I will prepare you with what to say tomorrow at the public appearance, but for now, enjoy yourself. There is someone I would like to introduce you to."

She nodded, swallowing the anxious lump in her throat.

He guided her through the chattering crowd of formally attired courtiers. Salma followed, remaining a mere few steps behind.

Ahead was a short woman with grey hair pinned neatly away from her face. Large blue eyes sparkled, and fine wrinkles stood out like crows' feet from the outer corners.

She curtsied before them, then kissed Adelina on both cheeks. "Ms. Orlova, what a pleasure it is to meet you."

Her stomach churned with nerves. She'd never been surrounded by so many unfamiliar faces before.

"This is Yelena Belsky. She will be your primary mentor when it comes to your magical training. She'll teach you how to harness your magic amongst other things, but I'll let her tell you about that. I've got to greet some of my benefactors, so I leave you in her capable hands," Filip said.

"Thank you," Adelina said. "It's a pleasure to meet you, Ms. Belsky."

"Call me Yelena, dear." She tucked a stray, grey curl behind her ear. Taking her by the arm, Yelena steered her towards a round table dressed with an array of platters, including cold cuts of meat, cured fish, mixed salad, pickled beets, tomatoes, mushrooms, and hard cheeses. "The cooks serve the most wonderful zakuski here."

Adelina gazed at the small dishes of food and her mouth watered.

"To eat before the feast, of course." Yelena smiled and gestured to a servant who carried a tray of shot glasses. She took two, then handed one to Adelina. "Take a gulp of vodka, then wash it down with a bite of this delightful food."

"I'm starving." She slugged the alcoholic drink, then popped a chunk of hard cheese into her mouth, relishing its pleasant, savoury taste.

"Some of the ladies and gentlemen here are known for polishing off at least four rounds of vodka and zakuski before dinner is even served!" Deep creases formed around the elder lady's eyes as a grin spread across her lips.

"I wouldn't want to embarrass myself in front of Filip and his guests, so I think I'll take my time," Adelina dipped her head, "and I don't want a headache while attending the public appearance tomorrow. Any thoughts on what I'll need to say or do?" She leaned towards her new companion, hoping to gain a useful insight into what was to come.

"I wouldn't worry, dear. He wants to show you off to his loyal supporters who've funded his cause for many years. You're a great asset, and he's thrilled to have you. Look at him beaming!" She pointed to Filip, who stood deep in conversation with three grey-haired men in the centre of the room.

"What do you mean, funding?"

"Well, his family is wealthy, of course, and he secured a considerable sum from his father. However, if Filip wants to remain in power, he needs support, people who believe in his cause, and men who will offer him weapons, coin, boats, you name it."

Adelina paused to process her words. It seemed Filip was well-liked, considering the many guests who flocked to his side.

"Do you believe in his cause?" she said.

"Certainly, dear, and you're going to help him on the way to greatness."

Filip tapped a knife against his glass at the back of the hall by the banquet room doors, catching the guests' attention. "Please take your seats. Dinner will be served."

The ladies and gentlemen slid into their chairs. Adelina sat beside Salma with Filip and Yelena opposite her.

"I hope you two have gotten acquainted—you'll be seeing a lot of each other over the coming months." Filip unravelled his napkin, then draped it over his lap.

Adelina raised an eyebrow. "A few months?"

"It's nothing to worry about." He smiled. "I want to ensure you have plenty of time to complete your training."

Yelena offered a reassuring smile.

Servants carrying cloches filtered into the room, positioned the plates in front of each guest, then lifted the metal dome, revealing a golden-crusted pastry, potatoes, carrots, and peas.

With her cutlery in her hands, Adelina tucked into the food, taking care to chew each mouthful as graciously as she could. She placed her fork on the rim of her plate, wiped the corners of her mouth with the napkin, then resumed eating.

Several hours after the feast, once plenty of vodka was consumed, carriages arrived to escort the guests to their homes. Servants tidied away the tables and bustled into the kitchens, while Filip retired to his drawing room after bidding Adelina and Salma good night.

Salma fell into step beside her as they climbed the grand staircase. "What a celebration."

"It was rather lovely," Adelina said. "Although I am feeling a little homesick. Perhaps I ought to write to my family, and Damir too."

"I'd imagine it would bring you comfort."

Salma kissed her cheeks briefly before entering her room. Adelina glided along the velvet carpet, then disappeared into her chamber.

The curtains were already drawn, and a fire crackled in the hearth, casting a warm, orange glow across the room.

She kicked off her shoes, then sank into the chair in front of her dressing table. While she tried hard to pull the pins from her hair, she'd drank one too many glasses of vodka.

Someone knocked on the door.

"Come in." Adelina swivelled around in the chair, and the sudden movement made her stomach spin.

"Good evening, miss." Natasha curtsied. "I've come to help you change out of your dress and remove the bed warmer."

"Of course." Adelina gestured for her to come closer—a wide grin on her mouth. "Did you enjoy the celebrations?"

"Oh, the household staff don't attend the celebrations, dear. But we were able to enjoy the leftover food," she said. "I came to prepare your chambers when the carriages came through the gates."

"You didn't have to go to such lengths but thank you." Adelina rose, then stumbled over to the bed. She rested her hands on one of the posters. "Can you help me get out of this corset? I'm afraid my fingers have turned to butter, and I won't be able to undo the laces."

Natasha smiled and went to her side. She worked on the laces, then drew the garment over her head.

As Adelina slipped out of the sarafan, she tripped over the hem, then fell onto the mattress. A laugh escaped her.

"Are you all right, miss?" Natasha pursed her lips.

"I'm fine." Adelina shifted into a sitting position and crossed her legs. "I think I might've drunk too much."

Natasha fetched her a nightgown from the wardrobe. "Here. Take off your silk underdress and put this on. I'll help you."

Wobbling, Adelina stood and stripped naked. Natasha didn't bat an eyelid, and lifted the nightgown over Adelina's head, guiding her arms into the sleeves.

Turning back the covers, Natasha removed the bed warmer.

Adelina slid into bed and flung herself back against the plumped pillows. "Thank you."

"You are most welcome. Sleep well, miss. I'll come to wake you in the morning." She glided out of the room, leaving Adelina alone, and enveloped with warmth.

FIVE

Embassy

The following morning, Adelina stretched across the mattress, yawned, then rose onto her elbows. Golden sunlight streamed through the gaps in the curtains and embers sparked in the hearth.

A frown creased her brows as a memory from the previous night's celebration resurfaced. Today, she'd be making her first public appearance with Filip.

Scratching the side of her face, she wondered what was in store for her. What did he expect her to say or even do? It'd been less than two weeks since the test revealed astral magic flowed within her, and she'd spent exactly none of that time practising her magic. Her training was yet to start.

Nonetheless, Filip's benefactors would be expecting to meet her. After all, each town and village in Toichrist, Temauten, and Saintlandsther would likely know. The problem was, Adelina didn't *know* what she could do, so how in the realm was she going to give a speech?

She dragged a hand over her face. Someone rapped on the door, jolting her from her thoughts.

She drew the covers over her chest as she lifted into a sitting position. "Come in."

"Good morning, miss," Natasha curtsied, beaming. "It's time to get you dressed and fed. You'll be meeting with Filip this morning. He'll want to talk to you before the public announcement later on today."

Nodding once, Adelina slid out of bed, then padded across the thick carpet towards the chair in front of the mirror.

"Do you know what I should expect?" she said as Natasha drew a brush through her knotted, bedraggled hair.

"As you know, Filip has been looking for you for a decade—he wants to show you off!" Natasha said. "More so, I think it is a way of showing his benefactors he does indeed mean business."

"What do you mean?" Adelina frowned.

"Well, he's found you for a start, miss." Natasha set the brush aside once she was done. "You are the beginning of some positive things. Preparations can be made, and treaties can be drawn between the countries. It doesn't matter if someone is from the rural towns of Temauten, or the highlands of Saintlandsther, but they'll surely know of astral magic and its importance."

"Shouldn't I speak with Yelena first?" Adelina swivelled in her chair, looking Natasha straight in the eyes. "She's going to be my primary teacher, right?

Perhaps she can explain the details of my training. I don't know what I'll be doing to help these people, but I *do* want to help."

Natasha patted her on the shoulder. "Don't fret, miss. I'm sure you will be fine."

After breakfast, Natasha escorted Salma and Adelina through the long conservatories at the back of the palace.

"Mr. Tarasov will be with you shortly." Natasha gestured to a stone bench in front of white rose bushes beside a water fountain. "Take a seat."

Adelina reclined onto the bench next to Salma, then tapped her fingers on her leg.

"It's a beautiful place, isn't it?" Salma's gaze travelled along the full rose bushes—butterflies fluttered through the open windows and landed on the delicate petals.

"It is." Adelina's gaze dropped to her gold embroidered sarafan skirt. "Although I wish I could share this with Damir."

Salma smiled and placed her hand on Adelina's knee. "This evening, once you've completed your duties, we'll call for some parchment and ink for the letter you need to write."

"I'd love that." Adelina squeezed her hand. "I'm glad you're here with me."

"Of course, dear," Salma said.

Natasha curtsied as Filip strolled through the conservatory towards them.

Unsure of how else to behave in his presence, Adelina rose, then smoothed her already creaseless sarafan.

"Good morning, Ms. Orlova." Filip beamed. "I'm sure you slept well?"

"Yes, thank you." She bowed her head.

"Will you join me for tea?" He gestured to a circular, white iron table and two chairs nestled between the rose bushes.

"Certainly," she said, smoothing her hair back from her face.

Salma remained on the stone bench, continuing her role as chaperone, but from a sensible distance.

Filip offered Adelina his arm, then escorted her to the table. Water on the fountain trickled, accompanied by the twitter of birdsong from the trees outside.

Several servants tended to the rose bushes, while another brought them a tray. She set the china teapot, cups, and saucers on the table, then took five steps back.

"I have a lot planned for you today, my sun." Filip poured the tea, the scent of bergamot and citrus wafting on the steam. "Before we get started, I want you to feel at home. You are not a stranger here, Adelina."

She smiled, then sipped her tea. "What should I expect from the public announcement?"

"This will be my opportunity to show you to the world, of course," he said. "I have a lot of support—financially and politically—from wealthy men in all three countries. They are all invested in my plan to reunite the people. It will be my chance to show them

A Ballad of Severed Souls

they weren't wrong for standing by me for the past ten years while I searched for you."

Trying to ignore her mounting nerves, she forced a smile. Filip's words sounded like a whole deal of pressure placed on her. "I want to help you. What can I do?"

"I'm glad you are as invested in this as I am," he said. "You won't be required to do anything except attend. Salma will accompany you, and Yelena will be there too. You'll have plenty of support."

"When does my training start?" she asked. "The sooner I learn how to use my magic, the sooner I can make a difference for people."

"Tomorrow." He sipped his tea. "As I mentioned, it'll last a few months, then afterwards, the real work begins. We will travel to Saintlandsther where you will see, first-hand, the poor living conditions and poverty. Toichrist, on the other hand, has vast, rich lands used for cultivating, and mines to explore. If I could make an agreement between the countries, I could set up trade deals and create a democracy to lead a united kingdom."

"You want to create one country?" She arched a brow.

"It is the only way to truly unite them. If all works, I will become interim President of the Republic lands." Filip's eyes gleamed with confidence.

"How do I fit into all of this?" A lightness filled her chest, and her pulse quickened. Could she help to make a difference for the people living in poverty and bring a balance between the three countries?

"Magic is power." Filip relaxed into his chair. "You'll see this during your training. The highest skilled sorcerers are assigned to one of the three governing bodies. You have the Temauten Congregation in Murtei not too far from your hometown, the Saintlandsther Council, and the Convocation of Toichrist, which I currently lead."

"And now you have found astral magic, you'll be at your strongest." Her lips parted as she connected the dots.

"Precisely. We will *both* be at our strongest when we are together." He stretched across the table and rested his fingers on her hand holding her mug. "Astral and nether magic are halves of one soul by nature. When the other governing bodies see us both at the public announcement, any doubt in their loyalties to us will be eradicated."

Adelina frowned. He spoke of their power as if it were a living entity—a concept she couldn't quite wrap her head around yet. Perhaps she'd believe it when she saw it in practise.

"Thank you for the tea." She sipped the last mouthful, then set the cup on its saucer. "Is there a clockmaker in town? I'd like to make a visit if time allows for it."

"There is. Tell the coachman to take you to *Francov's Clocks*, but ensure you are back by three."

She rose, flattening her sarafan with her palms. As she turned to leave, she realised she hadn't the funds to pay for the repairs on her grandfather's pocket watch.

"Have Natasha provide you with ruble," he said, perhaps noticing her pressed lips, revealing her inner thoughts.

"Thank you, kindly." She bowed her head graciously.

"There's no need for such formalities." He shunted his chair back, then rose. "After all, we will be working and living together. I want you to feel at ease around me."

She nodded—her lips curving up slightly. "I'd like to return to my chamber and write a letter home. My family will be happy to hear from me."

"Of course—I'll have writing implements sent to your room," he said.

As she turned to leave, Salma re-joined her, placing Adelina's hand in the crook of her elbow.

"Did he tell you anything important, my dear?" she asked—her large eyes sparkling.

"He did." There was a slight hop to Adelina's step as they left the conservatory and headed outside the main entrance of Kirovo Palace. "I'll tell you on the way to *Francov's Clocks*."

A servant cleared away the empty teacups as Filip left the conservatory and headed towards his office, which overlooked the gardens. The lawns were clipped short; the bushes cut into topiaries, and the flowerbeds bloomed. Sunlight drenched the Fernleaf peonies, royal azaleas, and the Lady Slipper Orchids.

Only the finest flowers for my garden.

He smiled as he leaned on the windowsill, watching a bird as it flew overhead, then disappeared into the aspens behind his property.

Then it was time to place his attention on more pressing matters—informing his father, Antanov

Tarasov, of his success after ten long, hard years. He paced the length of the thick, red carpet, his fingers pressed to his lips. Antanov was a difficult man—stern and a challenge to impress—and their relationship had always been strained. Growing up, Filip had taken to many different sports, such as jousting, fencing, and polo, yet even when mastered, Antanov would turn his nose up, and no words of congratulations were shared.

Climbing social and political ladders—that would surely win his father's approval.

Positioned a few feet ahead of him, on the parquet floor, was his solid oak desk. He slid onto the plush chair, plucked his quill between his fingers, then dipped it into the inkpot.

With his left hand, he held the parchment steady as he wrote.

Father,

I'm writing to share extraordinary news—astral magic has been found in a girl by the name of Adelina Orlova. We meet with the benefactors later today, and her training commences tomorrow.

If all goes to plan, their support will be indefinite, and their loyalties unwavering. I make a promise to you, my dearest father. I will unite the countries into one Republic, where I will rule as emperor for as long as I shall live.

May you continue to fund my mission, if it pleases you.

Your obedient son,
Filip Tarasov.

He folded the parchment, then slipped it into an envelope, sealing it with red wax.

A Ballad of Severed Souls

Creating a steeple with his fingers, and resting his elbows on the desk, he leaned forwards. He'd simply told Adelina his role was interim—a President, *not* an Emperor.

If he could turn her into the strongest sorcerer after training with Yelena, well…she would be indispensable. Her access to astral—sun magic—would prove invaluable in any wars to come, should there be any. To secure his position as Emperor, under the pretence and promise of uniting the countries into a democratic government, he'd fall into battle with Temauten and Saintlandsther. He'd claim them through war and force, but these were troubles for another day.

A servant came to take away his letter, so he turned his attention to a thick, leather-bound book positioned on the right side of his desk. He flicked through the parchment and landed on a page inscribed *Sorcerer Training*.

Tracing his fingers across the words written by Yelena, he absorbed the information—the exact teachings Adelina would learn. Nodding to himself in approval, he closed the book and left the room.

With his hand gliding along the banister, he ascended the grand stairs, then walked past the corridor leading to Salma and Adelina's bedrooms. He took the next corridor, strolling until he reached his own chamber at the back of the palace.

The only other thing he needed to do was find himself a wife, someone worthy of siring his children. If he was to maintain his position as Emperor of the Republic, he'd need an heir.

"Who better to entrust my kingdom with?" he said to himself as he sank on to his down-stuffed mattress.

He rubbed his hands together slowly, and a slight grin curved his lips.

Adelina, with Salma beside her, strolled along the cobbled streets of the bustling Toichrist town. Civilians filed in and out of seamstresses, markets, and shoemakers. A hearty scent from the local tavern wafted on the slight breeze.

They neared a stove maker store, and Adelina bit her lip—her heart swelled with longing to see her family.

Salma placed her hand on Adelina's shoulder. "Don't worry, dear. You can write to them later."

Adelina swivelled around and smiled. "I know. How will I survive months away from them? It hasn't even been three weeks yet."

"You'll be fine," Salma said. "I'm sure Filip will allow visitations. Besides, you know why you're here. Think of everything you're going to achieve."

"You're right." Adelina headed for *Francov's Clocks*.

She grasped the handle, then swung the door inwards, subsequently ringing a small bell hanging above.

The interior was filled with an assortment of clocks—wall fixtures, grandfathers, pocket watches, tabletop clocks, and, towards the back of the room, a workshop. Broken clock faces and hands lined the wooden workbenches. Polishing cloths were dotted about, beside pliers, and spare pendulum swings.

A Ballad of Severed Souls

An old man, with tied back hair, hunched over his current project, hummed to himself as he tended to the mechanism with care.

"Good morning, Sir," Adelina said as she neared the man. "Are you Francov?"

He whirled around—a gentle smile upon his face. "Ah, good day to you, miss! Francov is indeed my name. How can I help you?"

She withdrew the pocket watch from within her satchel, then handed it to the clockmaker. "Do you think you can fix it?"

"What a rare piece of gold you have here." He lowered his spectacles and inspected the timepiece. "Where did you find this?"

"It belonged to my grandfather, but it doesn't appear to be working." She closed her satchel and waited for the man to make his verdict.

"An heirloom piece, you say?" He raised a brow in fascination as he smoothed the gold surface with his thumb. "I'll have a look."

He beckoned Adelina and Salma around the front desk, and towards his workbench at the back.

"What do we have here?" He frowned as he popped open the watch and peered at the small gear train. With flat pliers, he removed the inner pieces. After a moment of closer study, the crease eased between his brows. "The mainspring is broken."

Adelina glanced at Salma, who shrugged. Neither of them were familiar with the intricacies of clock repairs and services.

Casting a glance over his shoulder, he said, "Fear not, miss, it can be replaced."

As the man got to work, dozens of clocks chimed, varying in tones. Adelina jumped—her gaze darting from one set of hands to another.

"Noon!" he chirped as he pieced together the heirloom, then guided them back to the front desk. "Are you new around here, miss? I don't think I've seen you before."

Adelina cast an uncertain look at Salma. Word travelled fast of the girl with astral magic, but not many people yet knew what she looked like, aside from the benefactors she'd met the previous night.

"I am." Once she'd checked the watch to see the little hands moving, she handed the man a dozen ruble from the pouch Natasha had given her. "Is this sufficient?"

"Indeed." He took the coins—an airy smile upon his face. "I bid good day to you, miss."

Together, Adelina and Salma left the shop and headed for the tavern. She wanted a cooked meal without the fuss of servants around her. A tavern would remind her of home.

"You should make the most of your anonymity while you can." Salma nudged her as they strolled along the winding path towards the tavern door.

"I thought the same." Adelina bit her lip. "It won't be long before everyone recognises me. I doubt I'll be able to enjoy simplicities such as these."

"Come," Salma said in a light tone as she heaved in the wooden door, and the scent of stewed beef and potatoes greeted them.

A Ballad of Severed Souls

A carriage beat along the path, taking Filip, Adelina, and Salma to the public announcement. *Where* that was exactly, remained a mystery.

She kept her hands clasped in her lap, ignoring her trembling fingers. She couldn't help the nerves racking inside her.

When the carriage came to a halt, the coachman placed a stool in front of it, then opened the door. He held out his hand.

Adelina flattened her skirt with her sweating palms, rested her hand on the coachman's, then lowered herself onto the steps with as much grace as she could muster. Salma and Filip followed behind her.

"Welcome to the Embassy." He gestured to the large, white marble building in front of them—its roof was domed and the colour of weathered copper. "You'll meet all the important benefactors, including the chosen leader of the Temauten Congregation and the Saintlandsther Council."

Her mouth dried and an empty sensation festered in the pit of her stomach.

"You've gone pale, my dear." Filip took her by the arm. "There's no need to worry. The people will be excited to make your acquaintance."

She gave a small nod and clutched his arm tighter than she'd wanted to. Although she knew frighteningly little about this man, she trusted him. There was no other choice.

"Perhaps we should get her some water." Salma's eyebrows knitted together in concern.

"I'll be fine." Despite her words, her chest tingled. She breathed in deeply, then followed the path towards the grand double doors.

Filip patted her hand as it rested in the crook of his arm.

"Good afternoon, Mr. Tarasov," the man posted outside said. "This must be Ms. Orlova?"

"She certainly is." Filip beamed.

"A pleasure." The man bowed, then opened the door.

Inside, two wooden staircases curved around both walls, meeting at a landing overlooking the entrance. In the centre of the foyer was a wooden table, and positioned on top, a large blue vase filled with fresh pansies.

"The men are gathered in the room ahead." Filip gestured in front of them. "Salma, there will be a seat for you on the balcony. Follow the stairs and the servant will show you from there."

"Of course," she said, then squeezed Adelina's free hand. "You'll do perfectly."

"Thank you." Adelina was grateful for her chaperone's kind words—they eased the knots in her stomach.

"Come." Filip guided her into the Embassy's main room—emerald chairs were positioned in a crescent moon shape around two large chairs at the other end.

Many faces looked back at her—their mouths slightly open.

Filip showed Adelina to her seat, then swivelled to face the crowd. "I thank you for gathering here today.

It is with great pleasure to introduce you to Adelina Orlova, the girl I have promised."

"Is it true?" one man said. "Did you see the dragon?"

Adelina glanced at Filip, who nodded with encouragement.

She cleared her throat. "Yes. Svarog presented himself to me."

Murmurs from the crowd echoed against the high ceiling.

"She will be working with our best trainer, Yelena. This will take time, of course—several months—however, her presence is vital to our cause. One she has completed her training and can use her magic, we'll be at our strongest and the countries will be united!" Filip's confident voice boomed through the room.

"How do you plan to utilise your power?" another man said, rising from his chair.

"It's good to see you here, Nikolay." Filip smiled, then turned to face Adelina. "He's the leader of the Temauten Congregation—perhaps you've seen him on broadsheets at your hometown?"

She nodded. "I believe so."

Filip returned his gaze to Nikolay. "When the wielders of astral and nether magic are together, no other form of magic can challenge it. Adelina and I will use our powers to oppose any threats that may rise up against the republic. Astral magic is sun magic—Adelina will have the ability to help plants and vegetation grow in even in the most stubborn terrain. She will be able to wield sunlight itself, which in essence, is fire."

"Which could wreak havoc across the countries." Nikolay frowned.

"So could nether," Filip said coolly. "As you are aware, I have the ability to cast a never-ending night over the realm of Kirromund, if I so pleased. However, my desire is not to destroy our countries, but to create a greater one."

"Haven't you claimed you are both stronger together?" Nikolay said. "Surely, this means you are *more* than capable of destruction."

"Pardon me, Nikolay, but what has brought on your doubt?" Filip said. "You have been a trusted benefactor of my cause for the last ten years. If you'd any doubt in your mind we were going to set the countries on fire or cast them into eternal darkness, you wouldn't continue funding our mission."

"As you said, it has taken you ten years. Now Adelina is here...well, it is all very real." He smiled, although Adelina couldn't be sure it was genuine.

"I assure you—I have no intention of bringing ill-will to anyone in *any* country," she said, then glanced to the balcony at Salma, who offered an encouraging nod.

"It's a pleasure to meet you, Adelina." A woman rose. "My name is Olga—I'm the leader of the Saintlandsther Congregation. Despite the concerns Nikolay has raised, I believe your abilities will be welcomed amongst the people in Saintlandsther. The country is in recession, crops struggle to grow and thrive in the polluted soil, and our resources are low because of it. There isn't enough food to feed so many mouths."

"It would be an honour to help restore your lands," Adelina said. "As soon as I've completed my training, of course."

"As interim President of the Republic, I promise your country will not go hungry again," Filip said—his tone full of conviction. "Trades can be set up between the villages, and our magic will prevent harm to our country. You also have your assigned sorcerer, who will ensure you day-to-day protection."

Adelina scanned the crowd, wondering who their sorcerers might be. They wore nothing that set them out from the rest.

"I have a question for you, Adelina," Olga asked. "Did you receive any signs you possessed astral magic before the test?"

"I did." Adelina arched a brow. "Vividly. There was an altar and a crow...I woke up with the sun mark on my shoulder."

Murmurs filled the room. Even Filip cast her a sideways glance. Neither of these came as a surprise to Adelina—she hadn't told anyone other than her mother and Damir about the dream.

"The sun mark is as old as time," Filip said, stifling the stirring crowd. "Proof of her magical abilities. We will not fail you."

Questions erupted, people demanding to know more, but Filip quickly escorted Adelina out of the room.

"What's wrong?" She glanced over her shoulder at the people left behind.

"Nothing." Filip opened the carriage door. "They know all they need to know. It's time we got you back to the palace where you can study and train. Any questions they have will be answered when they see how powerful you'll be."

"You have a lot of faith in me when I haven't even begun." Adelina climbed into the carriage. He hoisted himself in afterwards. They waited for Salma to return from the balcony.

The guests from the Embassy had already filed out of the building, clustering around the carriage—their questions booming outside.

"Shouldn't we speak to them? Settle their doubts?" She glanced out the window, overlooking the crowd. "We were there for the whole of five minutes. I was expecting something…more."

"A politician never gives all their answers." Filip smiled.

Frowning, she sat back against the cushions.

Once Salma reached the carriage, the coachman whipped them away, beating along the cobbles, leaving the Embassy and all its questions behind.

∾

Filip guided Adelina into his office, then gestured for her to take a seat in the velvet chair opposite his desk. He slid into his own chair and faced her with a pleasant smile. Salma waited outside the open door.

"Here's your schedule for the next week." He handed her a piece of parchment. "It's a summary of the contents in this book."

As he tapped his fingers on the leather-bound booked titled *Sorcerer Training*, Adelina held the parchment in her hands, scanning the cursive writing.

A Ballad of Severed Souls

"Combat training?" She glanced up at him.

"You'll be participating in a mixture of theory, practice, and physical classes," he said. "Followed by one-on-one sessions with Yelena specifically about your astral magic."

She gulped. "This is a lot. What could I possibly need combat training for?"

"As I've mentioned before, we could face opposition from neighbouring countries or anyone who poses a threat to us." He clasped his hands on the desk between them. "Even if war was not to happen, it is always best to be prepared. All sorcerers are highly-skilled fighters—they know how to use a sword as well as their magic."

"Am I needed for the rest of the day?" She rubbed the side of her head. "I've a bit of a headache and I'd like a bath before my training starts tomorrow."

"You may retire," Filip said. "Explore the castle grounds, read, or write—whatever you want to do. Natasha is at your disposal."

"Thank you." She rose. "I need to write a letter to my parents."

"Of course." He turned his attention to a stack of envelopes on his desk, perhaps the day's influx of mail he needed to sift through.

Turning on her heel, she left the room, re-joined with Salma, then headed to her chamber.

SIX

Prism World

Morning sunlight warmed Adelina's cheeks as she perched on the windowsill, overlooking the front entrance to Kirovo Palace. Birds sang nearby—their melodic tunes floating on the slight breeze through the ajar window.

She leaned her head against the wall. The silence in the palace, alongside the birdsong, reminded her of home and the quiet countryside. She sucked in a deep breath and stretched her arms.

Someone knocked, drawing Adelina away from her serenity.

"Come in," she said.

"Morning, miss." Natasha opened the door, strode in, then halted halfway across the plush carpet, and her eyes widened. "My gosh, what are you doing with the window open? You'll catch a cold."

"It's warmer here than in Temauten." Adelina shrugged, then hopped off the sill.

"Nonetheless, we can't have you coming down with the sniffles right before your training commences." Natasha gestured to the dressing table. "Take a seat—I'll brush and pin your hair back. You are expected to meet with Yelena and the other trainee sorcerers in an hour."

"Will there be time for food?" Adelina asked as she slid into her chair in front of the round looking glass.

"Providing we don't take too long here." Natasha worked quickly with the curls, pinning them into place, away from Adelina's face. "Now, pop on 'round the screen and get dressed."

A few moments later, Adelina was dressed and ready to leave.

Together, they exited the room, strolled along the corridor, and descended the stairs. Natasha guided Adelina to the dining room, where she was served breakfast. Once she'd eaten, Natasha ushered her outside.

"This is the training facility." Natasha pointed to a separate dome-roof building past the conservatories and gardens, nestled in front of a cluster of aspens.

As they drew nearer to the wooden doors, Adelina's previously calm demeanour was replaced with nerves. She tapped her fingers against her thigh as Natasha opened the doors for her.

Inside, Yelena and several other men and women waited.

"May I introduce Miss Adelina Orlova." Natasha gestured towards her, curtsied, then left the room.

"I'm glad you've joined us." Yelena smiled, crow's feet sprouting from the corner of her eyes behind her spectacles.

Yelena's welcome highlighted the shocked, wide-eyed stares from the other people in attendance. Adelina's gaze wandered from one person to another.

One woman leaned over from the desk she was sat behind and whispered something to the woman next to her.

"Settle down, all." Yelena waved her hands at the individuals murmuring. "We're all here to learn, Adelina included. Show each other respect in this classroom."

Adelina slipped onto the seat behind the vacant desk closest to her. The students formed a crescent shape around Yelena.

"Today, we will learn how to produce magic through a simple task," Yelena said in a clear tone. "Mastering the basics is essential—it creates a solid foundation from which your powers will develop. There is a match placed on your desk. Once you have lit it, you'll move on to the next exercise. Those who fail, will remain until they are able to do so."

Adelina glanced at the wooden surface in front of her, then curled her fingers around the thin, long match. As did the other students.

"How do we light it?" a young, fair girl said. Her auburn hair was tied back in plaits, and faint freckles dotted her nose.

Yelena smiled again, then began a slow pace. "Magic has existed for as long as time itself—it's powerful, difficult to control, but exceptionally extraordinary. Each one of you has the ability to channel it, in some form." She held a match in her hand. "Just because you can channel magic, does not mean you can control it. Light your match without striking it against another object. Produce a flame with your mind and contain it. You will do this by saying the words *areiras therasi*."

The tip of the match lit.

The domed room filled with the awkward sounds of students familiarising themselves with the outlandish words.

In particular, Adelina found the *r* sounds clunky, and she stumbled over them. Her cheeks burned with impatience, but she squashed this and focused on her task. She couldn't let Filip, the benefactors, or the three countries down—they were counting on her.

"*Areiras therasi.*"
"*Areiras therasi.*"
"*Areiras therasi.*"

The incantations continued for over an hour without any flames produced, yet Yelena remained calm-faced at the front of the training room, observing with a watchful eye.

Adelina's own gaze was caught by the ever so slight fizz and crackle of a match clutched between a dark-haired girl's fingers. Her eyes widened with excitement, fuelling her efforts to be the first to succeed.

Returning her gaze to the smooth surface of her desk, Adelina twisted her match between her fingers and frowned.

A few moments later, the satisfying pop of a lit match dragged Adelina's attention back to the squeaking girl, who hopped up and down on one foot, grinning widely at the flame flickering at the top of the stick in her hand.

Yelena, however, didn't share in the excitement—she simply clasped her hands in front of her, keeping her gaze on the girl.

The girl shrieked, dropped the match, which snuffed the flame, then lifted her fingers to her left eye. Adelina gasped as the student's eye turned milky white. A young man darted to her side.

"What's happened to my eye?" the girl's voice rose several octaves. "I can't see!"

"You did not contain your magic, Kira. This is the result. You should never let your ego exceed your abilities."

"Will she be all right?" The young man clutched Kira to his chest, a kind gesture towards someone he didn't know.

"The effect is temporary," Yelena said. "But let it be a warning to all."

Adelina let out a slow breath as she gathered her nerves and collected herself. Gripping the edge of her desk with one hand and clutching the match with the other, she focused her vision on the tip, willing for a golden flame to materialise.

Her temples throbbed as she shifted in her seat, encouraging her magic to flow through her body. Despite her best efforts, no flame came to life.

Glancing around her, she noticed several of the other students with lit matches between their fingers, to which Yelena praised.

Another hour passed, and Adelina and the young man who'd helped Kira hadn't produced a flame at all.

"Class dismissed," Yelena said. "After lunch, you will move on to the next task. Adelina, Kira, and Lev, you will continue your current work."

Adelina shared auspicious glances with Lev and Kira, then headed outdoors with them.

Together, they reclined on a stone bench in the shade of a tall aspen. The breeze was no longer icy but had the cool touch of winter. The fine hairs on Adelina's neck stood on end.

"We're a couple of hours in and my head is pounding." Lev rubbed his forehead.

"Me too." Kira blinked several times—the milkiness had faded from her eye.

"We'll get there, eventually." Adelina mustered as much conviction as she could, but she wasn't certain who she was trying to convince.

They watched the other students—standing amongst the flower bushes—praising one another and whooping with smug satisfaction.

"Ugh." Lev rolled his eyes.

"At least I'm not the only one who hasn't produced a flame yet?" Adelina's doubt made her statement sound more like a question, but she was glad she wasn't alone in her failure.

Kira's brows knitted, then her eyes widened. "You have astral magic. Surely, you should be able to do *all* of these tasks with ease."

This worsened Adelina's festering uncertainty. "I guess not. I'm starting to think the test was wrong, somehow."

"Don't be silly." Lev patted Adelina's knee. "The Seer has been conducting the test for ten years—there's no way she'd get it wrong. Not if you saw the dragon."

"I did." Adelina tapped her fingers against her knee. "I don't feel any different, though."

"You will soon enough." Lev smiled.

Kira sprung to her feet. "Come on, let's get something for lunch."

Once their stomachs were full and the hour break was spent, the students gathered in the training room. Each student who'd completed the first task had a glass lantern positioned in the centre of their desks.

"Your next task is to build upon the flame—light the lantern and contain it. Keep the fire from bursting from its glass container," Yelena said. "In order to do this, you must concentrate. The buzz you felt when you conjured the flame is what you will need to pass the next test. You'll do this by saying *illilriad*."

The spell came with the same consonant issues as the previous one—the '*l*' sounds clumsy in the mouths of those who tried to master it.

Adelina focused on the match in her hands. She drew it closer to her eyes and focused on the tip, willing it to light.

"I did it!" Lev called.

She glanced up as Lev flapped his arms, which snuffed his small flame.

"Well done," Yelena said. "You may move on to the next task."

She handed Lev a glass bottle.

"*Illilriad*."

"*Illilriad*."

"*Illilriad*."

Sucking in a deep breath, Adelina fought to block out the noise around her, then pushed her shoulders back. "*Areiras therasi.*"

Nothing.

Yelena drew nearer—her hands clasped—and watched Adelina.

"You're holding back," she said.

"What? No, I'm not—I'm focusing as hard as I can." Adelina sighed.

"Exactly—you're trying *too* hard. Clear your mind, allow the energy to flow through you. Be at peace with your magic." Yelena smiled before moving on to observe another student.

Adelina moved her shoulders and arms, loosening the muscles as much as she could before realigning her sight on the tip of her match.

"*Areiras therasi.*" Her words were clear and slightly haunted, as if the magic flowed through her vocal cords, straight into the match. The tip fizzed, spitting as if it'd been struck by the stars, before roaring into a flame. She grinned.

"There you go. Wasn't so bad, right?" Yelena gave her the last glass lantern. "Apply the same to this."

This incantation was more complicated than the last—their practice taking up a full two hours before even one person caught a flicker of light within their lanterns.

"Almost there," Yelena said to the student who'd made this breakthrough. "Keep going."

By the end of the day, one student completed their task—a bright, white-gold flame contained perfectly inside the lantern between her hands. She beamed from ear to ear.

"Congratulations, Vera." Yelena took the lantern, then placed it at the front of the training room for everyone to see. "This is what you are all striving to achieve. To the rest of you, go home, eat, sleep, and come back tomorrow, ready to try again."

The students filed out of the room, but Adelina remained, reluctant to abandon her task. Kira and Lev waved to her as they left.

Yelena crossed her arms. "My dear, you need to give your mind a break. Remember what I said—there are consequences to magic. This will be heightened if you do not regain your strength."

Adelina scratched the side of her head. "I know, but I don't want to disappoint Filip or anyone else who is relying on me to get this right."

"It's your first day." Yelena rested her hand on Adelina's arm and patted. "You have plenty of time to achieve great things."

"You're right," Adelina said. "Thank you. I'll see you tomorrow."

Yelena guided Adelina outside, locking the wooden doors behind her.

Salma met Adelina in the gardens, then strolled with her back to the palace. "How was your first day?"

"I'm not sure what I was expecting," Adelina said as a bird flew overhead and landed in its nest amongst the aspens. "Perhaps I assumed it would be a little easier seeing as I supposedly have an ancient form of magic no one else has."

"It takes time. It's day one, after all," Salma said. "Let's go for supper. Then how about we write those letters to your family? Maybe some needlepoint too."

Adelina smiled, reassured by her care. "I'd like that."

Filip's fingers curled around a letter addressed to Adelina. Shutting himself in his office, he dug the letter opener from his desk drawer, then slid it through the sealed envelope.

He flattened the parchment against the desk and sat on his chair as he scanned the cursive writing.

"This won't do," he muttered to himself, tapping the word *Damir* scrawled at the end.

A possible suiter for her would place a considerable block onto his plan to wed her himself and secure a line of heirs for the position of emperor.

Wandering over to the hearth, he tossed the parchment into the flames, and watched it burn. The fire crackled and swelled with its new fuel.

The corners blackened, and within moments, the whole thing turned to ash.

He rested his hand on the mantelpiece. Although he could burn the letters from Damir, he couldn't stop her from writing to him. Damir had already approached her father to ask her permission to wed her—at least as far as he could tell from the letters he'd read. There could be another letter on its way—from her parents, providing Adelina with the knowledge.

Crossing the length of the office, he flung open the door and beckoned the nearest servant. "Has any other mail come for Adelina?"

"No, sir." She curtsied.

"From now on, any mail comes to me first," he said.

"Yes, sir." She dashed off in the direction of the kitchens.

Two days passed before all the students successfully lit matches and their respective lanterns. The rest of the week was spent learning combat moves. Yelena had brought out training dummies made of cloth and stuffed with feathers. Boxes of batons were positioned close by, and Adelina spent her time getting used to the weight of it in her hands, the force of her blows against the dummies. Being the rural village girl she was, her muscles were not as defined as they should be. After an hour of exercise, sweat dripped down her forehead, and by the end of the first day, her muscles screamed in protest.

When Friday came, the students gathered in the gardens. They stood in single file lines, a metre apart, in front of Yelena.

Birds sung nearby and the rising sun warmed Adelina's cheeks.

"Today, you'll put into practice what you have learned over the past few days. The purpose of this exercise is to test your ability to sustain prolonged, substantial physical and mental efforts." Yelena's gaze wandered from one student to the next. "Your body and mind have been challenged up to this point, preparing you in the event of an emergency. There

A Ballad of Severed Souls

may arise a situation where you must escape quickly, defend yourself and others, and at worst, engage in combat with an enemy."

Adelina glanced at the boxes positioned beside them—wooden swords and batons were stacked inside. Every muscle ached and she longed for a hot bath, but she wasn't about to waste the strenuous efforts she'd put into learning combat skills.

"Once you're in your pairs, you will fight each other with a melee weapon in the boxes nearby. Use what you've learned, parry, and your opponent's strengths and weaknesses.. After lunchtime, you will embark on a unique challenge in the prism world."

Adelina frowned. Prism world? What in the realm was that? Several of the other students also shared puzzled expressions.

Yelena divided the students into pairs—Adelina and Lev stood opposite each other, both wielding a baton about two metres long.

"Ready?" Lev said.

"As I'll ever be." Adelina bit the inside of her cheek.

In one swift moment, Lev swung his baton towards her head, which she quickly parried, but his brute force sent her stumbling backwards. She teetered on the verge of losing balance. Of course, he was stronger than her.

Sweeping the stray strands of hair from her face, she lifted her baton and sucked in a deep breath.

They danced around the gardens—their weapons colliding, making mild clomping noises, which disturbed the nestling birds.

Lev's next strike caught her in the rib. She hunched over, wheezing from the pain.

"Sorry," he said.

A mixture of adrenaline and agitation pumped through her. She refused to yield.

Yelena observed nearby. "Remember what I said—learn your opponent's strengths and weaknesses. He is strong and considerably taller than you are. You are small and light on your feet. Time your blocks, dart out of the way when you can, and aim for his exposed spots."

Adelina nodded, her cheeks and lungs burning from exertion.

As Lev swung for her, she leapt aside, leading him on a chase around the bushes. When he came close, she parried his attacks. He panted, and his movements grew sloppier with each swing.

Ducking under an incoming blow, Adelina slid out of the way, raised her baton, then whacked it against his back, which sent him hurtling into a bush.

"Good," Yelena said. "You're learning."

They continued their training for another hour, until they were breathless and bruised from the baton's impact.

Sitting side by side on the stone bench beneath the aspens, Lev and Adelina gulped fresh water from their flasks. Once they were refreshed, they resumed their dance-like fight around the garden until noon, when they left for lunch.

Afterwards, they reconvened in the training room at the far end of the palace grounds.

"Now it is time to test your mind in the prism world." Yelena's steady gaze travelled from one student to another.

"Why do we need to use this prism world?" Kira asked. "We produced magic right here the other day."

"You did, but they were simple spells," Yelena said. "The prism world is a place where you can practise more complex magic. No collateral damage means no innocent civilians will be impacted by your errors. Consequences of failed and uncontrolled magic will affect you and you, alone."

"How do we access it?" Lev asked.

"I will create a passageway for each of you to walk through. It'll take you to a dimension that *is* a prism in essence, displaying your world identically on two shapes facing each other. This mirror reflection of your behaviour will educate you in better ways than I can. Learn from the consequences your actions create." Yelena stepped out from behind her desk at the front of the training room and lifted her sleeves.

She flexed her fingers, and with her right index finger pointed, drew it through the air in a large, circular motion.

The hairs on the back of Adelina's neck stood on end. A sparkling golden hoop zapped into existence beside Yelena.

"Go on through, one at a time. You'll each be taken to your own layer of the prism world," Yelena said. "When you are due return, another passageway will appear."

The students were hesitant at first, lingering behind their desks, until Lev led the way. Kira followed in afterwards, and so did the others, until Adelina was left in the room with Yelena.

"What are you waiting for?" she asked. "You'll do fine. Everything you'll learn will be for good and practical reasons. Take the match, for example—you might need this to light a fire, and once you can produce bigger flames, you can light a hearth or several camps if you're out in the wild with civilians. You can keep people warm."

Adelina nodded once, ignored the tense knots forming in her stomach, and edged closer to the flickering portal. She wiped her clammy hands against her breeches, then lifted her foot and stepped through the passageway.

On the other side, she appeared in the gardens of the palace, and as Yelena had described, the garden was mirrored on both parallel sides of the prism. Adelina could see her own reflection. There were three of her.

She tucked a stray curl behind her ear and wandered along the grass—the space in between the two shapes.

Glancing upwards, she noticed the prism world tapered into a point. She squinted her eyes to shield her vision from the bright, white light pouring from the top.

How strange.

Heading across the manicured lawn, she glanced from one side to the other, wondering how she would learn magic there. Previously, Yelena had told them the relevant spells, but alone, there was nothing to guide her.

Adelina halted. Ahead, two fair, golden-haired women appeared. They were barefoot, wearing white dresses with red embroidery along the collars and cuffs of their sleeves. They approached.

"Who are you?" Adelina edged towards the identical women.

"I am the Morning Zorya," the woman on the left said, then gestured to her sister. "This is my twin, the Evening Zorya."

Adelina arched a brow—she'd heard of the virgin goddesses before in the folklore of her country, but never in her life did she imagine she'd meet them. The same could be said for Svarog, yet she'd met *him* too.

Morning Zorya held a red light in the form of a ring in her right hand. In her left hand, a torch. From its tip stemmed a light green stripe of magic that transitioned into a deeper green, arching above their heads. The stripe ended in her sister's hand. A small bird fluttered from behind Evening Zorya, then soared across the sky. The magic dissipated.

"What was that spell?" Adelina gasped.

"We are sisters of the Sun," Morning Zorya said. Her voice was light and angelic, almost impossible to hear. "I release the Sun on its daily journey, and my sister waits until sunset to meet it. The green magic represents our connection to each other as sisters, and to our brother, the Sun."

"Why have you appeared to me?" Adelina asked.

"Astral magic flows within you," Evening Zorya said and clasped her slender fingers together. "So, you, as the practitioner, are also connected to us and forever will be, for as long as you appeal to the Supreme Power of the Sun."

"I'm not sure how." Adelina shook her head. "I know one spell, and it was difficult for me to master. How am I the person with astral magic? Why did it choose me?"

"We cannot answer those questions, for we do not know the reasons why the Sun God chooses his totem," Morning Zorya said. "The totem is you."

"I appreciate you saying so, truly, but it doesn't help me in learning how to use and control the magic," Adelina said. "Why would you appear to me if it wasn't to help?"

"We *are* here to help," Evening Zorya said—her golden hair billowing behind her on a phantom breeze. "Your fears hold you back, hindering your connection to the Supreme Power. You must clear your mind, liberate yourself from your worries, and *feel* our connection. Close your eyes."

Clamping her bottom lip between her teeth, Adelina obeyed. The twins' voices crept closer, as if they stood right beside her.

"Relax your arms, let your mind go blank," Morning Zorya said. "Then, you will feel us here with you, beside you—guiding you."

Adelina shook her shoulders and let her fingers uncurl. She drew in a breath. In. Out. In. Out. Her heart rate evened, beating a steady rhythm inside her.

A tingling warmth spread through her like sunrays enveloping her in a comforting embrace. She leaned into it, relishing in its protection and strength. Its own power fuelled her, ran through her veins, and prickled the fair hairs on her body.

She sensed a tether, like an invisible cord stretching from her, branching out, and on the other end...

"I can feel you," Adelina whispered. "You're here."

"We will always be here," Evening Zorya said. "Now, use this connection to fuel your magic. Produce a golden orb within your palms."

"I—I don't know the spell." Adelina's voice wavered.

"The word won't always be needed, but it will help you until you have enough control over your magic," Morning Zorya said. "*Linasriel.*"

"We must go now," Evening Zorya said, her voice fading towards the end.

"Wait!" Adelina's eyes flashed opened. "Don't leave me. Won't I need you?"

The twins grew farther away from her—their bodies disappearing from the prism world.

"We are always...with you," they said in harmony.

Surrounded by silence and totally alone, Adelina locked her gaze on her reflection in the prism pane. She wiped her hands on her breeches, then lifted and cupped them.

"*Linasriel*," she said.

Nothing.

She repeated the word several times, but nothing happened. Glancing around, she hoped the twins would return as a guide, but they did not emerge into her layer of the prism world.

"*Linasriel*," she said again. Her lips parted and her breath hitched as a spark flickered an inch above her upturned palms.

On her fifth attempt, a large flame shot out of her hands and bolted into the prism panel opposite her. The glass shattered, then reformed.

Stretching out her hand, Adelina leaned towards the prism panel—her fingers disappeared through the ethereal surface. She drew it out and glanced at her unscathed hand.

A portal crackled into existence beside her, and she saw Yelena smiling at her from the other side.

"Am I due to come back already?" Adelina asked. "I've been here barely ten minutes."

"Time works differently in the prism world." Yelena gestured to the dim lighting of the candles dotted around the training room. "It's almost evening."

"But I've just started learning the spell," Adelina protested—her feet rooted to the grass of the prism world.

"You have three months to perfect your art," Yelena said. "Come."

Somewhat reluctant to leave, Adelina stepped through the portal—her feet landing on the cold, stone surface of the training room floor.

SEVEN

Suspicions Arise

The first month of training passed quicker than Adelina expected. Her spells were successful, after considerable effort inside the prism world. Countless occasions of shattering the plains of the dimension and setting it alight with fire were endured before she held a ball of Supreme Power—astral magic—in her hands.

An icy trail of winter lingered through February, but with the promise of spring came the hope of progression in Adelina's own mind.

She tapped her fingers fast against the smooth wooden surface of her desk as she awaited Yelena's arrival. Into her second month of training, she'd be coached alone. After all, she was the only one with access to astral magic.

"Apologies for my lateness." Yelena swooped into the room in a soft glide—a stack of books in her hands. "I needed to ensure the other students were prepared to meet their mentors in their relevant country."

Adelina frowned. "They've been designated to Temauten and Saintlandsther already?"

Yelena's soft blue gaze fell on her, and a smile curved her thin lips. "Dear, don't worry. They each have been allocated a particular part of the Embassy, be it the Temauten Congregation, the Saintlandsther Council, or the Convocation of Toichrist. Regardless, they will be apprentices until a suitable role is given to them."

"Will any of them be staying here with me?" Adelina hoped Lev or Kira were remaining. Over the last month of training, they'd spent most of their time together between sessions.

Yelena placed her soft, wrinkled hand on top of Adelina's. "Maksim and Troian."

As her heart sank, Adelina's mind fixed on the names—people she knew from training but hadn't spoken two words to.

"Your mind is racing," Yelena said. "You're jittery and staring straight past me. Ground yourself. There is nothing for you to worry about. As for your friends, you can write to them."

Adelina concentrated on her breath, holding it in for a few seconds before letting it out. She repeated the process several times until her body relaxed. She'd received one letter from her parents, and nothing from Damir. Although she'd written to him too, she'd been ignored. She wondered if their goodbye had affected him more than she first thought.

"Where do we start?" Adelina gestured to the stack of books in an attempt to shift her attention from Damir and on to more pressing matters.

"Well, as you can imagine, I have no personal experience with astral magic—no one around here does—but we have plenty of literature on the subject, written by practitioners of the Supreme Power over the centuries. The next part of your training will require a great amount of researching, reading, and practise. I know the ins and outs of these books, so I can answer any questions you may have, but I will not be able to demonstrate any of the magic for you." She clomped the stack onto her desk. "First, the servants will move all these stones out of the way and drag the table into the centre."

Yelena poked her head outside the main door and beckoned two male servants. They shunted the students' furniture to the sides of the room, leaving one table in the middle.

Thanking the servants, Yelena dismissed them. She moved the books, laying them open in front of them. Sunlight streaming in through the windows lit the calligraphy well.

Adelina dragged two chairs over, then slid on to one and rested her arms on the table. "You know I told you about the twins—Morning and Evening Zorya? Well, they helped me conjure astral magic with a spell. Why do I need to research it when I can already conjure it?"

"There is a fair difference between being able to conjure and being able to control," Yelena said. "You are aware of your connection to the virgin twins, and such connection is your access to astral magic, but you do not yet know its relation to Filip's nether magic. Now it is time for you to learn how this…yin-yang entity exists, if you will."

"I've heard we are stronger together because of it." Adelina shrugged one shoulder.

"A fine balance between them needs to be maintained," Yelena said. "Like a weighing scale—it must be kept even at all times. If one side was to slip, even a fraction, the other entity will weaken and lose its control."

"Are you saying Filip had *less* control over his magic before he found me?" Adelina arched a brow.

"What I tell you must not leave this room." Yelena took Adelina's hands in hers. "Give me your word."

"You have my word," Adelina said.

"Filip's magic was volatile—the complete opposite of what yours was like when you were apart. Yours was dormant, and you were able to live a normal life in Aramoor," Yelena said. "Filip was not so lucky. A great deal of pressure falls upon him from his father—his wealthiest benefactor. Filip must not fail in his mission to reunite the countries, but with great pressure, comes consequences, in the same way uncontrolled magic can bring catastrophe."

"Another reason he needed to find me…" Adelina breathed, putting the pieces together. "Not only is he at his strongest when he is with me, but he also has better control over his nether magic."

"Precisely," Yelena said. "Take this as encouragement: you're not alone. Filip has struggled to master his own magic. He had to learn from books and theory, as there's no one else alive with nether magic to turn to for advice. Lean on him for support—share with him your worries. You will find a great deal of comfort in it. You both have a lot more in common than you think."

Adelina drew her lips into her mouth and mulled over Yelena's words. In her brief experience of living with Filip, she'd learned he was kind to her, ensuring she was looked after, but their conversations never exceeded pleasantries.

"Perhaps I will speak with him after our session," Adelina decided.

Yelena smiled. "Good idea. Now, start with this book here."

She gave Adelina a medium-sized, leather-bound book with a bulky spine, appearing new. "No one uses these books, as you can imagine, unless one is curious to learn about magic they do not possess."

Flipping to the first page, Adelina read while Yelena drew a piece of parchment, quill, and inkpot from her bag, placed them on the table in front of her, then set about her task.

"I'm documenting your progress in training so far—it'll be distributed to the benefactors to inform them," Yelena said. "Soon enough, you will have sessions with Filip to see how your magic behaves together."

"When?" Adelina peered up from the page. "I must be ready—I can't have Filip seeing me unprepared."

"Don't fret, dear, it won't be until next month." Yelena smiled, then tapped the book in front of Adelina. "Read."

Several hours passed and a chunk of the book was read. Adelina's brain hurt from absorbing the knowledge, ranging from the origin of astral and nether magic, its history, documentation of past tests, famous users of the magic, and a further acknowledgement of the fact astral and nether were halves of the same entity.

"It says here, *astral and nether, one being, one force, one soul—an ancient, powerful magic supplied by holy Gods and Goddesses,*" Adelina read. "What does it mean by *soul*? Is it really alive?"

"You have met the virgin twins—you know they supply you with Supreme Power. Filip has a similar connection with a different God, but I will let him tell you about it next month. The two strands of ancient magic are, in effect, the same, forever a part of each other," Yelena said. "You know there's reliance you will both have upon each other, now you know why."

Adelina had struggled to accept the fact she was receiving magic from the Goddess twins, now she needed to comprehend the notion her magic was alive, a being. A soul.

"Think of it as magical soulmates, if you will." Yelena set her quill aside. "Astral and nether, bound for eternity."

Leaning back in her chair, Adelina wondered what this meant for her. She'd hoped to return to her home in Aramoor after training, but the realisation of her fate unsettled her. A thick frown creased her brows, creating a dull ache in her forehead. No wonder Damir hadn't written to her—why would he want to? Maybe he'd known the reality—she wasn't able to leave Filip.

"You are homesick," Yelena said, tearing Adelina from her thoughts. "You have that long off stare you have when you think of your family."

"I've received one letter from my parents, but nothing from Damir. Salma says it is nothing to concern myself with as I'm to visit my family soon. Damir will be there, of course, and I can ask after his welfare, but something isn't right." Adelina shoved her chair back, rose, then paced the stone floor of the training room.

"It is the spring equinox soon," Yelena said. "A perfect opportunity for you to reunite with your loved ones. I'm sure all will be well."

"That's over a month away." Adelina swivelled around and fixed her gaze on Yelena. "What am I to do in the meantime to settle my nerves?"

"Turn your attention to more important matters—focus on your training. Learn as much as you can, gain control, prove yourself, so when you do return to your family, you bring honour to them." Yelena's words were gentle and full of reassurance, and her blue eyes sparkled.

Adelina relaxed her tensed shoulders and returned to her seat.

Over the course of her second month of training, Adelina found herself in the prism world —a place she'd grown accustomed to. There, surrounded by a false world, and the reassurance she couldn't do harm to anyone other than herself, a sense of peace washed over her.

Her connection to the virgin twins was strong, rushing through her like a powerful current, keeping her anchored in the great sea of uncontrolled magic.

Wielding a golden orb in her palms, she watched it spin, casting rays of sunshine over the manicured lawns.

The orb expanded to the size of a globe. She parted her lips—a warm sensation tingled her skin as she overlooked her growing power. Then the orb's surface crackled and sparked, the light flickering in and out of existence.

She stumbled backwards, losing control of her connection to the Supreme Power. The magic exploded from her hands, hurtling broken golden glass through the air and into the panels of the prism world. Shards erupted around her.

Dropping to the floor, she drew her knees to her chest, tucked her head in, and shielded her face with her arms. The sharp fragments rained onto her, tearing at the bare flesh of her lower arms. Her thick, dark curls covered her nape, but one piece slid past her cheek, nicking the skin. The surface stung.

She touched the wound on her cheek, then peered at her fingers. Drops of blood dribbled down the digits.

A portal zapped into existence, and a voice yelled from the other side.

"Adelina! Are you okay?"

Yelena hurried to her, wrapped an arm around her, and guided her out of the prism world and onto the solid training room floor.

Lips trembling, Adelina wiped her clammy hands on her clothing. She opened her mouth to speak, but the words were frozen somewhere in her throat. Spinning, she fixed her gaze on the spot where the portal had been and shook.

"It's all right," Yelena soothed, rubbing her back. "All is well."

"It h-happened again." Adelina's eyes were damp. "The p-prism world. I th-thought I had c-control of the s-spell."

Yelena helped Adelina into a chair beside the table, then fetched a flask of water for her. She unscrewed the cap and pressed it against Adelina's lips. A few gulps later, her shaking subsided.

"Are you feeling better now?" Yelena stroked Adelina's shoulder.

She nodded.

"I haven't seen your magic lose control this badly before." Yelena placed her fingers on her chin. "Perhaps we ought to find a way to make it less…volatile. Maybe we could ask Filip to join you tomorrow."

Glancing up through watery eyes, Adelina nodded again. "Do you think he'll help?"

"Of course," Yelena chirped. "His presence in the prism world should ensure your control over the Supreme Power. Yes…there should be no issues with that. Now, why don't you finish early for the day, hmm? Soak in a bath and have Natasha tend to these scratches of yours." She held Adelina's chin between her fingers, tilting her head to assess the injury on her face. "It shouldn't require stitches."

The next day, Filip joined Adelina and Yelena in the training room. There was an air of unease around him. Occasionally he'd check the time of his pocket watch, the ever so slightly curl of his fingers into loose fists, before flattening them against his dark breeches.

Adelina pursed her lips, following his moves. She sensed something was wrong—perhaps he'd had a stressful morning—but decided not to press him on the matter.

"I will conjure a passageway to the prism world," Yelena said. "Filip, you need to stand beside Adelina while she conjures the spell. We can observe how it behaves and see if there is a way to control her magic, even when you are not so close."

He nodded curtly.

Swiping her index finger through the air, Yelena drew a circle, materialising the golden, flickering circle of a portal.

Adelina puffed out a sharp breath, then crossed into the other dimension in quick strides. Filip followed her and the portal snapped shut behind them.

Stood side by side on the manicured lawn of the palace, Adelina flexed her fingers.

Pushing her shoulders back, she cupped her hands together.

"*Linasriel*," she said.

The golden orb flickered into existence, hovering a few centimetres above her outstretched palms. Filip's gaze rested on her.

A few moments passed, and the ball of magic hadn't crackled, sparked, *or* shot into the panels of the prism world.

"It's working." Filip's eyebrows rose.

A wide grin spread across Adelina's lips, and a burst of pride shot through her core. Yet her look of pleasure evaporated the second the ball fizzed and popped.

"Oh no," she muttered to herself. "Filip, drop to the floor!"

The golden orb shot into the sky, pelted into the top of the prism where the light shone the brightest, and glass exploded around them, littering onto the grass.

The portal zapped in front of them, and Yelena flapped her hands at them. "Hurry!"

Filip and Adelina dashed out of the prism world and stumbled across the stone floor of the training room.

"Damn," Adelina cursed. "For a second there, I thought it would work."

"So did I," he said.

Yelena pressed her fingers to her chin, a frown creasing her brows.

"What is it?" Adelina asked.

"Perhaps there is something that could help," Yelena muttered as she wandered over to the books sprawled across the table. She flipped through the pages, then tapped her finger on a section of calligraphy. "Ah, yes. An amulet."

"Amulet?" Adelina said. "Like a talisman?"

"Exactly." Yelena shifted, focusing her gaze on Adelina. "We could charm a piece of jewellery against evil forces. This would inevitably allow you to have better control of your magic."

"I have my father's necklace." Adelina's fingers wrapped around the locket hanging from the chain around her slender neck.

"Perfect." Yelena beamed.

"It seems you have everything under control here." Filip backed towards the door—the afternoon sunlight illuminated the beads of sweat along his hairline.

He disappeared from the room before Adelina could say a word.

She turned to Yelena. "Did something seem wrong with Filip to you?"

"He's had a busy morning dealing with the benefactors." Yelena waved the matter away.

"Didn't your letters deal with the benefactors' curiosity and demands for progress updates?" Adelina said.

"Yes, but Filip must still speak of his plans once you've completed training," Yelena said. "The benefactors want to know how he will reunite the countries and ensure it happens."

Adelina smiled, squashing her concern. Or was it suspicion? She couldn't decide.

"Pass me your necklace." Yelena held out her hand.

Unclasping the chain, Adelina dropped her father's locket into Yelena's palm.

"Now I'm going to need a few drops of your blood." Yelena wandered to the shelves positioned behind her desk, grabbed a bowl no bigger than a mortar, and a blade.

A chill tickled Adelina's nape as Yelena settled the mortar and blade on the table between them.

Yelena placed the necklace inside the bowl, then grasped Adelina's left wrist.

"This will sting a little, but it won't be deep enough to require stitches." Yelena ran the blade widthways across Adelina's wrist.

As she sucked in a sharp intake of breath, beads of blood blossomed from the cut.

Yelena tilted Adelina's wrist—four tiny drops of life splattered onto the cross and chain.

"*Tyleiri sinriyn,*" Yelena said while she drew a circular motion in the air above the mortar.

A sheen layer of light sprung from the bowl, like sunlight on floating dust. The blood was absorbed by the metal and a golden glow emanated from the locket.

When the glow faded, she scooped up the necklace. "Here. Put it on. This will reduce the chances of your magic losing control."

"Thank you." Adelina fastened it around her neck.

"Come back tomorrow morning and we shall test it in the prism world." Yelena gestured to the door—an act of dismissal.

Nodding once, Adelina slipped out of the training room, made her way across the gardens running the length of the conservatories, then entered the palace.

As she wandered along the high ceiling corridors, something called to her from Filip's office, like an unwavering compulsion. Other than the distant mutterings of servants, the palace was silent.

Finding herself outside the wooden door to Filip's office, she rapped on it.

"Not now." Filip's deep voice huffed from the other side.

Perhaps he'd assumed a servant had come to tend to his needs, and Adelina *did* need to speak to him if she was going to put her suspicion to rest.

She opened the door and peered into the sunlit room. "It's me, Adelina."

Filip, who was sitting at his desk, hands resting on a stack of parchment, glanced up. His cheeks were red. "Oh. What can I do for you?"

She edged into the room—her shoes sinking into the thick, red carpet—and made her way to the free chair opposite Filip.

Clasping her hands, she dipped into the chair and returned the smile. "Yelena has created me an amulet. I wanted to reassure you my magic will now be in control, and I can continue with my training. Will you be joining me for further sessions? I'm sure it will be beneficial to see how our powers work together."

"Unfortunately, I won't be able to attend your training." He moved his stack of parchment into the desk drawer and locked it. He slipped the key into his breast pocket. "My father requires a personal visit, so I am making the journey to his home in north Toichrist. I shall return in time for the spring equinox next month."

"What about the benefactors?" she asked.

"They have been made aware of this emergency," he said, rather nonchalantly. "Yelena will continue to send her letters regarding your progress. By the time we are reunited, you'll have completed your training."

"I do hope your father is well," she said, then mustered the courage to continue. "Although Yelena had said I'd be practising my magic with you."

"Your amulet controls your magic, does it not?" Filip's tone turned sharp.

Adelina flinched. "Yes."

Filip's tense features relaxed. "Apologies. My father is unwell, and the news has stirred…unpleasant emotions within me."

"Of course." Adelina rose, eager to leave the sudden taut atmosphere of his office. "I wish for your father's speedy recovery."

The final two weeks of Adelina's training passed in a blur. Her medallion helped her progress in the prism world, but with Filip away with his father, there was no telling how their magic would react together.

She took great comfort in the fact she'd mastered several other spells during her training. The skills required to produce a golden orb and a flame, developed into much larger flames, ones under her control. By the end of her training, she could manipulate the element with a wave of her hand, a flick of a finger, and with it, the flames would follow.

Adelina sat on her windowsill, tracing her thumb over the surface of her grandfather's pocket watch. Glancing through the window at the golden sunset, she bit the tip of her tongue. Filip's sudden departure hadn't filled her with confidence—how could she reassure the members of the Embassy of her magical powers when the other half of her soul magic wasn't there?

Natasha opened the door, then peered around it, bringing Adelina's attention to her. "It's almost twilight, miss. I've drawn you a bath. We should get you washed and prepared for your departure for the spring equinox. You'll need to leave tomorrow if you wish to arrive at the festivities in time. Remember, the journey takes two weeks."

"Oh, yes." Adelina slid off the windowsill, leaving the timepiece placed on top of the red cushion beside her.

"I've arranged for a new gown to be brought to the palace for you." Natasha beamed as she guided Adelina into the corridor and towards the bathing room. "I'll have it hung up behind the divider in your chamber this evening."

"Thank you," Adelina said.

She couldn't find the will to further the conversation with her maiden—her mind was elsewhere, wondering what she might say to her parents and Damir.

Her mother had promised her Damir was doing well—his apprenticeship with Alexei was proving fruitful, and their business was growing. Similarly, her father's stove workshop had been repaired and his supplies replenished due to Filip's generosity.

Yet in the three months since her departure from Aramoor, she hadn't received a single word from Damir. Not one. Her heart ached and her eyes burned. Had their kiss meant nothing? Their years of friendship tossed to the flames the second she left?

Natasha ushered Adelina into the steam filled bathing room, then urged her to strip and climb into the tub.

While Adelina soaked in the lavender infused water, Natasha headed to the door.

"I'm going to light the hearth," she said. "I'll be back in a few minutes."

A Ballad of Severed Souls

Left to her own devices, Adelina's troubled thoughts returned to Damir. Perhaps it was her own fault—she hadn't disclosed her feelings for him before they bid farewell. If she had, maybe things would've been different.

Perhaps, simply, her affection was not reciprocated.

"I won't accept it," she said, wrapping her arms around her drawn knees. "I'll speak with him soon—he'll have an explanation. Maybe he hasn't found the time to write."

When Natasha returned to the bathing room, she assisted Adelina into her nightgown, then led her back to her chamber. The room was already warm and drenched in the orange glow of the hearth fire.

On the first day of the weekend, Filip packed his luggage, and the servants loaded them into the carriage while he gathered his last-minute provisions from his office.

The key to the desk drawer was safely in his breast pocket—his journal stowed inside.

Pausing midway between the lit hearth and his desk, his mind returned to the dozen or so letters received from Damir over the course of Adelina's stay at the palace. He'd burned them all.

A soft knock snapped him from his thoughts.

"Come in," Filip said.

Adelina entered the room—soft brown curls framed her face and flowed down the length of her back. She wore a beautifully embroidered sarafan—its elegant stitching climbed her corset. The enchanted locket hung around her slender neck.

"Adelina." He smiled. "You look...well. Will you be taking your new dress on your travels to Aramoor? The one Natasha picked up from the seamstress?"

"Of course." She returned the smile. "I'll be changing once Salma returns from the market. She will be accompanying me to the spring equinox. Before you leave to aid your father, I wondered if I could speak with you about my magic."

He grabbed his coat from the nearby rack, then flung it over his shoulders, shimmying his arms through the holes.

"Apologies, but I mustn't be kept long. I'll be leaving shortly." His gaze landed on the door.

"It won't take a moment." She stepped closer to him, edging away from the wall. Her hand brushed her necklace. "Yelena suggested I speak with you. We are similar, after all, maybe there are things I can learn from you too. I'm worried my magic will be dangerous—you've seen what it did in the prism world."

He froze. He fought to keep his expression straight. "Your amulet will ensure nothing goes awry."

He needed her to believe it, at least for the time being

"Is it enough?" She frowned. "Will the benefactors trust me when they learn I must rely on a bewitched pendant in order to keep my magic under control?"

"All will be fine." Filip slipped past her, heading out of the room. "I must be going now."

A Ballad of Severed Souls

She hurried behind him. "Can you assure me I'm not dangerous?"

Halting, he sucked in a breath, then slowly faced her. "I trust Yelena's ability to teach you control. I also trust in Supreme Power—your connection to it is strong, and you are the only person to have such access to it in many years. Don't forget it."

He hurried out of the palace entrance before she could ask more questions. Once he was seated in the carriage, he glanced out the window—Adelina stood in the doorway, mouth open.

Slipping his fingers into his pocket, he withdrew a black, velvet box, then lifted the lid. A sparkling diamond ring lay between the cushions. He needed to wed her, and quick.

EIGHT

A Change in Circumstance

Adelina paced the length of her chamber floor, her hand planted on her hips. She needed answers. Something about Filip seemed off, but she couldn't put her finger on it.

She flung open her door, then hurried along the corridors in search of Natasha.

Natasha was in Salma's room—the door open—straightening the covers and plumping the cushions.

Salma, midway through tugging off her coat, glanced at Adelina. "Dear, you look like you've seen a ghost. What in the heavens is wrong?"

Smoothing the fabric of her sarafan, Adelina slipped into the room and closed the door behind her. "I must speak with you."

"Of course, dear." Salma gestured to the armchair opposite her. "Whatever is the matter?"

Blowing out a deep breath, heat rose in Adelina's cheeks. She sunk into the chair. "Can you promise to keep a secret?"

"Certainly." Salma slid into her own chair—a worried frown wedged between her brows.

Adelina's gaze wandered to Natasha. "I'm going to need your help, too. You've been my personal maiden for the past three months, and I believe I can trust you."

"Yes, miss." Natasha abandoned her cleaning duties, then positioned herself close by.

"I think Filip is hiding something from me—I'm not sure what, exactly, but I must investigate while he is away," Adelina said.

"What's given you this impression?" Salma kept an even expression, not a hint of concern on her face. Perhaps it was her way of maintaining a calm atmosphere until there was something to worry about.

"He's seemed...on edge around me." Adelina shook her head. "When I told him about my amulet, he sounded distant, irritable—I'm not sure."

"His mood could be caused by anything, dear," Salma said. "Why does it cause you concern?"

"I fear there's more to it." Adelina tapped her foot. "He's been courteous and pleasant for the last three months, but over the past few days, I've noticed cracks in his demeanour. Something is definitely on his mind. Natasha, has there been any gossip amongst the servants?" She glanced at her maid, whose cheeks were flaming red. "What is it?"

"It's just..." Natasha cleared her throat. "There has been some speculation—"

"Speculation of what?" Adelina jumped to her feet.

"Well, Filip—at least what the ladies have said—plans to wed you." Natasha's shoulders tensed as if she held in her breath.

"Wait. Did you say *wed*?" Adelina's gaze darted from Natasha to Salma, then back again. "What in the realm for?"

Salma's eyebrows shot skywards.

"I don't know." Natasha shrugged.

"I don't think your parents would take kindly to such a proposal. Especially from a man they hardly know," Salma said. "A marriage was not part of the agreement. After all, I have stayed with you throughout your training to ensure your virtue is not besmirched."

"Perhaps I could bring you his journal. I've often seen him scrawling in it," Natasha said. "I'm due to clean Filip's office now; I can hide the journal in my basket of dusting cloths. There's a master key to all the drawers and cupboards—I'll bring you what you need, then put it back. Filip wouldn't know."

"Won't you be caught?" Adelina said.

"No one will suspect me," Natasha said. "I'm often assigned to that part of the palace."

"All right." Adelina nodded. "Salma and I will wait here."

"I'll be quick." Natasha dashed from the room.

Adelina pressed her fingers to her forehead and paced the length of her chamber. "Can you believe this, Salma?"

"I'm sure there is some misunderstanding. Look how well Filip has treated you." Salma rested her palms on her lap. "Although his planned proposal has come as a shock, thinking about it, your parents might offer their blessing. After all, he is wealthy, has a good position, owns property and land. Perhaps he could be good for you."

Halting, Adelina shot her chaperone a stern stare. "Wait. You mean to tell me you *approve*? How has your mind changed in the last five seconds? This is absurd. I have no idea how old he is, what his intentions are. There will be no chance of a long and proper courtship."

"Marrying Filip will solidify *your* prospects as well, dear." Salma leaned forwards.

"What about...Damir?" Adelina's voice was small. Although she'd no idea what he felt for her, she couldn't disregard her own affection for him.

"Oh, dear, I know he is a good friend of yours, but he is only an apprentice," Salma said.

"I can't believe you're saying this." Adelina stared straight at Salma.

"Well, if Filip does mean to propose, it is my obligation to inform your parents," Salma said.

Natasha entered the room—her basket of cleaning supplies resting on her bent arm. She positioned the basket on the low, wooden table between the armchairs, then scooped the thick journal from underneath the cloths.

"Here you are, miss." Natasha handed the stack to Adelina.

"Thank you." Adelina smiled. "Please stand outside and ensure no one enters this room."

Curtsying, Natasha did as she was bid.

Adelina lowered into the armchair opposite Salma, then traced her fingers along the padded surface of the diary.

"Best get on with it, dear," Salma said.

Adelina opened it. The pages were full, covered with notes, with no blank pages or spaces at the end. He'd likely have started a new one, one he'd perhaps taken with him on trip to see his father, but she hoped she'd find useful information in the one in her hands.

February, training month one. Below notations to be written and distributed to my father and all benefactors at earliest convenience.

Adelina's time at the Embassy was a success. She was confident in answering questions, and I feel she will develop into the young warrior we need in order to succeed in our mission.

Her training is going as planned—I do not doubt Yelena's ability to teach her.

Next month, she will practise her skills in the prism world, where we will get a true reflection of the damage her magic can cause.

Gaping at the texture, Adelina fixed her stare on a single word. *Damage.*

"What is it?" Salma leaned forward, took the book, then scanned the cursive.

"Oh, this is harmless, dear." Salma waved her hand. "There is nothing to worry about."

Frowning, Adelina turned her attention to the next paragraph. Maybe Salma was right—there was nothing to worry about. Her fears were simply irrational.

A boy, by the name of Damir, has written to Adelina, wishing to take her hand in marriage. I plan to make my own proposal. My most pressing concern is to ensure a line of succession. This Damir will be dealt with. His letters will never be seen.

Personal notes: the Embassy believe I will hold an interim Presidential position while Adelina and I unite the countries. However, once we are in power, I'll assert a permanent Emperor title. Adelina can rule by my side, and our children will never be challenged—they'd inherit my position and estate.

Father's health: I have ordered the finest physician from Toichrist to visit him at once. I hope he can curb these pains of his, otherwise I'll need to make my own visit.

Adelina froze, each muscle tensing and tingling. She parted her lips, but no breath escaped them.

"What is it?" Salma grasped Adelina's hand. "You're shaking and your face has turned the colour of ash."

Adelina couldn't speak. Instead, she handed her chaperone the journal.

Salma scanned the writing. "Damir has written? Where are the letters? Natasha!"

The servant entered the room, her gaze flicking from Adelina Salma. "What is it, miss?"

"Did you find any letters in Filip's office? From a man by the name of Damir Litvin?" Salma said.

"No, miss," Natasha said. "There was nothing else in his desk drawers that would've interested to you."

"He must have destroyed them." Salma knelt beside Adelina, then clasped her hand. "Dear, why don't you read another of Filip's entries to see if there's more information?"

"I-it's a power play," Adelina muttered, her voice barely audible. "He wants to m-marry me to secure his position."

"I know, dear." Salma smoothed Adelina's hand lightly, keeping her voice light and level. "We must collect all the facts before drawing conclusions."

Shaking, Adelina gave the book to Salma. "I can't."

"I'll bring you some water, miss." Natasha dashed from the room.

Salma reclined into her armchair, flipping to the next page, then read its contents.

Her nerves settling, Adelina glanced upwards. "What does it say?"

"Well…it's about your magic."

"Go on." Adelina pressed her lips together as her stomach muscles clenched.

"He documents the amulet and…" Salma arched a brow.

"And?" Adelina shunted to the edge of her seat, gripping on to the armrests for dear life.

"He says it interferes with his plans to use your magic in its natural, uncontrolled state, and he must devise a plan to rid you of the amulet's hindrance." Salma shook her head.

"My magic's natural, uncontrolled state?" Adelina said. "What do you mean? It was never meant to be controlled?"

A deep frown formed between Salma's brows. "This is a big problem, dear. Further down, he mentions preparations for battle against Saintlandsther and Temauten—he means to take the countries by force, and with you by his side."

"What!" Adelina leapt to her feet, pinching the journal from Salma's grasp. She scanned the words.

Natasha entered the room with a tray—a pitcher of water and two glasses rested on it. She set it on the table, then poured the drinks. "Here you go, miss."

"You must put this back, straight away." Adelina thrust the diary towards Natasha. "Exactly as you found it, as not to rouse suspicion."

"Yes, miss." Natasha tucked it into her cleaning basket. "Right away."

She darted from the room.

"What are you going to do?" Salma frowned.

Smoothing her hair, Adelina thought for a moment. "We will go to the spring equinox as planned, so we do not draw attention from the palace servants. I'll find a library, see if there's any magical texts I can take, then I'll find Damir. He needs to know—my family, too."

"Gather your belongings," Salma said. "Enough to carry and nothing more. A change of clothes, a bag of ruble—you have an allowance from Filip, right? Now don't forget, we leave at dawn, so go to the library for reading material for the journey, and we'll leave as planned."

Salma whisked out of the room in swift movements.

Natasha returned moments later, and Adelina informed her of the plan. Her clothes, along with her grandfather's pocket watch, hairbrush, and other belongings were already packed for the journey. "There's enough clothing here to last you the two-week journey, so there's nothing for you to worry about. And of course, your new dress."

"Thanks." Adelina pressed her fingers against her temples, forcing her scattered thoughts to align. She was about to turn her back on her supposed destiny, but she couldn't agree to marry Filip and be used as his weapon. "But I doubt my dress is going to be needed, given the circumstances. Leave it here. It will take up unnecessary space in my bags. By the time Filip returns to the palace, I'll already be far away. It won't matter if he sees I've left it."

"Yes, miss." Natasha quickly unpacked the new sarafan, corset, and shoes.

"Can you escort me to the library?" Adelina said. "I'll need a few things before I leave. We must be quick."

"Of course, miss." Natasha bowed. "I'll load your bags into the carriage for you first thing in the morning."

Natasha guided her to the dome ceiling library at the back of the palace. Adelina's breath caught in her throat as her gaze fell on the spectacular, panoramic views of the gardens and aspen forest.

"Stay focused," Adelina muttered to herself.

As she surveyed the books stacked on the shelves, Natasha left.

Adelina made her way through the first few rows of books, all in alphabetical order, but none of them referred to astral magic. Hurrying over to the next aisle, she rummaged through books in search of Supreme Power, two of which referenced it.

Balancing them under her arm, she left the library and returned to her chamber, stuffing the tomes into her bag.

Later that night, she tossed and turned, fighting for sleep, yet unable to find any. At the first signs of dawn, Salma hurried through the door with Natasha on her tail. Within twenty minutes, Adelina was dressed and ready for departure.

Natasha carried her belongings, then stowed them into the waiting black carriage outside the palace entrance. Climbing inside, Salma slid across the seats.

Sitting next to her, Adelina leaned out of the window and smiled at Natasha. "Thank you for everything. Please tell Yelena I've borrowed these books to further my studying while I'm away."

"I wish you a safe trip, miss," Natasha said.

Adelina wanted to say more—a lot more—she wanted to thank her handmaiden for keeping her secret, for helping her flee without raising alarm, and for tending to her during her stay at the palace.

The coachman clicked his tongue, and the horses jolted the carriage along the path, through the gates, and away from Kirovo Palace.

Two weeks later, the carriage halted outside the entrance to Aramoor—the small, quaint village of her home. The snow had long since melted, and in its place, flowers blossomed. Buildings were bedecked with flower garlands for the spring equinox, and the strong scent of bonfires wafted on the breeze. As the sun sank towards the horizons, men and women lit the fire torches outside their homes, drenching the cobbled path in golden light.

The coachman hopped from his seated position at the front, then opened the door.

Adelina and Salma were greeted by Velinka and Daro.

"Oh, dear, I'm ever so glad to have you home." Velinka's eyes welled with tears as she drew Adelina into an embrace.

The coachman dropped the luggage onto the ground beside them, then guided the horses towards the field. He'd likely spend the night at the nearest inn, so Adelina would have to be careful if she didn't want word of her activities travelling back to the palace.

Adelina let go of her mother.

"We must speak somewhere private," Salma said, which was met with a concerned look from Adelina's parents.

"Oh?" Velinka arched a brow. "Come, I'll put the kettle on."

Once they were all inside the Orlov family home, Tihana bolted from her seated position at the dinner table, abandoning her schoolbooks to fling her arms around Adelina.

"I've missed you *so* much," Tihana said against the fabric of Adelina's corset.

"And I, you." Adelina smiled.

"Darling, why don't you have a break from studying? We need to speak with your sister in private," Velinka said to her youngest.

"Yes, Ma." Tihana dashed to her chamber.

Velinka brought a bottle of vodka and a tray of glasses to the table while the rest of them settled into their chairs.

"Salma, what is it you must tell us?" Velinka poured the drinks, then passed them out.

Adelina eyed her chaperone and tapped her fingers on the edge of the table.

"Best take a swig of your vodka." Salma clasped her hands and placed them on the table in front of her.

After Salma filled them in on Filip's plans, Velinka stared, wide-eyed and open-mouthed, from Salma to her daughter, then to her husband, Daro.

"You can't stay here," Daro said at last, slicing the silence. "Who knows—Filip could be on his way back to the palace right now if he isn't already there. You'll need as much of a head start as possible."

"Where do you plan to send her?" Velinka glanced sharply at him.

Adelina leaned forward, her hands planted on the table. "I'm right here, you know. Besides, I already know what to do."

"What?" her parents said in unison.

"I will marry Damir. Bless our union. Filip won't be able to force me to marry him. We'll pack our belongings—I have plenty of coin from the palace—and we will take a horse from the stables. We'll travel south into the pine forests away from civilisation and prying eyes," Adelina said.

"Surely not," Velinka said, her voice thin. "Flee like a thief in the night?"

"Damir is a carpenter apprentice and I'm good with needlework—we can find work in a small village, one less likely to recognise me," Adelina said. "I'll travel under an alias. It'll be harder for Filip to find me. Never staying in one place for too long will also help."

"Our eldest daughter living a life on the run?" Velinka laughed, her eyes wide. "Those are not the prospects we wanted for you." Her mother's lips parted, then closed again. She glanced at her husband.

Daro cleared his throat. "Perhaps we ought to involve Damir in this conversation. His parents too."

Adelina swallowed a large gulp of her vodka—if she was going to make this proposal to Damir, she'd need the liquid courage.

Sitting beside Salma, she waited while her parents left the house to collect Damir and his parents. A while later, the five of them returned.

Mirelle leaned over the back of the chair on which Adelina was sitting, then draped her arms over her shoulders.

"Oh, Adelina, your ma has told me all about your predicament." Mirelle squeezed her, then let go and slid on to the free chair next to her.

Adelina glanced from Mirelle to Damir, who stood awkwardly in front of the front door. An even more awkward silence fell over the dinner tables as both sets of parents observed the young ones.

"Shall we go for a walk?" Damir ran his hand through his hair, keeping his gaze fixed on Adelina.

"Yes." Adelina's voice was no louder than a whisper. A sudden and intense shyness flooded through her.

Velinka rose, then kissed her daughter on the head. "Be quick about it, dear. If you are both to go through with this union, we ought to do it fast."

Adelina nodded, slipping outside with Damir. They wandered, shoulder to shoulder, along the cobbled path towards the entrance of Aramoor, turning their backs to the cheerful chatter and merriment drifting from the centre of the village. The wooden sign could be seen in the distance, welcoming newcomers.

"How have you been?" She cast a glance at him, unable to find any other words in her vocabulary.

"Well," he began. "Ma has explained everything to me. I thought you didn't wish to hear from me. I awaited a letter from you, checking for post each day, but soon drew the conclusion you'd moved on with your new life in the palace."

"I'd written to you too, but I guess it was never sent," she said. "When I wrote to my parents, I also mentioned you but at the time, I'd no clue what Filip was planning. I found out right before making the journey here."

Damir halted, leaned against the stone wall, then rested his hands on the surface. He gazed across the field ahead of him—the corn crop golden under the setting sun. "He wishes to marry you," he said.

"Yes," she replied, falling into place beside him, an inch between their shoulders.

A long moment of silence hung between them.

Adelina glanced sideways at him, noticing the thick frown of concentration wedged between his brows.

"You don't have to, you know," she said at last. "If your feelings have changed."

He swivelled to face her. "If there's one thing I *am* sure about is that I *do* love you." The corners of his lips curved. "I regret not telling you the day you left."

She smiled too, her heart bursting. Was this really happening? This man, someone she cared deeply for, was prepared to accept her proposal and spend his life with her on the run. All she could do was hope she'd make him happy, because in truth, she'd grown to love him, too. "Then what?"

"I want to do right by you." He shook his head. "But a life on the run is not a good one."

"We'll figure it out." She placed her hand over his callused knuckles.

He paused again—she watched his gaze travel across the cornfield.

In his familiar presence, a calmness swept over her, like the gentle lapping of sea waves meeting the sand's edge. She didn't press him for an answer, despite their time constraint.

"I'll do it," he finally said as he wrapped an arm around her and drew her close. "I've known for a while I wanted to marry you. It'll be without the courtship we'd expect, the whole ceremony will have to happen quickly, but I'll do whatever it takes to keep you safe."

A heavy weight lifted from her chest. She buried her head against him and breathed in the scent of wood and the ever so faint tang of vodka clinging to his clothes. Even though it wasn't the life they'd planned, she could see happiness with him.

Back at the house, the newly engaged couple shared the news with their parents.

"We must send word to the house of worship," Daro said. "A wedding will need to take place at night once the stalls have closed and the festivities have ended—you two can't linger for too long in this village. When Filip realises you've been gone longer than the spring equinox lasts for, he will come looking for you."

"There'll be no time for traditions," Velinka said, a flicker of sadness in her eyes. "No week of celebrations. No dancing, singing, toasting, or banqueting."

If Adelina thought about her ideal wedding ceremony, she'd have a traditional *venchanie*, formed of a Betrothal; a prayer from the ordained, who blesses the rings during engagement and the Crowning, where members of the wedding party would place crowns on the bride and groom's head.

As if noticing her daughter's deep thought, Velinka rested her hand on Adelina's shoulders. "You will be married properly if we have anything to say about it."

"Which we do," Daro added.

Adelina clasped her mother's hand. "I'll have you both by my side, which is all I need. Have you told Tihana?"

"Yes. She won't come out of her room—she doesn't want to lose you again," Velinka said. "She will come 'round soon enough."

"Where has Salma gone? Is she not attending the ceremony?" Adelina surveyed the room.

"She's returned to her home," her mother said. "If Filip and his men come to Aramoor in search of you, they will likely find Salma. Don't fret, she has already sworn to say nothing about your wedding. If Filip questions her, she will simply tell him she saw you home for the festivities, and once you were returned to your parents, you were no longer her responsibility."

Adelina nodded. "I'll see if I can convince Tihana to come out."

Daro exited the house to call upon the ordained, and Adelina left Damir in conversation with his parents and Velinka while she padded across the floor towards Tihana's room. She rapped on the door.

"May I come in?"

Tihana sniffled and grumbled incoherently from the other side.

Taking this as an answer to her question, Adelina slipped into the room—her gaze falling on her dainty sister, wrapped in a bundle of blankets in the centre of her bed.

Kneeling beside her, Adelina placed her hand on her sister's shoulder, which poked out from the swaddle. "Tihana, do you want to come out from under there and speak with me?"

"Hmph…" Tihana grumbled again. "If you're to leave all over again, I can't bear to say goodbye."

Adelina rested her forehead against her sister's wrapped form—her heart ached. A few seconds later, she lifted her head and sighed. "I'm sorry, sis. Truly. But don't you want to join the celebrations? Damir and I are to be wed. Would you like to help me get ready?"

Tihana lowered the covers a fraction until one eye popped over the edge. She peered at her sister. "Can I put flowers in your hair?"

"There's no one else better for the job." Adelina squeezed her sister's shoulder.

Tihana scrambled out of the blankets, leaving them in a puddle around her, then flung her arms around Adelina's neck.

"W-will I ever s-see you again?" she whimpered.

"I hope so," Adelina said in a breathy voice, holding her sister close against her chest as she stroked her hair. "Do you want to see something cool?"

"What?" Tihana let go—her eyes alight.

"*Linasriel*." Adelina conjured a golden, spinning orb between her palms.

Her sister gaped. "Magic!"

"Yes." Adelina grinned. "Soon, I'll be strong enough to produce it without having to use the word."

"Can you teach me?" Tihana bounced on the edge of the mattress.

"*Linasriel*," Adelina repeated. "Your turn to say it now."

"*Linasriel, linasriel, linasriel,*" Tihana said without a breath. She hopped from the bed, then skipped around the room. "*Linasriel, linasriel, linasriel.* Does this mean I'm like you now, sis?"

"You are special in your own way, Tihana," Adelina said as her sister bounded into her, flinging her arms around her waist.

"I love you," Tihana said.

"I love you, too." Adelina's throat tightened around the words. How could she possibly tell her younger sister the inevitable—they truly may *not* ever see each other again?

Two hours later, when the moon drenched the village in a pale light, Velinka rummaged in her cupboards. She drew out a large wedding gown—its neckline was high, and the sleeves were full and long. Vine-like embroidery was stitched up the length of the skirt in silver thread, matching the delicate detailing on the veil.

"I know it's not what you imagined—wearing your ma's dress," she said as Adelina perched on the edge of the bed.

"It's perfect." Adelina clasped her hands together on her lap and fought to ignore the bubbling anxiety inside her. Her stomach muscles clenched and twisted, while her heart rate climbed.

The ordained agreed to perform the wedding ceremony on short notice, having accepted a small sum of coin from Daro, and awaited their arrival at the house of worship. Daro also reassured her the coachman wouldn't interrupt the wedding as he'd paid a trusted friend to keep him company at the inn.

Velinka helped her daughter into the dress, adjusting and tightening the corset, then pinned the veil into place over her curls.

Downstairs, Damir waited with his parents, Tihana, and Daro.

As Adelina descended the stairs—her train flowing behind her—she held her breath. Was she really going through with this? He'd admitted to loving her, and the fact he was prepared to wed her so hastily was enough to prove it. Warmth spread through her body, a mixture of nerves and realisation—she *could* be very happy with Damir, indeed.

Gripping the banister, her racing thoughts turned to what happens *after* the wedding ceremony. She halted on the stairs, her mother bumping into her.

"What's the matter, dear?" Velinka said behind her.

"I'm nervous, maybe a little scared, for what happens after we are wed." Adelina peered over her shoulder. "*Later.*"

Velinka squeezed Adelina's shoulder. "I'm sure Damir is, too, but you'll figure it out together. I've spoken with Damir's parents, and they've offered their home to you both for the night. It's best to keep you away from prying eyes while you're here."

Adelina nodded once.

When she reached the last step, Damir glanced at her, and his eyes brightened. "You look beautiful."

"Thank you," Adelina said—her voice timid as if she was looking upon him for the first time. He was about to become her husband, he would share her bed tonight, and the warmth ignited into a fervent heat inside her, spreading up to her cheeks. She took in the broad planes of his shoulders, the way the garment hung a little loosely around his otherwise defined body, and the warm, endearing smile spreading across his lips. "You look dashing yourself."

She grinned at his white jacket—its collar stood up, framing his face, and gold buttons ran the length of the garment and a quarter of the way up the sleeves. The fabric flayed outwards around his hips. Matching white breeches bunched slightly above his shoes.

"My father's wedding attire," he said. "It's a bit on the big side but was the best I could do on short notice."

"It's perfect," she said and meant it.

He drew two velvet boxes from his pocket, rested the smaller one on the table beside him, then opened the first. A golden bracelet lay upon the cushion—thin, curling vines wove into petals surrounding tiny rubies.

"It was my grandmother's." He clasped it around her wrist. "And it will belong to my wife."

"Beautiful. I'll cherish it." Adelina's breathing shallowed as she traced the delicate metal.

"It's tradition." He smiled. "To pay the dowry."

"A splendid offering." Velinka beamed.

"Do you have a ring?" Daro asked.

The tradition of paying the bride's dowry required two pieces of jewellery, if not money, and the latter piece must outshine the first.

"Of course." Damir picked up the second gift box, popped it open, and revealed a beautiful triple rolling ring—three interlocking bands made of rose, white, and yellow gold. "The bracelet and this ring are heirlooms, and they are very precious to me, and my family. I could not fashion you a new ring, given our haste, but it would be an honour if you wore this."

Adelina's eyes widened at the gift and realisation sank in—she and Damir would be married before the gods, and Filip wouldn't be able to do anything about it.

Lifting her gaze from the ring, she met Damir's gaze. "What you have given me is *more* than I could have asked for."

Nodding, a warm smile spread across Damir's own face.

"Let's get a move on." Velinka ushered them towards the door. "The ordained will be ready for us."

A Ballad of Severed Souls

When they arrived at the house of worship, candles were lit and dotted along the aisle and positioned on the sills of stained-glass windows, mingling with the silver moonlight. The ordained—a short man with greying hair—awaited them at the altar, while Adelina and Damir's family slid into the pews.

Adelina's body was numb, each of her limbs weightless, each step towards the ordained brought her closer to her married life with Damir. The prospect of it exhilarated her and terrified her at the same time. She wanted, above all else, to make him happy.

They stood, facing each other, in front of the ordained. His deep voiced echoed through the building. "The servant of the gods, Damir Litvin, will be married to the servant of the gods, Adelina Orlova, in the name of Lada, Goddess of love and fertility; may she bless your union. Damir, place the ring on her finger."

Nodding once, Damir drew the piece of jewellery from his pocket, held Adelina's soft hand in his, then slid the ring onto her fourth finger.

"A man will leave his father and mother and be united with his wife, and they will become one flesh. Therefore, what the gods have joined together, let no man separate."

Turning towards the altar, the ordained picked up two candles, handing one each to Damir and Adelina.

"Let these candles represent the eternal flame ignited in both your hearts, and may the gods guide and protect you as you begin your lives as man and wife. Now, Damir, hold your wife's right hand, so you may be united as one mind and one flesh. May you be blessed in the sight of all gods."

Adelina and Damir's hands remained clasped—he stroked his thumb along her skin, which soothed the pounding of her heart and the painful knots in her stomach.

"Drink from the common cup." The man took the candles from Damir and Adelina, and in its place, gave them goblets. "For it represents the mutual sharing of joy and sorrow. From this moment on, you will share everything in life, joys and sorrows. From this day, you will bear one another's burdens. Your joys will be doubled, and your sorrows halved."

Adelina sipped the wine—its sweet, berry contents tingling her tastebuds. All the while, she kept her gaze locked on Damir's, for she feared her knees would buckle. He kept a steady grip of her hand and gave her a reassuring nod before drinking from his own cup.

"It is my honour to pronounce you man and wife. You may kiss." The ordained took the cups and placed them on the altar.

The world around her blurred until all that was left was her and Damir. Her husband.

Damir bent and pressed his lips against hers. The hairs on the back of her neck stood on end as bolts of warmth shot through her core. He guided her out of the building, his strong arm around her waist, and she smiled as her family applauded. The moon shone between sparse clouds, a cool breeze tickled her cheeks, and with each step she took, the sturdier she became. No matter what they faced, they'd face it together.

NINE

Wedding Night

A fire crackled in the fireplace in the centre of the Litvin family room. Damir's parents had retired to Adelina's house, giving them space and privacy for the night. Stood beside the fire, Damir prodded the logs before setting the poker aside.

With a shy smile, he collected the blankets from the three-seater sofa, then draped them across the wooden floors. To hide her shaking fingers, Adelina grabbed the cushions and propped them on top of the sprawled blankets. Unpinning the veil from her hair, she set it on a bookcase.

"Will you take a seat?" He gestured to the cushioned chairs positioned around a small, round table. Removing his jacket, he rolled his white sleeves to his elbows.

She nodded, sliding into the seat—the flames beside her warmed her arms. "We had a beautiful ceremony."

Leaning across the table, he took her hand in his and kissed it. "Indeed, it was. It would've been lovely to see more of the spring equinox festivities, but we have many more years ahead of us for that."

Cheeks burning, she lowered her gaze and clasped the decanter of wine, pouring a glass for them both.

"Shall we make a toast?" Her voice was thin, almost inaudible. Her chest tightened—a combination of her tightly drawn corset and her nauseating nerves.

Flattening his shirt with his hands, Damir joined her at the table, then grasped his own glass. "To my beautiful wife."

She smiled as they clinked their glasses.

She gulped her wine in an attempt to rid the dryness from her mouth, but the alcohol provided no such relief. Yet it *did* numb the sickness in the pit of her stomach and her overwhelming desire to flee.

Her gaze caught her new husband, whose foot tapped the floor in a fast rhythm. He pressed his lips together, swallowing a mouthful of wine.

A loud crack and pop from the hearth made her jolt in her chair, sloshing the remaining wine in her glass onto the table.

Simultaneously, they both shot out of their chairs, heading in the direction of the kitchen branching off the main sitting room.

"It's all right, I'll get a towel." His eyes shone in the warm glow, and a calmness spread through her.

As he disappeared into the kitchen, she slipped back into her seat to hide the trembling in her legs.

Leaning forward, she propped her arms on the table and scanned the row of portraits positioned on a wooden shelf opposite her. Small paintings, and while their brushstrokes weren't wholly perfect, it was clear who they depicted—Damir and his parents through the years.

When Damir returned, he mopped up the spilled wine. He tucked a curl behind her ear and a tingling sensation shot up her arm. Her fine hairs stood on end, and her cheeks warmed.

While he took the towel back to the kitchen, her gaze flicked to the array of plump cushions and thick cosy blankets in front of the fire. She swallowed.

Readjusting her position on the chair, she shifted her attention to him as he strolled over and relaxed into the opposite chair. She desperately desired a distraction, anything at all to help the time pass before they inevitably ended up naked in each other's arms.

Despite her nerves, she longed to touch him, to explore him as his wife. More so, she wanted to understand him, and what it meant to be joined as one.

Leaning towards her, he stroked the triple stacked wedding ring on her left fourth finger. His touched lingered, tracing a light line on her wrist. Her breath briefly stopped, and any words she'd planned on uttering escaped her.

He cleared his throat, eyeing the almost empty wine decanter.

"Shall I get us more?" His voice was husky.

Unable to speak, she nodded.

In several strides, he was beside a wooden cabinet. Opening it, he revealed two bottles of vodka and three bottles of wine.

With his back to her, she puffed out the large gulp of air she'd held in for too long and collapsed against the back rest. She ran her hand over the top of her hair.

Pull yourself together. Don't be a coward.

Tracing her finger along her collarbone, a warmth bolted through her core. Her desire for his hands gave her the courage she needed.

She lowered her hand when he faced her and closed the space between them, bottle of wine in hand. Giving her a coy smile, he topped up her glass. Setting the decanter aside, he walked behind her. His fingers rested on her neck, then moved upwards into her hair.

She leaned into his touch—every nerve in its vicinity alight with fire.

He bent, pressing his lips to her head.

Fuelled by a need to be connected, she placed her hand on his arm below his rolled sleeve. As if the chair might disappear beneath her, she clung to him, the knot of nerves inside her tightening.

"We don't have to rush this." He swept her curls over her shoulder.

"No." She rose. "I want to do this."

Stroking her cheek, he explored her skin.

"Kiss me." Her words were light on her inhale.

Snaking his hand to the back of her neck, he bent and pressed his lips to hers. Tentative at first, with the soft tickle of his breath on her skin. Then his arms wrapped around her, pressing her against his chest, nothing between them except clothes and the glow of firelight.

She tasted the rich berry wine on his tongue, and the painful knots in her stomach unwound with each of his touches. His fingers against her arms. An eager kiss on her collarbone. A grasp of her hair.

Together, they lowered onto the strewn blankets, still clothed, their mouths exploring each other.

He drew back from the kiss, his lips barely touching hers. "I want more of you." He tugged at her dress and moaned. "More," he murmured again.

She pulled away and smiled, charmed by his words. "Perhaps we should undress first."

When he was on his feet, he offered his hand to her. She clasped it and allowed him to ease her up.

Trailing his fingers from her shoulders to her wrists, he kept his gaze locked on hers, a smile tugging at the corners of his mouth. The golden hue of the hearth fire cast shadows across the plains of his face and highlighted the bridge of his nose. His dark eyes appeared bottomless in the dim light.

"Laces," she whispered, turning to face the closed curtains.

He fumbled for the drawn laces of her corseted dress.

As he loosened the fitted garment, she remained still as stone, aside from the slight rising and lowering of her chest with each breath.

Lifting his fingers, he traced soft lines across her exposed shoulders, behind her curls, and to the back of her neck. She leaned into him.

Within minutes, he'd removed her corset, tossed it onto the floor, and began his work on removing her skirts.

Stood in her undergarments, she dropped her gaze—he was fully clothed.

Closing the inches between them, she pressed her body against him, and draped her arms over his shoulders, clasping her fingers at the back of his neck.

Stepping on to her tiptoes, she met his lips with her own, tasting the sweet berries once again. His tongue brushed hers, and the fibres of her being burst ablaze. An overwhelming combination of heat and chill spread across her skin.

He grunted as he broke the kiss, then drew his shirt over his head in one fell swoop, tossing it onto the floorboards. Undoing his breeches, he kicked them aside.

His hands traced the collar of her undergarment, guiding it towards the edges of her shoulders. It slid down the length of her body, exposing her pale skin.

Aware of her nakedness, she fought the urge to wrap her arms around her bare breasts, or dive under the blankets. Instead, she held her chin high, kept her hands rigid by her sides to mask their shaking, and fixed her unwavering gaze on his.

Chest raising and falling with sharp breaths, his lips parted as he absorbed the sight of the outline of her collarbones, her breasts, and her beaded nipples. Reaching out, he touched her, and as he kneeled upon the blankets, she lowered with him.

With one hand cupping her cheek, he leaned into her and whispered into her ear. "You are beautiful. And I am one lucky man."

He grabbed her by the waist, crushing his lips against hers.

"Your body..." he said, voice raspy, as his hands roamed the planes of her back, her buttocks, and her thighs. She weaved her fingers through his hair, unwilling to let go of him.

Slowly, he lowered her against the soft fabric beneath them. He propped himself on to his elbows, then planted light kisses along her collarbones, her sternum, each breast, down to her stomach.

Arching her back, she shivered from the pleasure of his touch. Any nerves she'd felt a moment ago were squashed with each move he made—together, they stumbled through this unknown experience, safe in each other's arms.

Her knees raised on either side of him as he edged into her. She gripped his lower arms, bracing for the sharp pain. Their mouths collided, and she inhaled the lingering scent of sawed wood and vodka clinging to him. He thrust into her, and she pressed her nails into his flesh.

"Do you want me to stop?" he asked, voice hoarse.

"No." She wrapped her arms around his back, drawing him close. She needed more of him, everything he could give her.

With each stroke, her pain subsided, and her body hummed with desire. A moan escaped her lips as his movements grew swifter.

He wound her hair in his hand, his lips parted, and he groaned deep and gravelly as she met him thrust for thrust. Raking her nails over his shoulders, she arched her back, wanting to rid them of any space lingering between them. As her core tightened, spurring her on to the edge of her pleasure, she pressed an urgent kiss to his collarbone. She guided his mouth to hers and his body spasmed with release.

Dropping onto the floor beside her, beads of sweat slid down his temples. He swatted them away, keeping his gaze locked on hers.

Turning on to her side, she stroked his jaw.

He kissed her on the nose, then fixed a serious look upon her. "Did you like it?"

Her cheeks burned, and her body trembled. Despite the short burst of pain, she hadn't wanted it to end. "Yes."

A wicked grin spread across his mouth. "How will we ever leave this house?"

"I'm sure your parents will want to come home *eventually*." She laughed.

"Then we shall enjoy every second until then." Getting to his feet, he padded across the room and grabbed their glasses. He handed one to her and sank down beside her.

Giddy and shaking with adrenaline, she sipped a large mouthful of her wine before setting the glass on the wooden floorboards beyond the fuzzy edge of the blanket.

"I don't know about you, but I'm ravenous." He laughed. "I'll raid the pantry and whip us up a meal. My mother usually goes to the market of a morning, so there'll be fresh vegetables and some meat, I expect."

He rose, threw his shirt on over his head, which hung halfway down his thighs, then headed to the kitchens. As she pushed herself up to help him, he stopped her, a warm smile on his face.

"No. Let me cook for you." His gentle voice melted her.

"How could I refuse?" She grinned, watching him disappear from the room.

She ran her fingers down the length of her abdomen, her skin flushed and hot beneath her touch. Somehow, she felt different, *new*. And she liked it.

Adelina stirred from her slumber and stretched. Shuffling to her side, she smiled at her sleeping husband. His dark hair was tussled from the cushions, and strands fell over his left eye.

She sat, letting the blanket pool around her waist, and gazed at her husband's bare torso. Tiny curls of hair on his chest looked caramel brown in the remnants of moonlight streaming through the gap between the curtains. Unable to resist, she brushed her fingers along his sternum, up to his cheek.

He grumbled, frowned, blinked several times, then fixed his gaze on her. "Morning."

"Good morning." She kissed his forehead.

Rubbing his eyes, he shifted into a seated position. His gaze travelled to her breasts.

"If you stay like that, we might never leave this room." He rose, nudging her down onto the pillows. Leaning over her, he trailed kisses up her stomach to her mouth.

Giggling, she played with the wisps of hair at the nape of his neck. "As much as I'd like to stay here with you, your parents will be wanting to come home. We should get dressed and head back to my parents'—we should say goodbye to our families before we go."

Collapsing on to his back, he puffed out a sigh. "And reality sinks in."

Swivelling on to her stomach, she rested her hand on his chest. "Hey, we'll be fine. We have each other and we'll travel south to one of the secluded villages past the pine forests, as planned."

He clasped her hand, then brought her knuckles to his lips. "You're my wife now—I won't see you without, but I don't have much more than my clothes to offer you, and I'm currently not wearing any."

She stifled a laugh.

Groaning, he rose from the floor and dressed. When they were both fully clothed, they folded up the blankets and stacked them, along with the cushions, on the sofa.

"I'll be right back." He dashed upstairs, then returned a few moments later with a satchel.

"I've packed what I could." He held out his hand to her. "Come on then. We should leave before the sun rises."

Smiling, she accepted his offer, and they headed out of the Litvin home.

The temporary bliss of their wedding night was shattered and their immediate need to hide from Filip was paramount. If anything, she should feel grateful they were able to enjoy their night together, having had no time to partake in the spring equinox festivities the previous day.

A cold shiver ran down her spine. They didn't have just Filip to worry about either—what about his father? She'd already discovered in Filip's journal he was securing power for himself and to please his father. Could the threat extend further? Members of the Embassy were promised her help in reuniting the countries, albeit a false promise, but surely, once they learned of her disappearance, they would demand for her to be returned to the palace at the earliest convenience.

Striding in through the front door of her family home, Adelina fought against the heat rising in her cheeks as her father glanced at her over the top of the broadsheet in his hands. He sat at the dining table, a steaming cup of tea in front of him, along with a plate stacked with rye bread and cooked sausages. Mirelle and Jasen sat in chairs next to Adelina's father.

Daro's gaze flicked to Damir. "I'm sure you looked after my daughter."

Damir nodded. "Yes, sir."

"Oh, my darling," Mirelle said to her son.

And no more was said about their wedding night. Velinka came down the stairs and drew Adelina into her arms, stroking the back of her hair.

When she let go, she blinked back tears. "Come with me. You'll need to change out of your dress. I have some riding clothes you can have."

In her parents' room, Adelina stripped out of her wedding dress and slipped into the cotton shirt and breeches her mother handed her. Sitting on the edge of the bed, she stuffed her feet into leather boots and knotted the laces.

"You're a woman now. My firstborn child. This time tomorrow, you'll be far from here, but the gods know I am glad you have a kind man to watch over you," her mother said.

Adelina lifted her gaze, her chest tightening. "I love you, Ma."

Velinka cleared her throat, then beckoned her into her outstretched arms. Embracing her daughter, she pressed her lips to her forehead. "I love you very much."

Adelina and Velinka returned to the living room to find Damir tucking into a plateful of sausages and bread.

"You'll want to eat something before you go." Velinka urged Adelina towards the table. "The breakfast should still be warm. I'll pack you more food for the journey."

Before Adelina could say anything, her mother disappeared into the kitchen. She could've sworn she'd heard the faint sound of sniffling.

"Don't worry about your mother," Pa said in a gentle tone as he set his broadsheet aside. "She knows you will be safe. I've given Damir an axe as he is likely to need one to cut wood for a fire, and your mother has already packed some clean clothes for you." He gestured to the same bags Adelina had taken to the palace.

"Thank you," she said around the lump in her throat.

"You'll find a map in there too," Pa said.

As she stared at her food, her stomach grumbled. She ate what she could, but the ache in her heart made it almost impossible.

When her mother entered the room, her eyes were red. She came to Adelina's side and kissed the top of her head. "Your pouch of coins and your grandfather's pocket watch are still in your bag, too. And here is some bread, cheese, and dried meat. It's not a lot, but it will last until you can hunt." She gave Adelina a cotton-wrapped bundle.

"Right, you shouldn't delay." Jasen shoved his chair back, grabbed his son's belongings and axe and handed them to Damir. "You should go while you can. The markets will open soon, and people will be out and about."

"He's right," Daro said. "My friend kept the coachman company last night, but I wouldn't hang around longer than necessary if I were you. If anyone should ask where you are, we'll say you were summoned back to the palace and left with the coachman—my friend said he's due to depart shortly.

"By the time Filip gets here looking for you, no one but us and the ordained who performed the ceremony will have seen you or know anything about your wedding. I've already secured two horses for you at the stables. You should head there now."

With a final embrace, Adelina bid farewell to her family. She glanced at the closed door at the end of the room—her sister's bedroom.

Velinka placed the strap of Adelina's bag on her shoulder, then squeezed her arm. "You know she loves you."

"I know," Adelina whispered, stowing the bundle of food in her satchel. "Tihana told me yesterday, and she knows I love her too, but I thought she would've come out to say goodbye this morning."

"She wept through the night," Velinka said. "It's been hard on her."

With a nod, Adelina peeled her gaze from the door and smiled. She took her husband's hand and left the house.

Damir carried their bags as he and Adelina hurried along the cobbled paths towards the stables. The scent of baked rosemary bread and aromatic mixed spices from the market wafted on the breeze. They passed the empty bathhouses. The place would be crawling with people soon.

On the way, she spotted the construction work of her father's stove-making shop. Stone walls were built, and new windows fitted, but the roof was yet to be replaced, and she'd no idea what the inside was like.

A sharp pain jolted through her chest. She couldn't stop to see what the shop was looking like inside, but she was grateful, nonetheless, her family weren't seriously harmed in the fire. She wondered if Filip would force her father to pay back the help he gave to fix the shop, and the thought of it made her sick.

Together, they hurried to the stables. As said by Daro, two horses were ready for them, saddled and bridled.

After giving his thanks to the stableman, Damir fastened their luggage to the back of the saddles, keeping the map out for a closer inspection.

Leaning against the stable wall, he flattened the map across his knee, then bent. A frown formed between his brows as he followed the trail with his finger. "This route will take us south through the pine forest. Beyond, there're several settlements dotted about, but days' travel in between each. We'll make camp along the way, and we'd better stay for only a few days in each town."

He straightened, then glanced at his wife. "Once we have an idea of what we're dealing with, we can decide if we can settle somewhere for longer."

She pressed her lips into a thin line. "Filip will never stop looking for me. I have no idea what lengths he will go to or what he's capable of."

"I won't let him take you." He cupped her cheek. "You're mine and I am yours. Nothing will get in the way of us."

"I trust you," she said, and meant it. "But if he hurts our family…" She shook her head.

"We can't do anything here for them, except leave and lead Filip and his men far away from this town." He urged her towards her horse. "Up you get."

Putting her foot into the stirrup, she hoisted herself onto the horse, then adjusted herself on the saddle. Clutching the reins, she waited for him.

When he was mounted, they rode along the cobble path, over the bridge, and into the pine forest, leaving their childhood home behind.

Tall pines rose from the earth to touch the sky. Sun-dappled leaves created flickering shadows on the ground. Animal trails disappeared into the undergrowth, and dead leaves and pine needles were caught in clumps of moss at the edge of the beaten path.

Bark frayed off broken branches, inches above fat burls. Moss wound around the trunks, and pinecones dotted the trail like spilled trinkets. Wood beetles bumbled across rotten, fallen logs next to the river meandering through the forest.

"Stay away from those." Damir gestured to the wind-damaged trunks leaning drunkenly against one another.

Adelina nodded.

"It's beautiful here, and so peaceful," she said. "Did you see the animal burrows amongst the roots over there?"

"I sure did," he said, then raised his arm. "Be still. There's a deer by the river."

The wind rustled through the leaves and the spongy layers of dead pine needles and twigs crunched underneath the horses' hooves. Birds called and animals rootled around in the underbrush.

For a moment, she enjoyed the serenity of the forest—her worries forgotten. The deer grabbed a mouthful of greenery beside the fern fronds.

"The idea of camping doesn't seem so bad now," she said in a hushed tone. "Imagine fireflies lighting the canopy of leaves at night. It sounds blissful."

"You don't want to use your magic for light?" He arched a brow.

She frowned, shook her reins, and resumed her ride along the path.

He caught up with her. "What's wrong?"

"My magic doesn't feel like a gift, but a curse," she said, her moment of peace shattered by a weight on her shoulders. "If I hadn't seen the dragon in my vision, if I'd failed the test like everyone else, then no harm would be brought to Aramoor. We've fled our home and for what? To bring Filip and his guards right to Aramoor's doorstep, anyway?"

"I understand how you feel, I do." His gentle gaze met hers. "But we've spoken about this—there's nothing more we can do for the people of our hometown, except get away. We'll keep riding until the sun sets—that'll put us at least twenty miles south of Aramoor."

"It doesn't mean they deserve the interrogation or threats I'm sure Filip and his men will come with." She dropped her gaze from his, fixing it on the winding path through the trees.

"All we can do is look after ourselves and take this one day at a time," he said. "Drink some water—you need to stay hydrated."

She nodded, hopped down from her horse, rummaged in her bag, then drew her flask. Unfastening the lid, she pressed it to her lips and gulped the cool liquid.

"Do you want some?" she said.

"No, it's okay, thanks," he said. "I have my own. Luckily, we have this river we can use to wash. Maybe there's a stream of freshwater somewhere close for us to refill our bottles when we need them."

She mounted her horse. "I'll keep my eye out."

"We'll ride until evening," he said. "Then we'll stop to make camp for the night."

―――

The forest darkened with each passing hour of evening stretching into night. Damir and Adelina hobbled the horses in a gravelly patch of ground ringed by trees and branches.

A pile of chopped firewood and scavenged deadfall lay beside Damir's handmade fire pit, while he skinned two rabbits he'd caught for supper.

Rifling through her bag, she found a lantern. She placed it on a tree stump. "Look what Ma packed for us."

Glancing over his shoulder, he smiled. "Very useful, indeed."

"*Areiras therasi.*" A light flickered inside the lantern, adding to the orange glow of the fire. "It's not much, but it'll help you see what you're doing better."

"Thank you." He shifted his position, soaking the game in light. "I'm almost done with this, then I'll set it to roast."

She lowered onto the springy grass beside him. The fire crackled as wood burned and sap popped. An owl hooted nearby, and tall trees creaked in the breeze. Firelight only extended so far, and beyond, the forest blurred into a black void, no longer the peaceful utopia she'd thought of earlier in the day.

"How can this place be so…creepy at night?" she said as a chill spread across her skin. She tugged her cloak tight around her.

"The forest comes alive at night, and we must respect it." He skewered the meat, then hung it over the flames. "From the wolves right down to the wood beetles—this is their land."

She leaned into him. "I'm lucky to have you."

Without him there, she could only wonder how she'd manage alone. She knew how to light a fire—her magic came in handy—and she could hunt. But she relied on his emotional resilience, and such a quality was essential when leaving everyone they loved behind.

Resting his forehead against hers, he drew her close. Together, they watched the flames flicker and the meat char.

Light streamed through the canopy of leaves and speckled the floor. Damir was already awake, tending to the horses, when Adelina stirred from her slumber.

Embers from the fire fluttered on the slight morning breeze, and with it, the lingering scent of burned wood and moss.

She swiped the tangling curls away from her face and shoved the blanket aside, one she assumed Damir had draped over her in the night. "Morning, my love."

"Good morning." He smiled over his shoulder at her while he fastened their bags to the horses' saddles. "We should ride as soon as you have eaten. I've already had my share of leftover rabbit, and while you slept, I refilled our flasks at a nearby stream."

"Thank you," she said. "Perhaps we will have enough time to bathe in the river?"

"We must be quick," he said. "I've checked the map and by tonight, we should reach the *Twelve Bells Inn*. We'll sleep indoors, my darling, and you'll have a proper dinner, I assure you."

"You needn't worry about my welfare," she said sincerely. "We managed well out here in the forest for the night. However, if an opportunity presents itself whereby we can enjoy the comforts of a mattress, well, who am I to decline?"

He laughed. "I see you're rather chipper this morning."

"Prospects of a new day is all." She rose, and in quick strides, came to his side. "Knowing I'm with you, we will overcome whatever Filip has in store for us. I believe we will be fine."

Her words were confident, and she hoped he believed them too.

Once she'd eaten her last few chunks of roasted rabbit, she swigged a mouthful of water, then headed for the river.

By midmorning, they'd broken through the edge of the pine forest, riding down a country lane stretching between rolling hills and open fields. They saw no settlements of any sort for miles, aside from small farm cottages and weathered stables.

Grass grew on the road's shoulder, beside the odd ditch. Yellow canola flowers sprouted from the fields where cattle grazed. Scruffy brush and stunted trees dotted fallow land, and a falcon flew overhead. Ahead, an old shack rotted, and barn structures remained forgotten in the fields.

"All this land and no one to tend to it," she said. "Aside from the one or two farmers this far south. You'd think they'd prefer the slightly better weather conditions."

"It's not so much the farmers' fault," he said. "There's a population crisis in this area—not enough families to work the land or children to take over from their fathers."

Wind feathered through the wild grass and sparsely sewn crops. Crickets and grasshoppers whirred and an animal, perhaps a mouse, rustled through clumps of weeds.

"Explains why there's limited crops growing," she said, and a pang of guilt shot through her. "You know, when I was staying at Kirovo Palace, I said to the benefactors I would help to solve issues within the three countries, and what am I doing? Running from them."

"You don't have a choice." He glanced at her—golden light illuminating the planes of his face. His dark eyes twinkled. "You were being tricked and deceived, and your life could've been at risk around Filip. He has already proven he can't be trusted."

She held her shoulders back and focused on the road ahead.

TEN

The Trace

Steam from the metal bathtub plumed, making the air thick with condensation. Adelina leaned against the surface, the water lapping around her collarbones. Closing her eyes for a moment, she inhaled the sweet, floral scent of lavender.

Damir knelt beside her, lathering her arms in soap.

She sat forward as he trailed his soapy hands up her back, to her neck, and along her shoulders. He kneaded her muscles, then grasped the jug on the counter nearby. Once it was full to the brim with foaming water, he poured it over her roots and the length of her brown hair.

Sighing in pleasure, she closed her eyes. "I've been looking forward to this all day."

"Hmm," he muttered. "We should go down for breakfast shortly before we set out."

"Of course," she said. "I have an idea."

"What is it?" He leaned against the tub.

"I borrowed a stack of books from the library at the palace." She twisted to face him—the water lapping around her chest. "If I can learn to open a portal into the prism world, I can practise my magic."

"Prism world?" He arched a brow.

"It's another dimension—a safe space for someone to practise their magic without repercussions on the real world." She smiled—a sense of pride filling her as she disclosed a piece of her magical knowledge. "While I have mastered several spells, I need somewhere to continue my learning away from prying eyes."

"Then a great plan it is." He offered her his hands, which she accepted graciously. When she was on her feet, she stepped out of the bath, water droplets splashing onto the floorboards. "Get dressed, my dear, and we will begin our search for a place for you to study this…prism world."

He winked, bent to kiss her forehead, then disappeared from the room.

Filip's carriage came to a halt outside the palace. Now his father was safely in the hands of an esteemed physician, he could return his attentions to Adelina. He'd need to act quick if he was to make her his wife—he'd already been delayed for too long.

The coachman opened the carriage door, Filip hopped from his bench, then strode through the open palace doors. The ring box positioned inside his breast pocket pressed against him—a constant reminder of his intentions.

He checked his pocket watch. Midday.

"Sir," a servant said with a nervous and too-quick curtsey.

He glanced up, meeting her bewildered expression. "What is it?"

"It's regarding Miss Adelina Orlova." She paled. "We wanted to wait for you to return home before bringing such matters to your attention," she rambled. "You see, a letter wouldn't have reached you in time."

"What's wrong with her? Has she fallen ill?" He glanced at the staircase, in the direction of Adelina's chamber. "Is Natasha with her? I'm sure she will tend to her every need."

"No, sir." She swallowed hard. "She has gone."

"Gone where?" His patience wore thin. "I shouldn't have to demand such answers."

"I'm sorry, sir. Truly." She flattened her skirts. "She and her chaperone, Miss Salma, have not returned from the festivities."

"I've been gone almost three weeks," he said. "Allowing two weeks for travel and a day of festivities, she should have returned a week ago."

He set into a quick pace through the palace, heading towards the training room at the back of the gardens. The servant scampered to keep up as they passed other servants who tended to the flowers and herbs.

"Sir, we have already spoken to Yelena—she has not seen the girl," the servant said.

Filip spun around, cheeks burning. "I will make my own enquiries."

Wide-eyed, the servant girl curtsied, then returned to the kitchens.

In quick strides, Filip burst through the training room to find Yelena nose deep in a pile of books lying open on the table.

She rose. "Afternoon, Filip."

"Where is she?" He ignored her pleasantries.

"I'm not certain," she said levelly. "I received word from Natasha that Adelina borrowed some books from the library. Perhaps you ought to check in with her."

He narrowed his eyes at her. "If I find out you are lying, there will be repercussions. Severe ones."

"There is nothing but the truth here." She smiled through gritted teeth. "I assure you."

Spinning around, he marched out of the room, across the gardens, then through the palace.

"Where is Natasha?" he asked a nearby servant who was tending to the vases of flowers in the foyer. "Send her to me."

He didn't give the servant a second to respond. Instead, he strode into his study, kicked the door shut, then planted his hands on the soft, wooden surface of his desk.

"Damn it," he muttered to himself.

If Adelina was truly gone, he'd need to locate her and return her to the bosom of the palace as soon as possible. Their union needed to be blessed and consummated. If his father learned the truth—the girl was lost—he'd be ridiculed, having found her after a decade of searching.

The door opened.

A Ballad of Severed Souls

He spun around to see Natasha stood a metre or so away from him.

"You wished to see me?" she said.

Narrowing his eyes on her expressionless face, he clasped his hands in front of him. "Do you have any idea where Miss Orlova is?"

"She went to visit her family for the Spring Equinox as planned, Sir," she said. "I know of no reason why she wouldn't choose to return."

"Are you quite certain?" His tone was sharp.

"Yes, sir." She curtsied, dropping her gaze from him to the floor.

Filip pressed his lips into a thin line. "I must find her. Call for the guards at once. It is time we paid a little visit to her hometown."

The rest of the week passed in a blur for Adelina as she and her new husband travelled from one tavern or inn to another. Within the next day or two, they'd need to move on to the next village, riding through the dividing woodlands to reach it.

When they rested, Adelina studied. Sat on one of the chairs at the wooden table beneath the window, she held the pages of her book flat and read each line over and over. Damir brought her a cup of tea and settled it on the surface in front of her.

"Have a drink," he said. "You've been staring at those pages all morning."

"I know." She sighed, then blinked several times. A dull ache throbbed in her temples. "But I need to understand this stuff. Yelena created the portal into the prism world with no issues whatsoever. I've never done it before, only practised my magic *inside* it."

"Why don't you crack open the window? Let the fresh air clear your thoughts," he suggested. "I'm going to visit the market to purchase some more meat and bread for the next few days. We'll need to collect the horses from the stable and depart within an hour or two, so we get a few miles of riding in before dark."

She nodded, stretched, then unlatched the window. A cool breeze tickled her cheek.

Bending, he planted a warm kiss on her forehead. "I'll be back before you know it."

With long strides, he left the room, the sound of his footsteps disappearing as he descended to the restaurant on the ground floor of the tavern. The wall vibrated when the entrance door clomped closed behind him.

She sipped her tea, and between each mouthful of sweet berry contents, she inhaled deeply, counted to three, then let out her breath of air.

"Back to work." She set the cup on its saucer, then scooped up her book.

Perched on the edge of the mattress, she returned her gaze to the portal spell. Each word was imprinted in her mind, meaning she was ready to put it to practice.

Rising, she flattened her skirt and flexed her fingers. With the book held in one hand, she positioned herself between the foot of the bed and the hearth, allowing enough space for the portal.

Casting another glance at the open page of the book, she cleared her throat in preparation of uttering the unfamiliar words.

Thaanariel malirasal.

"*Tha-thaanariel malir-rasal,*" she stumbled over the bulky, clumsy words of the complex spell. "*Thaan...ariel...mali...rasal.*" She tried again, pronouncing the words in smaller chunks to familiarise herself with the syllables and pronunciation.

Setting the book aside, she held her hand in front of her, then drew a circle through the air like Yelena did during training. "*Thaanariel malirasal.*"

A golden spark hissed into existence, then disappeared almost as quickly as it'd formed.

She frowned, pressed her lips together, then swiped her pointed finger through the air once again in a more exaggerated motion. "*Thaanariel malirasal.*"

Another flicker and pop of golden light. The portal formed tentatively, wobbling, and fading in and out of existence. It stabilised itself, shimmering around the edges. After a few minutes, a robust, perfect circle hovered a few inches above the floorboards.

The bedroom door opened, Adelina's concentration shattered, and with it, so did the portal.

Damir stared wide-eyed at the space between them. "Did I see a portal?"

"You did," she said a little tersely. "Just as I managed to open it."

"Well, perhaps a tavern bedroom isn't the best place for it." He wedged a bag of food inside his luggage. "Come on, we should get a move on."

Nodding, she tucked her books into her own bag, flung the strap over her shoulder, and followed him out.

Deep in the forest, Damir sat by the fire and watched the flames dance as their rabbits roasted. Stomach rumbling, he adjusted his position on the mossy log, then cast a glance at Adelina, who hopped out of the prism world portal.

She slid beside him on to the log, leaned against him, then rested her head on his shoulder.

He draped his arm around her and held her close. "How was it?"

"Good," she said. "I have full control over my fire magic—there's not so much of a concern there—but I *am* trying to master some other spells."

"Such as?" He peered at her with curiosity.

"Astral magic isn't just about fire or the sun—there are other elements to it. It's natural, remarkable. Beautiful." Holding her left palm up, she used her right index finger and swirled it through the air. "*Tyleiri.*"

A green stem sprouted from her hand, grew to the height of six inches, then blossomed into a rose.

He gasped. "So, now you can produce flowers."

She laughed. "I've read through almost all the books I took from the palace, and they all focus on nature and energy, which the sun provides. If you think about it, there isn't any limit to my power as long as it is natural."

Shifting to face her, one leg thrown over the log, he pressed his mouth into a tight line. The thought of Filip taking her away from him, forcing her to do whatever he pleased, sent hot waves of rage shooting through his core. He fought to keep his emotions in check as he said, "If there is no limit to your power, Filip could do anything he wanted with you. I swear it now, in front of all gods, I won't let him near you."

Despite the sturdiness of his voice, his chest tightened. He'd sooner rather tear Filip's throat out than let him press Adelina into his service. As if noticing his inner turmoil, she traced her thumb lightly over the frown between his brows. "We have each other now. As long as we're together, we will be all right."

He closed his eyes, taking her hand in his and pressing it to his lips. "Tell me more about your magic—whatever you know. Perhaps it'll quell my nerves."

"Well." She smiled as she picked up a stick and prodded the fire. "It's only a theory, but I think I could help farmers with their crops, help them grow more. I'm not sure if I'm strong enough yet to produce vegetation in large quantities and I'd need to practise more in the prism world."

His tense shoulders relaxed a fraction as he let out a breath. "I'm sure the farmers would be grateful for your help even if there is a population crisis."

Silence hung between them for a moment. Damir pictured what their life could've been like. A small cottage in the village, with him working as a carpenter, and she as a seamstress or whatever else she fancied. Together, they would help their neighbours with small yet bountiful harvests they grew in the fields near Aramoor. But as quickly as the pleasant image had formed, it disappeared, and he was left with an empty sensation in the pit of his stomach.

He dragged a hand down the side of his face. "I'm sorry, I can't shake this…rage. Filip spent so long looking for you, and he isn't likely to back down from finding you—and keeping you. Maybe it's selfish, but I've had you for a matter of a few days, as a wife, I mean. I have no intentions of letting you go."

"I know." She kissed him, stroking the side of his face. The taught muscles in his jaw relaxed beneath her touch. "I love you."

"I love you, too." He rose, then offered her his hand. "I've got a suggestion: Perhaps you can offer these villages something else instead. Some flowers here and there, a few more vegetables growing in their house gardens, a flame to light their torches, or anything else to make their simple days seem a little better or easier."

"A lovely thought." She accepted his offer, and he guided her into the centre of the glade.

With his arm on her waist, he led her in a slow dance, wanting to provide her with a moment of escapism as well as for himself. The orange glow of fire lit the bridge of her nose. The shadows turned her eyes to deep pools of brown.

"What are you doing?" She giggled. "We have no music."

"Listen closely," he said in a hushed tone, a playful grin tugging at the corner of his lips. "The rustle of the leaves and the undergrowth, the sigh of wind through the trees. An owl hoot in the distance. The life of the forest is our music."

"How poetic." She blushed, pushed on to her tiptoes, and kissed him again.

Filip's carriage came to a sharp halt on the path outside Aramoor. He leapt from the seat, landing on the cobbles with a dull thud. Several other carriages stopped nearby, his guards gathering around him like a small army.

"Speak to the locals. Extract whatever information you can via any means necessary," Filip said with as much calmness as he could muster. "Keep everyone alive. I'm going to pay my old friend, Pyotr, a visit."

The bustling markets of Aramoor were silenced by the heavy clomping of Filip's boots against cobblestones. Cautious gazes met his glare as the locals slowed to a halt, observing him as he wandered through the market.

His guards dispersed throughout the village but returned empty handed. Worse, no one had seen Adelina recently at all. It was down to him to find his own answers to her whereabouts.

Pressing his lips together, he considered where his old acquaintance, Pyotr, might be—his address unknown to him. There was no point in demanding answers from Adelina and Damir's family—they wouldn't give them to him. Although he could use techniques more persuasive in extracting information, it could amount to a lot of wasted time. If he could get his hands on somebody malleable—

someone like Pyotr—he could obtain information a lot quicker.

Filip understood, from his experience of working with Pyotr, that he was the type of man to do what he must to secure his own wealth and position. Surely, the man would be around here somewhere.

A whiff of hops and yeast wafted from the tavern near the market. It was the middle of the day, so the taphouse was almost empty. A few locals sat at wooden tables positioned outside, steins of beer in hand.

"Afternoon. Do you know a man by the name of Pyotr Lebedev?" Filip approached the patrons.

"He's inside, all right." A dark-haired man nodded towards the entrance. "You'll find him at his usual table."

Filip thanked the man, then slipped into the brightly lit tavern.

A middle-aged woman with tied back brown hair wiped the tables.

His heavy boots against the creaking floorboards broke the silence of the quiet room, and his gaze caught a man hunched over a pint.

Pyotr drew the stein to his lips and gulped.

"It's been some time," Filip said, which lifted Pyotr's glassy gaze from the table to him.

"Filip." Pyotr raised a brow, his head lolling to the side.

"Good to see you." Filip inhaled the stench of stale alcohol on the man. "May I join you?"

"Sure." Pyotr slurred.

"How've you been?" Filip slipped into the chair opposite.

"Well," Pyotr said.

A Ballad of Severed Souls

Filip checked his pocket watch for confirmation—it was barely lunchtime, and this man was drunk already. The local outside referred to this as Pyotr's usual spot, and if Filip could use his drunkenness to his advantage, he might have a smoother time in finding his lost sorceress.

"Are your family well?" Filip said.

Pyotr made a half-hearted attempt at narrowing his gaze on him. "W-what's with all t-the questions?"

Creating a steeple with his hands, Filip rested his arms on the table. "I can offer you a substantial amount of money for your cooperation, Pyotr."

"W-what would I n-need money for?" Pyotr gulped a mouthful of beer, then waved the barwoman over. "I'll take another. Bring one for my f-friend too."

She eyed him before trudging over to the bar to refill the steins.

"It's the middle of the day, Pyotr. What about your job?" Filip said.

"Turns out administration isn't for me," Pyotr said. "Used to manage the books in the post office, keeping track of the parcels and letters coming in and out."

"I need your help," Filip said. "And I'm willing to pay substantially."

"What could you p-possibly want m-my help with?" Pyotr wiped his mouth with the back of his hand as the serving lady arrived with their fresh steins of beer.

Filip nodded in thanks, then sipped his drink. "The local girl—Adelina—is missing. I need your assistance in locating her and reassigning her to the bosom of the palace where she will be safe. Should any ill befall the girl, plans to unite the countries will be implicated—she, and her powers, are being relied on, therefore, she is of great value to me *and* the kingdom. Do you understand?"

Pyotr shrugged. "I s-saw her the day of the spring equinox."

"Yes, she returned home for the festivities." Filip waved his hand. "What of it?"

"She and the carpenter boy…" Pyotr gulped his beer, collapsed back against the chair, and closed his eyes.

Leaning across the table, Filip snapped his fingers in front of the drunkard's face. "I've heard you have a great deal of debt now, Pyotr. My money can rid you of your problems. I'll send money to your wife and child."

Indeed, he'd been aware of his ex-employee's addictions. Gossip travelled between staff, even though Pyotr was no longer in service.

Pyotr's eyes flashed open. "Deal."

"Now, tell me what you know of Adelina and the boy," Filip said. "Is it Damir?"

"Yes." Pyotr swallowed another large mouthful of beer—beads of the liquid spilling from the corner of his lips.

"Go home. Sober up," Filip said. "Our horses need to be watered and fed, and the guards and I are yet to have dinner. You will meet me at the entrance of this village tomorrow at dawn."

"Will I be accompanying you?" Pyotr's eyebrow lifted.

"If you wish to receive further money for your assistance, yes." Filip rose, shoving his chair aside, then left the tavern before Pyotr could say another word.

Sighing, Filip dragged a hand over his face as he stepped into the sunlight. His patience had worn thin—Pyotr having tested his last nerve—and the sooner he could leave the dreary village, the better.

―――

Four days of travelling passed quickly. Adelina and Damir either camped under the stars, beneath a canopy of trees, or enjoyed the finer comforts of a tavern or inn room. Along the way, she experimented in the prism world, growing more comfortable with her magic, each time her amulet left a warm, tingling sensation on her neck.

They fell into a routine of stopping before dusk fell, so she'd time to practise her magic. If they camped, he hunted for food, set up a firepit, and collected supplies, she would disappear into her portal, but he never ventured too far away. On the nights they rented rooms, he made sure they had substantial meals brought up, and there was enough space on the floorboards for her to practice.

When she returned to the real world, she sank onto the mossy floor beside her husband. He handed her a skewer of meat, a chunk of bread, and a slice of cheese fresh from its market wrapper.

Placing the cheese on top of the bread, she balanced it on her knee, then scooted the charred rabbit off the stick and onto her sandwich.

Biting a large mouthful, she moaned in delight as she relished the smoky taste of meat mixed with the creaminess of cheese and the hearty, herby bread.

"Not as nice as the rosemary twists but definitely satiating." She wiped a powdery texture from the corners of her mouth.

"While I was in the village, I bought some more camping supplies and clothing." He nodded to the bags positioned on the ground beside the hobbled horses. "There're extra blankets, pots, bandages, some medicinal herbs. Oh, I also got something especially for you."

Jumping to his feet, he hopped over to his bags, rummaged inside one, then drew a wooden paddle brush with fine bristles. He handed it to her. "I'd make you one myself if I was back at the carpentry shop, but I saw it amongst some trinkets and thought it would come in handy. Saves your hair getting knotted while sleeping wild."

"It's lovely." She smiled and traced a line over the smooth surface of the pine handle. "Thank you."

"Well, thank Filip." He laughed. "It's his money that paid for it."

She narrowed her gaze on the flames of the campfire, and while it should've warmed her, a chill shot up her spine. "He could be anywhere—so close or further away than we expect. How can we know for certain?"

"We don't," he said softly. "But we are staying ahead of him and his men. We'll sail across the sea if we have to."

"He'll likely have sent word to the docks informing them I'm missing." She lifted a shoulder in a small shrug. "They'll know to look for me, and we won't get a chance to board a ship."

"Come with me—there's a stream through the trees, a couple of minutes' walk from camp. We'll bathe and watch the sunset." He rose, then offered her his hand.

She accepted it graciously, and as they walked to the pebbled bank of the stream, she finished her meal.

Damir had brought a bag with him, which he rested beside them.

Rootling around inside, he drew two towels, a pile of clothes, and a bar of lily soap wrapped in brown paper. He settled them onto the stones, then tugged his wife into his arms.

A bolt of desire shot through her core when he tilted his head to kiss her. His lips were soft against hers, the taste of roasted meat and cheese lingering on his tongue.

He slid her cape off her shoulders and let the warm fabric puddle on the ground at her feet.

"What are you doing?" she asked breathlessly, leaning back from him. "We can't—not out here." She glanced around as if she might spot somebody in the bushes or across the stream from them.

"No one will be this far away from a village, save a merchant or two, but I doubt even they would be loitering at this time of day." His voice was husky as he ran his fingers down her arms.

He brought her to the ground, the tiny stones shifting beneath their knees. One jabbed into her flesh, but she didn't care. His hand cradled the back of her neck, drawing her close. Her lips parted slightly as his mouth joined with hers. Her moment of hesitation washed away by her need to be one with her husband.

Together, they fell back against the towels and pebbles. She breathed heavier with each of his touches. They freed each other of their clothes and made love to the gentle sound of the rippling stream and birdsong.

Three weeks had passed since Filip left Aramoor with Pyotr and his guards. Horses' hooved clomped as they dragged the carriages along a beaten trail. Filip's already thin patience was almost depleted. Too much time had been spent trying to find signs of Adelina's whereabouts or an indication of where she was headed.

"We should make haste." Filip nodded to the coachman. "The longer we take in finding them, the further they're likely to travel."

In desperate need to stretch his legs and breathe some air that *wasn't* tainted by the lingering stench of alcohol clinging to Pyotr, Filip banged on the carriage roof.

When the horses came to a stop, Filip climbed out, sucking in a lungful of crisp, night air.

He turned to Pyotr. "You'll accompany me, but for the love of gods, stand down wind. No amount of bathing has rid you of the smell of hops."

Without a word, Pyotr obeyed.

A Ballad of Severed Souls

With one final glance at the coachman, Filip said, "Lead the others through the forest, stick to the path, so you don't damage the carriage wheels."

Turning on his heel, Filip traversed through the pine forest, the faint torch light of the carriages in the near distance. The deeper he and Pyotr travelled, the more noticeable and intense a tingling sensation became. It spread across Filip's arms and the back of his neck. The saturation of his vision sharpened, and the pitch of his hearing heightened.

He tilted his head to the side, observing his surroundings. The trees and underbrush *should* appear indistinguishable in the faint dim glow of torchlight, but he could easily make out the brambles and the berries.

"What is it?" Pyotr asked.

"I feel something…peculiar." Filip wandered closer to the brambles. "They say nether and astral are two halves of one soul. Naturally, we aren't supposed to be apart. It's like I can sense her."

"Do you think she's been here?"

"They would've camped nearby." Filip glanced over his shoulder, beckoning the guard nearest to him. Within seconds he, along with the others, were at Filip's side. "Search the trees. Report any signs of them to me."

They dispersed, crunching leaves and twigs underfoot.

Filip frowned. "Damn, why is everything so *loud?*"

Pyotr raised a brow. "I hadn't noticed."

"Of course, you wouldn't," Filip muttered under his breath.

He followed the path deeper into the forest, then halted, his peculiar sensations fading. Spinning around, he retreated towards his starting point, then stepped through the bushes, amongst the dense cluster of pine trunks. The prickling of his magic intensified.

"I must be getting warmer," he said.

"Wait up!" Pyotr hollered, thundering after him.

"Go back to the carriage. There's nothing you can do right now, except potentially crush evidence of Adelina under your booming feet." Filip held up his arm, barricading Pyotr as he plundered towards him.

"Sorry, sir." Pyotr froze mid-step beside the claw-like roots of a nearby tree.

"Over here, sir!" a guard yelled from a few yards ahead.

Filip hurried towards the guard, his magical sensation intensifying, the green of leaves now a bright and sickly saturated colour. He shielded his eyes. What in the realm was happening to him? Such a connection to astral magic would've come in handy during his decade search of the girl.

The guard knelt beside the remnants of a firepit—ashes, twigs, burned logs, and two rabbit carcasses.

A bright white scorch mark on the mossy ground next to the firepit caught Filip's attention the most. "What is that?"

"What's what?" the guard said.

"The mark, there on the ground. Can you see it?" Filip pointed to it.

"No, sir. I don't see anything." The guard shook his head.

Kneeling, Filip touched the mark—the moss scorched beneath his fingertips. The hues of his vision changed from sharp contrasts to a bright white against a black background. His veins pulsed and his temples throbbed.

He pressed his hands flat onto the ground to steady his wobbling body and closed his eyes. "Damn magic."

"What do you sense?" Pyotr asked, having *not* obeyed his direct order to return to the carriage. Insolent man.

"Astral magic. She was here." Filip didn't meet his gaze. "Her magic was dormant before, which explains why I wasn't able to trace her before she did the test. Now she's dropping clues in her wake. You can't see it, but there's a white, circular mark on the ground, right here." He tapped the mud. "She opened a portal to the prism world."

Pyotr nodded once. "Right. I'll take your word for it."

Filip rose and rubbed the side of his head. "We'll carry on our search, and if we're lucky, the trace will lead us straight to her."

ELEVEN

Set Sail

Adelina strolled along the cobbled path of a small, quiet village. Golden tinges of the setting sun glowed from behind the houses, stretching into a deep purple, then into dark blue, where stars came to life with the first touches of night.

Damir had taken the horses to the stables and paid the stable hand to keep quiet about their whereabouts before they settled into the inn for a few days before continuing their journey south, closer to the ports. Almost a month had passed since their wedding, and she'd begun to enjoy her life on the road. There was something comforting about their adventure—or at least, that's what she called it.

With a swirl of her finger, she relit the dwindling fire torches, no longer needing to utter the spell in order to use her magic.

She met Damir outside the tavern.

"I got some needles and thread from the market before they closed." She jostled the paper bag in her hand.

Along the way, their clothes had torn on brambles and branches. All four of Damir's shirts were dotted with holes, and so were hers.

"I'll start the mending in the morning," she said as he guided her inside the fire lit tavern.

A bard performed a song while strumming a lute. Patrons sat around tables, beers in hand and laughing.

She smiled, leaning into her husband's side as they watched from the back of the room. The crackling flames in the hearth warmed her stiff fingers. Taking off her cloak, she draped it over her arm and listened to the bard's melodic tunes.

A servant carrying a platter of steins, weaved through the crowd towards them. "Care for a drink?"

"Why not?" Damir smiled, handed one to Adelina, then clasped the last one. "Here."

He placed a couple of coins on the platter.

"Thanks, kindly." She returned the smile, then made her way around the tables, collecting empty steins.

A chair dragged across the floorboards as a patron rose, swayed, then ventured outside. The rich aroma of roasted meats wafted through the tavern as staff served bowls of food to some of the seated patrons. Adelina's stomach rumbled.

"Should we order something to eat?"

"Good idea." He led her to an empty table at the back by the window.

A single candle was positioned in the centre, its light flickering and casting a glow over the wooden surface.

They sat, and while he beckoned the server, Adelina propped her elbow on the table, rested her chin on her palm, and listened to the bard.

Adelina woke in the middle of the night—silver moonlight streamed through the gap between the drawn curtains of the tavern room. Her tongue stuck to the roof of her mouth.

Padding to the table between the armchairs, she lifted the jug and peered inside. Empty.

She glanced over her shoulder to Damir, who slept soundlessly between the white sheets.

Throwing a blanket around her nightgown, she carried the jug out of the room, closing the door quietly behind her.

Deep voices echoed from downstairs. There was something familiar about that clipped, rumbling tone, but she couldn't make out what he was saying from her position. Holding her breath, she edged across the floorboards.

"I require information about a woman and a man I believe are travelling through these villages. Mark my word when I tell you I want nothing but the truth."

Her breath caught in her throat. *Filip*.

She pressed herself against the wall, hoping to be swallowed by the shadows of the landing.

A Ballad of Severed Souls

"Filip does not give empty threats," the other man sneered. Pyotr.

What in the realm was Pyotr doing with Filip and his guards? Was it possible they knew she was here with Damir?

The innkeeper mumbled something in response, but she didn't linger to listen.

Pressing lightly on her tiptoes, she re-entered her chamber and locked the door behind her. After placing the jug on the cabinet, she rushed to Damir's side and shook him awake.

"Wake up, my love," she whispered.

He jolted and his eyes flashed wide open. "What is it?"

"Filip—he's downstairs. We need to go. Quickly." She spun on her heel, threw on her clothes, then grabbed their bags.

Within minutes, Damir was dressed and peering out the window.

"What are you doing?" she said.

"Looking for a way out." He unlatched it.

"We can't jump," she gasped.

"There's a ridge right outside—we can walk along the roof to the end of the building. I'll find the safest way for us to jump down. Pass me those bags," he urged.

She handed them to him, then peered out of the window at the stone ledge. Sucking in a deep breath, she climbed onto the sill, poked her legs through, then eased herself onto the ledge.

Dropping behind her, he followed her along the rooftop. She shuffled each step with consideration and thanked the gods it hadn't rained.

"Over there." He pointed to the edge of the roof at the end of the L-shaped building.

Some of the tiles were old, chipped, and weathered, yet none slipped loose under her feet as she made her way across the top. She ignored the tight knots in her stomach and her sweaty palms.

Other than a hoot of a nearby owl, the small village was silent. When she reached the edge of the roof, she lowered herself into a seated position.

"The vines?" She glanced over her shoulder to Damir.

"Good idea. You climb down first, then I'll pass you the bags," he said.

She nodded once, spinning around, and gripped the thick vines. With her foot, she tested the strength of the vines before making her descent.

Leaves and flower buds brushed against her. When she was approximately a foot above the ground, she dropped into the mud.

"I'm ready," she whispered, stretching onto her tiptoes and holding her arms towards Damir.

Kneeling on the roof, he lowered the bags to her, one by one. Once she'd piled them on top of each other, he hurried down the vines.

"This way." He grabbed their belongings. They kept within the shadows of buildings until they reached the stables. The stable hand was already on his feet, wiping his bleary eyes.

"I'm sorry to wake you," Damir said. "We must go at once."

"Be quick about it," was all the man said as he stood at the entrance, keeping watch.

Inside, Adelina and Damir saddled up as quickly as their sweating hands could manage.

"Up you get." He offered her a leg up onto her mount, then fastened her luggage to the back of the saddle.

He turned to do the same with his own bags, then lifted himself onto his horse. With a click of his tongue and a gentle shake of the reins, he rode on to the cobbles, Adelina following.

"Thank you." Damir nodded to the stable hand.

"Wait." She raised her hand, and with a swipe of her finger, flushed out the lights from the lantern.

In the darkness, they cantered away from the village, leaving Filip and Pyotr behind.

Trembling, she fought to steady her ragged breaths. They'd been close enough to catch her, to imprison her once more.

Clutching her cross amulet, she thanked the gods they'd escaped in time.

"Tell me where they are." Filip slammed his fist on the bar—his patience wearing thin. "Adelina Orlova and Damir Litvin."

"I'm sorry, sir, but I don't have no customers under those names," the innkeeper's wife said casually as she wiped the wooden countertop with a cloth.

"You are certain of this?" He narrowed his gaze on her and kept his voice stern.

"Yes, sir. We keep a ledger of all our customers, and they ain't written on today's sheet, nor any day this week. I'll fetch you the book for inspection, if you like," the woman said, unphased by his tone.

"All right, bring it to me now."

She shrugged one shoulder, disappeared into the back room, then returned with a large, leather-bound book. Placing it on the countertop, she flipped it open, then spun it around to face him.

"See, no Orlova or Litvin," she said.

Tracing his finger down the pages, he scanned each name. He turned the page to the previous day. He raised a brow.

"There. I've found them," he said, more so to himself than anyone else. "I recognise the handwriting—it's Damir's. I've seen enough of his letters to know. Alyona and Kirill Sirodov—an alias, no doubt."

"You think so?" Pyotr peered over his shoulder. "Let me take a closer look at this. Remember my days as your ledger clerk? It was part of my job to check for counterfeits."

"No need." Filip waved a hand to Pyotr. "I might've burned the letters, but I recall Damir's writing style. The Rs have long tails spiking across the page, and some of the Is are not dotted. He has a certain enthusiasm."

"It's the personality of the handwriting." Pyotr chimed. "If you're certain this is Damir's, then you've found him."

Filip gave Pyotr a sideways glance. "I much prefer you sober."

Pyotr's lips tilted into a fraction of a smile.

"Which room did you assign them?" Filip asked the innkeeper.

The woman returned her gaze to the ledger. "Says here second floor, third room on the right."

"Guards," Filip spun around, "Check the room, ensure this lady is telling the truth."

At once, the guards dispersed through the tavern, ascending the stairs.

"Hey, you can't barge through here like you own the place," the innkeeper's wife complained. "It's the middle of the night and we have guests upstairs asleep. You'll need a warrant."

Filip mindlessly handed her a pouch of coins. "Enough to keep you quiet?"

She eyed the money, then wrapped her fingers around it and she disappeared into the kitchens.

A while later, the thundering footsteps of guards drew closer as they returned to the restaurant area.

"Well?" Filip asked.

"No trace of the girl, sir," one said.

"They can't be far—search the village." Filip marched out of the tavern, then scanned the nearby buildings. She was within his grasp, so close.

***

At dawn, Damir and Adelina stopped at the top of a hill overlooking the busy docks and shipyard of the village named Bolvas. The stench of fish wafted on the breeze. She could only imagine the unpleasant smell when they rode closer.

"Are we to board a ship?" she asked her husband. "I know it's an option, but to be so far away from home…It's a strange feeling, to go so far from the only place we've truly known."

"Filip and his men will likely chase us all the way across the sea, but being on a ship a thousand miles away from him doesn't sound like an awful plan." He shrugged. "Plus, it's the only option we have."

"What about the horses?" She patted her mare's chestnut brown hide.

"We'll need to find one to house them in the lower decks with the goats, otherwise we'll have to sell them, and we won't get rid of our means of transportation until absolutely necessary," he said. "The streets will be packed at this time of the morning—locals purchasing their seafood and crews loading cargo onto the ships. We'd be best to dismount here."

Once they were both on the ground, they guided their horses along the path, which grew narrower as it descended into the port nestled between cliffs. The morning light shone through a low fog, and the streets came alive with the day. Shutter windows banged open, workers left their homes, and shoppers barged their way to the local markets through overflowing cobble passageways.

A fisherman sat mending his net, while another raised the sails of the small boat. Further along the harbour, bigger boats and ships prepared for voyages across the sea. Gulls squawked as they flew overhead.

In the centre of the docks bobbed a larger ship, its sails already lifted. Its crew thundered across the deck, wrapping ropes and stashing cargo. A long queue of people waited on the dockside to embark.

"Nope," Damir said as he steered his horse towards a vessel further along, weaving through the crowd and passed crewmembers loading barrels and crates. "It's too busy and with so many people wishing to journey, it's unlikely we'll be able to bring our horses with us."

"What about the *Senan*?" She gestured to a smaller ship, its frame a little weathered, but didn't appear to be unsafe.

"It could do." He nodded, then steered them towards the short queue in front of the ramp leading to the deck.

A tall, blond-haired man stood beside a pile of cargo, touching each item as if counting. "Take this below deck and be quick about it."

A crewmember dipped his head, hoisted a barrel, then hastened up the ramp.

"Excuse me, sir." Damir approached the blond man.

"No room," he said bluntly without looking up from his inspection.

"We can pay handsomely." Damir rummaged in his pocket, then withdrew a pouch of coins. "For safe passage for me, my wife, and our two horses."

The man glanced up, then narrowed his eyes. "How much?"

"Here." Damir grabbed a handful of coins from the pouch and handed them over.

"You don't even know where we're headed." The man laughed, although his gaze lingered on the offering.

"Does it matter?" Damir said.

"Why are you in such a hurry?" The man crossed his arms, looking from Adelina to Damir.

She tapped her foot nervously—surely, Filip would've sent word to the docks by now. They'd know she'd be here, looking for passage. How could she convince the captain to let them on board?

"You recognise me, don't you?" she said in a hushed tone.

Damir glanced at her sharply. "What are you doing?"

Ignoring her husband, she continued, "If you've heard about a certain sorceress, here I am. If you let us on board, I promise I will be of use to you for the entirety of the journey."

"We have no use for magic at sea," the captain said. "The deep waters have their own masters, and it isn't the likes of us humans."

"I can control natural elements—the sun," she clarified, a hint of desperation in her voice. "Perhaps, water too. I haven't tried, but if you provide us with a cabin, I'll learn. I can produce fire and conjure crops—your crew will not go without food or warmth."

The captain pressed his lips into a thin line, then cleared his throat. "Very well. The money *and* your service." He accepted the coins from Damir's outstretched hand.

"Your name, Captain?" Damir asked as he tucked the pouch inside his pocket.

"Burchard Brown," he said. "I shall not say your names out loud in honour of our deal, but if at any moment, I get a whiff of betrayal, I'll throw you overboard. Understood?"

Nodding, Damir gripped his horse's reins tighter.

"On you go." Burchard gestured to the ship.

As Damir led Adelina and their horses on board, he shot her a disapproving look. "What were you thinking?"

"I had to say something." She waved the matter away. "I'd rather secure his trust now before Filip finds a way to track us across the sea."

Carrying their luggage onto the deck, he led her past crew members who hauled the halyards, raising the sails, and others who filed the last of the cargo into the hull. Another member grasped their horses' reins, then guided the mounts below deck.

Damir scanned the ship. "This could be one of two options."

"What do you mean?" she said.

"Well, it could be a fruit schooner—quick passages, they'll take their cargoes to nearby islands and lands." He gestured to the man who carried the last crate.

"Or?" She leaned closer to him, the hairs on her neck prickling.

"It could be a pirate ship headed for the Hastehill Isles in the east, although they tend to have more cannons, and I couldn't see any at first glance." Damir adjusted the weight of the luggage in his hands and searched the deck once more. "In true pirate fashion, they'd likely have ten guns. This one has six, which barely scrapes the preferences of privateers."

"How do you know all this?" She pressed herself against the rail to let a crewman past.

"My grandfather used to work at the ports. Before he passed away, he told me about his adventures at sea. I picked up a thing or two." He winked.

She arched a brow. "After all this time of knowing each other, there are still things to learn."

He smiled, then bent to kiss her.

"None of that on deck." The rough voice of Burchard Brown rang in line with his booming footsteps as he passed the foremast. "You'll find a large berth area below deck in the forepeak, next to the galley—there'll be spare bunks for you."

"Thank you," Damir said.

Shielding her eyes, she glanced heavenwards, past the crosstrees of a large mast, to the cloudless blue sky. "Fine sailing weather."

"As long as there's wind." He nudged her arm gently.

Within half an hour, the captain was at the wheel, and the ship had left the harbour. From their position by the rail, the land soon appeared as an inky strip on the horizon. A sigh escaped her lips.

"A moment of relief."

He wrapped an arm around her, and they watched the lapping waves of the sea. "I feel it too. As long as we're together, we'll get through anything."

***

"A hat for you both." Burchard handed Adelina and Damir brown leather tricorns. "The sun is mighty mean out here."

"Thank you." She accepted the gift and placed it on her head. Her cheeks were already burning from the heat of midday. "Will you tell us where we're going now?"

"The Hastehill Isles in the east, which we'll reach within the month," he said. "Gods willing. Have you heard of Marina and Moryana?"

"The water maidens?" She arched a brow. "I've heard of them, but I'm unfamiliar with their stories."

Burchard wrapped his fingers around the wheel and resumed his steering. "Marina was a young widow from an old legend in which she drowned herself out of love. She'd sit along the shore, sadly looking at the house of her lover, who married another girl. In her heartache, she flipped boats, taking more men to their deaths."

"Ah, I remember her," Damir said, adjusting his own hat. "Didn't she charm her lover and take him under the sea, too? So she had her happy ever after."

"It may be." Burchard shrugged a shoulder. "I still don't trust her."

"And Moryana?" Adelina asked.

"She is beautiful—there's a figure of her carved into the mainmast over there." He gestured to the mast furthest aft. "Her hair is dishevelled and like sea foam. Most of the time, she'll swim deep in the waters, taking the form of fish. She is ruler of the sea winds, so we, sailors, pray to her each night. Depending on her mood, she could be either good or bad, eliminating storms or causing them."

"I'll add her to my prayers," Adelina said decisively.

"A wise decision." Burchard eyed her. "There are families on the coasts of the Hastehill Isles who practise offerings for the Vila Goddesses by laying baskets of fruit and flowers in the caves along the coasts, homemade cakes near wells, and assorted coloured ribbons hanged to the branches of trees. The goddesses are eternally young, dressed in white with eyes flashing like thunder. They live in the clouds and water and are rather well-disposed towards men. But all that can change—their moods are like tempests. Emitting a haunting noise of pipes and drums from the sky, they can strike men down with disease if they so choose."

"Sounds pleasant." Damir grimaced.

"Aye." Burchard nodded once, although seemingly unmoved by his recount of the disturbing deity.

"I'm not too certain this voyage was our smartest idea," she muttered to her husband.

Damir wrapped his arm around her and squeezed. "All will be well."

"Pray every night to all your gods," Burchard suggested. "It's the only way to get across this wretched sea in one piece."

"I think I might retire to the berths now," she said.

Burchard bid them farewell with a curt nod, then returned his gaze to the stretching sea beyond the boat.

Arm firmly around her, Damir escorted her below deck, weaving through the crewmen who carried out their duties, and to the small cabin next to the galley. Inside, a berth was positioned either side of a circular window. Water droplets splattered onto the glass as waves licked the ship.

He dumped their luggage onto one of the thin mattresses, then gathered her into his arms. His lips met hers, warm and tasting mildly of sea salt, and his breath warm on her cheeks.

Leaning into him, she draped her arms over his shoulders and buried her fingers into his tousled hair, the concern of meddling, dangerous sea deities shunted to the corners of her mind.

The ship bounced over jolting waves, sending them stumbling on to the opposite berth. Her head thumped the wall as he crashed on top of her.

"Ow." She rubbed her throbbing scalp.

"Sorry." He scooted off her, then inspected the back of her head where she stroked. "There's no blood. You'll be okay."

With their moment of intimacy lost, her thoughts returned to their close capture. "How long do you think we'll have before Filip finds us again?"

He shrugged. "A month, maybe more. He'll need to track us to the harbour, find out which ship we boarded, secure his own passage across the sea, then locate us on one of the many islands in the Hastehill Isles."

"I might as well make myself useful, then." She rose. "I gave my word to Burchard I would use my powers to assist him and the crew. I'll find out what needs to be done, and perhaps, you can find some work too. If we're going to be on this ship for the best part of a month, see if you can earn any extra coin."

"Yes, ma'am." He winked.

She smirked at him before turning on her heel and exiting the cabin.

On deck, she found Captain Burchard at the wheel.

The harsh sun beat against her face. Her cheeks were flushed and her lips dry. At least the hat prevented her scalp from burning. She'd need to pay a visit to the ship's physician for a medicinal concoction to protect herself from the rays.

"I intend to keep my word," she said as she approached the captain.

"Huh?" He glanced at her. "Ah, yes. Your magic."

"With any luck, Moryana will look upon our voyage kindly, but if any storms were to come our way, perhaps I can stop them," she said. "I'll need to practise, of course, but I haven't found any limitations to the use of my natural magic."

"You're saying your power rivals a deity's?" The captain narrowed his eyes.

She lifted one shoulder. "Well, I wouldn't have used those exact words, but astral magic is ancient. I can produce fire, make plants grow—who's to say I can't control the storm, or at least keep it away from the sails of this ship?"

He remained silent for a moment, as if to contemplate her words. Then he gave a quick, sharp nod. "You best get on with it, then."

Smiling, she returned the nod, then headed to her berth—the privacy of the small cabin would give her the space and quiet to open a portal.

Once the shimmering circle was formed, she slipped into the prism world, the manicured lawns of Kirovo Palace stretching in front of her.

***

"Check again." Filip narrowed his gaze on the man, who wrote the ledgers for the ship's passengers.

"As I've already told you, sir, there's no one aboard under the names you've provided." The man closed the book, then packed his belongings as the crewmen rose the sails behind him.

"What about the aliases I gave you?" Filip said.

"They weren't there either," the man said. "I must be on my way now. The ship's about to set sail and the captain doesn't wait for anyone."

A burst of anger shot through Filip's core. He grabbed the man by the scruff of his neck. "Check again."

"Let me go!" The man gasped. "I've done as you've asked."

"Perhaps we should find the harbourmaster." Pyotr stepped closer between the two men. "He'll have documentation for all the ships—and if they're carrying passengers. While Damir and Adelina might've bribed the clerks to keep quiet, the captains are required to list these things."

Filip let go of the man's collar, then backed away.

Pyotr and the guards followed him.

Scanning his surroundings, Filip found a single-storey building at the edge of the harbour. A flag billowed outside, and a man dressed in tailored shirt and trousers, paired with a black-rimmed cap, conversed with another man outside the door.

"Excuse me." Filip approached them. "Are you the harbourmaster?"

The man in the cap nodded. "I sure am. What can I do for you?"

"I require access to your logs," Filip said, keeping a tight leash on his bubbling impatience. "I'm looking for two individuals, who I believe boarded a boat here."

"I'm sorry, sir." The harbourmaster shook his head. "I'm not at liberty to disclose such information."

"Please," Filip feigned desperation. "The lady, she is my betrothed, and she has been taken against her will. I *must* find her."

The harbourmaster pressed his lips into a tight line, as if considering.

Digging into his pocket, Filip grabbed a pouch of coins and handed it to the harbourmaster. "Please. I only wish to escort her home safely. She must be returned to the bosom of her family."

Sighing, the harbourmaster nodded to the door. "Follow me. And keep your money. I do this only because I have a daughter myself, and a fair lady is never safe at sea."

The harbourmaster presented Filip with all his logs of the morning, and after a few minutes of flicking through the pages, he found their handwriting.

"Thank you." Filip met the harbourmaster's gaze. "When does your next ship depart?"

"*The Maiden* departs in fifteen minutes." The harbourmaster pointed through the window to a large vessel.

Filip strode out of the building, Pyotr at his side.

"Now, that's a fine ship!" Pyotr whistled as he and Filip approached it—the sails on its three masts already raised.

A carved goddess was mounted to the ship's bow—a wooden depiction of what Filip presumed to be Moryana. Many mounted guns could be seen from his position on the harbour.

"It certainly is," Filip said—his voice escaped his mouth in a light whisper, his breath almost taken from him by the beauty of the mammoth ship before him. "One such as this would be useful in laying siege to a smaller vessel, one which may be transporting Adelina and Damir. Find the captain."

"Yes, sir." Pyotr nodded once, then dashed towards the ramp leading to the deck.

His hands were raw from working the ropes and sails, but this didn't seem to bother him as he ate with a smile on his face.

"What are your plans for today?" she asked him.

"One of the new crewmen has fallen ill with a bad case of sea-sickness, so I volunteered to fill his place for routine maintenance." He wiped the corners of his mouth after he swallowed the last bite of food. "You?"

"I need to visit the physician—have you seem him about? Afterwards, I'll be back in the prism world. Burchard expects an update on my progress imminently." She rested her empty bowl on the wooden table beside her.

"You'll find Doctor Sullivan right there." He pointed to a grey-haired man on a bench a few tables over.

"You should see him too—your cheeks have blistered." She nudged his shoulder.

He rose, then kissed her forehead. "I need to get going—there's work to be done. Pick up some cream for me if it soothes your worry."

With a gentle squeeze of her arm, he turned, then headed for the deck.

Once she'd returned from the physician with two pots of salve in her hand, she ventured back to her cabin. She grabbed one of her spell books, then conjured the prism world.

Stepping through the portal, she returned to the manicured lawn of Kirovo Palace. She wondered why this magical dimension took the form of her former home. Perhaps it'd something to do with her connection to Filip—they were forever bound to each other, whether or not she liked it.

Grateful for the wealth of knowledge within the books she'd taken from the palace, she stroked the parchment pages gently.

She read through its contents, scanning sections she'd previously digested about astral magic and its solar properties. It was clear she didn't need to control the wind itself, but rather, interfere with it via the use of the sun.

"*Areiras nielasnal*," she said as she traced her finger along the written spell and the text beneath it.

This incantation, in conjunction with astral magic at its strongest, will intercept weather of a perilous nature. However, the conjurer should note such usage draws on the powers of whomever wields nether magic.

Slamming the book shut, she huffed. How in the realm was she going to draw on Filip's power when, hopefully, half an ocean separated them? She wasn't in any position to inform Burchard she would be useless in the event of a dangerous storm because of the give and take relationship between astral and nether powers. All she could do was hope the weather remained fair during their voyage at sea.

TWELVE

Captured at Sea

Three weeks at sea had passed and they would reach the Hastehill Isles within seven days. Adelina spent most of her time in the prism world, mastering the arts of harnessing the sun, although she hadn't the chance to utilise the power so far. She kept the torches burning, the food ripe, turned saltwater from the sea into drinkable liquid, and with it, the crewmen's morale remained high.

Damir spent most of his days fixing stuck doors, wonky chair legs, checking the conditions of the sails, and the lower deck for holes. He'd assisted the cook by sanding down the wooden table, which'd threatened to fall apart from long-term use. And whenever they both had time to spare, they sparred, ensuring she didn't lose the skills she'd learned at the palace.

Scorching heat beat against their faces. Captain Burchard remained unphased at the wheel.

Adelina nodded as she strode past the captain to enter the lower decks—the cook had become a decent friend within their three weeks of travel. She lit fires for him with her magic when the stock of logs ran low.

On her way, she passed Damir. She squeezed his arm gently, then leaned in for a brief kiss. Both kept busy by their duties, their moments of intimacy were few and far between and by the time they both retired for bed, they were too tired for anything but sleep.

After visiting the cook and igniting the fires for the dinner meal, she slipped into her cabin and rootled for her tubbed mixture of jasmine and rice. With her fingertips, she rubbed the thick, gooey texture onto the plains of her face and grimaced. It was slimy against her skin but was her only option of keeping the harsh sun and wind burn at bay.

A loud boom thundered. She jolted and dropped the pot onto the floorboards, which subsequently spilled a portion of her concoction. Bending, she scooped it into her hand, twisted on the lid, then put it in the drawer between the two beds.

She hurried on to the deck, weaving between gathering crewmen who filed between the masts. Rain fell heavier now, and a wind wiped through the sails. Waves crashed against the sides of the ship.

Damir grabbed her, and she startled.

"What's going on?" she asked.

"Look." Wide eyed, he pointed out to sea.

In the distance, but close enough to see, was a large, encroaching ship, perhaps twice the size of their own vessel.

"The bang was a cannon blast—they mean to board," he said.

She clutched onto him, and a bolt of panic shot through her core. "No. It could've been thunder. It can't be him."

"I pray to the gods it's not him," he said. His face had gone pale. "Thunder would be better. At least you can stop the storm. We can't stop Filip."

Burchard abandoned the wheel, rested his hands against the rail, and craned his neck. "A ship with so many guns means one thing—they want something, and they'll take it. Don't cause a skirmish."

A low murmuring rumbled across the deck.

"What could they want?" One man leaned close to another beside him.

His colleague replied with a shrug.

"We need to get you out of sight." Damir grabbed Adelina by the elbow, then whirled her down the steps below deck.

"How do you think this'll help? He'll surely come looking down here." She yanked her arm free of his grasp. "Where else do you expect me to go?"

"The prism world," he said without stopping his pace towards their cabin. "Open a portal and just…stay in there. I'm going to help the others and keep Filip the hell away from you."

She hesitated for a moment, drawing her bottom lip between her teeth. "Fine, but you'll need to be careful. As soon as Filip sees you on board, he'll know I'm here somewhere. He's powerful, and I wouldn't be surprised if he can sense me and my magic. Keep him busy so he doesn't conjure a portal right to me. Go, quick."

Urging him back the way they came, her heart hammered, and a line of sweat beaded along her hairline. She swatted it away with the back of her hand and sucked in a deep breath.

Drawing her finger through the air in a circular motion, the gold, cracking circumference of the prism world's portal snapped into existence.

Without lingering, she stepped through. She kept the portal open, showing the cabin on the other side.

From her position on the manicured lawn of Kirovo Palace, she could hear the thundering footsteps on the deck of the *Senan*.

She lifted her hands to close the portal, sealing herself inside, as the booming footsteps combined with thunder.

Thunder?

She frowned. They'd endured relentless heat moments ago. If she possessed the ability to end a storm, what in the realm could Filip do—was this *his* doing? She shoved her panic down.

The storm intensified and waves crashed against the ship, making the portal shake and flicker.

Her cheeks burned, flustered from her inability to do anything at present. There was no way she could help the crewmen without Filip and his men taking her hostage.

The portal wobbled, teetering, then disappeared altogether.

Hastily, she swiped her hand through the air to reform the connection to the *Senan* so she could do something—*anything*—to help Damir and the men in the storm, but despite her best efforts, the portal wouldn't reform. Nonetheless, she could *hear* the thundering, the deep yells of crewmen, and pelting rain. She was close, but not close enough to bring Damir to her.

In the prism world, she was rendered completely useless.

"Tell me where she is!" Filip demanded, his nose inches from Damir's face. The mid-castle rocked from side to side, but he was oblivious. In the few minutes it took to board and locate Damir on deck, his patience had disappeared.

"She isn't here," Damir said through gritted teeth.

A tumultuous wave shook the boat, sending both of them hurtling into the rail.

"Don't lie to me," Filip hollered. "I can sense her. She's using a portal, right? I can feel it!"

In truth, he couldn't sense it. The damned storm he'd caused was blocking out his connection to her. The saturated vision and other tell-tale signs of her magic usage were dulled by the crashing rain. When he tried to reign in his magic, calm the weather, his efforts were futile. Something was blocking him from undoing his spell.

Filip gripped Damir by the throat, then slammed him against the wall of the captain's quarters. "Call to her. Bring her back right now, or I will kill you all."

"I'd rather die, than ever tell you where my wife is." Damir stared him straight in the eyes.

"Wife?" Filip growled. "You wed her?"

"Yes." Damir's lips curved into a snarl. "Now you never can."

A white-hot rage shot through Filip. With a twist of his index finger, he produced black tentacles of nether magic, which wrapped tightly around Damir, lifting him into the air.

The tentacles branched out, expanding into thick vines hovering above the ship, stretching above the waves.

"You're coming with me," Filip said. "One way or another, she *will* pay for her disobedience."

His magic choked Damir unconscious, his face draining of colour. Throwing his body onto his own ship anchored nearby, Filip turned his head to the sky. Rain pattered against his cheeks. Whatever had stopped him from ending the storm he'd created was no ally of his.

Unwilling to spend another second in the prism world—useless and apart from her husband—she burst free from the portal with a mighty blast of gold magic. She ignored the shards nicking at her skin, drawing blood to the surface. When her feet hit the wooden floorboards, she marched through the lower deck, then ascended the stairs.

Rain hammered from thick, grey rainclouds, but the wind had subsided, and waves no longer raged against the walls of the ship.

Fixing her gaze on the heavens, she lifted her hands—her magic flowing through her and tingling her nerve ends. "*Areiras nielasnal.*"

The rain slowed to a gentle patter, then stopped altogether, and a sliver of sun broke through the clouds.

'The conjurer should note such usage draws on the powers of whomever wields nether magic.'

With Filip in close proximity, her spell would drain him. She hoped it was enough to keep him from harming Damir.

A pained grunt caught her attention. The physician knelt beside a wounded crewman with a ghastly cut to his forehead.

Scanning the deck, her heart pounded as she searched for Damir. She weaved through the gathering men, then hurried to the helm to get a better vantage point of the deck.

"You won't find him," Burchard said from his position at the wheel. His clothes were soaked through, and his hair clung to his face.

"What do you mean?" Her voice left her throat in a raspy whisper.

"He's gone," he said bluntly. "Take a look for yourself."

He pointed across the sea to a ship nearing the horizon. "He was here. I couldn't endanger the lives of my crewmen. Whoever the man was, he's too powerful. As he boarded, he cast his dark magic into the sky, thrusting us into a storm that threatened to rip apart this ship."

Reaching the side in quick, long strides, she gripped the rail, staring at Filip's vessel out at sea.

She covered her mouth with her hand, and her eyes burned.

"We have to go after them," she faced him and repeated her words again with more confidence.

"No can do." He shook his head. "We're headed for the Hastehill Isles, and we can't divert. You'll have to board another ship once we've reached our destination."

Her palms turned clammy, and a wet, cold shiver ran up the length of her spine. An intense nauseating sensation clenched and churned her stomach. Her knuckles whitened as she tightened her grip on the rail, and she wretched. Her eyes watered.

She wiped her mouth with her hand, her stomach muscles on fire, then eased herself into a seated position on the top step. Although her feet were on the ground, her knees were weak, and her body shook—she didn't trust herself to stand. Not yet.

The physician was busy making his way around the deck, tending to minor injuries, then headed towards her, a reassuring smile on his face.

"Are you all right, miss?" he said. "Here, drink this."

She lifted her gaze to meet his. He proffered his uncapped flask.

With a thin smile, she accepted and pressed it to her lips, slowly drinking the cool, fresh water.

"Thank you," she said. "How are…the crew?"

Forcing her attention on anything but her kidnapped husband, she gripped the railing, hoisted herself up, then descended the rest of the stairs onto the deck.

"As good as they can be after a storm, but the decks will dry soon enough under the sun. I could use your help in lighting fires for the men. The injured need to be kept warm and their wounds cleaned with boiled cloth and bandages."

"I'll get to it," she said, then headed below deck to the berths, trying her hardest to ignore the dull yet lingering ache in the pits of her stomach.

Reflexively, she twisted the triple stack wedding ring on her left hand. She needed to get to Damir as soon as possible. Free him from whatever Filip had in store. Knowing all too well it was Filip's way of luring her in, she clenched her teeth.

The ship would sail as fast as the wind could take it and there was nothing she could do until she reached the shore. She decided to keep herself—and her mind—busy with errands on board.

Over the next two days, her idea to stay busy kept her mind from dwelling on Damir. She worked closely with Doctor Sullivan and kept an eye on the crewmen who were wounded in the storm as well as treating new injuries.

She flicked her finger and produced a small, bright flame in the lantern, which swung on a rope above her head.

Doctor Sullivan patted a damp cloth on a man's bloodied forehead, having sustained the injury from getting into a drunk fight with another sailor on board.

"It won't require stitches," Doctor Sullivan said, then lifted the cloth. "See here? The wound isn't deep."

Adelina leaned towards him for a closer inspection. "It's likely he'll have a headache for a day or two."

"Certainly." He tutted. "Perhaps it'll teach him not to pick fights when intoxicated with vodka."

The crewman rolled his eyes. "Can I sleep now?"

"Off you go." Doctor Sullivan waved him away. "Don't be coming back to me tomorrow night with another cut to your head. And don't touch the bottles!"

"You know, my sister was injured in a fire. When she escaped, she caught her thigh on broken glass and my mother treated her. I want to help people." Adelina leaned against a support beam and crossed her arms. "This magic I have—Filip wants to use it for his own gain, but what if I can do more? What if I can prevent atrocities? I'm no healer, but what if I can learn to heal with my powers?"

He smiled. "You're a kind-hearted girl, for sure, and I'm betting anyone you offer your services to, will be happy to receive them. I must warn you, however—you cannot prevent everything from happening. Don't use your magic in an attempt to act the way the gods might choose to."

"Surely, you, being a physician, would do everything in your power to, say, stop an outbreak of disease?" She frowned.

"What I do is different. I tend to the sick with nothing but the skills of my hands." He tilted his palms upwards. "You, on the other hand, have a connection to great power. Understand its limitations, like I have with medicine. Go get some rest. I'll see you in the morning."

With a gracious nod, he left, heading towards his berth.

The ship lulled into silence as men went to bed. Limited light from the lanterns cast a warm, golden glow across the wooden floor and walls. Snoring men provided an oddly soothing rhythm to the ship's atmosphere, and her heart turned cold.

She pressed her hand to her chest, the coldness stretching through her body, yearning for Damir's presence—his touch, his warmth, everything he was. Retreating to the silence of her cabin, her breathing shallowed and her heartrate thrummed. She should never have retreated to the prism world, never let him get captured.

Resting her hand on a beam, she closed her eyes and puffed out a deep breath. When the thundering of her heart slowed, she wiped her hands on her thighs, then headed to her berth.

Casting a glance at the empty cot where Damir had slept, she slid on to her own bed and squeezed her eyes tight shut.

※

The rest of the week passed, and by the time the ship docked in the Hastehill Isles southern harbour, Adelina was itching to get herself onto another ship and make her way back to Damir.

"Thanks for all your help on board." Doctor Sullivan lifted his hat from his head and gave her a polite nod. "I hope you have a safe trip back. Here is the money I owed Damir for his services—and a little for you, too." He handed her a pouch of jingling coins.

She accepted it, smiling as he turned to disembark from the boat onto the worn wooden planks of the dock.

A crewman dumped her and her husband's bags beside her feet. While she waited for the civilians and crewmen to unload the cargo, she leaned against the rail, scanning the harbour for a decent sized ship suitable to make the month-long journey back to the coast of Temauten.

"Your horses will be brought up next," Captain Burchard Brown said as he approached her from the helm. "I'll help secure your belongings to their saddles, then you'd best hurry—there's a vessel further along the pier, about five minutes' walk, called *The Sundial*, which usually makes its rounds back and forth the isles and the mainlands. You might be able to secure passage."

"Thank you," she said, and meant it. "I wish you the best on your travels."

"Aye." He nodded. "You too, miss."

As he turned to leave, he paused, then glanced at her over his shoulder. "I hope you find your husband."

Swallowing a new-found lump in her throat, she returned the curt nod, grasped the handles of her bags, then hauled them down the plank.

When a crewman guided her horses off the ship, she stroked their noses. The brown mare—the one her husband had ridden—nuzzled closer to her. She leaned into the horse's side, feeling its warmth against her.

"You're not going to like this, but it's time for another sea voyage," she said soothingly to the two mounts.

With both reins in hand, she led the horses along the length of the quiet dock—a cool morning breeze fluttered through the shadows cast by tall buildings as the sun slowly rose behind them. It was barely dawn, and the scent of baked bread made her stomach grumble.

"Maybe a quick stop for food," she muttered.

She hobbled the horses to a post outside the bakery, then slipped into the shop, unable to resist the hearty scent reminding her of home.

"Good morning to you, miss." The baker glanced up at her while he kneaded a batch of dough and smiled. "What can I do for you?"

Eyeing the counters in front of her, her mouth watered. Five varieties of bread were laid out, ready to be purchased. Some loafs were dappled with poppy seeds, others with cinnamon, sugar, herbs, and even chilli.

"Which do you recommend?" she said.

He placed his fingers to his lips. "It all depends on what you fancy. It's early hours, so you won't be wanting any chilli flakes, right?"

She stifled a laugh. "Probably not."

"Perhaps...this one." He leaned across the counter, grab a toasted loaf, then popped it into a brown bag. "Tomatoes and mixed herbs. Down the road, you'll find the best dairyman this Isle has to offer. Ask for his goat's cheese—a bit of this with my bread...simply delightful."

"Thank you." She exchanged a couple of coins for the bread, then left the shop.

Once she purchased her cheese, she guided her horses towards the edge of the pier where *The Sundial* was docked.

Fastening the horses to a nearby post, she perched on the low stone wall, then drew her loaf from its brown bag and squished the goat's cheese on top.

It wouldn't be enough to barge her way back to Kirovo Palace without a plan. She needed to be at her strongest if she was to free Damir from Filip's clutches unscathed.

She forced herself to bite a chunk of her bread and swallowed it. Nostrils flaring, a flurry of emotions spun around inside her like an unhinged tornado. Gripping on to the edge of the wall, she clung to the fire burning within her.

If she was going to fight Filip for Damir, then she needed to understand his power, the way he used nether magic, and she must be prepared to go up against whatever he threw against her. If she could plan for any obstacles and strategise ways to overcome them, she'd stand a chance.

I'm going to do this.

With fresh bread-fuelled determination, she rose, grasped the horses' reins, then tugged them in the direction of the boat.

When she was aboard the Sundial and safely inside her cabin, she lay out her collection of candles she'd gotten from a crooked cabinet beside the cot. With a swirl of her finger, she lit them—their wicks popped with the orange and red colours of flames.

The books she'd taken from the palace were placed open on the floor in the centre of the candle circle. One had contained a blank chapter, a shimmering layer over the pages. It'd piqued her interest, but she'd look at it closer another time.

She hesitated for a moment, contemplating the prism world. Perhaps it would've been best for her to practise the spell first, in a safe environment. But she needed to trust in her own power, strength, and connection to both the Zorya sisters. She was made for this.

Flexing her fingers, she monitored her breathing, keeping it level and in time with her heartbeat.

Kneeling inside the ring of lit candles, she read the spell aloud. *"Rinaenelen trilriiel."*

At first, nothing happened, except a soft breeze stirring through the cabin. She took this as a good sign, seeing as the small, circular window was closed.

Clearing her throat, she focused on the elegant sounds of the spell, familiarised herself with the shape and feel of the words as they slid from her mouth. *"Rinaenelen trilriiel."*

A gold wisp of light spun out from the centre of her lower arm, weaving its way around her wrist, hovering an inch above her skin. It rotated like golden embroidery, delicate, yet strong and vibrant.

"Yes," she whispered. "Please work."

With her left hand, she swirled her fingers through the air, encouraging the golden magic to continue its weave until it locked itself into place. A thick, beautiful vine of astral power.

Trying to swallow her excitement, her gaze darted back to the spell book, pressing her fingertips onto the edge of the page.

"A spell which will draw on the eternal power of the Sun God, strong enough to combat ancient magic. A practitioner of astral may wield it." Adrenaline bolted through her core. This was it. She'd manifested her power, encouraging it into a weapon only she could hold.

Rising, she flexed her right arm—her gaze locked on the swirling vines. A bolt of fire shot from within the golden embroidery, collided with a mirror hanging crooked on the far wall, and shattered it.

Grinning, she lowered her arm and disengaged the magic. "Perfect."

Adelina spent the three-week journey back to the mainlands jittery and eager to press on with her mission. She practised and harnessed her new weapon—learning what it was capable of. After a matter of a few days, she'd discovered its defence capabilities—a golden shield sprung from the embroidery swirling around her arm, defending her from oncoming attacks inside the Prism World.

Using the Prism World was her chance to configure scenarios in which dark magic targeted her, and she could strengthen her ability to fight back.

Resting on a wooden box, she unravelled the bandages on her arm. Using the astral embroidery each day for long hours cut gashes into her flesh—blisters festered.

Her skin was red and puffy, but the blisters hadn't popped. Reapplying the ointment she'd been given by the former ship's physician, she sighed as the cool gel relieved the relentless itch. Once she'd readjusted the bandages, she shifted her focus back to the spell book.

Her fingers traced the etched, golden calligraphy on the cover. *A Practitioner's Guide to Ancient Magic, Astral Edition, Volume I.* She'd read other texts about astral magic while in training with Yelena, but there was something compelling about this book—the one chapter with enchanted pages *especially* interesting. The titled begged the question of whether a twin book existed for nether magic. Did Filip own it? Surely, he did if *this* version was from the Kirovo Palace library. The fact it was volume one suggested there were more.

Stomach fluttering with anticipation and the desire to learn as much as she could, she flicked to the introduction.

A being, pure of soul, is chosen by the Sun God, bears the sun mark, and holds an unwavering connection to the Zorya sisters. Through this, the practitioner wields an equally unwavering connection to astral magic. More so, at its core, astral magic is nature's perfect balance to the unruly magic that is nether. A yin-yang entity, two souls forever bound either in unity or in discordance. In power and magic, there must be balance.

Drawing her bottom lip between her teeth, she fixed her gaze on *"in unity or discordance"*. If Filip hadn't tricked her with false promises and deceit, she could imagine them working together in perfect harmony. But such an outcome was not possible for the man who wanted permanent power over the three countries and held her husband prisoner.

"In discordance, it is," she said, "and I'll be ready."

THIRTEEN

North Star

When the ship docked in the south of Temauten, Adelina guided the horses through the village. She'd need to sell Damir's. There wasn't any way she could travel quickly by herself with the two animals.

After a brief venture through the town, she found a local stableman and begrudgingly sold the horse. She stashed the bag of ruble, then mounted, riding fast onto the pastures stretching ahead. There was no time to waste—the quicker she rescued her husband, the better.

Galloping along the path, specks of dust plumed into the air, her hair billowed behind her, and the heat of the midday sun beat against her face. She shook the reins, urging her mount to carry her farther, faster.

In the pine forest, she hobbled the horse, then made camp within the trees. Crumpling to the ground, her heart stung with the memory of Damir. The silence overwhelmed her senses. She gripped a nearby tree trunk, and clutched her chest with her spare hand, while sucking in ragged breaths.

"Keep it together." Her voice was thin, but she injected as much confidence into it as she could. "He needs me, and I'm the only one who can help him."

Closing her eyes, she focused on her deep inhalation followed by the slow release of air. Her pounding heart rate slowed, and she set about gathering sticks for a fire.

Once the twigs and sticks were piled together, she flicked her finger—an array of gold and red flame burst from the construction.

She rummaged in her bag for her spell book, then knelt beside the fire. If there was more she could learn about her astral magic, she couldn't waste the opportunity. Landing on the page where she'd found the golden embroidery spell, she scanned the text again.

The text continued onto the overleaf—information she'd reread countless times since learning how to harness her astral power in the form of a weapon around her arm.

Frowning, she halted on the next chapter. A blank page with an ethereal shimmer. She'd seen this on the boat but had put all her focus on the golden embroidery spell. Now she wondered what this meant. Skimming through the book, she found only one chapter to be blank, each page shimmering.

She flipped the book to the last page—a reference.

To access concealed pages, one must prove their worth by finding the answer to the following riddle:

Jodie Angell

I never rest; I am never still. I am the keeper of the world. Without me, all will peril. And when I am not around, all is cool and darkness falls.

Adelina tapped the edge of the page; she was never one for solving them, but there had to be a connection between the riddle and her astral magic. Why else would it be etched onto the parchment?

Lifting her chin, she stared into the fire, searching her mind for an answer. Her magic was natural—she knew *that* much. But despite her best efforts, no obvious solution came to mind.

Resting the book on top of her bags, she wandered around the camp, fixing her tent for the night, all the while repeating those words over and over in her mind. She set up snares, and waited for a rabbit, then she slumped beside the fire again, drumming her fingers on her knee.

I never rest; I am never still. I am the keeper of the world.

The first line suggested mother earth, for she kept the world in its continuous cycle of life.

Without me, all will peril.

Such a thing could reference anything—the winds, the many oceans, even the endless forests.

When she finally settled down to skin and roast a rabbit from the snare, she considered the final line of the riddle and how it tied into the rest.

And when I am not around, all is cool and darkness falls.

Chewing the inside of her cheek, she searched her mind, trying to break down the words into something of meaning. Even long after she'd eaten her food, she was still without answers.

A Ballad of Severed Souls

With an impatient huff, she crawled into her tent, tossed the blankets over her, and closed her eyes. But her mind wandered, tried to decipher the message. She hadn't realised she'd drifted to sleep, not until she jolted upright in the dead of night.

As if her magic had stirred within her, continued its search during her subconsciousness, it led her back to the book. With a blanket thrown around her shoulders, she brought the pages closer, using the firelight to drench the parchment in a warm glow.

"Of course," she muttered. "The answer is light."

But the enchantment on the pages did not shift. Frowning, she placed her fingers on her chin. There must be a deeper connection to her magic. If the answer was indeed light, then perhaps using a spell to conjure a flame would reveal the hidden passage.

"*Areiras therasi.*" She swirled her finger, and a spark sprouted from the tip.

She grinned as the page's shimmer faded away, revealing neat calligraphy underneath.

Sword of Light, an enchanted weapon for the strongest of astral sorcerers.

Scanning the calligraphy, she absorbed the information as quickly as she could.

To obtain such a weapon, the wielder must complete three challenging yet deeply rewarding tasks.

Step one: Travel to the tallest peak in the Salken Mountains. There, the sorcerer must produce a sacrifice to Perun, God of thunder, justice, and war. Only then will He present himself, and if he deems the sorcerer pure of soul, He will present them with enchanted obsidian. This will be used to make the sword.

Step Two: Venture into the navel of the world—the deep sea. Find Uldan Island. The sorcerer is required to give blood to the World Tree, and in turn, they will receive Alatyr—father to all stones. Such a stone is endowed with healing and magical properties. It must be fitted into the sword's pommel.

Step Three: Cross the rocky terrain of the Svatken Peninsula and find the deepest cave. There, the sorcerer of astral magic will be reacquainted with an old friend. Call upon Svarog, God of the sun, fire, and forge. Present him with the obsidian and Alatyr stone, and the Sword of Light will be forged.

And in the footnote, further instructions were scribed.

To cloak these pages, conjure the spell 'Therasi anthilis'.

She said the words with a twirl of her hand, and the ink faded until the pages were blank, and the shimmering surface returned.

Collapsing onto her buttocks, her lungs tightened, and her chest ached as if the air had been knocked straight out of her. This was a crazy, absurd mission. Was it even necessary? How could she know for sure when she didn't know or understand the extent of Filip's magic? He'd refused to practise in the Prism World with her.

She tucked the book away, saving what she'd learned for later, should she need it. Her most pressing concern was Damir. What if she could find a way to get past Filip and his guards? Despite the stacking odds, she needed to do whatever she could to get her husband back.

A Ballad of Severed Souls

Galloping through the passing days, Adelina only stopped to water and feed the horse as well as line her own stomach and refill her flask. She didn't know for sure where Filip had taken her husband, but there was also no reason he wouldn't return to the palace with his captive.

As the sky shifted into an inky darkness on the third day of riding, she fastened her horse's reins to a branch and set up camp. Stifling a yawn, she grabbed a worn blanket from her bag, tossed it onto the ground beside the fire, and folded herself against it. Within a few moments of closing her eyes, she drifted into sleep.

A nearby rumble of laughter jolted her awake. She shot upright, scanning the shadows for any sign of threat. The fire had burned out, so if anyone *was* hunting for her, she wouldn't be easily spotted.

She rose and trod slowly to her horse, taking care over the leaves and twigs beneath her feet. The animal nickered.

"Shh," she whispered as she stroked its nose. Her gaze darted from one tree to the next.

A low-pitched voice muttered something close by. From her position, she couldn't make out the exact words. The southern forests weren't places people camped unless it was necessary. If she could get closer to the chattering men, she might be able to recognise the armour or a tell-tale sign linking them to the palace. If they were soldiers, perhaps they could lead her to Damir—or she could gleam information from them about his whereabouts.

Under the cloak of night, she couldn't rely on her golden magic, lest she reveal her stealthy position. Instead, if challenged, she'd have to rely on her combat training—her skills had improved thanks to her continued practice on the ship—and the small blade she kept in her bag. Withdrawing it, she gripped the hilt and followed the gravelly voices.

Bright orange light burst through the trees, and she darted behind a trunk. Holding her breath, she dared to glance around. Soldiers. Four of them. And a fire.

"Bloody hell, it's freezing," one soldier grunted as he shifted closer to the flames and rubbed his hands together.

In truth, she hadn't noticed the night breeze, for the adrenaline flooding her veins warmed her.

"Get the meat on to roast, will ye," another soldier said as he kicked off his boots and leaned against his bag.

The third soldier, who'd set about skinning an animal of some sort, chuckled. "We'll have to be quick to leave in the morning. Filip's patience is wearing thin."

Her back pressed against the trunk's rough bark. While there was no sign of Damir or Filip, those soldiers *were* his men. How could she get their location from them? She was outnumbered. But she had to try.

"I'm going for a piss," one of the men said.

Leaves crunched underfoot as he neared her hiding position. Veiled by shadows, she held an advantage.

When the man strolled ahead of her, ducking into the bushes, he unbuttoned his breeches. She pushed off the tree, for fear she might miss her opportunity.

Sneaking up behind the man, she held her blade in a tight grip and muttered the words, "*Reinisi amanir.*"

Amongst the several books in her possession, she'd catalogued a handful of useful spells, and she'd often wondered when a charm to ensnare the mind would come in useful. She couldn't fight the grin forming on her mouth as the man went rigid.

"Don't say a word," she whispered into his ear. "You do, and I kill you."

The man nodded, his hands freezing on his buttons.

"Tell me, *quietly*, where Filip is."

"He has men stationed up and down the country. Waiting for us to catch his *bitch*," he sneered, despite the magic forcing him to utter words of truth against his will. "You won't make it to the palace, girl."

"You best return to your little friends," she commanded. "You might want to tell them about our conversation, but this spell won't allow the words off your tongue."

The soldier nodded his obedience, buttoned his breeches, then strolled back to camp.

She hurried through the trees, back to her own camp and mount. Untying the reins, she fastened her luggage and mounted.

She rode long and hard through the night and didn't stop until the first signs of dawn painted the horizon in pink. Exhaustion wracked through her, each of her muscles heavy.

Tumbling off her saddle, she buried her face in her hands. She had to confront the truth—there would be no easy return to the palace if what the soldier had said was true.

She looked at the sun. The mark on her shoulder burned with ferocity, reminding her the dawn always broke after the dark, dark night. Her might must prevail. It must rise.

If she was to rescue her husband, she was going to need a better plan.

She rummaged in her bag for *A Practitioner's Guide to Ancient Magic, Astral Edition, Volume I*. The Sword of Light. But to obtain a weapon forged by gods would take weeks, maybe longer. She needed to learn more. If she was to stay away from Damir's side with the intention of becoming strong enough to save him from Filip, then she had to understand what she was up against.

On the last page, she found *Published and distributed by the Temauten Congregation Printer and Library*. Underneath was a list of other publications produced by them. Her gaze halted on a particular book: *A Practitioner's Guide to Ancient Nether Magic, Volume I*.

She puffed a breath through her lips as anticipation bubbled inside her. There it was. The twin book. If Filip owned a copy for astral magic, he'd more than likely have its partner in his possession. If she could get her hands on it, she could learn more about his powers. Then, and only then, could she determine whether the quest for the Sword of Light was needed. It was either that, or risk charging through the country, right into Filip's grasp.

Her mind raced. It would be dangerous to spend too much time in public areas of Temauten, and it would be *especially* dangerous to go to the building of the Temauten Congregation. Where even was it? She vaguely recalled Filip referring to the village of Murtei.

Flipping to the last page of the spell book once again, she found the address scrawled at the bottom: *Khasapa House.*

Laying the book flat on the ground, she rummaged in her bag for her map, then flattened it next to it. It'd taken her and Damir almost a month to reach the docks in the south, but they'd stayed in a village for a few days before moving to the next. If Adelina kept moving, she could be back to Aramoor in half the time.

Arching a brow, she found *Khasapa House* in Murtei positioned east of her hometown, possibly two or three-days' ride. From her current location, if she rode hard and fast, stopping for short bouts, she'd reach the Temauten Congregation's building in under two weeks.

She hoped to the gods Damir could survive long enough for her to get her answers.

Adelina's two-week journey to the Temauten Congregation in Murtei dragged by; each day, minute, and second filled with spirally thoughts of Damir's welfare. She fought to remind herself what she was doing—she needed to be at her strongest if she stood any chance of freeing her husband and defeating Filip.

Her current dilemma was to find a way into Khasapa House—the Temauten Congregation. Drawing the hood of her cape over her head, she hopped off her horse, then led it by the reins along the narrow, dusty path into the village. Keeping her gaze on the ground, she weaved her way through the bustling market streets and thanked the gods the library was situated in a village home to a busy market.

With her horse in tow, she passed stalls where merchants traded fruits and vegetables, spices, flowers and herbs, trinkets, housewares varying from vases to pots and pans, and even jewellery. The strong scent of cinnamon and star anise filled her nose, and the steady beat of the horse's hooves soothed her mounting nerves. If she ran into any more of Filip's men, her chances of increasing her strength before taking him on would be shot.

Keeping an even pace, she followed the winding path until it widened into a large fork, and beyond a tall, metal gate, stood an almost twin replica of the Embassy building. A fraction smaller, Khasapa House held all the appeal and lavishness the Embassy building in Toichrist had. There, she hoped to locate the book about nether magic.

She fastened her horse to a nearby tree, then joined the crowd of civilians filing into the building. The library section was open to the public, and if she travelled in dense crowds, she'd be able to get inside without concern or question. All she needed to do was keep her cool and not draw attention to herself.

After climbing white marble stairs, she followed the high-ceiling corridor into the large, dome-shaped library. Bookcases towered from floor to ceiling—

A Ballad of Severed Souls

there must've been tens of thousands of books covering the many shelves. People sat about, clustered around tables and armchairs. A middle-aged woman pushed a cart of books towards an aisle, then stuffed them back into their designated spots.

Adelina held her breath. Where would she even start? It's not like she knew a spell that would magically draw the book from its shelf. Even if she did, performing it in public probably wouldn't be the wisest idea. Her time in the library needed to remain inconspicuous.

Making her way down the first aisle of books, she scanned the spines. All fiction novels. At the end of the aisle, she turned a corner in search of non-fiction. She weaved her way between individuals who flittered through the library.

She halted. At the far end of the library, an entire wall of books was locked behind glass doors. Edging nearer, she strained to get a better look at the intricate carving in the metal panels around the glass panes. An unnatural, silvery hue shimmered from the shiny surface. Enchanted.

Her body tingled, and a compulsion to be closer flooded through her. As if her body was no longer her own to control, she touched the first door. A bolt of heat shot up her arm. She knew her astral magic shared the same soul as nether magic—perhaps this was the book's way of telling her she was close.

If the book on nether magic was locked inside a glass bookshelf, she couldn't perform any counter magic—not with so many people around. Instead, she yanked herself back, and scanned the shelves, one by one, following the warmth flooding through her body.

The pull of magic intensified—her skin blazed. Standing on her tiptoes, she spotted a black, leather-bound book positioned three quarters up the bookshelf. Although from her height she couldn't read the letters on the spine, the tingle in her limbs when she looked at it told her this tome was the one she sought.

"Can I help you, miss?"

Adelina jumped. Peeling her gaze from the shelves, she faced a middle-aged woman, who she assumed was the librarian.

"What time do you close?" Adelina smiled and kept her tone casual.

"Once the sun has set." The woman pursed her lips. "Meaning our hours vary depending on the season, but the days are getting longer. We'll likely be open until about 8 p.m."

"Do you find the library busy all day?" Adelina draped her arms across her chest, manifesting an air of casual interest. "The crowds—they make me anxious. I'd much rather come back when I can read in peace."

"Ah, yes." The woman rested a stack of books on the shelf. "We tend to be busy until about 5 p.m.—that's when folks go home for dinner. You'll find the library a lot more comfortable after then."

"Thank you." Adelina bowed her head, then left.

Once outside, she returned to her horse, unhitched it, then searched for a discreet tavern or inn. Her stomach growled. She was fortunate she hadn't drawn unwanted attention to herself.

A Ballad of Severed Souls

After eating a quick meal in the nearby tavern, Adelina hurried along the cobbled path back towards Khasapa House, leaving her horse in the small stables.

Squashing her nerves, she held Damir at the forefront of her mind—her love for him. As if he were there with her, he stretched out a hand to her, offering his guidance. A bolt of confidence shot through her, but she couldn't tell if it was from genuine faith in her plan, or the desperate need to save her husband. The image of Damir's warm, familiar face felt like home, and burned bright in her mind, acting as a north star.

Energy revitalised, she considered her next steps. She'd find another entrance to Khasapa House—*any* entrance except through the front.

She stayed close to the shadows of cottages, market stalls, and bustling taverns. The crowded cobbled streets allowed her to blend seamlessly into the village.

Ahead, the tall, wrought-iron fence surrounded the Temauten Congregation. People filed into the building, although in fewer numbers than before. Smaller clusters of men and women were dotted outside the entrance. Her gaze darted from one unrecognisable person to the next. She didn't find anyone who appeared to be guards of Filip's. Perhaps Filip's men *weren't* there, which begged the question: did he know she'd taken the astral book, and if he did, would he have questioned it? After all, she'd been at Kirovo Palace for training—taking a book to read wouldn't have been suspicious.

And yet, her whirling mind considered the possibility Filip could've sent anyone to find her. She didn't know all his benefactors or the men in his employ—she'd had the opportunity to meet a handful of them at the announcement party shortly after her arrival at Kirovo Palace, and a while later at the Embassy.

Her vision blurred, tilting her on her axis as she struggled to grapple with her warring thoughts. Sucking in a ragged breath, she forced herself to focus on Damir's image—a loving smile, an outstretched hand. Her north star.

Letting him guide her, she put one foot in front of the other and weaved her way between the gathered civilians of Murtei. Sunset cast a warm, orange glow over Khasapa House—spindly shadows from the iron fence stretched across the floor. A cool breeze chilled her cheeks as the temperature dropped.

She neared a set of double doors on the side of the building. A stone bench was placed beside it, overlooking a tended garden. Topiaries were carved into arrow points, rose bushes were round, and a circular fountain in the centre added to the peaceful ambience.

Smiling politely at the gatherers, she slipped past, then entered the building. From this side, she ascended a separate staircase from the one in the main entrance. When she reached the library, her shoulders relaxed, and she puffed out a sharp breath. The library was more or less empty, besides the librarian, and a handful of lingering readers.

A Ballad of Severed Souls

At the back of the library, she fixed her gaze on the black leather-bound book tucked into the glass-doored bookshelf. Casting a quick glance over her shoulder, she checked no one was looking, then grabbed a nearby stool.

Stepping up, she reached for the handle and gave it a tug. Locked. Not to her surprise at all. She dug her spell book from the bag slung over her shoulder, then flipped through the pages, looking for something—anything—to unlock the door. It wasn't as if she could simply ask the librarian for a key. Could she?

Paranoia shot through her. What if the librarian was a spy? She couldn't trust anyone. Her jaw clenched as a line of sweat formed along her hairline. After another brief glance over her shoulder, she returned her unblinking gaze to her spell book.

She found an interesting spell—a thistle vine strong enough to bend metal to its will.

Under her breath, she uttered the words, *"Rinorowlith."*

From the tip of her finger, sprung a thin yet sturdy green vine. It sprouted and twisted, thistles shooting from its stem. She held her finger in front of the lock and watched in wonder as the vine weaved itself into the keyhole. A golden hue shone from the hole, a byproduct of astral magic, and the glass door clicked open.

An excited laugh escaped her mouth. She clamped her hand over her lips and shot another wary look over her shoulder. Reassured no one was watching her, she pushed on to her tiptoes, then took *A Practitioner's Guide to Ancient Magic, Nether Edition, Volume I* from its shelf. Stuffing it into her bag, she quickly closed the door, then dropped to the ground. She told herself it wasn't stealing but rather borrowing the book to save her husband's life.

As she weaved her way back through the tall aisles, she passed the librarian. "Good evening."

"So, you came back after all." She smiled. "I didn't see you come in."

"I came to browse your collection of fiction titles. It's time for dinner now," Adelina returned the politeness, then hurried out of the library.

She made her way back to the inn, unhobbled her horse, mounted, then rode out of Murtei, the cloak of the pine woods a welcome relief from potential eyes. She hadn't known if it was her paranoia alone, or if Filip's men had been watching her all along, but she couldn't take the risk of staying there longer than necessary.

Riding until the village disappeared into the horizon behind her, Adelina clutched the horse's reins. She tugged them gently, slowing the horse from a canter to a walk. Deep in a pine forest, and with the sun setting, she was almost cloaked in shadows. With a swirl of her index finger, she cast a wisp of light. It hovered in front of her face, shining a warm golden, and expanded into a ball. Spinning slowly on its axis, it provided her with enough light to set up camp.

She untied her luggage from the back of the saddle, then dumped it on the ground. After leading the horse into the glade to feed on the dewy grass, she set about collecting twigs and sticks for a fire. Once she'd built the firepit in the centre of the glade, she produced a flame with magic. Holding her hair out of

A Ballad of Severed Souls

the way, she leaned closer, blowing on the flames, encouraging them to grow.

Happy with her work, she returned to her luggage, then grabbed a load of her clothing to use as a pillow. Her grandfather's pocket watch tumbled to the ground. Crashing to her knees, she scooped it into her hands and brushed off the dirt.

"How could I have forgotten about you?" she whispered as she inspected the clockface.

Bringing the metal to her lips, she pressed a kiss to the cool surface. It reminded her of home. A warmth spread through her, and tears welled in her eyes—for her mother, father, and sister, for Damir's parents. What she would give to envelop herself in the familiarity of Aramoor—her husband by her side.

As she lowered the clockface from her lips, a stream of light burst from the surface, startling her. She fell back on her buttocks, almost dropping the pocket watch. Clasping on to it for dear life, she steadied herself. Her lips parted as she gazed upwards, following the stream of light through the treetops.

"What in the realm?" she gasped.

She swirled her fingers through the golden beam. A warm, fuzzy sensation danced up her arm and through her body. The stream of magic lowered and rested on her bag.

Frowning, she scooted towards it, then withdrew *A Practitioner's Guide to Ancient Nether Magic, Volume I*. Barely grasping it, the covers flung open, powered by the magic from the pocket watch. Dozens of pages fluttered until they halted on one, three quarters through.

At the top of the page, she read *An Astral Sorcerer's Guide to Talismans.*

Sucking in a breath, she absorbed the words.

While an inanimate object may be used to control one's magic, a talisman has many other beneficial properties. An astral sorcerer may choose to store a sum of their magic within an object of their choosing. During the Great War of the Wielders, many sorcerers hid their magic in fear of being enslaved by the other half of their soul: nether sorcerers.

Her breathing hitched. The thought of people like her being pressed into servitude made her stomach heave.

Such talismans have the power of finding their way back to astral sorcerers, even if lost for generations, so they will never be far away from their own kind. The sorcerer may then choose to absorb the power stored within the talisman or protect it.

Her hand grasped the enchanted talisman around her neck. In her other hand, her grandfather's pocket watch lay in the centre of her palm.

Adelina returned to the passage.

While astral magic is not hereditary, it is not totally uncommon for multiple people across generations of the same family to possess such a magic.

She checked the book for the dates associated with the Great War of the Wielders. A breath caught in her throat. Less than a century ago. The pieces fell together inside her mind. Her grandfather was involved in the Great War. He'd been an astral wielder and had hidden his power in the pocket watch. Filip had spent the last decade searching for an astral wielder. The only way astral wielders could ensure their safety was to hide away their magic.

Meaning Filip had been searching for longer than a decade. How was that possible? He didn't look older than thirty, but she didn't know an awful lot about the man in possession of nether magic. She only understood he wanted her for his own political gain.

She was presented with a choice: put her own magic inside the pocket watch, so she could not be used by Filip ever again or absorb it completely.

Pressing her fingers to her lips, she pondered. Either way, she couldn't imagine Filip letting her go, and it wasn't just her involved in this anymore. He held her husband captive, and the gods knew what foul tortures he was inflicting upon him. His plan was much bigger—Filip aimed to control the three countries, meaning thousands of lives would be bent to his will.

An intense weight crushed her spirit. Swallowing her last ounce of anxiety, she tucked loose strands of hair out of her face and focused on what she must do. So much relied on her. She needed to do whatever it took to become as strong as Filip, to stop him at all costs. First, absorb the magic. Second, complete her quest and obtain the Sword of Light. Third, free her husband. Fourth, put a stop to Filip before he caused any great damage to the countries in which she called home, even if they were separated by borders.

Opening the pocket watch, she lay it flat in one hand while she read the book's description on absorbing magic stored within a talisman. Her fingers halted below the spell.

"*Tyleiri sinriyn,*" she whispered at first, then pronounced the words again with clarity and confidence. "*Tyleiri sinriyn.*"

The hands on the pocket watch clicked several times, shifting around the timepiece's face. Then, as if a mechanism somewhere inside unlocked, the face lifted into the air, separated from the rest of the object. A golden light poured out, casting a vibrant glow over the glade.

The freed magic enveloped her in warmth as it fused with her skin. An intense surge of power flooded her body, drenching every nerve ending and fibre. The fine hairs on her arms bristled, even underneath her cloak. Her nape tingled.

Closing her eyes, she breathed slowly and measured, allowing her body time to adjust to the wave of power settling into the depths of her bones. When the warmth of magic subsided, she grabbed the book she'd taken from Khasapa House.

This book would contain the secrets of Filip's power—a strength she didn't yet understand. Her fingers loitered on the cover, unsure if she was ready to learn how powerful he truly was.

Biting her lip, she flipped to the middle, pressing the pages flat with her hands.

Nether Wielders: A History.

During the dark times of the Great War of the Wielders, there was a surge of powerful nether sorcerers, often in the form of shapeshifters. Such a species was not considered a threat until it became apparent their access to nether magic was tenfold that of the average wielder. The Great War saw nether sorcerers enslave and condemn their lighter counterpart: astral wielders. The most famous and notable name from the War was Antanov Tarasov, who used his ability to shapeshift into an otherworldly creature—a demon, straight from the underworld itself, known as Nav.

She halted, stunned into a frozen, trance-like state as the words buzzed in her mind. Since when did shapeshifters exist? It seemed, with each piece of magic she learned, there was something else crawling out of the woodworks to surprise her. Antanov shared the same surname as Filip—could *this* be his father? If her speculations were correct, then Damir and the civilians of the three countries faced an unsurmountable threat.

What sent ice-cold chills down her spine was the mention of Nav. She'd heard stories of the underworld during her childhood. Somewhere deep underground, enclosed away from the world by a river with deadly currents, the God known as Veles ruled. In these stories, Nav was described as a green pasture, onto which Veles guided souls. The entrance to the underworld was guarded by a Zmey—*dragon*. The souls would later be reborn on earth, which rose the question in Adelina's mind: was this how demons found their way onto the living plane?

Underworld. Demon. Shapeshifter. Dragon.

Dizzy, she dug her fingers into the mud as her vision tilted and spots formed. She fumbled for her flask, shakily unscrewed the cap, then tilted it against her lips. The cool water slid into her mouth, washing away the bile. She closed her eyes, fighting the queasiness holding her body in a death grip. As if sensing her unease, her horse whinnied nearby.

You're going to make it through this. Damir's voice sounded in her mind, drawing her from the edge of panic. *You're going to be fine.*

She knew it wasn't him—not truly—but she let him guide her, focusing all her energy on the memory of him. His warmth and strength, the scent of sawed wood clinging to his skin. Her north star.

Her magic hummed inside her, settling her nerves. That, combined with the echo of Damir's voice, was all she needed. Even if it took everything she had—everything she was—she'd do what she must to make it back to him, to protect him and everyone else under threat.

FOURTEEN

Obsidian

A searing pain burst through Damir's head as he stirred awake. His left eye was swollen shut, and he winced when he opened it. He attempted to lift his hand to his face, but discovered his arms were restrained.

Glancing with his one good eye, a blood-stained rope bound his arms and legs to a wooden chair. Pyotr and Filip stood on the opposite side of the cell door.

"Coming around again, I see." Pyotr leaned against the bars, letting his lower arms rest in the gaps between. "Think the last blow might've been a bit hard."

A sadistic laugh escaped Filip's lips. "Ensuring you remained unconscious was the best way of escorting you into this prison without you trying to escape. I'd apologise for the bloody eye, but I'm not one for regrets. You'll stay down here until your wife returns because she *will* come for you." He turned on his heel, then left. "And thanks to the relationship my father and I have established with the High State means they'll turn a blind eye to what I do with you."

Damir grumbled at the mention of the High State. They were in charge of keeping crime under control in the three countries, but the prisons were already brimming with criminals. He guessed this underground prison was where Filip contained prisoners of interest to him, and he certainly found himself in a precarious position now he'd lost his most important weapon.

Once Filip's echoing footsteps dissipated, Pyotr shifted his attention back to Damir.

"Why?" Damir managed, barely keeping his head held an inch above his chest. "We're…neighbours."

"Doesn't mean shit," Pyotr grunted. "I don't need to explain myself to you."

"How much is he…paying you?" Damir tried to smirk, but a cut in his lip split, and a warm, liquid dribbled down his chin. "What is you or him who gave me a black eye and a split lip? I'll bet my coin it was him—I don't think you have the stomach for it. Can't say I blame you. You look at me and all you see is a child, right? Your friendly neighbour who never gave you any grief—someone who shared their vodka and food with you at the festivals. My own parents even housed you when you were too drunk to make it home to your wife and children."

"Don't you dare speak of them." In a flash, Pyotr gripped the bars in a white-knuckle grip.

"What would you do if someone was doing this to *your* wife?" Damir tested, feeding off the burst of confidence shooting through him. "Just imagine if it were *her* tied up here and being kept prisoner instead of me."

The colour drained from Pyotr's face. "Say another word and I'll kill you."

"I don't think Filip will be too pleased if he comes back here to see my neck half severed and my blood all over the floor." Damir fixed his unwavering stare on Pyotr. "You couldn't kill me even if you wanted to. You don't have the guts, nor do you want to risk your own pathetic life."

"I'd tread carefully, if I were you," Pyotr tried for a calm tone, although a vein bulged in his forehead. "You're *our* prisoner, at all, and you're at our mercy."

"You're a coward. A pathetic excuse of a man, who drinks and gambles his life away." Damir shrugged. "You destroy lives, and you don't seem to care. You burned Daro's workshop down even when he tried to help with your payments. Tihana, an innocent child, was injured. Do you know you could've killed her? She was there. Imagine if it were your own child."

Pyotr winced. A second later, his expression was as hard as stone.

Noticing the ever so slight reaction, Damir continued his jibe. "You're reckless with lives, even the ones you claim to love. And for what? Money? Actually, don't answer that. This conversation is dull. If I'm to be your prisoner, then leave me to my squalor."

Pyotr stared at him for a tense while. Silence. Then he shifted his weight, pushing himself off the wall. Within minutes, he was gone.

Shoving her book into her bag attached to the saddle, Adelina mounted her horse. According to *A Practitioner's Guide to Ancient Magic, Astral Edition, Volume I,* she needed to travel to the tallest peak in the Salken Mountains and offer a sacrifice to Perun. But who or what in the gods' good realm could she possibly use for it? Who was she to deem whose life should be taken?

It would take her another two weeks to cross the rocky border into Saintlandsther, and enter the highlands, where she'd find the Salken Mountains. Two weeks to find a sacrifice. Could she bring herself to kill something—*someone*—to save her husband and her family?

Her thoughts flipped—it wasn't just her loved ones anymore. Filip wanted to control everything, and everyone. Perhaps the loss of one life was the price to pay to save thousands.

She shook herself hard, ridding herself of the traitorous thoughts wrestling with her conscience. The sharp jolt of her body startled the horse, who gave an abrupt snort in response.

Leaning down, she patted his hide. "Sorry."

A week of sleeping under the stars passed painfully slow. Each night, she tossed and turned, contemplating Damir's captivity. The storm replayed in her mind, refusing to budge from her memory. Could she have done anything differently?

A Ballad of Severed Souls

By the time she reached the border, and the sharp incline of the highlands, her whole body ached, and so did her soul. Her silent loneliness of the past month gave way to all-consuming thoughts. The closer she came to the Salken Mountains, the sooner she'd need to find a sacrifice.

Giving a quick tug on the reins, she stopped her horse's gallop. Once she slipped off the saddle, she drew her book from her bag. Flipping open to the page about the Sword of Light, she reread the requirements.

She sighed in relief. Nowhere did it state the life give must be human. Perhaps an animal would suffice. Still, taking a life wouldn't be easy, especially for a girl who, at the beginning of the year, had never stepped foot out of her rural village, never laid a hand on *any* animal aside from hunting.

Tucking the book away, she glanced to the heavens. Thick, grey clouds swarmed the mountain peaks in the distance, and a cool breeze stirred across the pastures, chilling her cheeks.

She tugged her cloak tighter around her body, then mounted. She rode along the dirt path towards the small village nestled at the foot of the first mountain. How would she find the tallest one, when their tops were buried in the clouds?

Twirling her finger through the air, she produced an orb of golden light, which hovered in front of her, guiding her through the dimming atmosphere. Night was approaching, and she'd need to find somewhere to sleep. Perhaps there was room in an inn ahead.

As she approached the stone wall surrounding the dozen buildings making up the tiny, isolated village, she extinguished her light and dropped from her horse, leading it by the reins.

Torches were lit along the path, casting a warm glow across the wooden and stone structures. Candlelight gleamed in the windows of each house. She wondered what the village was called, never once in her life considering people would live somewhere so remote. The more time she spent away from home, the more she learned about the people of the three countries. Seeing them in their homes instilled a further concern for their lives. She didn't trust Filip's intentions, and she definitely didn't believe his promises to unite the countries and take care of the poor.

She bowed her head in greeting at a local man who walked past. Farther ahead, half a dozen people gathered around the small bathhouse, presumably the only one in the town.

Vegetables grew in a patch between two buildings. A fence was built to keep animals out, perhaps deer and rabbits, if they ventured this close to the mountains. At the front, was a small, wooden gate about hip high. As she wandered along the path with her horse, she glanced at the tilled rows of plants in various sizes and shades of green. The odd weed sprouted between the rows, in need of pulling. Pea vines and tomatoes grew up wooden posts, and ahead, frilly carrot tops and potatoes poked through the soil's surface. Near the back of the patch, tall corn stalks shuddered in the evening breeze.

As she wandered towards the edge, she spotted tall, thorny raspberry bushes loaded with red berries, strawberry plants dotted with delicate, white flowers, and bees buzzing here and there. Clouds gathered overhead, casting out the evening light. A gentle rain pattered against the nearby roofs, and the breeze sharpened.

Holding her cloak around her with one hand, and the other maintaining a tight grip of the horse's reins, she quickened her pace through the centre of the village.

She approached a weathered-beaten building with a wooden sign above the front door, flapping in the wind. On its surface, *Svante's Boarding House and Tavern* was etched. To the right, was a stone stable, perhaps big enough to fit four or five horses.

Once she hobbled her horse to a nearby post and gathered her bags, she entered the boarding house and wandered to the bar at the opposite end of the room.

"Good evening to ye, miss." The elderly man behind the counter tipped his hat in greeting. "Are ye in need of a room?"

"Yes please." She placed her bags on the floor, then drew her pouch of coins from the pocket of her cloak. "And my horse will require a loose box in your stable."

"You're in luck. A gentleman has not long checked out. Are ye wishin' for supper, too?" He propped his elbows on the surface and leaned forwards—a warm smile tilting the corner of his lips.

"That'd be lovely." She returned the smile.

The innkeeper wandered around the bar, then led her towards the stables. Once she'd unhobbled the horse, she guided him into its loose box.

"There'll be plenty of fresh hay for him." He gestured to the feed scattered all over the floor and stuffed into a wooden box fitted to the wall.

"Thank you, sir."

"None of that around here." He waved his hand. "Ye'll be callin' me Svante or nothin' at all."

She bobbed her head and smiled. "As you wish."

"I do so wish. Now, ye'll be followin' me to ye room. I'll be bringin' supper up to ye in an hour or so, once ye've bathed and set any affairs in order." He turned on his heel, grabbed her bags, and gestured for her to follow.

Inside, he headed for the stairwell. The wooden stairs creaked underfoot as he ascended. She followed behind.

Towards the end of the corridor, he stopped and opened a door, revealing a small yet quaint room with a fire in the hearth already lit.

He placed the bags at the foot of the bed. "Will this be suitin' ye?"

"Of course, thank you." Her gaze landed on the metal tub positioned near the hearth. "Can I trouble you for some hot water please?"

"I'll fetch it up for ye now, miss." He bowed his head, then dashed from the room.

Enveloped in silence, if one didn't count the crack and pop of flames, she wandered to the double bed. Tracing her hand along the cotton covers, her heart ached. Her eyes stung and an uncomfortable lump formed in her throat. She should've been with her husband—they should never have been separated.

Kneeling in front of the bed, she propped her elbows on the mattress, then clasped her hands in prayer. She closed her eyes.

"To all that is mighty, I ask you to look over my husband. Keep him safe and protected from the evils circling him. Until we may be reunited." She swiped the single tear rolling down her face and rose.

Clearing her throat, she straightened her skirts. Svante made several trips with buckets of water.

When the tub was finally full, she bid her thanks as Svante turned to the door. "Could you tell me where I could find the nearest hospital? I've some minor ailments in need of treatment."

"Oh, sure, miss," the innkeeper said, his hand resting on the doorknob. "Down the way, head north, and ye'll find the Salken Medical Centre. It's a modest place, but I'm sure ye'll find what ye're looking for there." With a smile, he slipped out of the room, clicking the door shut behind him.

She stripped, then sank into depths of the tub. Sighing, she let the water wash away her fears, her guilt for not being able to stop her husband from being captured. She pressed her lips to her triple stacked wedding ring.

"I love you, Damir," she said to the ghost of him guiding her. "Always."

The following morning, the narrow streets of the small village were bustling with town folk. Market stalls were open, and the familiar waft of baking bread filled her nose. If she hadn't already eaten breakfast in the boarding house, she might've been tempted to purchase some. Instead, she and her horse were about to embark on the journey deeper into the Salken Mountains, but beforehand, she wanted to top up her salve used to treat the burns on her wrists.

Following the innkeeper's instructions, she headed north, guiding her horse by the reins. When she spotted the billowing sign for the medical centre, she tethered the straps to a post and wandered to the small, terraced building. Its roof was weathered, moss covering the tiles, but the paisleys growing in the window boxes added charm to the otherwise decrepit place.

The door creaked as she entered, the ground floor long and narrow. Cots were crammed in rows against the walls, torches fixed above the frames provided additional light, and medicinal supplies were scattered across shelves and countertops. Each bed was taken by a patient, most of whom slept, despite the late morning hour.

"What can I do for you, miss?" a woman in a long gown and white apron asked as she approached Adelina. Her hair was scraped back into a tight knot and a pair of circular spectacles sat at the edge of her nose.

"I am looking to purchase some salve suitable for mild burns and blisters," Adelina said as she breathed in the strong, heady scent of garlic, ginger, lavender, and a variety of other herbs and spices she couldn't place.

With a swift nod, the woman stood on her tiptoes and withdrew a round tub from a cabinet fixed to the wall above a small desk. "Apply twice daily to the affected area."

Spotting the cost marked on the lid, Adelina rummaged in her pouch, then handed over the coins. "Thank you."

"If you'll excuse me, I have patients to attend to." The woman smiled. "Good day to you, miss." She turned on her heel and headed towards a barely conscious woman positioned a few strides away.

"It's good to see you awake, Sara," the woman said as she approached the sickly patient, whose eyes fluttered open and closed. From Adelina's position, she could see her collarbones protruding out the top of her shirt.

"Would you like some food and water?" the woman, who Adelina presumed was a healer, asked as she dragged over a cart, a tray with a bowl and spoon and cup placed on top.

"Water," Sara said breathlessly.

The healer handed her the cup, keeping a hand on the back of the patient's neck as she helped her to sip the contents.

Sara closed her eyes and moaned. When she reopened them, she rested her head against the pillow, all of her limbs limp and thin beneath the threadbare blanket.

"Is there something I can do to help?" Adelina asked as she wandered closer. For a reason unbeknownst to Adelina, she found herself drawn to the woman.

"It's all right, miss," the healer said. "I'm sure you must be on your way."

"I would be happy to sit with her while you attend to your other patients," Adelina offered, noticing the only other healer in the building was busy sponging down another patient.

The woman chewed her bottom lip, as if considering her response. "Only if you're sure. The other lady who works here has a grievance in the family and hasn't come in to work this morning. Understandable, but leaves the two of us, and with an influx of patients overnight, we're swept off our feet."

"It would be my honour to help." Adelina picked up the bowl from the tray, trying not to grimace at the stodgy oats inside.

"Thank you," the healer said. "And you may call me Molly. I won't keep you for too long. I have some wounds to dress, which should only take a short while."

"Of course." Adelina smiled as Molly nodded her thanks, turning her attention to the next patient.

Sitting on the edge of the mattress, Adelina scooped up some oats with the spoon and held it out for Sara. "Here. You should try to eat something."

Grumbling, Sara shook her head and swatted her away. "No, dear. I wish to be left in peace. If I am to die anyway, I shall not force myself to eat that mush they call food."

"Please," Adelina said in a gentle tone, unable to keep her gaze from the hollowness of Sara's cheeks. "You need your strength to recover."

"There is no cure for what ails me, dear." The woman smiled faintly. "Although, I thank you…for your concern. Now don't look at me like that…I don't want your pity. I have lived a good life."

"What about your family?" Adelina kept one hand on the bowl and rested her other on Sara's bony arm. "Can I get anyone for you?"

"My family…are no longer with me." The woman's words were laboured.

"You should rest your voice," Adelina said. "And drink some more water."

"I do not wish to be fussed over, girl." Sara sighed, closing her eyes. "Leave me in peace."

Adelina set the bowl on the counter but stayed at Sara's side. She'd already decided there was nothing in the gods' good realm that could convince her to take another human's life. But by the grace of the gods, she was presented with an opportunity to perhaps provide this woman with a fulfilling and quick death. She could complete the first step of her mission without losing her soul in the process.

"There is something I must tell you." Adelina rested her hand on Sara's arm again, in a gentle attempt to keep her lucid.

Sara opened one eye. "Oh? A story to make my journey…into the arms of the gods a little easier? You know, people often…take those they love…to a familiar place through kind words."

"That's not what I'm doing here," Adelina said.

"Don't tell me you're only here to tend to the sick and dying. A fine young woman such as yourself…will have plenty of opportunities, far away from this tiny village." Sara smirked, although it seemed out of place on her pasty skin.

Adelina leaned forward and lowered her voice. "Do you recognise me?"

"No. Why would I?" Sara frowned.

"My name is Adelina Orlova. The astral wielder, and I have fled from Filip. His intentions are not pure, and he holds my husband as his prisoner," Adelina revealed, keeping her tone hushed, so she didn't alert anyone nearby who may be listening.

"Why would you tell me…such things?" Sara said.

"Because I believe you can help," Adelina said. "Filip wanted to marry me to secure a powerful bloodline. He does not wish to reunite the countries but instead plans to dominate them through force and war. For the good, innocent people of these three countries, and for the sake of my husband and family, I am searching for the Sword of Light."

"I am no sorcerer; I cannot help you." Sara closed her eyes again.

Adelina clasped Sara's hand, urging her to listen. She chose her next words carefully. "Please hear me. The first step to require such a weapon is to give a life to the god of thunder, justice, and war. Perun. We will find him at the highest peak in the Salken Mountains. If you are determined to die, then let it be meaningful. I beg for your help. It is not just my husband I wish to save, but thousands of lives threatened by Filip."

"You wish to take me into the mountains...to die?" Sara peeked through her dusty lashes.

"Yes." Adelina squeezed her hand. "You will see the birds, and wildlife, the sun through the clouds and mist, and the gods will be through the veil. Peace is what I offer you."

"It is more than I am likely to get here." Sara smiled again. "But first, you will need to convince Molly to let me go."

"I'll get her to agree." Adelina headed over to Molly as she dressed a patient's abdominal wounds with fresh bandages. "When you're done, may I speak with you?"

"I'm just finishing up." Molly tied a knot, then as she turned, she flattened the slight creases in her apron. "I thank you for sitting with Sara for a while. She does not get visitors."

"Is there somewhere we could talk in private?"

With a frown, Molly gestured to the narrow door at the back of the room.

When they were through it, away from the listening ears of the patients, Adelina lifted her chin a notch higher. "I wish to take Sara with me."

"With you?" Molly's eyebrows shot upwards, eyes widening. "Why in the realm would you do that?"

"As you said, she does not get visitors," Adelina said, keeping her gaze fixed on Molly's. "I'm to join my husband's family on their farm beyond the mountains. We could offer her a peaceful life there."

Molly shook her head. "A patient as sickly as Sara will not survive the arduous journey through the mountains."

"My husband is sending a carriage for me." Adelina's lie tasted sour in her mouth. "It is due to arrive at the foot of the mountains in an hour. I can escort Sara by horse until then."

Molly was silent for a moment, then said, "Why would you offer such a thing to a woman you do not know?"

"I know what it is like to be without family," Adelina said, and meant it. The thought of her own family made her heart ache. "And it is within my bounds to give this woman what she wants: a peaceful ending."

"I will have to speak with Sara and ensure she is happy with this," Molly said. "In truth, we are desperate for vacant beds."

Adelina ignored the twisting of her stomach as the healer headed into the main room.

"Wait by the door, and I'll be over with you shortly," Molly said before striding over to Sara.

With a nod, Adelina made her way to the front of the building and tapped her foot. Molly spoke to Sara in a hushed tone, and Adelina bit her bottom lip as she waited for the decision to be made.

She let out a sigh of relief when Molly eased Sara onto her feet, wrapping the blanket around her shoulders.

"I have spoken with Sara, and she has graciously accepted your proposal," Molly said, guiding the patient over in slow, steady steps.

"It will be good to feel the sun on my face again." Sara smiled, warmer than before. "Molly, you should open the windows…it's awfully stuffy in here."

Molly patted Sara on the back as she opened the door. Turning to Adelina, she said, "Where is your horse?"

"Just outside." Adelina stepped through the door, unfastening the reins from the nearby post. "Here, let me help you, Sara." She hooked her arm around her, then helped her into the saddle. "I'll sit behind you to ensure you're comfortable."

Placing her foot in the stirrup, she flung her leg over and positioned herself as a support for Sara. She slipped an arm on either side of the frail woman, then grasped the reins. They bid their farewells to Molly, and together, they rode out of the dismal village, and along the path into the mountains.

When deep shadows formed along the path, and starlight peeked through the gaps between the gathering clouds, Adelina drew the horse to a stop. She dropped to her feet, then helped Sara down. At the side of the path, she spotted a sharp overhang jutting out of the mountainside. It would provide them with shelter from the icy winds the night would surely bring.

She guided Sara and the horse under the overhang, untied her bags, then dumped them on the ground.

"I'll be right back," she said to Sara as she eased her onto her feet. "I'm going to get us more food. We've shared what I'd brought on the way."

As she turned on her heel, she rubbed the horse's nose.

Staying close to the overhang, she climbed up the jutting side of the opposite mountain, and weaved her way between loose rocks, and clumps of grass. From her position a few feet above the path, she maintained a clear vision of Sara, the horse, and her belongings. Ahead of her was a cluster of aspen trees, clinging to the mountainside—their roots weaving in and out of the soil like thick claws.

When she reached the tree, she knelt, then ran her fingers over the cool grass. Amongst the blades, she found round mushrooms—their cap a tan colour, contrasting with their white stems. Recognising them from the markets in Aramoor, she knew they were safe to eat. She plucked a handful of them and stuffed them into her pockets.

In the opposite direction, continuing deeper into the mountain range, she spotted dense brambles, vibrant green leaves, and if her suspicions were right, she'd find berries amongst the thorns. She tugged a load of berries from the branches, keeping a tight hold of them while she descended the steep bank to the path.

By the time she reached the overhang, her teeth were chattering from the growing cold of the night. She set her food aside, went about gathering sticks for a fire, then stacked them together. With a wave of her finger, the fire was lit.

"I won't lie, I'm surprised you convinced Molly to let me leave. I was certain to die in that place." Sara wrinkled her nose. "What did you say to convince her?"

Adelina couldn't meet her gaze. "I offered you peace on my husband's family farm beyond the mountains."

"A beautiful lie." Sara shrugged one shoulder.

"Why did you agree to come with me?"

"I am dying anyway. What difference does it make?" Sara turned on her side, resting against the luggage.

Adelina let the silence hang for a moment, before finally deciding her words. "We will leave at first light. Thank you again. Your sacrifice means more than you know."

When the first signs of dawn cast streams of golden light across the mountains, Adelina woke. She rubbed her eyes, sat, then glanced at Sara who slept. Something seemed off about waking a dying woman from her final sleep to be taken to a god to be sacrificed. Instead of debating the morality of what she needed to do, she focused on her mission. She'd be giving this woman a peaceful death—better than what she could've hoped for in her village—and in return, she'd be granted the enchanted obsidian from Perun.

While Adelina munched on her foraged foods, Sara stirred. Rubbing her eyes with the back of her hands, Sara struggled to sit up. Her eyelids drooped, and her hair hung limp around her face.

"Are you okay?" Adelina's good-natured side couldn't resist asking, despite it being a stupid question.

"As good as one can be on their deathbed." Sara laughed breathlessly. "Pass over some berries...might as well eat before I meet the gods."

Nodding, Adelina handed her half a dozen wild strawberries. "When you're ready, we'll make a move."

After a while of watching Sara laboriously eat, she helped her onto the saddle. This time, she didn't mount but guided the horse with the reins.

"We'll only be able to go so far by horse," Adelina said. "When we reach the tallest peak, we'll have to climb the rest by foot."

"How do you...expect me to do that?" Sara asked—her body slumped forwards.

"I'll carry you."

"A fair maiden such as yourself...carry me up a mountain?" Sara said. "Aren't I lucky."

Adelina didn't respond, but instead, considered the inevitable array of emotions she'd likely experience in the coming hours. All she could pray for, and hope for, was that Sara kept her wits until the end.

Keep going. You can do this. I'm with you every step of the way. It wasn't Damir's voice inside her head, but the words she imagined him saying brought her comfort. A warmth burst from her chest. It would all be worth it.

"So, tell me about this husband of yours," Sara said, jolting Adelina from her thoughts. "Might as well…share a good tale…before I die."

"You should stop talking. Conserve your energy," Adelina said at first, then obliged. "We were wed recently. We arranged it so I could escape Filip's clutches."

"Do you love him?" Sara asked, ignoring her instruction to remain quiet.

"Of course. Very much so." The words left Adelina's mouth with unwavering certainty. "We were childhood friends."

"A perfect match." Sara smiled, which Adelina caught as she glanced over her shoulder. "You must miss him."

"Deeply." Every fibre of Adelina's body ached with the loss of her husband. She didn't know how long it would take to obtain the Sword of Light, and what she might face when she finally went to rescue him from the palace. Blinking back tears, she focused—it wasn't the right time to be overcome with emotion.

"I didn't wish to upset you," Sara managed, as she cleared her throat. "I'm sorry."

"Don't be." Adelina cleared her own throat, trying to rid herself of the firm lump lodged there. "You have done me and many others a great service by coming here."

The path steepened. Stones and boulders dotted the craggy cliffs. Shale and scree shifted underfoot as they made their way up the incline. Slate and pebbles covered the ground, and sparse trees lined with bits of moss marked the slope. Clouds hung low, blanketing the mountain tops in mist, and a narrow waterfall poured into a nearby ravine. Adelina made a mental note to stop there later when she'd need to fill her flask.

The odd bit of snow piled in shadowy spots, which brightly reflected the sunlight poking through gaps in the clouds. An eagle squawked as it flew overhead.

"Peaceful," Sara muttered.

Adelina glanced at her—the elderly woman slipped from the saddle.

"Whoa!" Adelina bolted to her side, grabbing her as she fell from the horse. The sudden jolt sent nearby rabbits darting into the shrubbery.

Kneeling, Adelina shifted Sara's weight into her arms. She attempted to lift her, but her calf muscles screamed in dispute. "Gods damn it."

Sara, unconscious, was practically dead weight in Adelina's grip. She hooked her arm under Sara's, then dragged her along the path.

"It's not very dignified," Adelina said, "but I'm not strong enough."

Of course, she was not given a response.

Each breath was laboured as Adelina hoisted Sara towards the top of the peak. She focused on the scent of pine needles and earthy moss, determined to ignore the burning sensation in her limbs.

By the time she reached the halfway point up the slope, she collapsed, almost toppling onto Sara's limp body. Adelina's lungs burned as she gobbled down brisk air, turning her throat raw. She grabbed her flask and gulped the water in a desperate attempt to soothe the fire in her oesophagus.

Panting, Adelina checked Sara's pulse. Alive, but barely. Grabbing the woman by the arms, Adelina let out a scream as she hoisted Sara up, her dead weight sagging against her chest. Staying in a lowered position, Adelina dragged her still body, bit by bit up the incline, stones sliding beneath her feet. Nonetheless, she dug the balls of her feet in, curling her toes inside her boots to keep her grip.

Adelina's spine barked in protest as she neared the top. Sweat streamed down her temples, and her hair clung to her face and neck. As she gripped the unyielding stone, grit drifted into her face as she threw Sara onto the flat peak. Crashing to her knees, Adelina wheezed. Her slight frame meant she was not built for heavy loads, especially not on such a steep incline.

Scrambling to her feet, she lifted her gaze to the dense clouds. "What now?"

Turning, she focused her attention on Sara, who slumped against the rocky ground. Adelina knelt beside her, then cradled her head, propping it into her lap. She stroked the matted hair out of the unconscious woman's face.

Sara stirred. "What in...the realm?"

"You fell from the horse, and I carried you up here. Well, dragged, but I don't suppose you mind." Adelina's voice was thin, overcome with emotion as she held the dying woman in her embrace. This was harder than she'd expected. "Look up."

Sara's hollow gaze lifted from Adelina's face to the sky. Her chest rose and fell with each breath.

A Ballad of Severed Souls

If Adelina could do one kindness for this woman as she made her journey into the arms of the gods, she'd do it.

Lifting her dominant hand, she swirled it through the icy air. Magic flowed through her body, coating each fibre and nerve ending. "*Areiras nielasnal.*"

Just like she'd stopped the storm and harnessed the sun while she was at sea, her magic dispersed the clouds, if only a fraction, and a bolt of brilliant, golden sunlight streamed through. Sara's face was drenched in the bright light. An eagle circled above.

"You will be with your family soon," Adelina managed, fighting against the burning in her eyes.

"My family…we lived on a farm…a field of golden wheat." Sara's voice was thin, almost lost on the wispy breeze.

A shot of pain jolted through Adelina's chest. Adelina had lied about taking Sara to a farm, had offered her a form of peace without knowing what it would've meant to her.

"A field of gold like the sun." Adelina stroked Sara's cheek tenderly. "They're waiting for you with open arms in the realm of all gods."

"I see them…" Sara's lips tilted ever so slightly, before her final breath fluttered from her pale lips. The light faded from her blue eyes.

Adelina closed Sara's eyes with her fingers, then closed her own, holding Sara close against her body. A tear rolled down her cheek. Silence enveloped them as Adelina's spell ended and the clouds cast out the light.

A few still beats passed before a low rumble ripped through the air. The wind whipped wildly, flapping Adelina's hair around her face. Several strides ahead of her, a groan rose from the rocky ground, and a stone pillar punctured the surface.

Laying Sara's head on the ground, she wandered to the pillar. Hovering in the centre, was a small, black stone. Glancing around, she saw no sign of the god she'd come to meet. Yet here it was—the enchanted obsidian.

"Do you want me to take it?" she asked the empty space surrounding her, unsure whether she should expect a response from Perun.

She stilled, her arms locked at her side, but her gaze on the stone. "I did what you required. A sacrifice. You have presented the stone to me, so I assume you deem me pure of soul."

The wind stirred, whipping into a form standing a foot away from the pillar on the opposite side. Faceless, but a form, nonetheless.

"Perun?" Adelina squeaked. "Is that you?"

Slowly, the parts of his body took form. Bright white eyes, matching the colour of his long beard and hair. Thick muscles, large hands. A metal helmet carved into the shape of angel wings. A chest plate etched with gold.

"Name yourself," his voice boomed, jolting her.

"Er…Adelina Orlova," she muttered. "Sir."

"You seek the Sword of Light," Perun, God of thunder, justice, and war, declared.

"Yes," Adelina barely managed the words—her gaze was fixed—no, absorbed—by the towering god in front of her. He was triple the size of her, rising high into the air.

"Take the stone." Perun gestured to the swirling black obsidian floating above the pillar.

A Ballad of Severed Souls

Adelina flicked a cautious glance at the god, then stretched her hand. The stone was smooth against her skin as she wrapped her fingers around it.

"That's it?" she asked hesitantly.

"I would not have presented myself if you were not worthy." His stern gaze fixed on her, unwavering.

"Right." She cleared her throat. "Thank you."

She turned to leave, unsure what else to say to a god, but her gaze dropped to Sara's still form on the ground, exposed to the elements, with no proper grave.

"She is with us now," Perun said in a softer tone, perhaps noticing Adelina's reluctance to leave Sara.

"Tell her I'm grateful. Truly." Adelina fought to keep her voice strong as the events of the day took a toll on her, pulling her heartstrings in every which way.

FIFTEEN

Aldercrown

Wind rustled the leaves of oak trees as Adelina rode through the forest near the eastern coast of Toichrist. Having left the Salken Mountains a week ago, she was on her way to finding Uldan Island. According to her map, it was off the northeast coast, but it would be another week of travel before she reached the docks.

The floral scent of windflowers mixed with the earthy smell of decomposing leaves and rotting wood. Branches scraped at her cloak as she wandered along the path's edge, plucking berries from between thorns. Her horse snorted behind her.

A river wound through the forest, and up ahead, Adelina spotted a frothy cascade of water filling into a plunge pool. Rocky outcroppings and lush grass lined the base of the waterfall. As she drew nearer, the vibrant green hue of lichen and moss reflected brightly in the water droplets splashed onto its blue-green surface. At the top of the waterfall, trees roots gripped the ledges.

She led her horse to the water's edge, where it bent to drink. Once she'd filled her flask, she guided her horse by the reins along the trodden path dotted with leaves and acorns.

On the outskirts of the forest facing out to sea, she sat against a tree trunk and munched on her berries and leftover rabbit meat from the night before. From her position, she kept a clear line of sight to the ocean. On the wind, the taste of salt carried. She swigged a gulp of water to rid the sharp flavour from her palette. As the sun dipped closer to the horizon, the temperature of the wind whipping across the ocean and through the trees dropped.

Tugging her cloak around her, she rose, then meandered to her horse, who grazed on a patch of grass. It wouldn't be long before the forest came to life with the orange glow of fireflies and the distant hoot of owls.

As she began her usual routine of setting up camp, a low rumble rippled through the forest, rustling branches and trees. Nesting birds shot from the canopy, darting into the sky.

Midway through gathering sticks for a fire, she halted. She decided she must've been hearing things, for all that surrounded her was the song of birds.

Once she stacked the branches and lit the fire, she set the snares around the campsite. Another rumble. She jolted, facing the direction of the sound. Under the dim light of the flames and the distant fireflies, she could've sworn a tree root moved.

Abandoning her task, she wandered to the large oak tree ahead of her. Its roots twisted in and out of the soil, and its trunk towered above her.

"Just a tree," she whispered to herself as she spun around.

The soil beneath her feet cracked and vibrated.

Jumping, she swivelled, fixing her gaze on the roots. They *were* moving—ripping through the ground, the trunk rising high above her.

Rubbing her eyes, she stared, dumbfounded, at the tree who literally grew legs in front of her.

"What in the realm…" she said on an intake of breath.

Amber eyes opened three quarters of the way up the trunk, sending a flash of fear through her core. She stumbled backwards.

The tree is alive...the tree is alive...

The tree thing bent, its expanse of green leaves shaking around what she presumed to be its head. "Who are you?" His deep voice boomed, vibrating her core.

She fell onto her buttocks, and her horse bucked behind her, tugging on its tied reins. All words escaped her. What *could* she say to a talking tree? She might know magic, but she'd been oblivious to the living forest. Did that mean others were too?

She put her questions aside, rose to her feet and stood her ground. Holding her palms in front of her to show she meant no harm, she cleared her throat. "Adelina Orlova."

"And what brings you to Aldercrown, Adelina Orlova?" The tree straightened its trunk spine, then used two lower branches, which acted as arms, to ruffle the full canopy of leaves atop its head. Loose twigs and fronds fell to the floor—one landed on her scalp.

"Aldercrown?" She arched a brow, unable to keep her gaze from wandering across the tree thing's body. A bird nested in a hole halfway along the trunk, seemingly undisturbed by its moving, talking habitat.

"The home of Treefolk." He glanced at the other trees. "Not all are alive, but we few who are...Aldercrown is ours."

"Are you magical?" Although a part of her knew she should be concerned about this new, unfamiliar creature in her presence, she couldn't ignore the lulling sensation wrapping around her like a fuzzy blanket.

"We are but one being of magic." His voice reverberated, rippling the nearby trees and shrubberies. "Are you not one yourself?"

"Well, yes," she said, almost at a loss for words. "I've not seen your kind before. Come to think of it, I've never even heard of you."

Thick bark above his amber eyes moved, imitating the action of knitting brows. "And for good reason. Only those who possess light magic can enter the forest of Aldercrown. An ancient charm protects the Treefolk clans from dark sorcerers."

The hairs on her neck stood on end as her mind wandered to Filip, his father, and whoever the nether wielders were before them.

"Does this have anything to do with the Great War of the Wielders?" she said.

"It has everything to do with it." The Treefolk lowered his hand to the ground, held his palm open, and nodded. "Hop on. I shall show you Aldercrown as I tell you our story."

"Y-you trust me?" She hesitated—her gaze locked on his thick, trunk-like fingers.

"You are an astral wielder, no? A form of light magic. The people of the forest trust you even if they do not know you," he said.

She swallowed, stepping onto the uneven, barky surface of his palm. In one fell swoop, he lifted her several feet into the air. Her stomach flipped.

With his free hand, he plucked her luggage from the horse's saddle. As his footsteps thundered through the forest, drowning out the flow of water and nearby critters, he tilted his chin to look at her. "During the time of the Great War of the Wielders, the astral sorcerers were all but wiped out. Many lived in fear."

"They put their magic in talismans for safe keeping," she said, recalling the passage about it in her book.

"Yes, but before they did, they protected Aldercrown, so the Treefolk could not be used as a pawn by those who hungered for power," he said.

"Nether wielders." Coldness swept over her body as she imagined an army of nether wielders plundering the forest. Such thoughts raised an important question. "Forgive my ignorance, but how did they use you? You are large, mighty creatures."

The Treefolk chuckled. "There was a time when many nether wielders joined forces—such a significant amount of power is more than enough to overcome clans of the forest. And with the help of the astral wielders they'd enslaved—"

"They were at their strongest." The realisation hit Adelina like a sledgehammer. She wondered if this was part of Filip's plan to control the three countries.

"The charm stops us from being exposed to such otherworldly magic. *Dark* magic." The Treefolk shuddered, sending loose leaves spiralling to the ground around them. "We were almost brought to extinction. The last few decades under concealment have given us time to thrive once again."

She smiled, his deep words replacing the chill in her bones with a comforting warmth. "You have a beautiful home."

"It is. Yet we live in fear of what may come. Filip is a powerful man and if he finds you…" The Treefolk cast her a sideways glance.

"But there is only one of him. Even if he captured me, the two of us wouldn't be strong enough to repeat what happened in the War." She frowned.

"One can never be too sure." The Treefolk carried her to a clearing. A jagged cliff overlooked a dramatic waterfall plummeting into the ocean beyond. "After all, he is a demon."

"Wait." She spun to face him, peeling her gaze from the natural view. A sudden cold sensation swept through her core, and her skin tingled with discomfort. Time slowed, tick ticking, until it halted altogether. That singular word echoed in her head, causing a throbbing in her temple. She grinded her teeth as she fought to pull herself together. If this was true, she'd need all the information she could get. "Did you say demon? I read Antanov Tarasov was a shapeshifter—a demon. He's Filip's father, isn't he?"

"Yes." The Treefolk blinked, and his bulky eyes remained closed for a few seconds before they opened. "If Filip has you in his possession, he will not need a dozen other nether wielders. All it takes is for him to tread into the darkness, sink into the underworld, and bring his demons back with him."

"I won't let him hurt you," she said at once, overcome by a strong urge to protect this harmless Treefolk. "What is your name?"

He laughed. "We do not have names in Aldercrown, little one. But...you may call me Ironpine."

She smiled. "Ironpine. It suits you. How did you choose it?"

"It is the name of my clan." He gestured to the wandering trees on the other side of the waterfall. "They are my family."

"I'll do everything I can to protect you from Filip," she promised. "I'm headed to Uldan to retrieve the *Alatyr*—father to all stones. This will be fitted into the pommel of the Sword of Light."

Ironpine raised his crooked eyebrow. "It sounds most enchanting. I shall take you to the coast. There is a boat, and you can continue your search for this...Alatyr."

"Thank you." At ease, she lowered herself into a seated position in his hand as he continued the journey around the body of water, and through his home in Aldercrown.

The sun began to set, and her eyelids were heavy. She slumped against the ridges of his hand, falling closer to sleep.

She jolted.

"What is it, little one?" he said as softly as a giant tree could.

"What about my horse?" She widened her eyes.

His amber eyes sparkled with what she deemed as amusement. "He will not stray too far. Animals tend to like it here."

Nodding, she nestled into his palm, dragging her knees to her chest in the foetal position, and closed her eyes. His thick fingers curled around her, shielding her from the sharp, evening winds of the north.

By morning, they'd reached the northern edge of Aldercrown. Ironpine knelt near the coast, then lowered his hand to the ground.

"It is time for you to leave, little one." He nodded to the boat at the dock.

"Thank you, Ironpine." She hopped onto the dirt path. "I will see you again soon."

"There's one more thing," he said with a smile.

"Yes?"

He raised his hand to a hole in his chest, and with his forefinger, he scooped out her luggage. They were the size of stones in his mighty palm as he placed them next to her.

"Thank you," she said as she heaved the strap of her bag over her shoulder.

"Of course." He bowed his head. "You have made a friend in me, Adelina Orlova, astral wielder. Little one."

"I'll see you again soon." She smiled.

"And I'll see *you* from afar." He turned to leave, his footsteps booming as he retreated into Aldercrown.

Sand bars and descending slopes stretched ahead of her. Half-buried shells poked through the white sand. Caves and caverns lined the cliff edge, facing the ocean, and a singular wooden boat was fastened to a post at the beach dock.

Casting a glance over her shoulder, she wondered who it belonged to. There was no one in sight. She wasn't about to sit around and wait for someone to pop out and question her either—there was a mission to fulfil, and she'd deal with the consequences later.

She jogged along the pier, dropping into the boat, unfastened the rope tethering, then pushed out with her oar. The shoal bottom and sea grass were clear in the bright water, but as she rowed out to sea, darker spots formed as shafts of light filtered down. She was lucky Uldan Island wasn't more than half an hour's row from the beach.

A variety of coral waved in the current, which leaked into limestone trenches. Octopi slid among the rocks and across the floor, and as the sea deepened, the life below was masked by drifting seaweed.

Lifting her gaze, she focused on the repetitious movement of rowing. Left. Right. Left. Right. Her breathing magnified as she maintained a steady rhythm. Even so, she couldn't ignore the burning sensation in her arms and the ache in her curved spine.

Having been focused on her rowing, she hadn't realised the gathering clouds. They'd gathered *too* quick. Dark, thick heavens threatened to burst with rain. Despite the island's beach being a short distance away, she couldn't afford to be caught in a storm at sea. Swimming wasn't one of her strengths. Being a village girl hadn't warranted the opportunity to ever learn the skill to any great degree. Despite the definition of her muscles, she couldn't trust her ability to swim to shore, fighting against a possible lethal undercurrent.

She shoved the thoughts aside, and kept her sight fixed on the solid ground in the distance.

When she approached shallow water, she dropped the oar, scrambled into the thigh deep ocean, then heaved the boat onto the pebble beach. Stones churned underneath as they scratched against the wooden underbelly.

From what she could see, Uldan Island was tiny—she could walk its circumference within an hour or two. Sandy white beaches stretched along the coast, palm trees leaned against each other, and lush undergrowth clustered at the bottom of their trunks.

There were no footprints in the wet sand, an indication people did not tend to venture to the island in the north. She wondered why—it's not like it was difficult to reach.

As she walked, she passed seashells and seaweed strewn along the sand, driftwood washed up on the shore, and stray coconuts dotted here and there.

In the centre of the island was a winding hill dense with trees, and somewhere in between, a waterfall sheeted down a rock wall. The soothing swish of waves lulled her, removing any sense of caution she should have. Birds cawed overhead as they nestled in the trees, and palm fronds scraped together in the slight breeze.

Jodie Angell

The sun bore heavy against her skin, and as she entered the forest, she welcomed the relief brought by the shade. Flies buzzed around her head, insects hummed and chirped in the undergrowth. Even as she walked farther away from the beach, the taste of salt water lingered on her tongue.

Her stomach rumbled. When has she last eaten? Instantly in need of food, she scanned her surroundings. The loose coconuts wouldn't do—she hadn't anything to crack through the tough exterior. She spotted a tree up ahead, sporting bright orange fruits. Dashing to it, she plucked one from a branch, then turned it over in her hand.

"How long it's been since I've seen an apricot," she gasped before sinking her teeth into the fruit. She moaned with delight.

Apricots didn't thrive on the Hastehill Isles because the weather was too extreme in the south, but *here* on Uldan Island, the heat was warm enough for the tree to prosper, but not strong enough to kill it.

Unfastening her cloak, she plopped a bunch of apricots inside, holding her garment like a bag. It would do nicely if she were to find any other food along the way. Next on her list of things to do was to follow the sound of running water, and hope to the gods it was fresh.

Keeping her hearing attuned to the rippling water, she meandered between dense trees and foliage, across uneven ground, and to the grassy bank edging a shallow stream. Rocks created drifting along the sun-dappled surface. Kneeling, she cupped her hands, then lowered them into the stream.

Here goes.

Lifting them to her face, she drank. Cool, fresh liquid slid down her throat, relieving her of a sandpaper texture.

Damn it.

She realised she'd left her flask with her baggage, having been too distracted by Ironpine to notice or prioritise.

Rising, she headed to a bush with large, splayed leaves. Ripping one from its stem, she turned on her heel and returned to the bank.

Using the leaf as a cup, she drank until satisfied. With nothing else in her possession to use as a flask or drinking tool, she placed the leaf with the apricots inside her folded cloak.

As she followed the wounding path up the hill, she recalled the passage about Uldan Island.

"The sorcerer is required to give blood to the World Tree, and in turn, they will receive Alatyr—father to all stones. Such a stone is endowed with healing and magical properties. It must be fitted into the sword's pommel."

It wasn't a lot to go by—where exactly *was* the World Tree in this place? She hoped she was heading in the right direction. To her, it made sense such an important tree would stand out from all the others, so surely, it would be somewhere near the top. And obvious.

A while later, she reached a break in the trees, and at the peak, the ground levelled. The dirt and grass were dry from exposed sunlight, but in front of her stood a towering tree, its roots weaving in and out of the mud like talons, journeying right to her toes.

From her position, it almost seemed like the tree glowed. A golden hue emanated from the trunk, branches, even the green mass of leaves shrouding it.

She edged closer. In front of the trunk was a stone pillar, similar to what she'd found on the highest peak of the Salken Mountains. Around the base of the tree were stones and fallen twigs.

With no blade or sharp weapon on her person, she knelt and gripped a jagged stone. With her wrist held above the pillar, she sucked in a deep breath and dragged the sharp edge across her skin, drawing blood. She winced, shaking the blood until it dripped onto the surface.

Tearing a piece of cloth from her shirt, she wrapped it around her wound and tied it in place. She waited for her blood to do something—call upon the gods, fizz and pop from magic, any sign to suggest she'd been granted the Alatyr.

A harsh wind whipped across the island, rattling the trees, and in the distance, large waves stirred in the ocean. Clouds darkened above her, threatening to unload a storm. A brisk chillness swept past her, sending a shiver shooting down her spine. Her bare arms prickled with gooseflesh, and she fought the urge to abandon her picked fruit and sling the cloak back around her.

Instead, she gritted her teeth and waited for the mystical stone to appear. Her blood had already soaked into the stone pillar and disappeared—something like that wouldn't happen to any ordinary pillar, or in front of any ordinary tree. Right?

The ancient roots of the World Tree moved, like claws pulling themselves up through the ground. She jumped back, avoiding each tendril as they whipped into the air. Falling, she watched as the roots spun, whipping the air into a tornado around her—she wasn't sure it wouldn't grow legs and walk like the Treefolk.

One root gripped her, forcing a high-pitched yelp from her throat as it lifted her high into the air. She clung onto it for dear life as she hurtled through the sky, the root drawing her nearer to the towering trunk. The base of the tree raised, revealing a shaft travelling deep into the ground. Wide-eyed, she braced herself for the plummet.

The root threw her into the tunnel, and the sunlight behind her was swallowed as the tree repositioned itself. Sliding deeper underground, she whizzed past twigs, leaves, and what might've been bugs in her hazy vision.

She soared off a ledge, and her stomach lurched as she landed on her buttocks at the bottom. Heart hammering, she grunted and scrambled to her feet. High arched ceilings of rock surrounded her. Shafts of light slipped in through the tree roots acting as a ceiling to this strange, magical grotto. Moss and lichen were dotted here and there, and the smooth rock walls were worn by water trickling from the ground above. Stalagmites hung from the curved rocks intertwined in the ceiling.

Barnacles and small fish lived in the body of water in the centre of the grotto, directly underneath the trunk of the World Tree. Silt stirred underfoot, muddying the water, and dead leaves and debris had worked its way underground, either from above or through the tunnel she'd flown through.

Water droplets pattered onto the surface from the stalagmites, and crumbles of rocks dislodged underfoot as she wandered the length of the grotto. The strong scent of mildew filled her nose.

Using the strands of golden light filtering in from above, she made her way across the loose stones. Ahead of her, she spotted one stone dazzling even in the reduced light. It hovered, floating alongside dust particles dancing in the golden stream of sunlight.

A guttural roar rumbled from the shadows. She jolted, scanning her surroundings, every inch of her body urging her to *get out*. Something pawed the ground, scraping the stones, dried leaves, and twigs. Without hesitation, she conjured her golden whip, the twirling embroidery-like magic dancing around her wrist, singeing the skin beneath.

Ignoring the sting, she held her arm out in a defensive position. Aside from her panting, silence engulfed her. Like a predator hunting its prey. Adelina refused to be *anything's* prey.

The beast lunged from the darkness. Her back was slammed into the ground before she could blink, the creature pinning her beneath its mighty paws. She would've thought it a wild dog or wolf if it wasn't for the festering darkness swirling in its eyes. Whatever animal this was, it wasn't natural. Her assessment was stifled by a blaze of pain firing up her arm as sharp claws dragged through her flesh. She screamed.

Pushing through the blinding pain, she covered her face with her limbs like a blockade, pushing back against the snapping jaws. The golden whip drove the beast partially off her, sparks of fire slashing into its snout and cheeks. It growled, tossing its head from side to side. Using it to her advantage, she shoved hard, tossing the weight off her. Within a heartbeat, she was on her feet, prowling towards the creature.

A Ballad of Severed Souls

Where had it come from? Who'd conjured this monstrosity?

She didn't have time to consider the particulars. Instead, she took in every detail of the large hound, scanning it for weak spots. Its towering body was covered in thick black fur, draped over hard, defined muscles. That, combined with two-inch claws that could possibly disembowel her and the sharp canines, made it a worthy—and challenging—opponent.

Shaking out her limbs, she straightened her spine, keeping one foot in front of the other as she circled the beast, maintaining a healthy distance from its paws and jaws. She couldn't afford to be trapped underneath it again; she wouldn't survive it a second time. With a quick glance at her magic, she supposed now was as good a time as any to put its velocity to the test. She uncurled it like a lasso. It hit the stony ground with a sharp thud, sparks of fire erupting from it. The beast growled in response as it dived out of the way.

Sucking in a breath, she went on the offensive, luring the creature towards her as she walked backwards to the grotto wall. It curled back its lips, baring its canines.

She grinned, baring her own teeth, and lashed out her magic. The whip struck true. Black blood sprayed from the neck as the severed head hit the floor. Blinking rapidly, she could do nothing but watch as the animal—and its blood—vanished. *Vanished.*

She swore. "A ward. You have got to be kidding me."

Despite the creature's disappearance, the injury to her arm remained. Tearing a strip of cloth from her shirt, she wrapped it tightly around the wound, gritting her teeth through the pain. She'd need to assess it properly to determine whether it needed stitches, but first, the stone. She wasn't going to leave empty-handed.

Taking careful steps towards the hovering stone, she reached for it. She wrapped her fingers around it, and a bolt of warmth shot through her hand, up her arm, and overwhelmed her body.

Dropping to her knees, she cradled the stone against her chest, waiting for the paralysing heat to subside. She clamped her eyes shut, forcing herself to breathe deeply through the uncomfortable pain. Spots swarmed her vision, and her limbs grew limp and weak.

A few moments later, she opened her eyes. She frowned. When did she lie down? She didn't remember. Glancing at her palms, she uncurled her fingers, revealing the glistening stone within her grasp. There it was. The Alatyr. She was one step closer to obtaining the Sword of Light. One step separated her from reaching the end of her mission. *'Cross the rocky terrain of the Svatken Peninsula and find the deepest cave.'*

No matter her determination, she couldn't move. It wouldn't hurt to sleep for a little while, would it? The mystical grotto would protect her from whipping winds and the threatening storm outside. She *did* need to sleep. As if the rocks underneath turned into a feather blanket, her body relaxed, and she closed her eyes.

A Ballad of Severed Souls

She stirred sometime later when the sunlight faded from the grotto. She'd need to find her way back to ground level soon if she didn't want to do it blind. Not only that, but pain radiated through her arm, and she needed to assess the injury. Clean it out and cauterise it if necessary. Scrambling to her feet, her vision tilted on its axis. She gripped the rocky wall for support, then headed for the tunnel. At least, if she crawled up it, she wouldn't worry about falling to the ground on the threat of fainting.

Grinding her teeth, she focused on the path ahead, forcing herself to remain conscious, no matter how much the pulsing, magical stone in her grasp threatened to throw her back under. She didn't understand the control it held over here but hoped it would wear off.

With her pulse pounding, she edged into the tunnel. On her hands and knees, she climbed towards the tree roots. They opened for her like a pair of curtains. Clambering out, she rose, feet on the ground above. She spotted her cloak—she'd dropped it earlier when the roots had thrown her underground—and grabbed it. The leaf was a little crumpled and the apricots flattened, but they were edible.

Placing the Alatyr stone inside her pocket, she made the descent to the beach. Focusing all her energy on the last part of her mission—making it to the Svatken Peninsula—she charged ahead. It seemed, with the stone out of her direct hand contact, it held less control over her consciousness, so using it to her advantage, she could centre on her objective.

I can do this. I'm one step away from getting my hands on the Sword of Light. From there, I can save Damir, my family, and everyone else threatened by Filip. I'll put a stop to him, and he won't threaten anyone else ever again.

She homed in on her thoughts of encouragement and threw herself into the boat, rowing with as much determination as she could muster. The image of Damir's face appeared in front of her like a vision. She smiled, overcome by a warmth spreading through her entire body—as if he were right there with her.

"I'm coming," she said aloud.

Adelina's injury wasn't to the bone, to her relief. Before climbing back into the boat, she'd cleaned the wound with water from her flask, wrung out her makeshift bandages to clean it as much as she could, then tied it awkwardly with one hand. She prayed she would not be hindered by infection. When she finally reached the north-eastern shoreline of Toichrist, Ironpine awaited her. Body aching from the strenuous trip, she all but collapsed into his lowered palm.

With a warm smile, he lifted her into the air.

"Look up," he said. "You'll have a wonderful view of the sunset from here."

Peering over the tip of his curved thumb, she rubbed her tired eyes. Moments later, they widened. Deep orange on the horizon cast a glow over the rippling ocean. Further into the sky, purple transitioned into midnight blue, and beyond, stars twinkled. With no light pollution from burning torches or nearby villages, the stars were bright and vibrant, like diamonds stitched into fabric.

"Beautiful." She swallowed a yawn.

He chuckled. "Sleep, little one. I will take you to my clan in Aldercrown. Your horse and belongings are safe—you can ride tomorrow."

Knowing she'd be no use when overcome with exhaustion, she nodded and curled into a ball in the palm of his hand. The deep sound of his heavy footsteps lulled her to sleep.

The sound of songbirds flittered through the trees and stirred Adelina from her slumber. She grumbled, stretched, and gazed at her dark surroundings.

"What the…" She frowned.

Sunlight streamed through the hole in the…what was it? A trunk?

"Ironpine?" she called. "Did I sleep…inside you?"

"Warm in there, isn't it?" His deep chuckle vibrated the trunk in which she rested.

"Um, I guess so." She shrugged, although knowing he wouldn't see it. "Can you get me out, please?"

She peered through the hole, spotting his palm upright in front of her. Hopping out, she landed in his hand, then swirled to face him. "Thank you."

"Ready for some breakfast?" He wiggled his brows.

"Sure," she said. "Although, what do you eat? You're a tree. No offence."

"None taken," he said. "We don't need to eat, but you, on the other hand, do."

Her stomach rumbled. She'd snacked on her apricots in the middle of the night, but that wasn't a substantial meal.

Placing her on the ground, Ironpine gestured towards a crooked firepit—a goofy grin tugging at the corner of his bark lips.

"You made a fire?" A warmth burst through her chest. This person—if one could call a Treefolk such a thing—had accommodated her: a human.

"Such a task is challenging when I have large fingers." He lifted his hand, each digit bulky and covered with moss. "I knocked it over at least a dozen times, and I swore more than I wish to reveal, but the fire cooked some meat for you. Humans eat meat, right?"

She nodded. "Thank you."

Eagerly, she hopped towards the makeshift skewers of meat. She didn't comment on the fact the *whole* rabbit was impaled on the branch, with half of its skin attached.

Nearby was a pool of standing water. Lily pads floated on the pond's surface, reeds and long grasses poked out the top, and a mixture of dandelions, daisies, and clover blooms grew along the edge. The muddy bank was strewn with rocks and pebbles, broken branches lay half in the water next to floating leaves, and frogs leaping into the shallows.

She smiled, each of her muscles relaxing as a wave of calm washed through her. Her gaze rested on the birds bathing and preening, and the rustle of leaves on the nearby trees removed any sense of urgency she should've possessed.

"It's peaceful, isn't it?" Ironpine said, breaking her from her trance.

"Yes," she breathed. "Very. I can understand why you would want to protect the forest as much as yourselves from harm. I couldn't imagine anyone wanting to harm this place."

"Unfortunately, that did happen, as you know." He sighed. "We are protected now, though, and as long as you stay out of Filip's clutches, it'll remain so."

She nodded sharply. Although the scent of wild mint and sweet clover encouraged her to stay at the pond's edge forever, she shifted her attention back to her mission.

"I'll eat, then I must be on my way. I have everything I need to forge the Sword of Light." She grasped the roasted rabbit, then tore a leg from the body. She needed to line her stomach before moving on.

"You will find your horse and belongings in the glade five minutes from here." He pointed to a fork between the trees. "But before you go, there is something you should always remember. Keep these words close to your heart, for when times get dark, and you lose your way. You are not a slave, Adelina. You are not, and never will be, enslaved to Filip. Everything you are, your power, is opposite of everything *he* is. Where your magic is natural and wondrous, his is cruel and unpredictable. Violent at times. Never forget those differences. I must go now, little one. You will always have a friend in me."

A bubble of emotion welled inside her, threatening to leak tears from her eyes. Indeed, she tucked his words somewhere safe and secure inside her. For when she needed them. "Thank you for your kindness, Ironpine. I'll see you again soon."

He bowed as graciously as a solid tree could before thundering through the forest, the canopy of leaves around his head blending into the sea of trees around him.

SIXTEEN

Sword of Light

Venturing into the mainlands of Toichrist, Adelina rode to the rocky terrain of the Svatken Peninsula. There, she'd find the caves. In the deepest cave, she'd be reunited with Svarog—the god who'd presented himself to her during the test.

As she approached the cluster of caves, she tried to determine which would be the right one. Some had smaller openings, which she ignored. Further along the track, she spotted a large swell in the mountainside.

She guided her horse through the opening, then dismounted. At least with the horse sheltered, they'd less likely be spotted by Filip's men should any be stationed nearby. Patting the horse on its hide, she scanned her new surroundings. Bumpy stone walls with fingerlings of tree roots growing through made up the structure of the cave. Dirt and dead leaves had been blown in by the wind. Faint tracks marked the dirt of some animal living there. Stalactites hung from the ceiling, and water dripped from cracks, pooling onto the dusty floor.

Venturing into the cave, she followed the passageway, which led her deeper underground. The wind whistled through breaches in the stone, and the skittering of what she assumed to be animal paws made her jump.

Swirling her fingers through the air, she produced an orb of orange light. It illuminated the crevices in the walls, and the water slick surfaces. She grimaced at the stench of stale air and stagnant water.

She slipped on a patch of wet rock, sliding into a tall boulder. Her heart slammed against her ribcage. Jamming her fingers into the fissures for handholds, she hoisted herself up and over the boulder blocking her narrow path. She bumped her head on the low ceiling in the dim lighting. Lifting her dusty covered hand, she prodded the injury on her crown.

"At least there's no blood." She sighed as she inspected her fingers.

Water dripped from a crack somewhere above her, then slid down her nape, making her shiver. She tugged her cloak tight around her.

Damir's face flashed in her mind—she jolted back into the rough, jagged wall. Her breath caught in her throat. This wasn't like her other visualisations of her husband. This time, it was tangible, as if he were real in front of her.

Clasping a hand over her mouth, tears prickled her eyes.

"Damir?" she whispered.

She focused all of her being, power, and will on the image. The walls of a prison came into view as if she'd been transported there. The prison bled into the peripheral of her vision, where it blended with her true surroundings in the cave. Her magic had seemingly given her a foothold in two areas at once. She'd worry about the logistics later. Right now, her concern was Damir.

Stretching an arm, she reached for him, but her fingers couldn't quite pierce the veil of the true distance between them. A shimmering surface separated them, like a window. She couldn't help him.

A thick lump formed in her throat and her chest tightened.

"Damir?" she asked again.

He said nothing.

Even though she'd known it impossible, she'd hoped he'd heard her. Instead, he remained slumped against the water-slick wall, his clothes caked with dirt.

Adelina's blood ran cold. A sickly sensation made her stomach somersault as she surveyed his pale face, sallow cheeks, and sunken eyes. His hair was matted, hanging limp around his face. There was no comfort in his cell, not even a bed of hay to sleep on.

"Perhaps she doesn't love you enough." The grating sound of Pyotr's voice dragged Adelina's attention to the bars. He leaned against it, arms casually draped through the gaps. What was *he* doing there? "I would've thought she'd have come for you by now. I know Adelina is close with her little sister,

Tihana. I'm sure *she* will be sufficient bait." A callous smile spread across his lips.

Damir ground out, "Don't touch her."

"As soon as we have her within our possession, you, on the other hand, will have outlived your use. I'm sure Filip will agree."

Footsteps drew nearer, thundering along the stone path.

"Speaking of which, he's come to join us," Pyotr said.

"I want an update," Filip said abruptly, without casting a glance in Damir's direction. His icy stare focused on Pyotr, who Adelina realised to be his accomplice.

"We've kept him here for weeks, and nothing. There is no sign of his wife. We must move our sights to Tihana," Pyotr said. "Adelina may have stayed away on her husband's order, but she will not refuse the calling to save her sister."

Filip nodded once. "Get it done. Kill him."

He turned on his heel, his black cloak flapping behind him, as he disappeared from the prison.

"No!" Adelina screamed, clawing at the veil separating her from her husband.

The image dissipated like dust in the wind, and she fell to her knees. Ignoring the hard crunch of stone beneath her kneecaps, she clamped her hands over her eyes and sobbed. She didn't understand how she'd been able to see events as they transpired. Her previous visions of Damir were more like memories than they were real, but this one shook her to her core.

There was no reason for Filip to show her false images, even if he was capable of doing so. She had no way of knowing when the conversation took place.

For all she knew, Damir could already be dead, and her sister held captive.

Her tears subsided, and in their absence, her eyes ached. Lowering her hands, a white-hot rage bubbled underneath the surface of her skin, spreading like wildfire through her veins. She dug her nails into the gritty floor and ground her teeth.

Rising, she charged deeper into the cave, overcome with a need to call upon Svarog. He'd chosen her for a reason, entrusted her with astral power, and she'd use every drop of it to save her sister and husband—if he lived. But a part of her knew Filip wouldn't hold back.

"Svarog!" she called—her voice echoing through the channels of the cave. "I have everything you need to make the Sword of Light."

Her words were met with silence.

"Svarog, *please*." Her body trembled as she scanned the dimly lit cave for the dragon.

Nothing but the sound of her own breath and the distant skitter of insects answered her. Unable to bear the deafening quiet cloaking her, she dropped to the gritty cave floor. With a half-hearted flick of her finger, she cast a golden orb to provide further light. She needed to rest. All she wanted to do was *rest*, to shut out the ache in her heart, the utter *helplessness* seizing her body. Without the Sword, she had no hope.

None at all.

Curling in her a ball, she closed her eyes and shut out the world.

Unaware of how much time had passed since she'd fallen asleep, Adelina pushed back the loose strands of hair from her face as she scrambled to her feet.

Swallowing her anger at being ignored by the god—she'd had no other choice but to believe it *was* ignorance, and he hadn't abandoned her for good—she sucked in a ragged breath, clamped her eyes shut, and steadied the thumping of her heart. After she'd counted to ten, she opened her eyes and injected as much patience as she could into her tone. "Please, Svarog. I need your help. You chose me for this, and while I may not understand the limitations of my powers, or can even begin to comprehend Filip's, I'm here. I'm ready to serve you, the innocent people of these countries, and my family. The Sword of Light is my only hope."

A bright, golden light drenched the jagged rocks and reflected in the pools of water. The almost translucent body of Svarog took form, his giant wings expanding the full width of the cave.

Fire blazed from his skin, illuminated the rows of red scales. He lowered his wings, curling them into his sides, and his tail wrapped around him. The fire reduced to a gentle glow.

"You came," she breathed. Every muscle in her body relaxed, the heavy load weighing on her shoulders lessened, and the ache in her heart dulled to a slight throb.

A Ballad of Severed Souls

"Yessss," he said in his hypnotic tone.

She hadn't seen him since the test a few months ago, and she'd forgotten how regal this dragon God was.

"I need your help," she repeated, flattening her hands against her legs. "We all do."

"You have the obssssidian?" He flicked his forked tongue out of the corner of his mouth.

"Yes, and the Alatyr." She drew them from the folds of her cloak, then stretched her hand. "It's everything you need."

"Sssso it issss." His voice was almost a whisper—a lullaby on the gentle whistle of wind through the cave. Her whole being calmed in his presence.

The dragon closed his beady eyes for a moment, and a golden shield popped out around him, spinning slowly on its axis. It expanded until she was in the dome with him. Beyond the veil of the golden dome, the cave walls were almost invisible.

The two stones burned in her palm. She dropped them and stumbled back, falling onto her coccyx, which sent a sharp jolt of pain up her the base of her spine. A cool breeze whipped around her, throwing her hair in every which way.

Clawing her hair back, she pushed onto her knees. Her gaze was transfixed on the dragon, God of the Sun. The sword's handle materialised, forming itself from magic—the obsidian rose from the ground and fixed itself into the pommel. Sparkling into existence, the blade expanded, glinting in the golden light. Finally, the Alatyr stone took flight, and fused itself with the glowing sword. A stream of white magic burst from the metal, all but blinding her.

Closing her eyes, she waited for the light to subside. When the brightness behind her eyelids dimmed, she opened her eyes. Hovering in front of her was the Sword of Light, and Svarog smiled.

"Usssse it well, Adelina Orlova," he said.

Tentatively, she stretched her hand, then wrapped her fingers around the pommel, its surface warm. A current shot up her arm and through her body. Dropping to her knees once again, she threw her head back as the same white light burst from her and illuminated the cave.

A strangled scream escaped her mouth as the magic set each of her nerve endings alight. Her body convulsed as if every inch of her skin burst with flames. Her vision blurred, black spots formed, and once the searing pain in her core dimmed, she fell forwards, crippled over the sword she held in her hands.

"You c-could have w-warned me."

"I mussst caution you," he said deeply, ignoring her prior scorn. "Thissss weapon issss powerful."

I was kind of relying on that.

"You mussst tread carefully," he continued. "For Filip will know."

"How?" she said, overlooking the jelly like sensation in her limbs.

"You are two halves of one soul," he said. "A part of both of you now lives inside this sword."

Lowering her glance, she stared at the engraving along the blade—a foreign language she couldn't understand.

"He will want it assss much assss you."

"Are you serious?" She scoffed. "After everything I've gone through to get this sword, you tell me he will want it? I made it easy for him to take it from me?"

"There issss much to tell you sssstill," he said—his voice as calm and soft as before.

"Tell me." She couldn't refrain from injecting a sense of urgency into her words.

"Assss you were the one to forge the sssword, it will only anssssswer to you for now. But the clossser you are to Filip, the more unpredictable itssss loyaltiessss will be."

"You have got to be kidding me." She laughed hysterically. "I need to save my sister *and* my husband—if he hasn't already been murdered. Many other lives hang in the balance, but now I cannot go near him?"

"There issss one other thing." His gaze lowered to the talisman around her neck. "Remove your necklacsssse. Let your magic free."

Her hand clasped the pendant. "This is the only thing ensuring I have control over my magic. If I take it off, I have no idea what could happen."

"The connectionssss you have with Filip meanssss you will alwayssss be each other's equal, thussss alwayssss looking for a way to be sssstronger than the other," he said. "You abssssorbed the magic from the pocket watch, did you not?"

"Yes, but...how did you know?" She arched a brow.

"I am a god." He grinned, revealing sharp teeth.

"You have the collected astral power of countlessss generations, and the Sssword of Light in your possession. But you cannot fathom your true capabilitiessss until you remove the one thing hindering you." Although he was tempting her into something she hadn't even considered, his voice remained soft and gentle. He was someone she could trust.

As if compelled to do so, she unfastened the talisman from around her neck, then placed it into her pocket. A chill shot down her spine, a welcome contrast to the blazing fire she'd previously endured.

"I hope you're right," she said. "I'm trusting in you, God of the Sun."

"And I am trusssssting you too, Adelina Orlova, wielder of astral power," he said.

As she turned on her heel, a memory resurfaced in her mind.

'Somewhere deep underground, enclosed away from the world by a river with deadly currents, the God known as Veles ruled.'

"Do you know much about Veles, God of the underworld?" she asked. "I read about it. Filip and his father are shapeshifters. Their souls were reborn in the real realm—the living realm—weren't they?"

Svarog lowered his head, and something flashed in his eyes. From the drooping lines forming around them, she determined it to be sadness. "Yessss."

"How?" A sickly, icy sensation rippled through her body, making her shiver. *'The entrance to the underworld was guarded by a Zmey—a dragon.'* "I don't understand. Why would Veles allow them to be reborn—what is their bigger purpose? And what about Zmey—the dragon guarding their lair? Surely, he wouldn't let them leave without a reason." She wrapped her arms around her, and her mouth dried. The threat loomed over her like a giant shadow, and she clung to the thought that she was the light.

"If I knew all the anssssswerssss, I wouldn't need a warrior." He tipped his scaled head towards her.

"Why did you choose me?" The question poured from her mouth without thought. "What is so special about a small-town girl? I was young, naïve, and held such small knowledge of the world. How could you be certain I would be good enough to become a wielder?"

"You have a pure heart," he said simply, as if there was no argument on the matter. "But I musssst clarify it is not as simple as me—or any God—choosing you. Before you were born, your ssssoul was but a twinkle of life waiting for a chancssssse to blosssssom. We do not undersssstand how or why, but wielderssssss are born one half of each other."

"Are you saying my life was predetermined? I already shared a soul with Filip before I was even born? How is it possible?" Her head pounded from the dozens of questions spinning inside her mind.

"Can we ever travel through time? Is thissss universssse the only one to exissssst? What exactly is a consssssciousnessss?" He smiled. "Thessssse are all big, unansssswered questionssssss."

"But you're a god. You know everything." She narrowed her eyes. "All the gods and goddesses we know, love, worship, or even hate—are you saying no one decided astral and nether wielders would be one half of the same soul? No one *chose* to link them?"

"While I may have exissssted for thoussssandssss of yearssss, I wassss not the beginning of time." He chuckled. "Inssssstead of focussssssing on riddlessss you may never solve, turn your attention to what you musssst do on behalf of the Godssss you love. For every light, there issss darknessss, and Filip is your darknessss. You musssst overcome him."

"He's going after my sister," she said through gritted teeth. "My astral powers let me see things. I'm not sure how, but I *saw* Filip and Pyotr. They were with Damir, and he looked exhausted. Filip ordered to have him killed and I don't know if he lives, or when the conversation took place, so he could have my sister already in his clutches."

"Try to reach out to them again through your powerssss," he suggested. "Let them guide you through thesssse dark timessss. You musssst go now, young warrior."

As soon as his last words left his mouth, the sparkling form dissipated.

"Wait. I still have questions." She stepped forwards, stretching a hand in front of her.

"Trusssst in yoursssself as we trusssst in you," he said—his voice whisper thin on the breeze.

He disappeared, and she was alone.

Filip relaxed into his chair, propped his elbows on the cushioned arms, then created a steeple with his fingers. He'd sent Pyotr and a dozen armed guards to capture Tihana, and in about four weeks, their carriage would come barrelling through the palace gates.

A burst of pain shot through his core. He jolted forwards, slamming his body into the table, almost knocking him out of his chair. His vision filled with

A Ballad of Severed Souls

black dots, and the world spun on its axis. Gripping onto the edge of the table, he fought to steady himself, not at all sure he wasn't about to collapse. What in the realm was going on?

The furniture in his office tapered into a fuzzy image in front of him. A vision formed. He rubbed his eyes, forcing his gaze to focus on the scene materialising. Adelina.

He jumped to his feet, then stumbled backwards. Every muscle in his body turned to jelly, aching and throbbing from the earlier burst of pain.

Supporting himself against the wooden desk, he watched as she held a golden, glowering sword in her hands. Her surroundings were dark. Where was she?

Fighting against the dizziness flooding through his body, he forced one foot in front of the other as he stepped around the desk. Stretching his hand, reached for her, but his fingers fell through the empty space between them. Scanning the vision, he sought something—anything—to hint at her location. But the shadows cloaked her.

The image dissolved, and when the ache in his body subsided to a dull throb, he arched a brow.

Well, that was new.

His train of thought shifted to the weapon she'd wielded. A strange sensation urged him towards his shelf of personal books. Wrapping his fingers around the spine, he drew his copy of *A Practitioner's Guide to Ancient Magic, Astral Edition, Volume I* positioned beside its partner for nether magic.

Flipping through the book, he halted on a blank page. Strange. From his knowledge of magic, charms and spells were only cloaked if they were of significant importance. And to *his* advantage, he had experience with such wards. It took him a matter of minutes to solve the pitiful riddle, and ink materialised on the parchment. The Sword of Light.

"Huh," he breathed. "This has got a whole lot easier."

He carried the book back to his desk, then settled into his chair, keeping his gaze fixed on the writing—a guide Adelina must've followed in order to obtain the sword. She'd gotten her hands on the one thing that would've given her an advantage against him, but *he* knew such a powerful weapon possessed a mind of its own. It was loyal to its wielder, and if he could take possession of it, no one would ever challenge him again.

Four weeks later, Adelina clutched the horse's reins in a white-knuckle grip as she approached the eastern entrance to the city of Kirovo. By then, her wound had healed, leaving a faint scar in its place. Sooner or later, it would likely fade. Running her teeth along her lower lip, she searched her brain for a logistical way in which she'd find her husband and sister and get them both to safety. She couldn't dwell on the idea he may be dead, and the gods only knew what condition Tihana could be in. The thought of anyone arming a single hair on her sister's dainty head shot waves of heat through her body.

A sharp pain rippled through her lip as her teeth punctured the soft skin. A drop of blood slid against her tongue, coating it in its iron taste. Loosening her grip on the reins, she fought to swallow her anger. She needed to remain focused and devise a plan before reaching the palace. If she could reach the servants' entrance, she could find Natasha, have her convince the other staff she was a newly employed maid. But even dressed in the proper uniform, her face would be recognisable by guards passing by, and certainly Filip if he were near.

Flinging herself off the horse, she guided it towards the market. Rummaging in her pocket, she drew her pouch and poured the remaining coins into her palm. She used them to purchase a pair of scissors and round wire-rim glasses. Tucking the items into her pocket, she headed to the closest tavern, her chin tilted to the ground, and the hood of her cloak up. The hem of the fabric hung below her brow.

Once she'd hobbled her horse, she entered the tavern, weaving her way between patrons. A musician played a violin, providing the evening's entertainment, and keeping unwanted gazes from her. Using it to her advantage, she hurried along the back wall, towards the restroom at the other end. Through the wooden door, she slipped into the stone-built structure and thanked the gods no one else was inside.

The restroom was bare aside from a basin and chipped mirror hanging haphazardly on the wall. A small window allowed for ventilation and the dispelling of any foul smell, which she was also grateful for.

Turning on her heel, she locked the door, then braced her hands against the basin, staring at her reflection in the worn mirror.

Take a deep breath. You can do this.

Pursing her lips, she slowly drew the pair of scissors from her pocket. With a wad of brown curls between her fingers, and the scissors in her other hand, she snipped off the locks. Eight inches of hair fell into the basin. Her heart hammered and her hands trembled with urgency as she quickly made her way around the back of her head and to the other side of her face.

When she was done, she stared at the bundle of locks discarded in the basin. As if she'd removed a part of her femininity, her heart panged. But there were more important things to be concerned about.

She grabbed the curls, then tossed them into the toilet, holding her breath. The wooden seat didn't look at all comfortable, and she was glad she didn't need to use it.

Before leaving the restroom, she placed the wire-rimmed glasses on her face and unlocked the door.

The musician sang melodically while picking up the tempo, driving fierce and dramatic notes through the atmosphere. Sliding through the narrow passage between patrons at the back of the room, she headed for the door.

When she was outside, she kept a tight grip on the pommel of the sword at her waist and didn't slow her pace. Grabbing the horse, she mounted, then turned towards Kirovo Palace.

Instead of riding in through the grand entrance, Adelina rode along a narrow, cobbled path leading to the eastern servants' entrance. From her position near the treeline behind the market and houses, she spotted the gardeners tending to the flowers and shrubs. Yelena strolled down the path between the manicured lawns towards the training building.

Adelina fastened her horse to a tree branch inside the forest, then discarded her robe and slung it over the saddle. What was she to do with her sword? If she was going to disguise herself, she couldn't exactly stroll through the gate with a weapon.

Turning on her heel, she made for the fallen tree stump. She dropped to her knees and clawed back the dried leaves and mud. Hastily, she stashed the sword, still in its sheath, into the crevice between the log and the ground. Once she'd shunted the leaves and mud on top, she rose.

Tucking her hacked curls behind her ears, she straightened her shoulders and headed to the iron gate ahead.

The entrance was wide enough for one person to slip through the gate, and a handful of steps later, she was in the stone-floored hallway. Daylight streamed through the small, square window, filtering into the kitchens through the archway.

Servants flittered back and forth. A hanging rack with pots and pans dangled from the ceiling near the brick stove in the centre of the room. Heat radiated from it as food cooked inside. One cook chopped a bunch of vibrant green herbs against a wooden block, while another ground a fragrant mixture with a mortar and pestle. Garlic wafted off a sauce bubbling in the open stove, and the pleasant blend of basil and rosemary stirred a hunger inside of Adelina. Her stomach growled.

Shoving her thoughts of food aside, she strolled through the kitchen as if she walked this place daily.

"Where did you come from?" the cook who chopped vegetables said—her cheeks tinted red from the sweltering heat. "Are you the new chamber maid who was hired? And where are your clothes?" She wrinkled her nose at the breeches and dirtied, cotton shirt Adelina had been wearing for quite some time. "Natasha! The new maid is here."

Natasha came bundling through the kitchen, skidding to a halt in front of Adelina and her eyes widened. "I was about to head to the chambers when I heard your call. Ah, yes…she is the new chamber maid, indeed."

"Yes, yes, she is quite filthy. I'm sure she will be of use to you once you have her cleaned and dressed."

Unable to peel her gaze from Adelina, she simply nodded, then grabbed her by the elbow. As she steered her away, Natasha lowered her voice to a whisper. "What are you doing here?"

"I had to come back." Adelina's heart thrummed and her stomach somersaulted. "I'm so glad to see you. I need your help. Filip threatened to kill my husband—I don't know if he lives—and I think he's captured my sister. We don't have much time to get them both out of here without raising the suspicion of the guards, and the gods only know how long it'll be before Filip spots me."

"Fear not—he's been locked in his office all day. Something about arranging living quarters for his father." Natasha tugged her through a doorway and up a spiralling staircase, presumably to the servants' living quarters.

"His father? You mean Antanov Tarasov?" Adelina asked.

"Yes. Filip wants him housed nearby as his health deteriorates," Natasha said.

"Why isn't he living here in the palace?"

"I suppose Filip doesn't want his father sniffing around in his work. As much as Filip does what he can to please his power-hungry father, Filip likes his *own* control." Natasha flung open a bedroom door, then ushered her inside.

Adelina knew the truth of it—while Antanov's lust for power might've spurred on Filip to crave the same thing, she knew they were both spawn from Nav, allowed to be reborn in the real world by Veles. She hoped the Sword of Light remained hidden and away from their clutches. If it was to fall into their hands, she couldn't be sure she'd keep a firm hold of the sword's loyalties, and there would be no stopping Filip or his father.

"Can you get me into the prison?" Adelina caught the maid uniform Natasha threw at her. Quickly, she stripped out of her dirty clothes, then redressed, flattening the crumbled skirt.

"The cells are directly below the ground floor and the entrance is through a passageway off the kitchens. I've been down once or twice to provide food to the guards, and it's a maze down there." Natasha tossed her a pair of black canvas shoes.

"I can bring the guards food, but then what? How will I get past them?" Adelina flipped her hair and hastily combed her fingers through it in an attempt to align her disguise as a servant, or more truthfully, to ignore the tightening sensation in her throat.

"Here, put these lifts in the shoes—it'll make you appear taller and more unlike your true self." Natasha grabbed a pair of wooden blocks from inside a bedside drawer, then handed them to her. "The prisoners haven't been fed yet today, so you can bring something to them too. From what the cook says, the prisoners were on a strict regime of burned bread only. Seems they were being starved. On the odd occasion, the guards allowed leftover stew passed them, so it didn't go to waste. They won't question it."

Nodding, Adelina slipped on the shoes. "How do I look?"

Natasha smiled warmly, dispelling the tension in the air. "Like you fit in."

SEVENTEEN

A Deal with a Demon

Carrying a tray in hand, Adelina followed the instructions given to her by Natasha and headed down the steps springing off the kitchens. Torches affixed to walls cast a warm glow across the stone, contrasting with the icy prickling of her skin as she descended into the prisons.

Squashing the building nerves flipping her stomach, she kept a tight grip on the tray, steadying the rattling bowls and plates. A crust of bread threatened to roll off the edge. She slowed her pace.

Remember, you work here. You know these corridors, these staircases. These guards. Act like it's the thousandth time you've done this, and you'll be fine.

Releasing the inside of her cheek from between her teeth, she approached the first guard.

"Here's your lunch." She plastered a bright smile on her face.

The guard clasped a bowl with his bulky hand and took a spoon in the other. "Thank the gods. I'm starved."

As he slouched onto his chair, she made her way towards the next guard, who was stationed further along the corridor.

"Are you hungry?" she asked pleasantly.

"Always," he said, then narrowed his eyes. "Wait, I've not seen you down here before. Who are you?"

Tilting her chin a little higher, she fought to keep her tone level. "I'm the new maid under Natasha's training and guidance. What better way to introduce me to the guards than to bring them food?"

"What's your name?" His watchful gaze travelled from head to toe.

Her body trembled, and her knees locked.

"Ana," she lied.

"Very well, Ana. Are you to feed the prisoners, too?" He took his bowl and cutlery from the tray.

"Yes. We burnt some bread this morning," she said, recycling Natasha's line.

"The filthy vermin don't deserve it." He wrinkled his nose. "Although they are quite docile—no fight left in them." He shrugged. "Even so, keep your wits about you and call me if you need anything."

"Of course." She bowed her head.

Holding her breath, she made her way along the narrow passage between cells—iron bars shiny in places where hands had gripped them, and sparse furniture fastened to the stone floor. A continuous drip of water echoed, and she wrinkled her nose at the smell of mildew. Under the dim orange glow of torchlight, she could make out the thin mattresses, pillows, and old, tattered sheets in the cells she passed.

An inmate whispered to his neighbour through the bars—theirs faces covered in dirt, and their clothes threadbare. She didn't recognise them. One man turned to face her and cocked an eyebrow. Heart thrumming, she hurried along, clutching the tray for dear life as her nerves mounted, and her stomach knotted.

Swallowing several times, she fought to rid the dryness from her mouth. A cough ahead froze her in her tracks.

"When can I go home?" A timid, quiet voice. One Adelina knew all too well. Tihana.

Adelina's chest tightened, and her limbs tingled. Closing her eyes, she thanked all the gods for the sound of her sister's voice.

"I'll find a way to get you home soon—I promise," Damir said hoarsely.

Heart soaring, Adelina fought the urge to bolt forwards, blast the door down, and throw her arms around her husband and sister. Tilting her head to the ceiling, she whispered a prayer of thanks, then edged towards the cell. There they both were. Alive. Together. She didn't bother wondering why Pyotr hadn't killed Damir as Filip had demanded.

"Food for the inmates," Adelina said as levelly as possible. She cast a quick side glance over her shoulder to make sure the guards weren't watching.

"Adelina?" Tihana whispered.

"Shh, don't call me by my real name, sis. It's Ana. Come to the bars—I have food." She lowered the tray, then slid it under the bottom metal rung.

In a swift movement, little Tihana held the bars in a tight grip. "I'm starving."

"Here. Eat up." Adelina slipped her arm under the bar and nudged the tray closer to her sister. "Damir? Are you okay? Can you come here?"

"He's not doing too well." Tihana's lip quivered.

Adelina placed her hand over her sister's. "It's okay. Don't worry. I'm going to look after both of you."

"What did you do to your hair?" Tihana tilted her head to the side.

"It was the only way I could get into the palace without bringing attention to myself. It'll grow back." Adelina squeezed Tihana's knuckles. "Go on—eat."

Nodding once, Tihana dropped to her buttocks and scoffed the bread down in less than a few minutes. Beads of liquid rolled down her chin, but she didn't seem to care. Adelina's heart ached for her—how long had her sister gone without food, water? All she wanted to do was wrap her in a blanket and hold her close.

"Done." Tihana wiped her mouth with the back of her hand. "Thanks...Ana."

Adelina gave a half smile—there wasn't anything to smile at, but she hoped it soothed her sister.

"Damir?" Adelina tried again. He hung back in the shadows, and she couldn't tell from the dim lighting what sort of condition he was in.

"My...love," he croaked.

"He's exhausted." Tihana looked at Adelina with round, wet eyes. "They've been starving us, and we are given little water."

"Can you help him come to the bars?" Despite the gut-wrenching sensation in her stomach, Adelina

A Ballad of Severed Souls

wrestled with her emotions, fighting the shakiness in her voice. She couldn't show her sister how she felt—they both relied on her to get them the hell out of there.

"I'll try." Tihana scrambled to her feet, exposing her dirtied knees and torn dress.

Disappearing into the back of the cell, she grumbled and shuffled. Adelina strained her eyes—two shadows lumbered across the floor.

Damir, one hand on the water-slick wall, and one arm around Tihana, hobbled to the bars. His eyes were half closed, and dirt covered every inch of his exposed skin and clothing, and clumped hair hung over his forehead.

Gripping onto the bars, he slid into a seated position and stuck his hand out to Adelina. She clasped it between hers. Ignoring the filth on his hand, she kissed it, and tears threatened to fall from her eyes. She couldn't break down—she'd lock her emotions in a box and stuff them into a far corner of her mind until she'd gotten them to safety.

"I've brought you some bread. I'm sorry it's not more, but I couldn't raise suspicions." She leaned closer, resting her forehead on the bars. "Please try to eat."

"I'll try." He smiled weakly—even such a small movement exerted him. Slouching against the wall, he resembled an aged ragdoll. Tihana handed him a crust of bread, which he ate in slow bites.

"I had a vision of you both—I don't have time to explain now—but I suspected you'd be here, and I'm going to find a way out of here. Sit tight. I'll bring you more food and water." She fixed her gaze on him and injected as much confidence as she could into her words.

"What's the plan?" His eyes fluttered closed, and his words were no louder than a whisper, but the sound of his voice sent a flood of warmth through her whole body, burning away her nerves. Reminding her of who she was. She was a wife, a sister, and a wielder. And she'd make Filip pay.

"Yelena was my teacher here—I'll find her. She'll help us," she said.

"Is everything all right down there?" A guard said, and his footsteps neared.

Adelina hopped to her feet, letting go of the bars.

"I'm fine!" she called. "Be right there."

"I love you," Damir whispered. "So very much. But if it comes down to a choice between me and your sister, get Tihana out of here."

Tihana cried and buried her head in his shoulder. "No!"

"Don't say such a thing, Damir. We're all getting out of here. I'll be back. I love you too. Both of you." Adelina carried the empty tray and paced towards the staircase where the guards were stationed.

"Did the prisoners give you a fright?" One of the guards frowned. "Your eyes are puffy, and your cheeks are as red as tomatoes."

"Not to worry." She lifted her chin and gave what she hoped was a measured smile. "I must be returning to my other duties. Good day."

Before the guards could question her further, she hurried up the steps and squinted from the brightness of sunlight streaming through the windows. With her back pressed against the wall, her heart hammered, threatening to unleash a tidal wave of guilt, fear, and sheer panic through her body. Clasping a trembling hand over her mouth, she sobbed, and the floodgates burst open. The box she'd fought to stuff her emotions into exploded inside her chest.

She stuffed her hand into her pocket and clasped her father's locket—her talisman she could no longer wear if she wished to heed the sun god's advice. Withdrawing it, she stared at the gold chain.

Bringing it to her lips, she kissed the locket, then wiped her tears. She pushed off the wall, straightened her shoulders, and headed to the kitchens.

Setting the tray on the counter, Adelina grabbed a pitcher of water, some rolls, cheese, and slices of cured meats. Turning on her heel, she started towards the gardens. If anyone questioned her, she'd simply tell them she'd gone to serve food to the trainer. She needed to secure an ally if she was to succeed in saving her sister and husband, and her most likely one was Yelena.

Inhaling through her nose, exhaling through her mouth, Adelina beelined for the training room at the back of the gardens, positioned in front of the aspens behind the property grounds.

The door was open, letting daylight flood and the mild, spring breeze in. Yelena stood hunched over her desk at the front of the room, her elbows propped on the surface, nose buried in a knock.

"I've brought you lunch...ma'am." Adelina added the pleasantry for good measure.

"I didn't request food." Yelena raised her head. "Send it back—" Her eyes widened.

Adelina tilted her lips into a slight smile.

"What are you doing here?" Yelena dashed to the door, peered her head out, glanced both ways, then locked it. Spinning on her heel, she looked Adelina up and down. "What in the gods' good realm are you wearing?"

"I had to get into the palace without being recognised."

"You are most fortunate he hasn't been strolling the grounds. Come with me." Yelena gestured for her to follow as she headed towards the row of bookshelves behind her. Lifting a hand, she gripped a green book and tilted it.

A lock popped.

"A door?" Adelina gasped.

Yelena gripped the bookcase door with both hands and hauled it open. "Hurry inside."

Books were stacked on wooden chests against the walls, and a desk at the opposite end was covered in rolls of parchment. Quills were stashed in a pot, and a small chandelier hung from the ceiling.

"What is this place?" Adelina spun around to face Yelena. "Why have I not seen it before?"

"This is my private office." Yelena paced around the desk, then rummaged through the parchment sheets. "Filip has never had cause to doubt my loyalties before, so has not seen fit to inspect it."

"And where *do* your loyalties lie?" Adelina ran with the bolt of courage the adrenaline gave her.

Yelena lifted her gaze and fixed an unwavering stare on her. "My loyalties lie with what is pure and good, and I assure you, what Filip has planned for you and the three countries is far from it."

"How do you know?" Adelina asked.

"I have remained in contact with the leaders of the Saintlandsther Council, and the Convocation of Toichrist—Nikolay and Olga. You met them at the Embassy," Yelena said.

Adelina recalled their meeting—Nikolay had questioned Filip's intentions and was concerned her magic would wreak havoc across the countries. Olga, on the other hand, seemed positive about Adelina's arrival and the involvement she would have in uniting the countries and tackling poverty in Saintlandsther.

"Yes, I remember. What about them?"

"Nikolay has always been suspicious of Filip—he knows nether magic and fears for what Filip may do with his strengthened power with you by his side. Nikolay is a sceptical man and does not tend to trust those who make promises left unfulfilled." Yelena placed her palms on the desk and leaned forward. "It wasn't too long before he convinced Olga to consider the repercussions of Filip being at his full power and *not* being used to fulfil the promises he's been spouting for the last ten years."

"I'm not sure what you're getting at." Adelina took a step forward. An ache throbbed in her temples.

"Nikolay and Olga have been sending me coded letters for months. Filip's father played an instrumental role in the War. Antanov Tarasov should have been imprisoned for his crimes—he used his powers to shapeshift into a demon. Many astral wielders were enslaved during the War. Many sacrificed their magic, so they escaped a life of servitude. They were killed.

"Antanov has been funding Filip's campaign for years, which is rather clever if you think about it. Filip is a likeable, charismatic man, and no one would think he is capable of repeating his father's mistakes. Filip promised he would find you and do good with your magic. Many people believed him. Even I, for a time, believed him—and you—to be the true answer to all our problems." Yelena gathered a stack of letters and held them in her arms.

"Wait…from my understanding, Antanov wasn't using his powers to shapeshift. He *is* a demon, sent to Kirromund by Veles. Filip is one too. I learned this recently when I read about it. Why would anyone let these two men roam free when they have a direct link to the underworld?" A cold chill rippled across her body.

"People were desperate after the war. Astral magic was lost. Many wielders were killed or sacrificed their magic. Filip used this to his advantage, convinced people once he'd found you, everything would be made right again. No more poverty, no more unfair taxes, or poor trade routes. He promised democracy—a fair vote for everyone, no matter your status." A deep sadness resonated in Yelena's eyes, accentuated by the dark circles forming around them. "Now he has you. Have you seen any of this happening?"

A sudden guilt gripped Adelina's heart and twisted. "I fled the palace because he wanted to marry me. He wanted me to conceive his heirs, so the powerful bloodline didn't end with us. I learned his true intentions by reading correspondence between him and his father—after uniting the countries into a republic, he would've assumed role as permanent

Emperor. A role that would've stayed within our family forever."

"I wouldn't condemn you to such a fate, and neither would Nikolay or Olga. Here, take these letters." She handed the pile to Adelina.

Dropping to her knees, Adelina lay them side by side across the carpeted floor. "I don't know how to read code."

"It's complex and detailed enough to give you a headache, but I'll help you." She smiled. "The words were initially written backwards, then random numbers and letters were inserted between each of the original letters in the message. After several weeks, we changed it, adding in symbols and runes. We kept to this pattern over the last few months, changing our code in case anyone *was* intercepting our mail. The wax seals didn't appear to be tampered with, but we couldn't take the risk."

"What now? They know Filip is powerful, and they know what he intends to do with me. What are we going to do to stop him?"

The clock on the wall chimed, making Adelina jump.

"I have to go. It is time for my meeting with Filip—he wants to speak to me about a weapon forged by gods." Yelena's gaze narrowed on Adelina, but she let it fly over her head. No matter how much she trusted Yelena, she wouldn't tell her about the Sword of Light. Not until she was absolutely certain about her loyalties.

"Natasha will be expecting me to carry out my chores. When can I see you again?" She rose.

Yelena shook her head. "I'm afraid I can't answer. It is not safe for you to stay here."

Adelina refused to accept this. An idea bloomed inside her mind—a plan that sent shivers down her spine and turned her blood to ice. "I could give myself over to Filip. Offer myself in exchange for Damir and Tihana. He would let them go free, and in return, I would do his bidding. We could use this as a façade while I train in secret with you. Haven't you noticed I no longer wear my talisman? I am now the wielder of uncontrolled astral magic. If you help me—prove your loyalties—then we can put a stop to him."

Yelena placed her fingers to her lips. "You'd willingly put your life on the line? He is not likely to let Damir go—why would he? If he kept him a prisoner, he'd be motivation to ensure you did whatever he asked of you."

"I love and trust my husband. He would want me to do whatever it takes to keep our families—and the countries—safe. If you doubt Filip will free Damir, then he will remain a prisoner as he is now, but at least I can use my connections with the servants to safeguard his welfare. I will keep up my end of the bargain until I am ready to end him." Adelina straightened her back and tilted her chin a notch higher.

"It seems you have made your choice," Yelena said. "Now go at once. Don't come back here until you've revealed yourself to Filip."

A Ballad of Severed Souls

A sickly sensation wracked Adelina's entire body, churning her insides and dousing her nerve-endings. Her skin blazed as if someone struck a match and set her afire. With her tongue stuck to the roof of her parched mouth, and her nails dug into the palms of her hands, she marched across the manicured lawns.

She tossed her spectacles to the ground, no longer needing or desiring the disguise it gave her. Storming through the kitchen doors, she headed for the servant room in which she'd changed earlier. If she was to hand herself over to Filip, she would not do so gently.

Ignoring Natasha's calls from behind her, Adelina tore off her maid outfit, then threw her breeches and shirt on.

"What are you doing, miss?" Natasha gasped. "You will be spotted."

"Precisely what I intend." Adelina marched past Natasha, through the steaming kitchens, along the wide corridor to Filip's office.

While adrenaline flooded her body like wildfire, she flung open the door. It banged against the wall. Filip shot a glance at her.

"Ah. You are here." He created a steeple with his fingers and leaned back in his chair. "Perfect timing."

She couldn't help but notice, despite his cool demeanour, his gaze travelled over her body. He wouldn't find the sword in her possession.

"I've come to make a deal." She held her posture straight and tall.

"I did wonder what it would take to get you here." His voice was calm, which sent a shot of rage through Adelina's core. "It seems I have found the right price."

"Let's not play games," she said, matching his cool tone with her own, no matter how disingenuous. "You have my sister and husband. I want them set free. Unharmed."

"Ah, your husband. Yes, the cells have done him no favours." Filip's lips curled up in a callous grin. "You'll have to excuse me—games are in my nature. What do I get in return?"

"My servitude." The words tasted sour in her mouth, and every fibre of her being fought for her to take them back. But they were spoken, and by the gleam in Filip's eyes, she assumed his interest was piqued.

"Do tell." He gestured to the seat opposite him at the desk separating them.

With hands flat against her thighs, she slid into the chair and fixed her unwavering stare on him. Black hair was slicked back from his face, and his equally dark stare met hers.

"If you give me your word to set my sister and husband on the path home—unharmed in any way—then I pledge myself to you. You will have my obedience, my power, and strength to do with as you see fit. We will take the three countries together." She added her final sentence for good measure, knowing it was the one thing he wanted most.

"Quite the proposal you are making." Filip leaned forwards. "How do I know you won't betray me?"

"It is a matter of trust, after all." She crossed her arms over chest and forced a nonchalant energy into the air. Despite how difficult it was, she would not give him the satisfaction of knowing the turmoil tearing at her insides. "You have the lives of my loved ones in your hands."

"Rightly so." He cocked a brow. "Little, sweet Tihana. Yes, I could send her back to the squalor of Aramoor. Her whingeing and crying are *most* tedious."

Adelina ground her teeth. "What of my husband?"

"He is another matter altogether. Without him here, I will have no way to guarantee you will hold up your end of the bargain." He stretched in his chair, oozing an air of confidence and control. She was submitting herself to him, and he could do whatever he wanted with her husband. "He will remain here."

"I implore you to reconsider." She sat forward.

"Make me a better offer." His words were sharp like a knife.

She rootled in her pocket, grabbed the talisman, then threw it onto the desk. Lowering his head, he stared at the necklace.

"You took it off," he said.

"Yes. I am no longer restricted by this piece of metal. Destroy it if you must, but know I have full access to my powers, and you know what that means." Her heart pounded. She prayed it would be enough to influence his decision. There was no way she'd be handing over the Sword of Light. Not unless he held a knife to her throat. And even then…

"Very well." He rose abruptly. "You may return to your original quarters, but guards will be stationed with you at all times. You understand."

Fighting the urge to throttle him or launch a candlestick at his head, she nodded.

He called to the three guards in the foyer, who entered the office at his command.

"Keep a watchful eye on Miss Adelina Orlova. She is not to be let out of your sight at any time.

Before she bathes, ensure all windows are barricaded, and remain positioned outside the door. Escort her to and from her chambers, for meals, and bring her to me when it is requested."

The guards nodded.

"You." He lifted a finger to the tallest of the three guards. "Bring Tihana and Damir to me at once."

The man slipped out of the room.

Turning, Filip shifted his gaze to Adelina, and a slight smirk tugged at the corners of his lips. Tense silence hung between them—their gazes locked. Adelina refused to lower her own.

Moments later, the guard returned with Tihana and Damir in tow—their hands bound with rope. Damir's head hung forward and his body sagged. The guard shoved him into a nearby chair.

Tihana dashed to Adelina and flung her arms around her waist. "Sis, what are you doing?"

"I'm sending you home." Adelina stroked her sister's back while watching Filip for any sign he may change his mind.

"I'll arrange for a horse for you, and you'll be on your way," Filip agreed.

Tihana glanced over her shoulder but clung to her sister. Her bottom lip quivered.

Smoothing Tihana's hair, Adelina flicked a glance between her barely conscious husband and his captor. "And what of my husband? He needs medical attention."

"Ah, he does." Filip clomped his hand on Damir's slumped shoulder.

Damir grunted but didn't try to shove him off.

A Ballad of Severed Souls

"I am prepared to keep up my end of the deal, Filip." Adelina enunciated the syllables of his name harshly. "Let him go."

Filip gestured to the guard. "Take Tihana to the stables. Put her on the path home."

The guard moved towards her.

"No, I'm not leaving you," she squealed, squeezing Adelina's waist.

Adelina swallowed her anger, and instead, smoothed her sister's hair in an attempt to sooth her nerves.

"She cannot ride to Aramoor alone and without food. It will take her two weeks to reach home," Adelina said. Her blood ran cold as ice. "Providing she doesn't get lost."

Filip waved his hand as if the subject was of no concern to him. "Fine. The servants will give her a bag of food and a map. Now get her out of here."

The guard gripped Tihana's shoulder and plied her from her tight grip of her sister. She screamed, tears rolling down her face.

"You need to send Damir with her," Adelina urged as she lunged for her sister. She grasped Tihana's arm and held her tight. The guard pulled her other arm, trapping Tihana in a tug-of-war. "It is part of our deal."

In a swift movement, Filip drew a knife from his pocket, gripped Damir's body against his, and held the blade to his throat. Black shadows poured from Filip's limbs like sharp talons, wrapping around Damir's body and puncturing his skin. Damir swallowed a grunt of pain.

So, that's what nether looks like.

Adelina grimaced, and her heart pounded. Her husband was too weak to fight back, and even if he was at full strength, how would he fight against the power of nether? He couldn't.

"Let the guard take Tihana away or I will slit his throat," Filip said through gritted teeth.

Adelina froze—blood drained from her face and a sickly sensation somersaulted through her core. "Lower the knife."

"Let. Tihana. Go." Filip enunciated each word as sharply as the edge of his knife.

Unable to swallow her emotions any longer, Adelina's trembling hand let go of her sister.

The guard hoisted Tihana off the floor and flung her over his shoulder. He strode to the door as Tihana thrashed and kicked against him.

"Be strong, Tihana. I love you." Adelina managed around the lump in her throat as the guard dragged her sister out of the room. Her cries rung through the hall.

Although her heart bled, and every fibre of her body urged her to wrestle her sister free of the guard's firm grip, Adelina needed to let Tihana go. She blinked back tears. It was the only way she could guarantee her safety.

"I've done as you said. Lower your weapon." Adelina's body coursed with the burning sensation of astral magic firing through every vein, nerve, and cell.

A spell which will draw on the eternal power of the Sun God, strong enough to combat ancient magic, only a practitioner of astral may wield it.

Just like before, a gold wisp of light weaved around her wrist, hovering above the skin's surface.

Like sparkling, golden embroidery, it glowed, pulsing with magic. She flexed her arm, fixing a deathly stare on Filip. "I said let him go."

He tutted. "I wouldn't do that if I were you. Without your talisman, your magic is uncontrolled. You promised you would be subservient, and now I ask you to prove it. Dissipate your magic or I will slit his throat."

Adelina, feeding off the high her magic gave her, let the gold embroidery brighten, surging with power.

"I will do it." Filip gripped Damir tighter, pressing the tip of his blade into his neck. A bead of blood popped from the surface, and Damir winced. "Just because you fled the palace and married this man, does not mean my plans are thwarted. I could kill him now. You'd be a widow, and there'd be nothing stopping me from making you my bride."

Adelina's rage flared like a beast inside her, eager to rip through her body and bolt all its energy into her enemy. The notion of marrying him, of conceiving his spawn made her sick to her stomach. But the thought of losing her true love, Damir, was even stronger. She lowered her arm a fraction, but the magic didn't dissipate.

"Adelina." Damir's raspy voice ripped her icy stare from Filip, back to him. "My love."

His words sent shockwaves through her heart, and she could no longer hold back the tears.

"It's okay," Damir said soothingly. "I'll be all right."

She dissipated her magic, and the golden embroidery vanished, leaving blisters on her wrist in its wake.

"Damir will stay as my prisoner to ensure you keep your promise. Any toe out of line and I will take my frustration out on him. Or I might get Pyotr to torture him." Filip shrugged as if the decision was as simple as choosing what to wear.

Adelina had forgotten about Pyotr—the neighbour she'd known for most of her life. He'd threatened her father, burned his workshop to the ground, and had become Filip's accomplice.

"Where is he?" She seethed, bunching her hands into fists.

"Now, now." Filip's tone was condescending at best, vicious at worst. "I'm sure you will see him soon. But remember, best behaviour."

With a callous grin, he grabbed Damir, hauled him to his feet, and practically threw him to the two remaining guards. Damir crashed to the floor.

"Take him back to the cells," Filip demanded.

The guards pulled Damir to his feet. He cast a glance over his shoulder as they towed him towards the door.

"I love you," Damir said as he was carted out of the room.

Biting hard on her bottom lip to prevent herself from shouting at Filip, Adelina swatted her tears away and straightened.

"Now I've proven I can keep up my end of our little deal, it is time for you to keep yours." Filip strolled to the desk—an air of ease about him—and slid into his chair. "Take a seat. We must discuss strategy."

"For what?" Adelina lowered into her chair. She feared the answer he would give, but deep down, she knew he meant war.

"How I plan to lay siege to Saintlandsther and Temauten, of course." He grinned. "With you and your uncontrolled magic in my possession, and me at my strongest, the countries will fall. Now there is only one more thing I need to succeed."

"What?" she managed. Her stomach twisted.

"The Sword of Light." He crossed his arms and leaned back. "Bring it to me."

EIGHTEEN

In Deception we Thrive

Adelina led Filip through the servants' entrance at the narrow metal gate. A pulse throbbed in the side of her neck, and a numbness spread through her chest. She blindly followed his instructions to retrieve the Sword, while the crippling sensation of defeat clutched her heart.

He'd won. Filip had won. And she was about to give him one more tool to aid him on his quest to conquer and raze the countries to the ground. Her name would be dragged through the dirt with him—she'd play an equal part in destroying homes, taking lives, fuelling Filip's crave for power. And what was to say he wouldn't kill Damir and force her into an unwanted marriage? To spawn his children, who he'd shove onto the same, dark path on which he strolled?

"If I'm to do your bidding, then I want to know what role your father plays in all this," she said to Filip as they headed towards the treeline.

"My father?" He laughed—the sound slicing through the air. "Don't play coy with me. I know you know what we are."

She whirled to face him. "You're demons. Shapeshifters from the underworld."

"Clever. Keep moving." He nudged her forward, and she stumbled over a thick tree root.

"Why would Veles send you both to the living realm? Your father played an instrumental part in the last war—enslaved many astral wielders. But he failed, didn't he? Otherwise, you wouldn't be here to do his bidding." Adelina matched his sharp tone with her own equal one.

"My father was responsible for countless murders, and the needless sacrifice of astral magic, which resulted in the near extinction of astral wielders." Twigs snapped underfoot as he followed her towards the fallen tree in which she'd hidden the Sword of Light underneath.

She bit her tongue—she would never tell him about the pocket watch and the stored astral magic within. The power she'd absorbed. While she'd been born an astral wielder, according to what the Sun God had told her, she was far more powerful than she was a few months ago. Her thoughts spiralled—he hadn't answered her question about why they were sent to the living realm in the first place.

"My father was reckless." He spat on the ground. "He squandered his opportunity for complete power and nearly rid this world of the one thing we need to be at our strongest: astral wielders. As penance for his crimes, Veles has weakened him."

"What do you mean?" She frowned. If she was to play his servant, she may as well learn everything she needed to. "Wait, is this something to do with your father being ill all these past months?"

"I promised my father, and by extension, Veles, I would correct his mistakes," he said. "Otherwise, my father will be dragged back to the underworld."

Not a single ounce of her felt bad for Filip *or* Antanov. Whatever the God of the Underworld had in store for them, they deserved.

"What does Veles gain from you laying siege to the countries and creating a republic?" Adelina couldn't quite fathom the final piece of the puzzle.

He simply grinned. "Now if I told you, there would be no fun."

She shivered.

"It's here," she said as they reached the trunk.

"Get it for me."

Kneeling, she rifled through the dirt, then drew the Sword of Light. Despite every ounce of her body screaming at her to not hand it over, she had to in order to keep Damir alive. He could have him killed on a whim. And what about Tihana? If Adelina didn't follow Filip's orders, what's to say he wouldn't have her sister dragged back to the palace or harmed in some way?

Reluctantly, she handed it to him.

He grasped it, turned it over in his hands, and inspected the glinting, metal surface with a steady gaze.

Chewing her bottom lip, she studied him. He did not cripple over in pain as she had in the cave. No white light burst through his body. He stood perfectly still, not a single dark hair on his head out of place. She wondered what it could mean.

"Finally," he mused. "Come. We have work to do. Preparations need to be made."

Instead of voicing her thoughts about his rather subtle reaction to wielding the Sword of Light, she bit down on her tongue. The Sun God had been right about the sword's loyalties, and she wasn't about to clue Filip in on it.

Filip rested his hands on the large wooden table as he scanned the map of the three countries. Three other men gathered nearby. A sickening sensation flipped Adelina's stomach. They were planning their attack, and there was nothing she could do to stop it. A dark part of her mind tempted her to unleash her magic. If she killed Filip and his puppets then and there, the war would not happen. But she was not a murderer, and she could not risk the wrath of Veles. For all she knew, he could simply summon another demon to carry out Filip and Antanov's unfinished work.

"We follow the route through the mountains into the north of Saintlandsther. From there, we march through the Salken Mountains, travelling south until we reach the city of Pike. We will lay siege to the city and take down the Saintlandsther Council." Filip's voice was as charismatic as they come.

"You'd previously promised the leader of the Saintlandsther Council your support in ending poverty amongst other things. They will not be expecting your attack, sir," a middle-aged man with sharp facial features said.

Adelina knew otherwise—the coded letters sent back and forth between Yelena, Olga, and Nikolay suggested they would be anything *but* unsuspecting. She hoped they would be ready. Yelena wouldn't have time to send them a coded letter to inform them of Adelina's presence, so they would likely see her as an enemy too, especially if she opened fire on them.

"Precisely. We have all the power we need to take them down." Filip stood back from the desk. "We'll rally the soldiers and prepare to march at first light."

Heart rate spiking, she scrambled through her thoughts for a sound reason for him to postpone his attack. She hadn't planned for him to order it so soon, and she needed time to practise with Yelena. Instead of letting Filip use her as a weapon, she had to find an advantage against him, since she could no longer rely on the Sword of Light or her talisman to keep her magic in check.

"Perhaps it is wise I spend a few days training with Yelena. Since removing my talisman, my magic is tumultuous. While this is what you want, maybe there is a way Yelena and I can weaponise my magic further." She kept her voice level. "I am sure there is a way for me to master the element of fire. It would help when we reach the city walls. We could burn them out."

Filip arched a brow. "Adelina Orlova, I am surprised by your sudden enthusiasm in our war efforts."

She needed to think of something, and fast, if she was to stop Filip and his men from ever setting foot on their march south.

"Fire is the best way to ensure a quick capture of the Saintlandsther Council. It means we lose fewer soldiers, weapons, and cavalry on our end. We will be in a better position for when you plan to move onto Temauten Congregation." The mention of her home country seized her heart in a deathly grip, but she fought to keep her facial expression neutral. "Combined with my freed magic, the fire will spread quickly. And wildly."

Filip stroked his chin, but from the spreading grin on his face, he'd already made up his mind. "I will give you three days to master this. Get it done and I will ensure Damir is fed well. If you are fooling me, he will face punishment. Understood?"

"You have my word," she said, lying through her teeth. "I will head to Yelena's right now."

Shooing her away, he returned his attention to the three men. "Prepare the cavalry and gather the supplies. We must face no further delays."

Whatever responses were given were drowned by her clomping footsteps as she hurried out of the palace, through the gardens, and towards the training building. She found Yelena hunched over an open book, uneaten food on a tray beside her.

"What have you got there?" Adelina asked as she neared her.

Yelena jolted. "What is it with you appearing out of nowhere, unannounced?"

"Sorry, but we don't have much time. Filip has given orders to invade Pike. I've persuaded him to postpone, but he has only agreed to three days." Adelina raked her hand through her hair.

"Gods be good, I thought we'd have more time." Yelena's eyes widened as she discarded her book. "Tell me what else was said."

Adelina spurted out the details of the training she'd spoke of with Filip, all the while pacing the floor. When she was finished, a silence formed between them.

"Well?" Adelina halted.

"We need a spell strong enough to disable Filip and his men from ever leaving this palace." Yelena grabbed a load of books from the shelves, then scattered them along the floor. "We must be quick if we are to find something *and* learn it in such a short time."

Dropping to her knees, Adelina helped her teacher rifle through the pages in search of *anything*. Books were flung to the side if deemed unhelpful.

Although Adelina fought to keep her attention on the task at hand, she couldn't resist the thought of Damir creeping into the centre of her mind. His life was on the line. If Filip cottoned on to the fact she'd no intention of ever helping him take Saintlandsther or Yelena's loyalties did not lie with him, he could discard of Damir as easily as breathing.

Her vision blurred, heart pounded, and each breath was ragged.

"Steady there," Yelena soothed as she wrapped her hand around Adelina's wrist. "We'll find something."

"It has all become so real. My husband rots in a cell, his life in Filip's hands. If I fail, I could lose him, and many other lives could be taken." Adelina trembled as she clutched the open book in her lap.

"We will not let that bastard succeed; do you hear me?" Yelena shook her, forcing Adelina's gaze to meet hers. "Too much is at stake."

Swallowing the hard lump in her throat, Adelina nodded and forced her attention to the text in her hands.

After two hours of rifling through all the books on Yelena's shelves, Adelina puffed out an agitated breath. "There's nothing here."

"And three days isn't enough time to search the library at Saintlandsther Council." Yelena shook her head—her shoulders slumping.

Adelina sucked in a breath. "That's it."

"What?" Yelena's gaze searched her face.

"The library is where I found the book about astral magic—it's what told me how to obtain the Sword of Light. Surely, they will hold other texts, a much more extensive collection than what you have here. They're bound to have what we're looking for." Adelina rose. "And the only way Filip will let me go to Saintlandsther is if I am a part of his army."

"You mean to say you want him to go ahead with the attack?" The colour in Yelena's face drained, leaving a pasty, grey tinge to her skin.

Adelina resumed her pacing. "How else are we going to get what we want?"

Yelena placed her fingers to her chin. "I am aware of the extensive collection of books in the library, and it probably *does* have something of use. But to put so many lives at risk? How in the realm will we get you in and out without raising suspicions? Didn't you say to Filip you'll burn the place down? If you go with him to Saintlandsther, he will expect you to do it. There will be no going back."

Pulling at her hair, Adelina clamped her eyes shut and wracked her brain for a plan. After a few moments, she peeled back her hands and opened her eyes. "I don't see any other choice. Besides, I am playing him at his own game. I will think of something—no one will lose their lives by my hand."

Yelena pursed her lips. "Well, let's hope not."

Over the course of the next three days, Adelina trained in the Prism World. Despite her best efforts to control her magic, it was as wild as it had been the first day she'd set foot in there. When she returned to the training room, she dragged a hand over her face.

"You'd have thought my magic would behave," she muttered.

"You haven't had enough time without wearing your talisman to truly understand the ways in which your magic *does* behave." Yelena emerged from her secret office and closed the disguised door behind her. "Unfortunately, the only way you will learn to control it now is through practice."

"By burning down buildings and laying siege to innocent cities." Adelina frowned.

The door of the training room burst open as Filip strode inside. The Sword of Light hung from a baldric around his waist. "It is time to leave."

"I'm ready." Adelina injected as much confidence into her tone as possible. Before she left, she cast a final glance over her shoulder at her trainer.

Yelena gave her a nod of encouragement, then disappeared from sight.

Without slowing his pace, Filip led her into the palace, straight for the entrance. Outside the palace, carriages were prepared, calvary in line, and foot soldiers gathered. Wagons were stashed with canvas tents and large bags, which Adelina presumed to be filled with food and medicinal supplies.

She halted, her heart lurching into her throat as she caught a glimpse of Damir, wrists bound, held in position by a guard in front of the leading carriage.

"You're bringing him with us?" She couldn't hide the tremble in her voice.

"Consider it your motivation." Filip fixed his hard stare on her. "Not a single toe out of line, or I'll kill him."

Unable to resist the urge to comfort her husband, she flung her arms around him, drawing his filthy body against her chest. He rested his chin against her shoulder, his warm, ragged breath on her neck.

Filip gripped her arm and yanked her away. "None of that. Get in."

The guard all but shoved Damir into the carriage. Adelina climbed in after and positioned herself between him and Filip. Although she couldn't fight Filip, she'd do whatever she could to put as much space between them as possible.

Thumping on the roof, Filip gave the signal to move out.

With a sharp jolt, the carriage was on its way. Through the thin glass window, the sounds of clomping horses' hooves and marching soldiers rung.

"We'll be stopping at the garrison on the way south." Filip's voice broke the silence. "More soldiers will be joining us."

Although she'd opened her mouth to speak, no words came. Instead, she cast a sideways glance at Damir. He'd not been bathed in what she'd guessed as weeks. Even in his current condition, his eyes shone. Hope. She rested her hand on top of his bound ones and squeezed. Beneath her fingers, the cool surface of his wedding ring pressed into her palm. Their locked eyes spoke a thousand words. They'd survive this together.

Two weeks of heading south and camping in endless rain dragged by. Each day a painful reminder of what was to come. She'd spent her time silent, aside from the sparse conversations she was allowed to hold with her husband. He'd been kept apart from her, bound to a tree trunk. At least the rain had washed away the thick layer of mud from his weary body.

When she passed Pyotr, who'd travelled in their company, she fixed a glare on him, as if her gaze might rip through his wretched chest. He'd simply walked by, returning to the side of his master—Filip. But she knew the truth. If put to the test, Pyotr would prove to be a coward.

When the city of Pike was in sight, she turned her glance skywards and prayed to all the gods she ever knew, needing their guidance on the dark path on which she trod. Turning around, she scanned the horizon in the north—the highlands of the Svatken Mountains. Svarog had presented himself to her then, warned her to be careful.

"From here, we ride." Filip approached her—the reins of two horses in hand. "We will return to the carriages when the city has fallen."

Grimacing, she accepted the reins, placed her foot in the stirrup, then hoisted herself onto the back of her black mount.

"The soldiers and calvary will charge ahead," he said. "And we follow. I am counting on you to do as you promised."

As the words left his mouth, the foot soldiers marched towards the city. One dragged Damir along by a stretch of rope.

"My husband is unarmed." She found her voice. "He has nothing to defend himself with."

"My men will keep him out of harm's way," he declared.

She didn't trust a single word he said, so she said, "You want to see this city burn, get my husband out of here."

"I cannot afford to keep some of my men back with Damir," he said. "If you do as you've promised, I will ensure he stays alive."

Thick, grey clouds cast ominous shadows over Pike. The calvary and foot soldiers held their position, waiting for their signal to attack.

Filip's booming voice ripped through the cool air. "Charge!"

Galloping horses kicked mud into the air as they thundered towards the city gates. Soldiers ran, their hollers ringing. She lost sight of Damir.

"Shouldn't we move?" she swung an urgent glare at Filip.

"We head straight for the Council. Stay close." He shook his reins vigorously, and his horse set off in a gallop.

Urging her own horse to follow, she rode hard into the city, Filip ahead of her.

Soldiers fought all around—the clank of swords and screams ripping through the air. Pike was not unprepared after all—their fighting men littered the streets.

Charging straight ahead, Filip ignored the battle. Cavalry tore through the crowds, their swords slicing through the mob with ease.

Where the hell was Damir? She hoped he'd got hold of a sword and cut himself free.

"Filip!" she called. "Give me command of a handful of men, and I'll strike the eastern wing of the Council building."

He cast a sceptical glance at her, but after a beat, he nodded. "Burn it down, or you know what will happen to your husband."

After he'd given the order, ten armed soldiers followed her towards the iron gate surrounding the Saintlandsther Council. She'd used the entrance when she'd visited the library before. As she approached from the eastern side, she cast a glance to her left—Filip dismounted and wielded the Sword of Light. He sliced through men as if he used a normal weapon. It wouldn't be long before he realised something was wrong with the weapon, and she wanted to be far away from him when he did. Thick, black talons burst from his body. His nether magic carved through his enemies, sending severed limbs and blood through the air.

She peeled her gaze from the gory scene and rode ahead. If she could get into the library, she could search the books for something she could use to stop Filip. But she'd need to be quick.

Throwing herself off the horse, she sprinted through the entrance. The soldiers in her command sliced down men surrounding her. Ignoring the screams and fighting, she forced herself forward.

When she reached the library, she flung open the door. The soldiers filtered in behind her.

"What are we doing here? We must return to the fight," one said.

Backs to them, she produced the golden embroidery around her arm—its magic surging through her body, drenching the room in a bright, golden light. Spinning, she extended her arm in a sharp jolt—the thread unwound, lashing out like a whip. It slashed through the soldiers in one quick, bloody strike. Severed heads hit the floor and rolled.

Panting, she stared at the pooling blood, and decapitated bodies. People she'd murdered. But she couldn't let herself feel anything about it—if she did, she would break, and there would be no hope for her husband, family, or the countless innocent lives Filip threatened to snuff.

Jogging between the aisles, she hastily grabbed book after book. Her hands trembled, her knees weak, but her mind forced her onward. The building shook with the impact of an explosion, sending her hurtling into a bookcase. She crashed to the floor; stacks of books tumbling on top of her. She pulled herself free, ignoring the pain shooting up the side of her ribs.

Taking a turn to the back of the library, she sprinted to the shelves where she'd found the astral magic book. She froze. Each of her muscles tensed, and she was unable to move. They were gone. They were *all* gone.

She fell to her knees. An overwhelming charge of anger shot through her body, dousing each of her nerve endings in wildfire. She screamed. Golden light ripped through her and blew out of her in an explosion, decimating the bookcases.

Digging her nails into the palms of her hands, she rose. Charged with a newfound abhor for Filip, she climbed over broken shelves, scattered books, and bodies of the soldiers she'd killed.

Her gaze locked on a battered, dusty grey book poking out from between splintered shelves. Bending, she scooped it up. She wiped away the dust, revealing it's faded title. *A Practitioner's Guide to Ancient Magic, Nether Edition, Volume II.* Flicking through the pages, she frowned. Unlike the first volume, this one was written in a different language—one she didn't understand or recognise. If she wasn't going to get help from astral magic books, she sure as hell would take the one about nether. She shoved it into the inside pocket of her cloak.

Another explosion rang, ripping through the wall behind her. The impact sent her hurtling through the air. She collided with the doorframe.

A searing pain shot through her scalp. Wincing, she raised her hand to the top of her head. Glancing at her blood-covered fingers, she groaned. Hoisting herself onto her hands and knees, she fought with every shred of energy to rise. Her vision swung wildly on its axis.

Tilting, she fell into the wall.

"Gods damn it!" she shouted.

With a mighty yell, she pushed through her pain and stood. Prodding her ribs, she growled. Probably fractured, but there was nothing she could do about it right now. Readjusting her eyes to the dusty dull light of the corridor, her lips parted. Chunks of stone from the explosions littered the long hallway. Paintings either hung crooked on the expanses of wall still intact or lay buried beneath the rubble. Broken glass dotted the floor, having blown in from the impact. Glancing down, she spotted a pair of booted legs sticking out underneath the full weight of a collapsed stone beam.

Covering her mouth, she gasped. Their blood pooled around them, soaking into the carpet. Although she suspected they were dead, she grabbed at the beam. With every ounce of her strength, she tried to lift it off the person crushed. Despite her best efforts, it wouldn't budge.

Glancing at her hands, she considered using her magic to blast the stone, but what good would it do? If anything, her magic was more likely to cause harm.

Cursing, she spun on her heel and jogged through the winding corridors towards the way she'd entered. Her route was blocked off by a blown-in wall. A thick cloud of dust hung in the air, giving a haziness to the sparse light shining into the building. While it was still midday, the clouds cast out the sun, and darkness fell in its place.

Hurrying through another corridor, she found the main staircase. The banister was ripped off, and several steps had caved in. She dashed down them, jumping over the broken steps.

A new wave of pain shot through her ribs from exertion. She clutched her side, flung open the main door, and stumbled outside.

The city of Pike stretched ahead of her—charred, blackened, and blazing with fire. She shivered as a howling wind cried, mingling with the grunts and screams of fighting men. A lone horse neighed, galloping along the cobbles, retreating. Bodies littered the floor—blood coating the ground.

Through the commotion of sparring soldiers, she caught a glimpse of Filip. Black tendrils spun from his body like giant tree roots, and talons formed at their tips. His nether magic snaked through the serried enemies, encircling them, choking out life. With quick flicks, the talons discarded severed bodies, flinging limbs to all corners.

Her stomach heaved. Doubling over, she wretched. Wiping her mouth with the back of her hand, she darted towards Filip. Within seconds, the gold embroidery erupted from her arm, wrapping itself round her wrist like a rope. Its burst of light shone over the courtyard of the Saintlandsther Council.

His piercing gaze found her, and with swift movements, his talons cleared the path for her, removing men as if they were no more than pesky flies. Soldiers surrounded Filip, although she didn't understand why. It's not like he needed the protection—he was more powerful than anyone there.

"Where are my men?" he hollered—a sharpness to his tone.

"Dead. They fell in battle while we took out enemies inside." She would never admit she killed them.

Pressing his lips into a pale line—fire burning in his eyes—his talons shot upwards, whipped through the air, and into the crowd. She spun on her heel, staring at the nether magic as it recoiled. In its clutches was Damir.

"One thing you should know about nether magic—it does its master's bidding." Filip snarled. "If I command it to find and kill, it will execute my orders precisely."

The black shadows held her husband in a death grip. His face turned purple from suffocation.

"No!" she shouted. "Let him go."

"Do you think I would allow you to come to the Saintlandsther Council without removing any and all tools of support from your path?" He laughed. "I had a vision you were going to produce the Sword of Light, and such a book is only held in this grand library. I removed the whole collection, of course."

You were too busy stealing all the astral books, you forgot about your own.

"Please," she choked out. "It's not his fault. I'll do whatever you say."

"You'd already promised your obedience, and you have now proven your word means nothing." His black stare pierced straight through her.

As more of his soldiers marched into the courtyard, one approached him.

"What is it?" he snapped. "Can't you see I'm busy?"

"The city has fallen, sir," the soldier said. "Saintlandsther is yours."

Filip nodded once. "Find the Council members. Bring them to me."

The soldier spun on his heel, then headed inside the building. Moments later, six unarmed individuals filed outside. She recognised two of them. The elder woman was Olga—the leader—and the second was Kira. The girl she'd quickly befriended during her training. She hobbled—her leg covered in blood—but held her chin high.

"As punishment for your treachery, you will kill them." Filip's words sliced through the air like knives. "If you don't, I will snap Damir's neck, rip off his limbs, and throw each of them to every corner of the world."

Her magic surged, urging her to lash out at him. To snuff the life out of *him* instead of the countless innocents he'd slaughtered in his quick and bloody battle.

"Don't even think about it." His lips curled back as his gaze fixed on the golden rope around her wrist. "You have no control over your magic—if you use it, what's to say you won't kill everyone here anyway? Actually, you'd be doing me a favour. Go on. *Do it.*"

Every inch of her body crawled with the desperate need to lash out, to scream and let her magic erupt. For everything he'd done and threatened to do. She didn't belong to him, and every fibre of her being wanted to fight against his control. Those soldiers she'd killed—that was out of self-preservation. But *this*—this was cold-blooded murder. She would not risk lives for sake of letting out her anger. Lives would be lost for nothing. She couldn't kill Filip.

"Time's ticking." His hard voice interrupted her thoughts. The nether magic lowered Damir a foot or two, bringing him closer to her. His eyes bulged from the restricting talons. "He doesn't have much life left in him."

She flicked her gaze from Damir to Olga, Kira, and the other council members. Her eyes watered. How could she take their lives? Who was to say they meant less than Damir's? She shook her head profusely.

I am not a murderer.

"It's okay." Olga's voice was soft, almost inaudible. "I am quite prepared to die for my cause, and someday, Adelina will rise from the darkness in which you keep her."

Adelina could no longer fight the quiver of her lips or the tears in her eyes. "I won't do it."

"You must," Olga said sharply. "You must stop him, and we are but one sacrifice to ensure it happens."

"Do it now!" Filip hollered.

The soldiers shoved the Council members forwards, forcing them onto their knees, then stood back.

"Do it now, or so help me, I will kill them all. Every last one, including Damir, and your entire family." A feral growl escaped Filip's throat. "I will not pay a single thought for any civilian. Man, woman, or child."

Rage burst through her body, drenching her skin in wildfire as tears fell from her eyes. Golden light exploded from her, and the embroidery lashed out like a whip. Six severed heads hit the floor.

She fell to her knees, gaze locked on the bodies in front of her. Her hands were weak—no anger left in her to bunch them into fists. But her heart and her soul ached. How did this make her any different from Filip?

Damir thudded on the ground, tossed aside by Filip's talons.

Groaning, Damir crawled to her, wrapped his arms around her, drawing her against his chest. His act of comfort burst open her floodgates, and she wept. Mourned.

"Get up." Filip seized her by the arms and hoisted her off the ground.

Damir lost his balance and fell against the stone path.

Filip ordered a portion of his army to stay behind to ensure Saintlandsther remained captured, and any surviving man was slaughtered.

To her, his words were drowned, sounding distant and detached. The face of each council member burned in her mind. She was broken, and by his hand.

Chosen foot soldiers and cavalry prepared to leave the beaten city of Pike. As Filip left the courtyard, he halted, peering at a body slumped by the gate. With his booted foot, he turned the man's bloodied face. Pyotr.

"Pity," Filip muttered. "I suppose you have fulfilled your purpose."

As he hoisted himself onto his horse, Adelina stared at Pyotr. Although he'd betrayed her and her family, his death meant a wife without a husband, children without a father. She peeled her gaze from him, put her foot in the stirrup, then flung her leg over the saddle of her own mount.

"Return to the carriages," Filip ordered the army. "We must make way for Temauten."

A Ballad of Severed Souls

The foot soldiers shoved Damir along the path as the cavalry left the city. Filip rode ahead. But she could not rid herself of the gore and death surrounding her. It would haunt her on her journey to her home country. The ghosts would follow her. And she could not escape the fate awaiting her there. Home. Family. Everything she'd ever loved would be destroyed.

The world blurred. A dull ache shot through her chest. Her heart shattered.

NINETEEN

An Imbalance in the Scales of Nature

As they rode into the night, Adelina's ribs tightened. She wasn't at all sure if it was from the fracture or the shame holding her in a tight grip. Her head and muscles ached, and all she wanted to do was sleep. To rid herself of the hellish nightmare in which she lived.

The constant motion of riding did nothing to soothe the nausea churning inside her, or the gritty sensation in her eyes.

When they finally stopped to make camp, a handful of soldiers set about their hunt for food, while she conjured a fire and with the sluggish help of Damir, built her canvas tent. A gentle rain patted against the fabric.

Filip remained close by, keeping an eye on her and her husband. Since she'd done as he'd commanded and killed the council member and her apprentice, it seemed he was rewarding her with time with Damir.

They should never have died in the first place.

Damir rested one of his bound hands on her wrist, dragging her away from her sour thoughts.

"Thank you," he said softly. "For saving my life. I can't even begin to think about what you must be going through."

She looked at the ground, unable to meet his gaze. "Don't thank me. I am no better than he is."

"Hey." He tilted her chin until she faced him. "Look at me. You are *nothing* like him. Don't ever let him make you believe it. He wants to break you."

She shook her head as her eyes prickled. "He already has."

Brushing him off, she set about collecting sticks to keep the fire burning through the night. She couldn't bear to face him or hear his words. Shame consumed her, and it wouldn't be long before he saw it, too.

Once the sun set and their bellies were full, Filip and the soldiers retired to their tents. Damir was kept away from her—concealed within a tent manned by those on watch for the night.

Tossing and turning, unable to rid her mind of the images of severed limbs and bloodied bodies, she groaned and sat up. Dragging a hand over her face, she strained her eyes in the dim light of the fire shining through the thin walls of her tent.

She rummaged in her cloak pocket, then drew the book she'd taken from the library. With a flick of her finger, she conjured a ball of light, which hovered over her shoulder. Flicking through the pages, she frowned as she traced the unfamiliar words with her finger. What could they mean, and more importantly, why would this volume about nether magic be written in a different language to the first one? Checking the front and back pages, she searched for a clue—anything to help her understand the book's contents—but came back equally mystified.

Tucking the book away, she collapsed against the ground and clamped her eyes shut. She knew, if she were lucky enough to find sleep, she'd be haunted by the faces of those who'd perished. There'd be no escaping the nightmares awaiting her.

She found herself in the cave again. Water dripped from the walls, patting the floor in a steady rhythm. Darkness blurred her vision, making it almost impossible for her to make out the jagged surfaces of the cave. Why had her dream brought her here—to the place where Svarog had shown himself to her?

"Hello?" she called—her voice echoing onwards, distant and detached from her body.

Somewhere ahead, a golden light popped into existence, then spun and swelled. She shielded her eyes from its brightness, and when the light dimmed a fraction, Svarog stood in its place. The mighty dragon, God of Sun, yet she did not feel his benevolence.

"Why have you brought me here?" She crossed her arms. "I presumed you preoccupied with whatever it is you gods do in when you're not in this realm."

"I can ssssensssse the ache in your heart," he said tenderly as his tail wrapped around him. "I am ssssorry for the pain you endure."

A Ballad of Severed Souls

She scoffed. "Forgive me, but I don't believe you. You chose me, yet you have left me to face this darkness alone."

"I may be a God, but I have no physsssical being in your realm—you manifessssst me in your mind when I need you to ssssee me," he said—his gaze gentle on hers. "However, I have sssssenssssed the sssscalessss of nature are imbalancsssssed."

"You're late on your assumption." She rolled her eyes. "Many have already died. More are likely to."

"I undersssstand your contempt, but I have appeared to you in your dreamssss for a reasssson, Adelina," he said. "You oncssse assssked me why Velessss would allow Antanov and Filip to be reborn into the physsssical realm. I have ssssincsssse pondered your quesssstion and believe I may have your ansssswer."

Despite her prickling annoyance, her attention piqued. "Tell me."

"Much like how you and Filip are each other'ssss natural balancsssse, Velessss issss mine." His voice deepened with a note of what she considered disdain for the God of the Underworld. "He alssssso doessss not have a physsssical presssssencssse in your realm for issss sssshackled to the realm in which he rulessss. I have come to believe hissss dessssire for dominion liessss elsssssewhere."

He let his words hang in the air, allowing her to draw her own conclusions.

"You think Veles wants to dominate the living plane?" She raised a brow. Despite her scepticism, her blood cooled.

"Why elssssse would he be concssssserned about the three countriessss? Why would he care whether Filip

or Antanov ssssuccsssseeded in gaining control?" he questioned.

"I asked Filip the same things, but, of course, he avoided them," she said.

"Asssss godssss, we are sssseparate from the living plane, but I have causssse to believe Velessss hassss grown bored. He sssseeksss a new kingdom." His wings flared, whipping a breeze through the cave.

"He wants to break through to the living realm." An icy shiver jolted her.

Nodding, his beady eyes fixed on hers. *"I ssssee you have found ssssomething to confirm our sssssuspicionssss."*

"The book?" she said. "Well, perhaps not. It's written in a different language unless you know how to translate it."

"I can blessss you with the knowledge." As his slippery words left his mouth, a golden light shone from him, enveloping her. *"Conssssider it my way of adjusssssting thossse sssscalessss."*

"Let's hope it's enough." She straightened her back, rejuvenated with a new sense of purpose. He'd helped her, after all. "And I hope your words prove true. Otherwise, I will add your trustworthiness to the list of things I have already lost on this dark path."

His forked tongue flicked out the corner of his mouth. "Farewell, Adelina Orlova."

She bolted upright, a layer of sweat lining her forehead. Feeling the warmth of his magic on her skin, she could've sworn the dream had been real.

Leaning forward, she grabbed the book and flipped through the pages. She couldn't afford to draw any attention in her direction. When she landed on the centre page, she squinted. Smothering a laugh of amazement, she watched the letters shift and reorganise themselves into words she could comprehend. If the god she'd trusted could do one thing to help her, it was surely that.

Her breath caught in her throat.

The passage spoke of the living plane, the Underworld, of Svarog and Veles—two halves of the same soul. A mirror image to her and Filip. Yet the difference was the gods had been at war with each other for centuries. The text spoke of Veles' failed attempt to break through the barrier between realms a millennium ago. And history was repeating itself—he was using Antanov and Filip as his emissaries. If they succeeded, a hole would be ripped through the barrier. Veles and the demons of the Underworld would be free to roam the realm.

Mind reeling, she stashed the book away and fought the urge to scramble out of her tent and go to Damir. This was yet another secret she must keep from her husband—keep him safe—and find a way to stop Filip. More than ever, she longed for the one book she needed above all else—the one Yelena swore was in the library in Saintlandsther Council. The one Filip had likely stolen when he'd cleared out the entire astral magic collection.

She prayed a quick thanks to Svarog for reminding her of her purpose.

Songbirds woke her. Sunlight shone through the thin canvas of her tent, and the early morning breeze made her teeth chatter. Whipping on her cloak, she tugged it tight about her shoulders. When she climbed out of the tent, a waft of roasting meat filled her nose. Her stomach grumbled.

Soldiers sat around a fire, eating their meal. Damir was positioned nearby, hunched over a small portion of burned scraps. She beelined for him.

Glancing up, he gave her a tired smile. "Morning."

"Morning to you, too." She lowered onto the ground beside him. "Where's Filip?"

"Off speaking with some General, I think." His gaze hollowed. "There's been talk amongst the men of the siege planned for Temauten. There's no way for us to even warn our families."

"No," she admitted. "But when the attack starts, head straight to your home. Get our parents out of Aramoor. Urge them into the forest, and as far away as they can get. I don't want them to be there when Filip forces my hand."

He nodded, then clasped her hand and squeezed. "I'll make sure they're safe."

Within the hour, the camp was dismantled, the horses saddled, and Filip led the army back to the meandering dirt path leading to the forest along the Temauten border.

The following ten days' journey to the border passed at an excruciatingly slow pace. The serenity of the forest was a welcome sight for Adelina—its peacefulness cleansed her mind of the trauma she'd faced at Saintlandsther and gave her a moment of respite from what was to come.

They rode steadily along the trail passing between sheer rock faces. Tree roots crisscrossed the path, and branches hung out—soldiers dipped their head to get by. Overgrown sections swallowed separate routes whole, seemingly disappearing altogether. One could easily get lost there, and she wondered if it was such a bad idea.

Half-buried stones and pebbles shifted underneath horses' hooves. Fallen, dewy leaves clung to twigs at the sides, and wildflowers poked through the tall grass. Sun speckled areas broke the darkness of the forest in random places. Tilting her face to the sky, she let the light warm her cheeks for the few seconds she rode.

A low footbridge over a stream ahead held them up for half an hour while each soldier coaxed their horses along the worn, creaking bridge, and again later, when they rode through a shallow creek. Fallen tree trunks and decaying branches blocked several routes through the forest, testing Filip's patience as he navigated the way through.

Adelina remained close by, biting her tongue. Every muscle of her body ached from exhaustion—each of her nights plagued by nightmares she couldn't seem to shake. She was in no mood to deal with Filip's displeasure, nor did she possess the effort to poke and prod at him, either. Instead, she focused her attention on the small animals moving in the underbrush, and the splashing of water over rocks. As soon as they broke through the edge of the forest, her thoughts would return to the siege laying ahead of them, but until then, she let her mind wander.

The pungent scent of decaying wood and leaves filled her nostrils.

'The thought of you leaving, leaving me, is crippling. If you told me you wanted to run away to

escape Filip—if you feel this mark has sealed your fate—then I would go with you.'

Damir's words all those months ago echoed. She wondered what would've happened if they *had* run away before the test. Would Filip have found her anyway? There was no way of knowing for sure.

When they broke through the treeline and the afternoon heat of early summer warmed her cheeks, she refocused on the task at hand. Reach Aramoor. Keep Damir and her family safe. She could not fail. *She would not fail.*

~~~

Drums boomed over Murtei—the city of the Temauten Congregation, not too far from Aramoor. The sound of thundering drums would carry on the wind. Her family would hear them. Adelina hoped they would heed its warning.

Filip led the march into the city. Murtei's soldiers were already in position—shields raised; swords pointed. Her breath caught in her throat. Another bloodbath would ensue, and she could do nothing to stop it.

"Attack!" Filip's booming voice sliced the air.

All foot soldiers and calvary charged forward in formation. The bright red banners of Murtei waved in the breeze. What seemed like hundreds of narrow spears shot through the air, ultimately landing in the hearts of his men.

Adelina couldn't help the surge of joy shooting through her heart. Temauten were prepared for this attack—they'd ensured their defences were in line, and perhaps there was hope they wouldn't face the same ending as Saintlandsther.

The people of Temauten—her beloved hometown—were prideful, and they weren't about to let their home be taken down without a fight.

She stayed out of Filip's line of sight and sought civilians. Instead of committing murder, she'd save those she could. She'd prove she was not the same as Filip. While she may share half her soul with him, he was not half the person she was.

Jumping from her horse, she guided a quivering family inside a building. She ushered them under a table. "Stay low and keep your heads covered. Don't come out. There may be explosions."

As she turned to leave, a child grabbed her arm. "Wait. Don't go."

"You will be fine here," she reassured him. "I must help other families."

His mother held him, stroking his head. "Thank you."

Adelina smiled, then dashed outside. Damir waited, wielding a sword.

"Where in gods' realm did you get that?" she gasped.

"I saw you slip off, and I wasn't about to lose you in the fight like last time *or* let myself get throttled by Filip again. I knocked out a soldier and stole his weapon. Here, I have a sword for you." He grinned, tossing it to her. "We stay together. Always."

"Always," she repeated. "Stay behind me. You don't have any true experience with a sword, so follow me and copy what I do."

She'd need to rely on her combat skills if she was going to use the blade instead of unleashing her magic. Chewing on the inside of her cheek, she squashed her nerves. There wasn't time to dwell on her newly acquired abilities to fight with fists and weapons. With a tight grip on her weapon, she led Damir into battle.

She swung her sword, cutting a path through the battlefield. With a brief glance over her shoulder, she found Damir slashing his weapon this way and that—clumsy and not always accurate, but she was in no place to complain or criticise, especially if it kept him alive.

The iron scent of fresh blood filled her nose, making her grimace. Another wave of arrows *whooshed!* overhead as archers on the walls unleashed them from their bows. Instinctively, she flung up her arm to protect her head.

Screams punctured the air as men hit the ground like tumbling dominoes.

While the army of Murtei was smaller than the number of men at Filip's command, they did not back down. Adelina, unwilling to thrash her weapon through men of her own country, ducked and dived out of the way, dashing through shadows, and drawing families away from the conflict. Damir, on the other hand, stayed close to her, and flung his sword up to meet any attacking blows.

Sweat stung her eyes like tiny vipers as she re-emerged into the chaos outside. A blur of colour. A whirlwind of disorder. Her parched mouth collected dust from the cloud stirred into the air by heavy footfall. Blood pounded in her ears, drumming to the ferocious beat of her heart. The sound wasn't enough to drown the screams of men, the cries of children separated from their mothers, or the thunder of steel striking steel.

"Head straight for the gates of Temauten Congregation. Let no man stand in your way!" Filip's barked ordered pierced her ears.

She spun, searching for his face amongst the crowd. His black talons snaked through the air, tossing bodies aside as if they were nothing, severing limbs like snapped twigs.

Fuelled by rage, her golden embroidery zapped into existence around her wrist. She raised her arm, ready to fire a bolt of unrestrained magic in his direction.

"Don't." Damir grabbed her. "It's not worth risking innocent lives. Remember what you're here to do. Help people."

Swallowing her wrath, she nodded.

One of Filip's soldiers snatched a longbow from a nearby stand and unleashed an arrow. It punctured a man on a roof opposite them. He toppled over, descended two storeys, and crashed onto the porch below.

Adelina ground her teeth. Filip was ordering needless murders of people who were defending their home.

Heading deeper into the packed streets of the city, it wasn't long before she and Damir were separated. She'd no choice but to parry oncoming attacks. She blocked what blows she could as she darted through the crowd, all the while keeping one hand pressed against her fractured ribs. She gritted her teeth through the pain. These moments of agony in her side would be worth it if it meant getting her family to safety and getting her hands on that book.

One of Filip's men threw a punch into a Murtei soldier's neck. He stumbled backwards into another of Filip's army.

He gripped him by the neck and sliced it.

"You didn't need to kill him!" she raged.

"It's either kill them or they will kill you. And Filip will never let me see the light of day if I let you die," he grunted before countering another attack.

Spinning, she searched for Damir. Disoriented by the packed crowd, the constant clatter of metal, and the sharp shoves and jolts of charging men, she fought her way through the battle.

Gripping onto a nearby, blood spattered beam, she panted, catching her breath. She needed to get a better vantage point if she was to spot her husband. Taking in a moment, she scanned her surroundings. The beam was connected to a wooden floor directly above her head. Following it with her gaze, she spotted a staircase.

Dashing for it, she sprinted up the spiralling steps and onto the balcony overlooking the onslaught crammed into the narrow cobble street. "Damir!"

Despite screaming his name at the top of her lungs, the sound would not carry over the battle below.

Her gaze darted about, and she cursed the fact his dark hair blended in with the rest. Thankfully, he was armed.

"Gods damn it," she said under her breath.

As she hurried down the stairs and through the door, she found herself in a sea of fighting men. Cramped, she shoved her way between jostling limbs and swinging swords. Her ribs screamed in protest as people pushed and shoved her. Blinking back stars, she ignored the pain, keeping her spare hand clamped against her side as she sought her husband.

Rising onto her tiptoes, she craned her neck and searched for him again. As she surveyed the crowd, a sharp blow landed on the back of her head. The street wheeled, and the blood-spattered cobbles rose to meet her.

She awoke to a silent city. Her eyes fluttered open, and a concerned Filip frowned at her. With a disorienting jerk, she tumbled out of his embrace.

He let her go but remained kneeling by her side. "Victory is ours."

While the words brought a proud grin to his face, it made her sick to her stomach. Ignoring him, she absorbed her surroundings. Bodies littered the street as far as the eye could see. Filip's men stood nearby, one keeping Damir's arms bound behind his back.

"What...what have you done?" Her tongue was thick, and her mind muddled from the blow.

"I have done what I set out to do. The city has fallen, and the three countries now belong to me." He approached a soldier, muttered something she couldn't hear, then turned back to her. "We will stay here for the night. If there's anything to eat in this gods-forsaken city, we'll feast—celebrate our victory—then make our way to Kirovo Palace tomorrow."

If her head didn't hurt so much from the blow, she'd have wondered what he'd said to the soldier.

"You mean to say you've done Veles' bidding," she spat. "He's got his claws so deep in you, hasn't he?"

Something flickered in his eyes—she couldn't decipher what it was—but a stony expression returned to his face just as quick. "Despite Veles' involvement in this, the cities belong to *me*."

She scoffed. "Keep telling yourself so. You're a pawn in his game. He is bored with his own realm, and he's using *you* to get what he wants: a new kingdom."

Pressing his lips into a thin line, he clenched his fist. His anger amused her. Despite the atrocities Veles orchestrated through Filip, he'd given him a taste of his own medicine.

"And what makes you any different?" He strode towards her until his nose was mere inches from her face.

Damir thrashed against the soldier, who kept his arms restrained. While she appreciated his concern, she could defend herself. And she would never let Filip use her again.

"If I am Veles' pawn, then you are but the same for Svarog." Filip curled his top lip in a snarl. "Two gods at war with each other for centuries, two halves of the same soul. Don't take me for a fool, Adelina. You see him too, don't you? I know what it takes to forge the Sword of Light. Svarog would've come to you. The same as Veles comes to me."

She rose on her tiptoes to meet his spiteful glare, matching it with equal measure. "If you think Svarog and Veles are the same, you are sorely mistaken."

"Stand *down*, Adelina. Or so help me gods, you will regret it." His steely voice sliced the air.

Shaking her head, she took a step backwards. "So be it."

Filip was in denial—he couldn't see what she could see. And when Veles was successful at ripping a hole through the barrier between the realms, he'd be dragged so deep into darkness, there'd be no saving him. She wondered why the concept of saving his soul came to her mind. Perhaps there was an element of pity she held for him. Considering all he'd done, she didn't think he deserved even that.

Filip stormed through the corridors of the Temauten Congregation building. She'd gotten under his skin. Perhaps there was weight to her words—something to consider. No—he'd done what Veles demanded to correct his father's mistakes. But *he* was powerful, and he would not be used and discarded by a god. If Veles wanted out of the underworld, he'd need to learn to cooperate. Filip was not about to hand over the cities he'd claimed. The next time Veles presented himself, Filip would make his intentions clear. He'd assume his role as emperor as planned, and if Veles didn't like it, he'd ensure he'd never cross the threshold into the living realm.

Resting on the windowsill of a chamber in the Temauten Congregation, Adelina watched as soldiers stacked bodies into carts and wheeled them out of the city. Even through the window, the stench of death reached her nose.

She yanked the curtains closed, then paced the wooden floors. Damir was being detained separately from her, and Filip had locked her in her room. She'd challenged him, poked, and prodded the fire raging inside him.

Biting hard on her bottom lip, she wondered if she'd made the right decision. She should've kept her mouth shut. Someone would pay the price for her treacherous words.

In the middle of the night, Adelina jolted. The entrance doors of the building banged open. Screams of protest rang through the halls.

Flinging back the covers, she scrambled out of bed, tugged on her breeches and shirt, then rattled the door. Locked. But she recognised those voices. Her family. What in the realm were they doing there?

Shoving her hand through her hair, her mind spiralled. Was this Filip's way of punishing her for challenging him? If so, she'd throw herself at his feet for mercy if it meant keeping her family from harm.

Hurrying to the other end of the room, she tugged on the window to see if she could pry it open. It wouldn't budge. She returned her attention to the door.

Scanning her mind, she searched for a spell to unlock it. She'd once used a thistle vine to pry open the glass cabinet at the library. Surely, that could work here.

Fighting to keep control of her voice, she said, "*Rinorowlith*."

Heart hammering, she tapped her foot in a fast rhythm. Nothing happened. *Nothing.*

Filip be damned.

He must've warded the lock—some sort of counter charm.

Cupping her hands together, she conjured a blinding ball of golden light. Without hesitation, she fired it. The magic snuffed, little embers drifting to the floorboards. Aside from a scorched surface, the door remained standing.

Shoving loose strays of hair out of her face, she took a deep breath and produced the golden embroidery. Her skin on her wrists stung as blisters formed, but the magic spun like fine thread. She uncurled it and lashed it against the wood. It creaked and groaned, but not enough to break through completely.

Placing one foot ahead of the other, she balanced herself. She rolled her shoulders, raised her arms, and encouraged the swelling magic inside her until it set her skin alight.

As she whipped out her magic in another blow, she covered her face with her free arm as the wood shattered on impact, sending fragments hurtling in her direction. The door was ripped clean off and half the stone wall was blown in.

Trampling over the rubble, she strode out of the room, setting a quick pace down the hallway. She followed the high-pitched yells of her sister and her mother's fragile attempts at soothing her.

Coming to a halt at the top of the grand stairs, she absorbed the sight of her family, arms bound behind their backs by soldiers.

"Let go of them!" Adelina barrelled down the stairs but stopped when Filip stepped out of the shadows. "Filip. Whatever it is you're thinking right now, I implore you to reconsider."

He watched her closely, not a hint of emotion on his face.

"Earlier on," she continued, forcing the words from her mouth. "I overstepped. I should not have questioned you as I did."

"No." His single word was abrupt and cold. "You shouldn't have."

Gaze flicking to her crying sister, Tihana, Adelina fought to keep it together. The fate of her family was in Filip's hands, and she must tread carefully.

"Let my family go. Please." She refocused her stare on Filip. Her heart pounded against her ribs. "They have done nothing wrong."

"No?" Filip tilted his head. "I beg to differ."

He strolled towards her father and stopped in front of him.

A Ballad of Severed Souls

Daro lifted his chin a notch, refusing to lower his gaze. Adelina's stomach churned, threatening to upheave the minimal contents of inside it.

"Filip." Her words were no louder than a whisper. A desperate plea. "*Please.*"

He shot an icy stare over his shoulder. "Be quiet." He returned his attention to Daro.

"When the test confirmed Adelina was a wielder, we did not resist. We let you take her in peace," Daro said.

"And this is where your obedience ends." Filip narrowed his eyes. "After all, you condoned a marriage between Adelina and Damir. Correct?"

Anger burst through Adelina's core. She wasn't about to stand by idly while Filip took his wrath out on her family. Golden magic shot from her wrist, casting a bright light across the foyer.

"Adelina, do you always have to be such a constant annoyance?" With a flick of his hand, Filip conjured a nether talon. It snaked towards her and bound her in place.

She fought against it, but its grip was unbreakable.

"Do not harm my daughter," Daro growled. "I allowed what any good father would—a happy and *consummated* union between a man and his wife."

"Damir is a wretched excuse of a man. Constantly in my way. You know, he is confined to a room upstairs. I could have him killed and be done with it. Your daughter would be free to wed again." Filip was goading her father.

Adelina prayed he wouldn't walk straight into Filip's trap.

Daro didn't speak.

"Ah, silence." Filip sighed. "No, it won't do. As much as Adelina might do anything in her power to save her husband, he is not the one who has a true hold on her heart."

Daro frowned.

Adelina fought as hard as she could against the nether talon wrapped at her torso. It's sharp blades punctured her skin in several places, but she didn't care. She needed to break free. "Filip, wait—"

The talon extended, coiling itself around her face. Her words were choked.

"What do you mean?" Daro questioned.

A second nether talon lashed out from Filip's body. It shot straight for Tihana. She cried as it rocketed her into the air. The tip of the black tendril throttled her.

Adelina screamed, but the sound was muffled by her own restraints. Her parents fought against the soldiers.

The nether talon constricted, and Tihana's neck snapped. The crunch of bone pierced Adelina's ears. Her vision blurred as the tiny fragments of her heart disintegrated.

Tihana's body dropped to the floor in a mess of limbs as the nether magic slithered away. Her parents shrieked, Velinka screaming wildly, Daro swearing viciously, both of them clawing at the soldiers as they dragged them out of the entrance. They towed her parents away from her sister's body. Away from her. Their demands and pleas echoed until they faded altogether.

Adelina, bound by the last nether talon, fell to her knees. She fought against her constrictor, crawling her way towards her sister's body.

A Ballad of Severed Souls

Filip's magic dissipated. He stood by idly as she scrambled to Tihana.

Shifting Tihana's motionless body, she rested her head in her lap and stroked the curls away from her face.

Almost eerily, Filip's clomping feet echoed through the foyer as he retreated into his study.

Tears dripping onto her sister's face, Adelina's clutched her tight. Leaning forward, she pressed a kiss against her temple. Gently, as if not to wake her from the peaceful slumber Adelina pretended her sister was in, she laid her head on the floor.

Two soldiers emerged, presumably to remove the body, to be taken wherever they'd dumped the fallen from the earlier battle.

Even as she stood, she couldn't stop looking at the pale, colourless cheeks of Tihana's face. Her closed eyes, and her tiny button nose. Her sister seemed younger than her years—death stripping away the small amount of life she'd experienced. And there was nothing Adelina could give her, nothing she could do to comfort her as her soul made its way to the afterlife.

Adelina thought of the bunny Tihana had taken everywhere, and what she would've given to tuck it into her arms. Instead, she tore the peonies from a vase positioned on a sideboard, then lowered beside her sister.

She rested the flowers on her still chest, then placed her sister's hand on top, as if she were holding them.

Heavy footsteps drew closer, but she ignored them, unable to tear her blurry stare from her sister's still-warm body. Even when large hands wrapped around her arms and yanked her from the floor, she did not look away.

"Goodbye, Tihana," she whispered as the guards dragged her up the staircase.

More soldiers filtered into the foyer and was all the confirmation she needed. She'd never see her sister again.

TWENTY

The Ghosts of Her Heart

Filip kept to himself and didn't stop Adelina from going straight to Damir. Even the guard positioned outside his door moved aside and allowed her in. She couldn't comprehend why they'd given her time to share grief with her husband, but she didn't care. She needed him.

He met her gaze with his own hollow one. Instead of offering words of condolence, he simply held his arms out for her. She suspected he'd heard the screaming—the sound would've carried. It echoed in her mind like a ghost and would live there for eternity.

"These walls aren't as thick as they appear," he whispered, confirming her suspicions. "I'm so sorry."

She buried her face against his chest. A thick lump wedged itself in her throat, an intense ache gripped her insides, and her eyes stung. She hadn't thought her heart could break further—she was wrong. The fragments turned to dust.

"I'm with you. I've got you." He stroked the back of her head, holding her tight. He began to pick up each grain of dust, and while she knew he'd try everything he could to find a way to piece them back together, she didn't think such a task was possible.

Even with her eyes clamped shut, she couldn't rid herself of the image of her sister's still body. Her pale skin. She was a child. Filip murdered her sister. A *child*. How could she rise against him? Inflict her revenge on him?

Although each of her muscles ached from weariness, she wanted to do something—*anything*—to make him accountable, to show the world she was *not* Filip's pawn, she wouldn't bend to his will, nor allow anyone else to fall by his hand. Tihana was more than a piece in his game, and so was she. And she'd make sure he remembered it.

Withdrawing from their embrace, she tilted her chin up to meet Damir's soft gaze. "We have to do something."

"I know." He stroked her cheek with his thumb. "We'll be heading back to Kirovo Palace soon."

"I didn't find the book in the Saintlandsther Council building. Yelena believes there's something that'll help me—some spell to finally put a stop to Filip." She wrapped her fingers around his hand as he traced a line down her cheek. "We'll find it. Filip will pay for his crimes."

"I believe you." He bent to kiss her, and the softness of his lips and the warmth it shot through her core dulled the ache in her fragmented heart. "I'll be with you every step of the way."

She hadn't told him the full extent of what Filip was up to, nor disclosed the contents of the book she translated and Veles' involvement. There was no point in worrying him when there wasn't much he could do. It was up to her, and as long as her husband was by her side, she'd succeed.

A thundering knock on the door broke them apart.

"Time's up," the soldier hollered from outside. "You're both needed up at dawn for the journey to Kirovo Palace."

Damir grasped her hands and squeezed. "We'll be fine. I promise."

She nodded, unsure whether she truly believed it. After a final kiss, she let go and headed out of the room.

※

Sitting in her saddle, Adelina waited for Filip to give the command to move out. Their supplies were packed and strapped to the horses. A handful of soldiers were ordered to stay behind, to maintain control of the city until Filip could position someone trustworthy—*and easily bent to his will*—in the Temauten Congregation.

Filip hadn't cast a glance in her direction, nor said a single word to her. He was lucky he hadn't—she wasn't at all sure she could keep her rage in check. The sight of him made her want to vomit.

Within half an hour, they'd ridden out of Murtei and along the dirt path heading north. They'd cut through the mountain and follow the route back to Kirovo.

Casting a glance over her shoulder, she looked a Damir. He rode close by, under the watchful gaze of surrounding soldiers. He nodded at her, which she took as a sign he was okay.

It took them two weeks to reach the gates of Kirovo Palace. Adelina couldn't shake the weariness in her bones, nor the black cloud following her. The only hope of light was Yelena, and the help she could offer.

Damir was escorted back to the prison cells beneath the palace, and Filip sent orders for his father to be brought there. Shortly after, he disappeared into his study. She headed straight to the training room, then slipped into Yelena's secret office.

"You look dreadful." Yelena shut the disguised door behind her. "What happened?"

"My sister died." The words tasted sour in Adelina's mouth.

"Oh." Yelena lifted her hand to her chest. "I'm so sorry."

Adelina shook her head, blinking back tears. "Don't be. It's not like you forced Filip to murder her."

"He's a vicious monster," Yelena spat. "Did you find the book?"

"No." Adelina set in a pace across the wooden floorboards. "All the astral books were removed. Filip was two steps ahead of me—he *knew* I'd look for them. He was testing me, and I walked straight into his trap. As punishment, he forced me to kill the Saintlandsther Council. Olga and Kira are dead."

Yelena's mouth opened. "I...I don't know what to say."

"I'm sorry." Adelina pushed the words out—the lump in her throat made her voice thick. "Olga was your friend."

In quick strides, Yelena closed the space between them, grabbed Adelina's hands, and halted her pacing. "Don't ever apologise for that bastard. It's not your fault."

"I'm not sure," Adelina whispered. "Filip said I'm not so different from him, and well...maybe I'm starting to believe him. The person I was a few months ago would never have let innocent people die. No matter the cost."

"Even if the cost was Damir or your family?" Yelena raised her brows. "I'm sure that's how Filip got you to submit, right?"

"Yes," she breathed—her grief clawing at her throat, gripping her. "My sister's death isn't even the worst of it. There were so many people who died. Soldiers. Civilians. Filip has his men stationed in Pike and Murtei to ensure they remain defeated. What about the people who survived, still living there?"

"Hey, calm down. Focus on one thing at a time." Yelena's voice was feather-light. Soothing.

Adelina tried to heed Yelena's advice, but her mind darted back and forth. Between one problem and the next. "I think he's suspicious of the sword too."

"What do you mean?" Yelena frowned, and crow's feet sprouted from the corner of her eyes.

Resting her hands on the back of a chair, Adelina attempted to get her thoughts in order. "He's been using it this whole time…to kill people. There was no reaction when he first touched it—not like what I experienced when Svarog forged it for me—and there was no effect when he used it to cut down his enemies. He might as well be wielding a normal weapon. There's nothing remotely magical about it."

"It doesn't make any sense," Yelena said. "The Sword of Light should've changed its loyalties when you gave it to Filip. After all, it possesses both of your souls."

"Even so, I'm telling you, something isn't right."

"Well, let's see it as a good thing." Yelena straightened. "Filip doesn't need more power than he has."

Adelina couldn't see it as a good thing, no matter how hard she tried. Filip wasn't stupid. He'd question her about it, eventually. If anything, she wondered why he hadn't demanded answers already.

"If we go based on the assumption that he *does* know something is off with the sword," she said, voicing her concerns, "why has he not spoken of it?"

Yelena shrugged. "Why would he? It would show he relies on you for information—no book is going to tell him. If the answer *was* in a book somewhere, he'd know by now. After all, he has the entire astral collection in his possession. He's not going to want to appear weak, or less in control, in front of you. He'll try to figure it out on his own."

"Veles speaks to him like Svarog does to me," Adelina said. "Perhaps Veles will tell Filip something about the sword's allegiance."

A Ballad of Severed Souls

"Possibly." Yelena's lips twisted as she pondered. "There's no way for us to know what goes down between Veles and Filip. Since the sword is in Filip's possession now, they won't worry about you using it against him."

"He has control of all three countries, at least through their council buildings." Adelina's eyes widened as her memory shifted to the council leader of the Temauten Congregation. "Wait…Nikolay wasn't in the battle. Do you know where he is? Has he sent you a letter?"

"No, it's too dangerous to send letters right now." Yelena shook her head. "Filip will be intercepting everything sent between the countries. How better to stomp out any rivals than to always remain two steps ahead? Any whiff of treason—revolt—he'll kill them."

It was too much. It was *all* too much. She walked a blade's edge between keeping her sanity and falling to the floor, overcome with grief and heartache. If she did, it would consume her and there'd be no getting back up.

"What are we to do?" Adelina said breathlessly.

"We need to find the book." Yelena lifted a finger. "I'm not even sure *which* one, but it's likely Filip would've hidden them somewhere close to him. When you were both away, I had a quick snoop around his office, and I couldn't find anything. We'll need to pay close attention to anything that looks out of place—creaking floorboards, strange latches, anything that looks like it could be a place to hide an important object from unwanted attention."

"It would make sense for him to keep the book in his office, seeing as he spends so much of his time there," Adelina said.

"Yes, but exactly *how* are we going to get an opportunity to go rifling through it?" Yelena began a slow pace back and forth across the floorboards. "He'll have to be away for at least an hour for us to have enough time to search for the books and ensure we've taken the right one."

"We'll need to cause a distraction—lure him away from his office, so we can check," Adelina suggested as adrenaline flooded her body.

"There will be no *we* about it. You'll stay with him, so he doesn't suspect you," Yelena said. "I can search through his office, find the right book, then return here. He won't suspect a thing if I ensure everything remains undisturbed."

"Won't he eventually notice the book was taken?" Adelina said.

"We'll have to be quick. I'll bring it to you, learn what you must, then I'll put it back," Yelena added. "Now we need to figure out a way to get him and you away from the palace."

Adelina rubbed the side of her head as she searched her mind for a plausible distraction. "I'll give him what he wants. At least for a short while. I'll practise my magic in the gardens. No prism world."

"You could set the place on fire." Yelena narrowed her eyes.

"It'll be worth the risk—Filip needs to see me using it, believe I'm serious, broken to his will since he murdered my sister. He'll want to spectate, witness how uncontrolled my magic can be. I'm sure he won't mind some torched bushes." Despite the confidence she forced into her voice, her hands shook. Filip was always a step ahead of her—would she outsmart him this time?

Yelena smiled. "You haven't given yourself a second to grieve, and yet you remain focused on stopping Filip. I admire it."

"I don't have time to grieve." *Or the strength to.* "If we don't succeed at this, Filip will rip a hole through the barrier, and Veles will have his kingdom. Filip already has the three countries under his thumb—he has access to all armies, resources, you name it. No one will try to stop him."

"It will be dinner time soon. Dine with Filip. Ask him to accompany you to the gardens. When I see you, I'll go to Damir," Yelena said.

"What about the guards? Won't they see you?" Adelina frowned, aware of a potential fault in their plan. If they were caught, it would be all over.

"I'll deal with the guards in the prison and let Damir out. We can use him as part of the distraction—have him make a run for it. The guards positioned on the ground floor will assume he is trying to run away." Yelena's words tumbled out of her mouth with haste.

Adelina nodded before she processed the words. "How can we ensure Damir's safety? He's been through too much. I've risked *everything* to protect him, and I *won't* risk his life as collateral."

"Trust me. For this to work, ensure Filip joins you in the garden. It's not enough for him to simply see you from his office window. He *must* be by your side for me to allow enough time for Damir to cause a distraction." Yelena inspected her watch, then lifted her gaze. "Once I've grabbed the book, we'll meet first thing in the morning. If Filip sees you sneaking off to the training room late at night, it might ring alarm bells in his mind."

"Okay." Adelina swallowed, ignoring the sickly sensation crawling up her neck. "I'll see you later."

Hurrying out of the training room, she headed for her chamber. Keeping a neutral expression so she didn't draw attention to herself from patrolling guards, she slipped into her room and prepared herself for dinner.

―――

Adelina clamped her fingers together underneath the large table. The banquet served was enough to feed the entire household, yet only she and Filip were seated, each of them at either end. Instead of curling her lips in distaste at the waste of food when there were thousands of people starving in Saintlandsther, she plastered a smile on her face.

"You look as radiant as ever." He eyed her over the rim of the glass in his hand. Swilling the liquor, he sipped it, then lounged back in his chair.

"Thank you," she said, ignoring the nausea in her stomach. He made her skin crawl, but if false pleasantries and surface level dinner talk was enough to get him into the garden, then so be it. She'd stroke his ego if she needed to. "So do you."

"What are you waiting for?" He nodded to the spread of food platters. "Eat."

Picking up her cutlery, she ate only enough to line her stomach, to ease the cramping there. Anything more, and she might vomit. Taking the napkin from the table, she dabbed at the sweat on the back of her neck.

"All is well?" he asked.

She set aside the napkin and folded her hands in her lap. She wasn't gullible enough to think he genuinely cared for her welfare, not unless it posed a threat to *his* plans. He could bait her all he liked, but she refused to fall into any of his traps. "Yes, thank you. Perhaps it is the alcohol."

She glanced the goblet beside her plate—she'd taken several large gulps to quell her nerves.

"Perhaps," he mused, his stare burning into her.

"I was thinking you might like to join me in the garden," she said, keeping a casual tone to her voice. "I would like to practise my magic, and it might be wise to see how our powers interact with each other. After all, we are strongest together, aren't we?"

He arched a brow. "I'm sure at the very least it will prove entertaining."

She smiled again. "Of course. Care to escort me now?"

He flicked his gaze to his unfinished glass of liquor, then nodded, setting it on the table. Shoving his chair back with feline grace, he strolled over to her and held out his hand.

She accepted it and allowed him to guide her into the moonlight.

Adelina strolled into the centre of the garden, with Filip at her side.

Closing her eyes, she coaxed her magic, urging it to drench her nerve endings in fire. The warmth of her power grew, intensifying, until it emerged as golden embroidery twirling around her wrist.

With one foot positioned slightly ahead of the other for balance, she raised her arm. The golden light shone, covering the gardens in bright sunlight—a stark contrast to the dull, cloudy sky.

Letting go of the loose grip she maintained on her magic, the embroidery shot out like a whip, severing the tips of nearby topiaries, the stumps charred. It wasn't enough. She needed more. *Fire.*

She sucked in a deep breath, giving her body over to the burning sensation coursing through her veins. Sunlight streamed from her skin as if she'd become the sun herself. The whip shot out again, this time plunging straight through the conservatory window, raining glass onto the flowerbeds.

"You've destroyed the topiaries." Filip smirked. "Entertaining, indeed. Although I'd much prefer if you didn't destroy more of my carefully tended garden."

"You've proven you're smarter than me," she said. "And you have proven you will take what you want by force. I'm not prepared to sacrifice anyone else I love, so I will do what you say without resistance. I will show you more of what I'm capable of, then we can see how our magic behaves together."

He didn't speak or move for a moment, but then he nodded and reclined onto the wooden bench nearby.

Straightening her back, she mustered another lash of energy. The tail of her whip thrashed.

Within seconds, Filip was on his feet, the tip of his black nether talon wrapped around her golden embroidery.

"I wasn't attacking you," she said quickly.

"It aimed for me," he spat. "Do not test me, Adelina. You know what happens when you challenge me. Unless you want me to march right downstairs and slit Damir's throat."

"I'm sorry." Her heart pounded, threatening to burst from her chest. "I didn't mean to. I'm not in control."

His talon let go, and her magic recoiled, fading from existence.

He walked towards her, positioning himself right behind her. With his cold breath on her shoulder, she locked her muscles. Her stomach churned with the threat of wanting to vomit. He made her skin crawl.

Ever so slowly, he touched her, wrapping his fingers around her palms. "Let your magic go."

His words were soft, gentle…and confusing. It was like Damir was talking to her, encouraging her. But she wouldn't be fooled into thinking his soothing tone meant anything other than deception and manipulation.

Obeying, she conjured the golden light again, letting it spin around her wrist.

"Aim for those bushes when I say. I do not care if you destroy *those* ones." His lips brushed her ear, and she swallowed to stop herself from heaving. "Now."

Training her eyes on the bushes, she fired her magic—it shot straight for them. His nether magic seeped from him like dark shadows, manifesting into a talon at the tip. It weaved with hers, seeping the light from her. Gold and black fought against each other for a moment, until she could *feel* him. Feel his power. Nether and astral flowed together, streaming as a single entity towards the bushes.

Power surged through her core, and if she thought fire danced on her skin before, this was another level. But it wasn't painful. Her nerve endings *tingled* with heat, singing with the euphoric sensation of mingled power. This is how she was *supposed* to feel. Nether and astral were two halves of the same soul—they were never *meant* to be apart.

"Feel it," Filip whispered against her ear, and she was no longer repulsed by his breath. She liked it. "This is how strong you can be. How strong *we* can be. Don't you want more of it?"

His chest was pushed against her back, his hands on hers. She turned her chin to look over her shoulder, and her gaze met his. The distraction caused her magic to snap, and with it, the desire for power disintegrated.

She scrambled away from him. Her cheeks flamed. "What did you do?"

"This is what our magic is like when we are together. Imagine the things we can do." His voice was husky—a fire burned in his eyes. "We'd be unstoppable."

Sifting through her jumbled thoughts, she shook her head. This was wrong, so *very* wrong. The sickening sensation returned to the pit of her stomach. He was manipulating her, using their magic to lure her, to draw her further into his dark, evil clutch.

For good measure, she took several steps back, widening the gap between them. Her skin crawled as if a dozen bugs skittered across her flesh. How could he, one minute, make her feel invincible, and the next, repulse her?

She ran her hand through her hair and flicked a glance over his shoulder, through the window. Yelena was inside, and Adelina needed to keep Filip distracted for as long as possible.

"I'm sorry." She cleared her throat. "I wasn't expecting the magic to be so...intense."

It wasn't *technically* a lie.

"How about we try again?" He smiled, and she frowned. It seemed genuine.

Managing a nod, she repositioned herself, and held her breath, waiting for the critter sensation of bugs crawling across her arms as he moved closer.

As he placed his hands on her wrists, she coaxed her magic forth, encouraging it to flow from her in golden beams. The beams coiled, forming the embroidery whip she was familiar with. His nether magic poured from him like black smoke and shadows swirling around her own. They merged.

Intense power shot through her, and when she looked over her shoulder at Filip, her disgust washed away. If anything, she *desired* him. All memories of the past horrors caused by his hands disappeared from her mind. Her sister's memory disappeared. Damir disappeared. Him and her, their infinite power, remained.

This time, their magic bolted to the distant tree—it blasted against the trunk, sending bark hurtling. The tip of her whip lashed upward, slicing through several dense branches. They clambered to the floor.

"Impressive," he breathed against her cheek.

She leaned into him, feeding off his magic, relishing in the strength it gave her. She wanted *more*. But he withdrew his magic and stepped away.

Stumbling backwards, her mind reeled. She was a married woman, and yet he tempted her with power lust, drawing her into his web of manipulation. Clutching her abdomen, she heaved, throwing up the contents of her stomach onto the manicured lawn. At least he disgusted her again.

"It will take time to get used to," he said.

Alarm bells rang in her brain—he'd lured her with darkness, showed her how powerful she could be if she stayed on this path with him.

An image of her sister shone brightly in her mind's eye. A reminder of what he'd done. He was *not* someone she could trust. She clung onto the thread of sanity for dear life because she couldn't afford to lose herself to the addictive power of merged astral and nether magic.

She needed to get away from him, and fast. As far as her legs to carry her. The flight response kicked in. But her legs were jelly, and she knew she had to keep Filip distracted until Yelena grabbed the book.

A loud clamber came from inside the palace. Filip jolted his head to the door.

Adelina's heart rate spiked. Probably Damir's fake runaway attempt to distract the guards from Yelena.

Filip lifted his foot and stepped towards the palace. Holding her breath, she clasped his hand, drawing his attention back to her.

"Stay," she whispered. "I want to learn more. Show me."

A Ballad of Severed Souls

His lips curled into a pleased smiled. "I'm liking this new side of you, Adelina. But I don't want to destroy any more of my lovely garden." He laughed.

Although her stomach churned with revulsion, she needed to keep his focus on her, and away from Yelena and Damir. She would do whatever it took and worry about the consequences of it later.

"What about the prism world?" she suggested. "It would give us a safe space to practise using our magic together—the way it was intended."

She hoped he hung on her last words, and by his expression, he seemed intrigued. But she knew what he was like—always ahead of her, calculated and strategic.

Not wanting him to have too long to consider it, she conjured the portal. It spun and crackled. Swallowing the urge to vomit, she held her hand out to him.

His gaze landed on her upturned palm briefly, as if questioning her motives. But he accepted it and followed her into the prism world.

Inside was a perfect reflection of Kirovo Palace's immaculate gardens. She wondered for a moment why exactly they looked that way—why not a field, a mountain, a beach? Why was it a constant reminder of what she was shackled to?

Filip wasted no time—he was behind her, hands on hers, intertwining his fingers with hers. There was something possessive about his stance, the way he pressed his body to her back, his warm breath on her nape.

Their magic fused together, hit the glass panels of the prism world, and rained fragments onto them.

She covered her head with her hands.

"Magnificent." He laughed.

"How?" She frowned. "It is no different to when I trained here without my talisman. I've shattered the prism world several times before."

"Maybe so, but this is the beginning. You can feel the current of magic surging through you when we link hands, don't you? It's addictive. It makes you feel free, powerful, *superior*. Doesn't it?" He didn't say his words like questions, but as statements of truth.

As much as she despised it, she *did* find truth in his words. And it shocked her to the core. She didn't want to follow him deeper into darkness. Yet she'd tasted what her magic was like with him by her side, and she couldn't deny it *did* feel good.

She dipped her head, stepping away from him. "Maybe that's enough for tonight. I don't want to tire myself out."

He tilted his head and surveyed her. "You are quite curious, Adelina."

Unsure how to respond to his strange statement, she nodded, then hopped out of the prism world. Yelena strolled along the path, her gaze connecting with Adelina's.

Adelina rose a questioning brow.

Nodding once, Yelena wiggled her arm as she held something under her cloak.

Filip exited the prism world, and it snapped shut behind him. A guard approached him from the doorway.

"A prisoner tried to escape, sir," he said.

Filip met his gaze with his own stern stare. "Who?"

"Damir Litvin, sir," the guard said.

"I presume you have reincarcerated him?"

"Yes, sir."

"Then what is the problem?" Filip's words were blunt, and he'd pronounced the consonants sharply. Adelina interpreted it as his frustration at having his attention pulled from her.

"Nothing else, sir," the guard said.

"Your husband ought to stay in line." Filip shifted his stern gaze to her. "Perhaps he needs reminding not to get on my bad side. Or has he forgotten what happens when someone does?"

"If you'll allow me, I will speak to him. He won't do anything like it again. I'll make sure of it," she said.

"No," he said. "You will not."

She kept her unwavering gaze on him because she couldn't find the words—she knew what would happen if she challenged him.

"It's late," she finally breathed. "I'll be going to my chamber."

Filip nodded. "Off you go."

She slipped past him and the guard, hurried through the foyer, and up the marble staircase. When she was inside her room, she pressed her back to the door. Her heart hammered in her chest. She'd tasted her magic at full power, and she'd *liked* it. Worse, it'd made Filip desirable in her eyes.

Lifting her hand to her chest, she thought of Tihana and her parents. There'd be no funeral for her sister, no goodbyes. A sudden chill swept over her, and she wrapped her arms around herself.

Wandering to the cabinet, she lit a candle, then sat on the windowsill beside it.

"I love you, Tihana. With all my heart," she whispered around the lump in her throat. Tears pricked her eyes. "I will make this right. I promise."

She went to bed with a heaviness in her chest, and a crippling need to be with her mother and father. Even her own husband was left below ground in a dark, damp cell.

Pulling the covers over her head, she clamped her eyes shut.

TWENTY-ONE

Visions

The following morning, Adelina met Yelena in the training room. Dark circles had formed underneath Yelena's eyes, and she still wore the same clothes as the day before.

"Is everything all right?" Adelina frowned.

"Come with me." Yelena urged her through the bookcase door, into the secret office.

Walking around to the other side of her desk, she unlocked the drawer and drew out a book. "Here. I think this is the one we need. It's written in a different language, whereas the others were not."

Taking the book, Adelina flipped through the pages. She raised her brows. "I know this language."

"You do?" Yelena's words were emphasised with surprise. "How?"

"Svarog presented himself to me in a dream." Adelina scanned the cursive writing. "He gave me the knowledge of the language, so I can understand it. It's an ancient tongue used in nether magic books."

"Then you mean to say, the spell we'll need is nether magic?" Yelena shook her head. "You won't be able to use it."

"Not quite." Adelina removed a folded slip of paper from the centre and held it up for Yelena to see. "It's a great place to hide something we *do* require. I'm guessing Filip tore this out of the original book and stuffed it in here, knowing it would be the last book I'd look for."

"It won't be long before he notices it's missing. It's been gone all night," Yelena said. "If you know the language, then you best be quick and read what it says. As soon as you're done, I'll need to figure out a way of putting it back exactly when I found it."

Adelina sunk into an armchair beside a stack of books, then unfolded the paper. She scanned each line, absorbing its information.

"Well?" Yelena probed. "What does it say?"

"Huh." Adelina brought the paper closer to her face. "It's a spell to store power in inanimate objects. My grandfather's pocket watch was full of astral magic—put inside by wielders from the War—and I absorbed it. This looks similar except…it's a way of overcharging the magic so the objects become dangerous. They're used as weapons because they can explode on impact."

Yelena placed her fingers on her chin. "While I'm shocked you didn't tell me about the astral magic in your watch before, that's not the main focus here. We can overcharge some objects around the palace, perhaps the guards' swords and shields and some of Filip's belongings."

A Ballad of Severed Souls

"It would need to be enough magic to cause a big enough explosion to kill Filip." Adelina shifted her gaze back to the page in her hands.

"Sacrificing some of the astral magic you absorbed will be worth it," Yelena said. "I'll go to Filip, tell him you'll be using the prism world to practise. Use the time to learn *this* spell."

Adelina nodded as Yelena left the room. Pacing back and forth, she ran her hand through her hair. This was her opportunity to obtain revenge for all the horrid things Filip had done, the death of her sister, one of them. His death would mean freedom for the three countries, and a new leader could be elected. She could go home with her husband and live the life she wanted with him.

Something niggled inside her, though—Nikolay wasn't at Murtei when they attacked. Who would've sent word to him? It wasn't Yelena, and she doubted Olga would've sent a coded letter between them arriving in Pike and her death. Her *murder*. At my hands.

Mastering this spell and getting rid of Filip was one of many things she needed to do to atone for her sins—as much as she was forced, she still *did* whatever he commanded. Her actions were imprinted on her conscience along with his, and she had to prove to herself she was nothing like him. Filip lived in darkness—*thrived* in it—whereas she walked a dangerous line between darkness and the light. She didn't have a choice then, but she'd prove she didn't belong to him.

When Yelena returned a while later, Adelina conjured the prism world. Positioned outside of the golden, swirling portal, she faced her.

"Did Filip seem suspicious at all?" Adelina asked.

"It is not uncommon for you to use the prism world to practise your magic. Besides, he's too busy celebrating his victories to care." *Did Yelena roll her eyes?*

Adelina couldn't help but smile. "Thank you. Let's go master the hell out of this spell."

As Adelina took a step towards the hovering portal, a sickly, ice-cold sensation skittered up her spine. Her vision swung on its axis. She stumbled into a nearby chair, and a searing pain shot through her temples. Tossing the page onto the nearby table, she clamped her eyes shut and cradled her head in her palms.

"Adelina?" Yelena's voice was muffled by the roaring in Adelina's ears. "Take deep breaths and tell me what's happening when you can."

Behind Adelina's eyelids, a vision materialised, as bright and vivid as if it were happening in real life. "I see a forest...so much fire."

Flames licked trees wildly, growing more brutal by the second. Thick, black smoke churned into the sky.

"Ironpine!" Adelina covered her mouth with her hand, her eyes still closed.

"You know a Treefolk?" Yelena asked in a soothing manner.

"Yes, he helped me get to Uldan Island for the Sword of Light." Adelina's heartrate soared. "We have to help the Treefolk. The fire will ravage their home, it could kill them all."

Opening her eyes, she attempted to rise, but stumbled into Yelena, who gripped her arm.

A Ballad of Severed Souls

"What are you doing?" Adelina tried to shake Yelena off, but she maintained a firm grip. "We have to go."

A crease wedged itself between Yelena's thin eyebrows. "We can't. I believe you were having a vision."

"What do you mean?" Adelina trembled. "It was so *clear*. I could've sworn it was real."

"Why don't you sit down while I explain it to you?" Yelena gestured to the seat.

Adelina obeyed, grateful for the solid wood beneath her. The shakiness in her legs did not subside.

"It's a rare ability, but not unheard of," Yelena said. "My sister, Ivanna, is a Seer with the ability to see slices of the future. But visions can be of anything—past, present, *or* future. Have you seen things before—things so close you could almost touch it but weren't there?"

Adelina nodded, gripping on to the armrests. "I had a vision of Filip—that's how I knew about Damir and Tihana being his prisoners. There were right in front of me, and I could do *nothing*. I had to come back. Is there a way for me to see *more* of this vision? I need to fully understand what is expected to come to pass."

Yelena placed her fingers on her chin, then dashed to her box of medical supplies. She withdrew a vial of cloudy liquid. "Drink this. It will allow you to tap into the part of your mind connecting you to certain slices of the future. You might not be able to see everything, and it is unlikely to last long, but it should give you more clues."

With a swift nod, Adelina accepted the vial and downed the contents. It left a tingling sensation in her throat. Reclining in her chair, she shook out her limbs, trying to relax as much as possible.

"Close your eyes and focus on what you saw," Yelena said.

Letting out a steady breath, Adelina waited.

From her position on a grassy hill, she could see Aldercrown stretching on the horizon—the treeline approximately three-hundred feet away. The edge of the forest was untouched by fire, but the deeper into it, the more ravaged it became. The flames and black smoke were relentless.

Instead of staying at the top of the hill, she hurried down the slope and into the forest. She didn't know how long the vision would last, and she needed to learn as much about it as possible.

"What do you see?" Yelena's voice sounded distant and close at the same time.

Adelina jogged over fallen twigs and dead leaves. Coming to an abrupt halt, her whole body stiffened. She stared at a man ahead. A man she recognised was mounted, surrounded by cavalry.

"I think Nikolay is here," Adelina said on an intake of breath.

"What about him?" Yelena probed, keeping her voice level, although Adelina detected the ever so slight wobble.

Adelina swallowed the bubbling worry inside her. "It is too convenient he wasn't at the Temauten Congregation—he just so happens to not be there when Filip attacks. If this vision is showing the future, then Nikolay is definitely alive."

"You think he is responsible for the fire?" Yelena asked.

"There's one way to find out. I'll see if I can get closer—confirm it's him." Adelina rushed through the forest.

A heaviness expanded through her core. Ahead, a cloud of smoke flittered through the trees, filling her nose. *This isn't real.*

She pushed onward, weaving through trunks.

Ahead, fire raged, engulfing tree trunks. A deep groan echoed, and an oak snapped in half, toppling to the ground with a loud thud.

"You need to hurry, Adelina," Yelena warned. "The vision won't hold for much longer."

Could Nikolay betray them? If he had, it meant Filip would also know about the coded letters, incriminating Yelena.

As brambles and bushes caught at her cloak, she ran back to where she'd left Yelena. She, too, was gone. Frowning, Adelina tried to find a sense of direction amongst trees all looking the same. Finding her way onto a beaten trail between stumps and fallen logs, she froze.

"It's definitely Nikolay." Adelina's gaze travelled from Nikolay to the fallen Treefolk, lying on the ground. The trunk making up his body flickered with fire, and the leaves on his head turned to ash. Her heart panged as she thought of her friend, Ironpine. It could've been him. She'd no idea if he was alive.

The vision disintegrated and Adelina opened her eyes, her heart pounding. She blinked rapidly, trying to process everything she'd seen. "What's the likelihood of this coming to pass?"

"I'm not sure. I haven't heard Filip speak of the Treefolk before." Yelena shook her head. "What could he possibly want from them? They are a calm, peaceful people."

"Aldercrown is enchanted." Adelina's mind spun, recalling Ironpine's words. *'The charm stops us from being exposed to such otherworldly magic. Dark magic.'* "Yes, Aldercrown is protected from dark magic—how would Filip get through it?"

A haunted look appeared in Yelena's eyes.

"What?" Adelina's stomach knotted and churned as nausea flooded through her.

"He would need something to break through the enchantment." Yelena's voice was thick with worry.

Adelina's mind darted back to the conversation she'd held with Ironpine. *'There was a time when many nether wielders joined forces—such a significant amount of power is more than enough to overcome clans of the forest. And with the help of the astral wielders they'd enslaved...'*

"Filip wouldn't be able to break through the enchantment with his power alone. When the Treefolk were enslaved during the War, the magic of many nether wielders was used, as well as astral wielders. Filip doesn't have access to any astral wielders except me, and I certainly won't help him." Adelina's words tumbled from her mouth. Heat rose in her cheeks.

"The most frightening part is the nether wielders." Yelena crossed her arms. "There's his father, Antanov, but he is too sick to be of use."

"Veles is responsible—he's keeping him weak to ensure Filip stays in line," Adelina said. "Unless…"

A cold, sickly sensation flooded through her body, and her heart leapt into her throat. Sweat formed on her nape. "Oh, dear gods."

A sudden light-headedness swept over Adelina. She rubbed the back of her neck to rid herself of the forming tension.

"What is it?" Yelena said.

"Veles. It's got to be him." The words tasted sour in her mouth. "A God of the Underworld would surely be powerful enough to rip through the enchantment. The barrier between planes needs to be torn for Veles to have physical form in this realm, but there's no stopping him interfering if it works in his favour. He wants to dominate the living realm, so this does him a service. If he succeeds, he will be able to roam this plane and could bring countless demons with him. And we have Zmey, the dragon, to worry about."

"Even more reason for us to learn the spell. We must do everything we can to prevent that vision from becoming reality." Yelena pointed to the piece of paper on the table.

"Maybe the Zorya sisters wanted me to see this vision?" Adelina shrugged. "Or if it wasn't them, it could've been Svarog."

"Either way, we need to stop Filip." Yelena grabbed a stack of books. "We'll have to train in the prism world, regardless."

"The quicker we learn this damn spell, the quicker we can stop him," she said through gritted teeth as she rose from her chair and stepped into the prism world—the manicured lawn of Kirovo Palace sprawled ahead.

"We'll use these books as objects to overcharge," Yelena said as she rested them on the grass. "Your magic is free from the talisman, so it shouldn't be too difficult. Instead of firing your magic like a whip, you need to concentrate on the object in front of you. Imagine you are pouring it inside the book, allowing the pages to absorb your power."

Adelina nodded as she read over the spell again. The words she needed to say were rather simple, but controlling her powers would be the test. She'd grown used to it lashing out at whatever she set her mind to.

Setting the page aside, she positioned herself opposite the first book. Straightening her back, she cleared her throat. *"Merindasriel tyrasnerael."*

Like most astral spells, the syllables were clumsy in her mouth. She repeated it several times until she was familiar with the shapes and sounds of the words.

Her magic bolted from her wrist in a stream, incinerating the book. Ashes and tiny fragments of burned pages remained. She jolted backwards, casting a wide-eyed look at Yelena.

"It's all right," Yelena said. "It will take time. Try again with another one."

Grabbing a book from the pile, she set it in front of her.

Adelina closed her eyes and cleared her mind, which was difficult seeing as Aldercrown burned in the distance. Encouraging her magic, it grew and swelled inside her, warming her limbs. Instead of the golden embroidery she was familiar with, she coaxed her astral power into the form of water. With the clear image of streaming liquid in her mind, shining brightly with sunlight, she opened her eyes and aimed for the book.

The book jutted on the ground as it absorbed the light. Several sparks burst from the cover, but not fire.

"There you go!" Yelena chimed.

Adelina's magic disconnected, and the golden light faded. A sudden dizziness washed through her, and she stumbled.

Yelena gripped her arms and steadied her.

"It's unsurprising you feel weak," she said softly. "You're shifting some of your magic out of your body and into an object. It will likely have an adverse effect on you."

"Will I be strong enough to do this on multiple objects?" Adelina rubbed her throbbing temples. "I'll need to overcharge a dozen or so swords or items belonging to the guards."

"We'll stay here for a few hours. Overcharge as many of these books as you can. You'll have to take frequent breaks to regain your strength, but over time, it will be less tiresome," Yelena said.

"How do you know all this?" Adelina frowned. After all, the spell was written in an ancient tongue used to conceal nether magic.

"I know a lot of our history," Yelena said. "As you know, astral wielders did the same thing during the War, and I did a lot of research to better understand it for when Filip eventually found you."

"Thank you," Adelina said, sensing the truth in her words.

Adelina spent the next several hours in the prism world, infusing her magic with a variety of inanimate objects, from books, ink pots, and quills, to random plates and mugs brought from the kitchens. In between practice, she sat to eat and drink, regathering her strength before returning to her work. Yelena stayed with her the whole time, offering words of encouragement, and by the end of it, Adelina didn't have a single doubt over where Yelena's loyalties lay.

Sitting with her back pressed against the wall of Yelena's office, Adelina rubbed the side of her head. "What are we going to do about Aldercrown? We can't let them die."

"Filip knows you're training in the prism world—you could speak to him," Yelena suggested. "Ask him what he needs the Treefolk for."

"While he may give me answers, he may still deploy his troops, especially if it's beneficial for him to send them. He's doing all of this because of Veles." Adelina groaned. "He says he wants power for himself, *he* wants to rule, but he has no clue how much of a pawn he is. Instead, he thinks he's a king. Veles is using him, and I know that what's in store for Aldercrown is to serve a greater scheme than he has in mind."

"You'd best not say anything of the sort to Filip—he does not like being referred to as a pawn." Yelena placed her hands on her hips. "I'm not sure there's anything more you can do to help, not without risking your parents' or Damir's lives. Besides, you're learning this spell quickly. If we kill Filip, Veles will have no emissary, and the vision will be unlikely to come true."

"What's stopping Veles from simply allowing another demon into the living plane?" Adelina asked.

"It doesn't work like that. There has to be a balance. Filip exists in this realm because of you. You share the same soul, you *are* each other's balance. Another demon can't roam the living plane without the barrier being down," Yelena explained.

"Even if we do kill Filip, Veles' plans will have contingencies, and his contingencies will have contingences." Adelina rose. "He's not going to let Filip's death destroy his desire to rule the living plane. We should overcharge a bunch of the guards' weapons as we planned. It'll blow up the palace, but it's the only chance we have at stopping Filip. Do you know if there's a way I can contact Svarog? Maybe he can help the Treefolk—after all, the balance of nature is threatened. He's presented himself to me in a dream, in the test too, but can I bring him to me?"

"I know the ritual the Seer performed for the test," Yelena said. "We'll have to do it at night, so we don't raise suspicions."

"Are you okay?" Adelina frowned as she stared at Yelena—her eyes darkened, and shadows circled them.

Yelena shook her head as she sank into her desk chair. "Nikolay fooled me for months. Olga too. She would be alive if it wasn't for him."

"We don't know for certain." Adelina didn't want to remind her it was *she* who killed Olga. "Although, there is a possibility Filip will know about your letters *if* Nikolay has been relaying information to him. Do you ever leave your office for long periods of time? It's likely Filip has come in here to see them as evidence."

"There's no need for him to come looking." Yelena waved the matter away. "If we suspect Nikolay is betraying us at this very moment, he's probably been resending the letters to Filip with a decoding guide, for gods' sake."

"He's incriminating you." Adelina's mind reeled. "Why in the realm hasn't Filip arrested you? Of course, I don't want him to, but surely, he would've thrown you in the dungeons, or worse…"

"He wants to see how it all plays out." Yelena placed her hands on the table. After a minute of staring at the door, she lashed her arm out, hurtling all the coded letters into the air. They fluttered to the floor. "Damn it. Always one step ahead."

"Well, if that is truly what he's doing, then you need to act like you haven't figured it out." Adelina kept her voice soft in an attempt to reassure her teacher. "Act normal. I'll find Natasha and see if she can gather some items the guards won't notice are missing. Try to keep calm. I'll be back tonight as planned."

Adelina headed for the door. When her hand rested on the handle, she glanced over her shoulder. "I won't let anything happen to you."

Although her lips were pressed tight together, Yelena managed a small, sharp nod.

Slipping out of the door, Adelina set in a quick pace towards the kitchen. She found Natasha kneading a ball of dough, flour dusted over her apron and face.

"Adelina." Natasha's eyes widened. "What are you doing here? You shouldn't be in the kitchens. If you're hungry, I can bring food to you."

"I'm wondering if you can prepare a bath for me." Adelina tilted her head slightly, hoping Natasha would pick up on the signal.

"Right now?" Natasha frowned.

Adelina gestured to the door. "It's quite urgent. My muscles are sore…from the training."

Natasha turned to speak to the head cook, then escorted her into the foyer. "What's wrong?"

"Not here," Adelina whispered as she followed Natasha up the marble staircase towards the bathing room.

Closing the door behind them, Natasha went to prepare the tub. "I'll boil the water and bring it up, miss. I wasn't expecting you to request a bath in the middle of the day."

"I don't require a bath." Adelina grabbed her hands. "There's something I need you to do for me."

"What is it?" Natasha asked.

"You must swear you won't say a word. I'm counting on you, here. What I'm about to ask of you will potentially save hundreds of lives, including my husband." Adelina couldn't help but wrinkle her nose at the fineries around her. When she'd first come to the palace, her breath was taken away. But the exquisiteness had soured for her—her sister's ghost would forever haunt the place, and she'd never forget the hardships her husband had endured.

Natasha nodded sharply and gripped Adelina's hands. "I helped you once. I will do it again. What can I do?"

"I need you to collect some items for me. Without raising suspicion. Go to the barracks when the guards are sleeping—take swords, shields, arrows, anything they use." Adelina kept her voice low. "You'll have to do it in several trips—the items are large, and we can't risk you dropping things and making a noise. Can you do this for me?"

"Yes, of course, but what for?" Natasha's eyebrows knitted together.

Adelina hesitated—the words dancing on her tongue. Natasha *had* helped her before—if it wasn't for her, she would be none the wiser about Filip's intentions to wed her and sire his children. If Adelina was going to cause an explosion, she didn't want her caught in the blast. "I'll overcharge them with my magic and put them back before the guards wake. The overcharged state will last for a few hours, so they will explode as soon as they're touched by the guards. If I overcharge enough weapons, it'll likely destroy the palace, bringing Filip down with them. You'll need to grab a horse from the stables, and ride away from here."

Natasha stared at her blankly.

"Natasha." Adelina shook her hands. "Do you understand?"

Closing her mouth, Natasha nodded and blinked several times. "Yes, I…I understand."

"You can't speak a word of this," Adelina said. "Countless lives have already been lost, Filip might be starting a war with the Treefolk. I can't explain all of it right now, but this is serious. I've already lost my sister, and I haven't seen my parents since the day she died. I won't let anyone else be hurt or killed by Filip. Including you, Yelena, or Damir."

"A war—with the Treefolk?" Natasha's eyes widened.

"Look, I don't have much time," Adelina said urgently. "Please, do this for me, for us. Then get yourself *out* of here."

"Okay." Natasha breathed. "I'll go to the barracks tonight. Where shall I bring the items?"

"Come to the training room, and don't get caught," Adelina said. "I'll see you tonight."

Natasha flattened her skirts, tucked loose strands of hair behind her ears, then left the bathing room.

Blowing out a deep breath of air, Adelina pressed a hand to the wall and focused on her hammering heartbeat. They had one shot at this. And they couldn't afford to get it wrong.

When the sky was black with night, Adelina slipped through the door and tiptoed along the manicured garden towards the training room at the back. She clung to the shadows cast by the conservatory to keep out of potentially watchful eyes.

When she reached the building, she grabbed the handle and slipped inside. The room was dark to avoid any light leaking from the windows. Keeping her hand on the wall, she let her touch guide her towards the secret office.

The door was left ajar, and a tiny sliver of light shone through. She quickly opened it and hurried inside. Pressing her back to the door, she sighed through her nose.

"Just in time." Yelena glanced at her from behind her desk. In front of her was a stash of sage and a box of matches. She gestured to the armchair opposite her. "Take a seat."

Adelina slid onto the chair, shuffling until she was comfortable. "I've spoken to Natasha. She will be bringing items for enchantment tonight, but she'll only be able to bring a few at a time."

Yelena nodded. "While we wait for her, I'm going to re-enact the test—it'll be exactly like what you went through with the Seer."

Swallowing, Adelina gripped the arms of her chair.

"Try to relax," Yelena said in a soothing manner. "I know your mind is shifting through everything else going on, but you need to let go if you want to see Svarog."

"Okay." Adelina tilted her chin a notch higher. "I'm ready when you are."

Yelena clasped the bunch of sage, lit the end, then danced around the office. She waved the burning sage as she hummed and circled Adelina. As the Seer had done, Yelena's tune shifted to a melodic chant.

As Adelina's mind turned foggy, the song grew distant, like she was falling farther and farther away from the living plane. Her vision blurred, and her muscles relaxed. Yelena's song dwindled as Adelina fell asleep.

She plummeted into a trance, but the aroma of burning sage tickled her nose. Behind closed eyes, a vision materialised. This time, there was no outstretched hand to guide her through the darkness—she didn't need it anymore. She ambled through the smoke circling her feet.

A Ballad of Severed Souls

A golden spark flickered against the endless blackness. Instead of Svarog's slow emerge from the shadows in her test, he popped into sight. She shielded her eyes from the sudden burst of golden light blazing from his body and wings.

"Adelina," he said as his long tail lowered to the floor, wrapping itself around him.

"Svarog," she said. "I need you."

"I am aware of what might come to pass." His forked tongue flicked out the corner of his mouth.

"Can you help them?" Adelina stepped forwards, coming closer to him than she ever dared before. "Please. You've mentioned the balance of life before, and surely, this violates it."

"I already have a plan." *Did a dragon god just grin?*

"What do you mean?" she asked.

"Sssshould your visssssion come to passss, I won't be able to sssstop the fire or bring back thosssse who perissssh, but I *can* usssse my magic to make a ssssafe haven for the Treefolk who sssssurvive," he said.

"How?" Her interest piqued. "Like what the last astral wielders did for Aldercrown? How will it stop Filip and his soldiers from figuring out a way to break it? They could get Veles involved again."

"Lasssst time, the Treefolk did not have the help of a god to keep them ssssafe. Do not worry about Velessss—leave *him* to me." His lips curled back, flashing his long, sharp teeth.

"Easy for you to say." She couldn't suppress a nervous laugh. "You know what his plans are. I'm doing everything I can to stop him from tearing down the barrier. I'm going to need a little help."

"Velessss and I have been at war for centuriessss—we are the ssssame assss you and Filip. One ssssoul to fight over." He flapped his wings, sparking golden light.

"I already know all this." Adelina's voice was blunt, fuelled by her impatience. "What are you going to do about it?"

"I will enssssure the Treefolk are protected, but I do not have a physsssical pressssencsssse in the living plane. You mussst do whatever you can to thwart Filip, remove Velessss' emissssary."

"My plan is already in motion," she said. "Just please, do what you can to save the Treefolk. They are innocent and don't deserve to die."

Silence formed between them.

His eyes softened as much as a dragon's eyes could.

"I'm ssssorry about your sssssisssster."

She nodded as tears prickled her eyes. "There's something else I need to talk to you about."

"What is it?"

"The Sword of Light—it's not behaving in the same way for Filip that it did for me. When I gave it to him, he experienced no pain, no burst of light. He's going to figure out what is wrong with it. Perhaps you might know something, seeing as you created it." She rubbed her arm—there was no chill where they stood, but the idea of facing Filip's wrath again made her hairs stand on end.

"Curioussss," he said. "The ssssword may be conflicted. With you both sssso clossssse by, it may not be able to determine where itssss loyaltiessss lie."

She shook her head. "I'm not sure. He used it during battle, and it acted like any other sword. You wouldn't have been able to tell it was forged by gods."

The dragon god remained silent for a few moments, as if lost in deep thought. "I have forged one other ssssword like thisssss in all my centuriessss of being. An old tale, no doubt, but the detailssss are intact in my memory."

"What details?" She shifted her weight from foot to foot, itching to get back to the living plane—back to her mission with Yelena and Natasha.

"There lived another sssssoul pair—like you and Filip. The male wassss a powerful asssstral wielder, and he came to me in ssssearch of the Ssssword of Light. He brought me the materialssss, I forged it, and he wassss on hissss way," he said. "A woman, the other half of hissss sssssoul, killed hissss wife and children becausssse he refusssssed to combine their magic. The woman wanted to rule, but during thosssse timessss, ssssuch a thing wassss frowned upon—ssssshe needed a husband, a man to be king."

"She desired nothing more than to marry him." Adelina put the pieces together.

"I'm ssssure it ssssoundssss familiar." He arched a brow.

"Filip wanted to marry me, but I refused. Ever since, nothing but bad things have happened." She shivered.

"Except in this sssstory, the man wassss already married, with children. There wassss no way he could posssssibly leave hissss wife and family. Even though he was an asssstral wielder, he did not want to usssse it, certainly not to rule a kingdom," he said. "You know what happenssss next."

"She killed him and his family for it," she whispered.

"Yessss." He nodded. "But before that, he did everything he could to protect hissss family from her. He wanted the ssssword to end her life, remove her as a threat to hissss family."

"Then what happened?" Her attention was rapt by the story so like her own.

"Well, sssshe ssstole the Sssword ssstraight from him. When sssshe tried to usssse it to take down her enemiessss, it did not work," he said, "Now I sssee history repeating itsssself with you and Filip, I wonder if the sssword only *truly* givessss itsss loyaltiessss to thosssse whosssse intentionssss are pure."

"You know, we speak of the sword as if it is alive," she pointed out. "You're the one who created it. Did you intend it to have a mind of its own?"

"The Ssssword of Light issss made of everything pure and natural in life," he said. "It embodiessss ssssunlight and life. It would make sssensssse for it to act in itssss own way. I hadn't consssidered it in ssssuch detail until now, with you and Filip living a ssssimilar ssssstory. And sssince thissss issss only the ssssecond time thissss weapon hassss been forged, the depth of itssss loyaltiessss hassss not been recorded by wielderssss."

"There have been thousands of astral wielders to exist over the centuries, right?" she asked. "Why did you only make two?"

"Two have been pure of heart." He smiled warmly. "And only two who've required it."

She couldn't help but return the smile—his presence soothed her.

"This means the sword will never truly obey Filip," she said. "And when he finds out…"

"You know what to do, Adelina." His gaze narrowed on her.

Sensation prickled her arms and legs as she returned to her body. When she opened her eyes, her vision was foggy, and she couldn't lift her head from its resting position against the back of the chair.

"I'll make you a medicinal concoction to help with the dizziness." Yelena's voice echoed as if she'd spoken underwater. "Orpin rose flowers—it's what the Seer would've given you after the test."

Adelina tried to nod, although she wasn't sure she'd managed to. As her eyes adjusted to the faint light of the office, she waited as Yelena approached.

"Sit there for a little while, and drink this." Yelena handed her a vial of steeped, crushed petals. "I brought this to a boil before you came."

Blinking slowly, Adelina took the vial and unscrewed the cap. Her muscles were heavy, so the movement of bringing it to her lips was slow. She tipped the contents into her mouth and breathed in the fragrant aroma.

The last time she'd drank it, she was desperate to sleep. Although her eyesight was somewhat blurry, she was conscious.

"It gets easier." Yelena smiled as if she'd sensed Adelina's thoughts.

Adelina spent the next hour stretching her arms and legs, walking around the office to stimulate the muscles. With each passing moment, she grew more anxious. Where in the realm was Natasha?

"You're making me nervous, dear." Yelena frowned. "Natasha will be taking her time. Or she risks getting caught."

"We're going to have this anxiety all night." Adelina dragged a hand over her face. "Natasha will be taking several trips back and forth from the barracks while I overcharge things. Then they'd all need to be put back before the guards wake up. Who knows if I'm even strong enough to overcharge so many objects?"

Yelena chuckled. "You are an astral wielder—the sun god's chosen one. You will be strong enough."

TWENTY-TWO

Yelena

Another half an hour passed before there was a light knock on the door.

Rushing over to it, Adelina welcomed Natasha inside. "Did anyone see you?"

"No." Natasha beamed, seemingly proud of herself.

"Thank you." Adelina returned the smile.

"This time you'll need to do the spell without the prism world." Yelena gestured to the handful of swords Natasha placed on the floor. "And before you do, Natasha and I will need to touch every single item *before* you overcharge them. Since she brought them here, her fingerprints will already be on them. This prevents them from exploding from our touch."

In quick succession, Yelena pressed her hand to each item before standing out of the way.

In her mind's eye, Adelina pictured her powers taking the form of water, fused with golden light. She encouraged the magic to swell inside her and seep from her skin. "*Merindasriel tyrasnerael.*"

The magic poured into the first sword. It jutted, threatening to explode on the spot. She fought to keep control of the spell, urging it forward in a continuous stream.

Sweat trickled on her brow as she forced every ounce of concentration into fusing her magic with the sword. The magic snapped with a fizz and a pop, and the sword wobbled.

"How are you feeling?" Yelena asked.

"I'm all right." Adelina's limbs were strong, her mind clear. "I'll keep going, but I'll let you know if I become faint or weak."

Yelena nodded. "We must be quick."

For the next half an hour, Adelina poured parts of her magic into the items on the floor. Each time she sacrificed some of her astral powers, her limbs became heavier. It felt as if life itself was being sapped from her.

By the time she'd overcharged the fifth sword, she pressed her arm against the wall, her knees threatening to buckle. Yelena wrapped her arm around her, guiding her to the chair.

"Natasha, why don't you sneak these back to the barracks? Place them exactly where you found them and bring more. Adelina needs a break," Yelena said. "And don't get caught."

Nodding, Natasha scooped up the items and was out the door in a flash.

"Sit down." Yelena eased Adelina into the seat. "I'll bring you some tea."

Within a few minutes, Yelena whipped out another vial of liquid and handed it to her. "This tea is made from steeped rhodiola root. It will boost your energy and encourage your body to recover quickly."

Adelina removed the stopper and sniffed it. "It smells like roses."

Yelena grinned. "While it may smell lovely, it has a strong, bitter taste to it."

Grimacing, Adelina pressed the vial to her lips, tilted her head back, and poured the contents into her mouth. She swallowed, shuddering at the sharpness of the plant's taste imprinted on her tongue.

With a deep breath, she lifted herself out of the chair and shifted her attention to the remaining two swords. By the time she'd overcharged them, Natasha returned with a stash of arrows in her arms.

"These are a lot lighter, so I'm able to carry more of them." Natasha laid them on the floor.

They repeated the process throughout the night—overcharge, more tea, overcharge, more tea.

Halfway through the night, Adelina had overcharged two loads of swords, three dozen arrows, and several crossbows. Slouched in her chair, she struggled to keep her eyes open, even after drinking five or six vials of foul-tasting tea.

"I'm sorry, Adelina, but you don't have time to sleep." Yelena gripped her shoulders. "If Natasha is going to take this last batch of arrows back to the barracks right now, you won't have long to get Damir out of his prison cell."

Despite the fact her entire body sagged against the chair's frame, and a fogginess filled her head, she fought against her fatigue. Pushing onto the armrests, she hoisted herself onto her feet.

"There's something I need to give you." Yelena rushed around to the other side of her desk, then rifled through a drawer. She withdrew a book, then thrust it into Adelina's hands. "This is my own personal book of research. Inside, is everything I know about herbs, magic systems—not just nether and astral, but what other sorcerers use, like Kira and Lev—and much more. Hide this in your cloak and take it with you. Leave now before the servants wake. They are usually up and about a couple of hours before dawn, so you have no time to waste."

"Wait." With her free hand, Adelina gripped Yelena's wrist. "You're coming with us, aren't you?"

Yelena's face paled. "I will do everything I can to make sure we bring that bastard down and you and your husband get away from this place. If it means I don't make it, then I have done my duty to you, and when I stand in front of the gods, they will know."

Adelina shook her head sharply. "No. This isn't the day you die in an explosion *I* cause. I'm not letting it happen. You're coming with us."

Although she nodded her head, Yelena pressed her lips into a thin line, and practically shoved Adelina towards the door. "Find your husband. When the first explosion sounds, I'll keep Filip away from you."

Throwing her arms around her teacher, Adelina held Yelena in a tight embrace. "Thank you."

When she let go, she spun, shoved the book into her pocket, and hurried outside. The full moon drenched the lawn and flowerbeds in silver light. Slipping through the kitchen door, she made her way across the stone path and disappeared down the stairs to the cells below ground.

A Ballad of Severed Souls

Drawing forth her magic, she let it flood her veins and fill her with a fiery warmth before she conjured the golden embroidery. She ignored the tingling sensation and the blisters forming.

"What are you doing down here?" the guard on watch said as he halted at the bottom of the steps. His stern gaze lowered from her face to her wrist.

Her magic lashed out like a whip, slicing through his neck. Blood spurted from the wound as he lifted his hands to clutch his throat. He'd be dead in minutes.

"I'm sorry," she whispered. "I really *am* sorry, but I need to get the hell out of here or far more people are going to die."

When the guard hit the floor, she rummaged in his pockets and withdrew a set of keys.

Sprinting to the end of the corridor, she halted outside Damir's cell. With shaky fingers, she fumbled for the right keys. Dazed, she struggled to get a grip on the small piece of metal.

Damir was already at the bars, his fingers wrapping around her hand. "I'll do it."

He took the keys from her, fed his arm through the gap, twisting as he unlocked the door, and flung it open.

In a quick stride, he'd gathered her in his arms, pressing her head to his chest. She breathed him in, not caring he smelled of dirt and damp. Her whole body shook, and she clung to him. There he was, the love of her life, and he was *whole*. It was her mission to keep it so.

"We need to go," she whispered.

With a nod, he clasped her hand, and together, they jogged towards the staircase. His gaze dropped to the body on the floor, then flicked back to her.

"I didn't have a choice," she said quietly, although she didn't quite believe her words.

"Don't worry," is all he could say before the impact of the first explosion sent them hurtling into the stone wall.

Plumes of dust and stones dripped from the ceiling and rubble thundered to the ground above them. As she clawed to her feet, she spotted the opposite wall completely caved in, crushing whoever was imprisoned in the cell there.

Damir grabbed her by the arms and scanned her body. "Are you okay?"

"I'm fine." She touched the crown of her head and winced. It throbbed. "We need to get you a weapon—something to defend yourself with. We'll have to fight our way out of here. I've overcharged a bunch of items belonging to the guards. There will be more explosions."

Bending, he tossed chunks of stones aside, then drew the guard's sword from underneath. "What's the bet this is one of few you *haven't* tampered with?"

"Come on." She clasped his hand and climbed over the rubble, heading up the stairs.

The back entrance of the palace, leading to the kitchens, conservatory, and gardens, was destroyed. Pillars lay broken and caved-in. Doors were ripped from their hinges, halls collapsed, and shattered glass littered the floor. Any paintings still hanging were crooked, and chandeliers lay crushed underneath stone.

A Ballad of Severed Souls

"How many explosions can we expect?" he said as he led the way around the rubble in search of an exit point.

"Two or three, depending on how quickly the guards picked up their items. I can't imagine they will grab their swords and arrows at the exact same time." Adelina came to a halt as she stared at the crushed body beneath the fallen beams, his face bloodied, eyes closed.

Her attention was ripped from the corpse when a dozen guards charged into the building through a hole in the external wall to the left-hand side of the palace. A split second to conjure her magic—there wasn't time to think, to consider their lives.

The golden whip lashed out, swiping through the row of bodies in one fell swoop. Their bodies were sliced in half, hitting the ground to join the debris.

"Do I even need a sword?" Damir eyed her.

She didn't say anything—she couldn't—bile rose in her throat. Each time she killed someone, the more scared she was of losing herself to Filip, becoming more like him.

An almighty *boom!* ripped through the air, vibrating the ground as the second explosion erupted from somewhere in the gardens.

Damir threw out his arm, holding her in place as the conservatory shattered.

Grabbing her, he pulled her to the floorboards, shielding her head from the glass shards hurtling towards them. She winced as something sliced her cheek.

"We need to find Yelena." She scrambled to her feet. "I'm not leaving her here."

"We should head towards the barracks—the rest of the guards will be there, right?" he asked. "How much time do we have between explosions?"

"I'm not sure." She pinched the bridge of her nose as she started towards the barracks past the training grounds. "The guards would've walked from the barracks to the conservatory and the gardens for the explosion to happen, which means their overcharged weapons aren't exploding as soon as they're picked up. There's probably about a fifteen- or twenty-minute window. A guess, at best. The next one could occur at any moment. And where the hell is Filip?"

She couldn't help the rise of panic inside of her. Surely, she would've come head-to-head with him by now. Unless he knew all along. Wherever he was, Yelena would be with him, and there was no way she was leaving her with him.

Four more guards appeared. They held their swords forward as they rushed for her. She lifted her arms, ready to unleash her golden whip.

"Are you all right, miss?" one guard said as he approached. "We're not sure what's causing the explosions, but we are trying to get to the bottom of it. You should get somewhere safe."

Raising her brows, she found no words. She'd thought they were going to attack her. Seeing as they hadn't, perhaps it meant Filip hadn't told them he suspected it was her behind the explosions. She doubted he wouldn't have figured it out, considering he knew how astral magic worked.

"We're headed to the barracks." Adelina found her voice. "I believe my teacher, Yelena, is already there for her own safety. I'm to join her."

A Ballad of Severed Souls

The servants hadn't been in the kitchens when she'd dashed through them to reach the prison cells beneath the castle, but she also wasn't going to tell them she suspected most of them were probably crushed by the impact of the first explosion. After all, it'd detonated through the back right wing of the palace, which would've ripped straight through the servants' quarters.

The guard nodded. "Filip will be in the barracks too—it's the safest place for you all. Go to him."

Adelina grabbed Damir's hand, then towed him away.

"Wait." The guard lifted his arm to block them and frowned. "Aren't you the prisoner?"

"Uh..." Damir cleared his throat. "The first explosion tore through the prison cells—I'm not sure how many prisoners survived, but I got out of there before the ceiling caved in. I'll stay with Adelina—make sure she's safe—until we have all clear to return to the palace."

"Not happening." The guard narrowed his eyes on Damir. "I'll be taking you into custody—"

A thunderous *boom!* ripped through the air, shuddering the nearby trees. Large chunks of mud and grass hurtled around them. Stone and brick whizzed as the third explosion tore through the training room, the impact sending them crashing to the ground. *Yelena.*

Scrambling off Damir, Adelina forced herself onto her elbows, urging her eyes to focus through her blurry vision. The guard was unconscious, bits of debris lying across his chest.

Heart lurching in her chest, she forced herself up. Damir was on his feet in an instant, taking a firm grip of her hand. They sped along the lawn to the western edge of the property, where the barracks were located. Most of the area hadn't been impacted by the explosions, meaning she was right about her theory of the time it took for them to detonate.

"If there are more guards at the barracks, we need to get them away from us, or we need to get away from *them*," she said. "If they are holding overcharged weapons, they'll have fifteen minutes or so before they explode, and we'll be crushed."

"Calm down," he said. "The guards aren't likely to remain at the barracks, are they? Not when they believe the threat is outside. They've no reason to suspect you."

"If they've seen Filip, he would've told them. He doesn't like it when I challenge him." She halted, grabbing Damir's arms. "You need to leave. Head to the stables, grab a horse, and ride to the forests on the Temauten border. I'll meet you there."

"I'm not leaving you." His voice did not falter. "I don't care if he comes for me—let him."

"He won't hesitate to kill you. I won't risk losing you, too." A thick lump formed in her throat, making her words sound hoarse.

"Besides, even if Filip suspects you, he would never order his men to kill you. It completely defeats his goal. He needs you."

She shook her head. "You don't understand. He murdered my sister because I opposed him. He will do the same to you. You *have* to go."

He gripped her arm. "We're *both* getting out of here. *Right now.*"

"We get Yelena first." As she prepared to push off in the direction of the training room, Damir tugged her in the opposite direction—towards the barracks.

"No. It's not safe for you to go there," he said.

"Yelena could be there." Her thoughts spiralled. "I will not let her die."

"Do you have any reason to believe she would hide there while you rescue me?" he said.

She dragged her hands through her hair, thrusting it away from her face. "No…I…She said she'd distract Filip while I got you out."

"Exactly," he said, a degree softer. "You already know this. Keep your mind on what is logical. She wouldn't betray you."

Sucking in a deep breath to steady her wild heartbeat, she climbed to her feet, joined hands with her husband, and continued to the barracks.

When they reached the rectangular shaped building, she braced herself. Having not seen Filip at all, she feared he was inside.

As she approached the entrance—the door a mere handful of feet away—Yelena came outside. A sullen smile spread across her lips.

"Yelena!" Adelina gasped as she lunged towards her.

Yelena tossed her the sword, and with a flick of her hand, she conjured a line of fire blocking her path. Adelina stumbled backwards, clutching the weapon. Her teacher didn't have access to astral magic, so any form of fire magic would take its toll on her.

"What are you doing?" Adelina frowned. "We need to get you out of here."

Through the tall, thrashing flames, Adelina's gaze caught sight of a bunch of arrows in Yelena's hand.

"Filip is inside. He's unconscious, but he won't be out for long—my magic isn't enough to hold him. You need to go. Leave. Now," Yelena said.

"No." Adelina shook her head profusely as she scanned the fire, looking for a way through. She took a step forwards, prepared to walk through it if it meant saving her.

Damir grabbed her arm and pulled her back.

"Get off! We have to help her."

"Adelina," Yelena called, drawing her attention back to her. "I am so proud of you. I know your parents and sister will be too. Thank you…for your determination. And your friendship."

"Wait!" Adelina's scream was drowned by the final explosion.

A blast tore through the building, annihilating the walls. The roof caved in. Fire burst from the ruins, hurtling thick, black smoke into the air.

"Yelena!" Adelina screamed so hard it ripped at her throat.

"Adelina, we need to go." He yanked her away from the fire. "You can't help her."

Tears fell from her eyes as she watched the flames engulf the building with her teacher, Filip, and anyone else who was inside.

With a firm grip on her arms, Damir practically dragged her in the opposite direction.

She swiped the tears from her face as he stitched his fingers together and bent. "Give me your foot. I'm going to hoist you over the wall. We'll head to the stables from there."

Unable to manage any words for fear she might vomit, she nodded. She placed her foot in his hands, and with all his force, she was pushed up towards the top of the wall.

Gripping onto the top bricks, she brought her feet up, then lunged to the ground on the other side. He climbed up. It'd taken him mere seconds to scale it, but it'd felt like an eternity to her as the image of Yelena disappearing in erupting stone, brick, and fire burned in her mind's eye.

When he landed on the grass beside her, he grasped her hands and pulled her to the path. "I know you're going through a lot right now. But I don't know where the stables are. You'll need to lead us there, so we can get a horse, and get the hell out of here."

She nodded, forcing her attention onto her husband. She looked up at him—her eyes wet. But Yelena would not want her to cry for her, she'd want them to get to safety. Otherwise, she would've died for nothing.

"Natasha—She..." Adelina cleared her throat. "I sent her to the stables, so she didn't get caught up in the explosions."

"Then she will be safe," he said.

"The stables aren't far from the barracks," she said, maintaining a tight grip on his hand. If she let go, she feared her legs might give way. "Follow this path."

The route ran parallel with the perimeter of the palace grounds. A few strides ahead and they were at the paddock fence.

"Through here." She pointed to a gate.

They made their way through, hushing towards the stable entrance, when Natasha popped out, towing a horse by the reins behind her.

"Natasha, why are you here?" Adelina gasped. "I told you to get away."

"I didn't want to leave you, miss," she said, wide-eyed. "I made my way here as you ordered, but there were so many explosions. I feared you—"

"I'm fine." Adelina squeezed her shoulder. "Me and my husband are both fine, but you should've gotten out of here. I'm not sure how many of the household staff survived. I haven't seen anyone else."

"What about Yelena?" Natasha asked. Perhaps it was easier to ask about the trainer's life than the lives of the people she'd spent every day working with.

Adelina shook her head—the words lodged in her throat.

"She didn't make it," Damir said. "She brought the barracks down with Filip inside."

"Filip is dead?" Natasha's eyebrows shot skywards.

"There's no reason for us to think otherwise. Nobody could survive that," Damir said. "We should ride to Temauten, but we'll need to stop to hunt. The explosions didn't allow us any time to gather provisions for the journey."

With a sharp nod, Natasha thrust the reins into Adelina's hand.

Shoving her foot into the stirrup, Adelina hoisted herself onto the saddle.

When they were mounted, they galloped along the trail behind the palace, leaving the fiery wreckage behind.

A Ballad of Severed Souls

By the time they'd reached the border of Temauten, a week had passed. There'd been no sign of Filip, no sign of his men.

Adelina bit her bottom lip. If he'd survived the explosion, he would've searched for her. He would've sent men to find her if he were incapable. Perhaps Filip's death marked the end of her and her loved ones' suffering.

When Damir returned to her, he pressed a warm kiss to her temple. "You're frowning."

"I know." She slithered her arm around his waist and held him close. "We're heading home—to Aramoor—and I can't help but think of my sister. I'll see her face everywhere I look."

"Filip is dead. The man responsible for your sister's murder is *dead*," he reminded her. "You can finally put all this behind you. You can grieve with your family, and when it is time, you can live the life you always wanted. With me."

She rubbed her eyes, then dragged her hand around to the back of her neck where she squeezed the muscles. "You're right. I have no reason to doubt he didn't die in the fire. This is it…he's truly gone."

"Yes. It's finally over. We can go home. Together." He lowered his head, pressing his lips against hers. A shot of warmth bolted through her core. She'd missed him—she needed him in every way a wife needed her husband. His touch relieved the ache in her heart, the ever-present pain since her sister's death. The agony reignited with Yelena's sacrifice.

A fire burned in his eyes, giving her the impression he needed her too. Her hands travelled up his chest.

"The fire is lit." Natasha's voice sliced the silence, startling Adelina. "Sorry, miss. I didn't mean to frighten you."

Adelina cleared her throat as she stepped back from Damir. "No, don't be. You should've asked me to light the fire—I *do* have magic."

Natasha smiled. "I don't mind. It's the least I could do."

Returning the smile, Adelina clasped hands with her husband, then walked over to the fire.

He impaled the fish he'd caught earlier on sticks and hung them above the flames on makeshift brackets.

Once they'd eaten, Adelina left him in Natasha's company and headed for the stream. Kneeling beside the water's edge, she cupped her palms and brought the cool contents to her face. She splashed it against her cheeks, forehead, and nose, then breathed in the fresh scent. The chilly water made her shiver, but she didn't mind. She needed to feel *something*, anything besides grief, guilt, and heartache.

Sitting on a boulder, she watched the stream trickle, having flown from some spring in the mountains. The quiet, harmonious sound of crickets soothed her, and the rising moon cast a silver shine across the stream's surface.

Peeling back her sleeve, she inspected the blisters on her arm. They weren't infected or painful, but she hadn't given them a chance to heal. Each time they'd calmed down, more appeared because of her constant use of magic. Having been on the road for the last week without having to use her golden whip, the red tint and the itchiness had subsided.

She rested her forehead in her hands, closed her eyes, and breathed deeply. What she would give to have her sister here, safe with her. What she would give to save Yelena from the fire, and all the innocent people who'd lost their lives in the battles of the past few weeks. All for Filip's desperation to rule. She could only thank the gods he'd perished in the fire—he'd certainly paid the price for his crimes.

Grabbing the Sword of Light from its sheath around her waist, she held it between both hands, the moonlight glinting on the metal surface.

"Hey," Damir said softly as he approached her.

She turned to smile at him over her shoulder.

"What are you doing?" He rested on the boulder beside her.

"Contemplating the use of this sword," she muttered. "If I threw it into the ocean right now, would I really, *truly* miss it? It has been of no use to me so far."

"You didn't have a choice but to hand it over to Filip." Damir drew her against his chest. "Yelena stole it back. You have it. And if you haven't noticed, it's a stream, not an ocean." A hint of humour flickered in his eyes as his smile widened into a grin. One she'd sorely missed.

"You know what I mean. But I guess you're right. Yelena ensured our safety and gave it back to me—its creator." She traced a finger along the inscription on the sword. "It never worked for Filip, you know—not in the way he'd hoped. The sword has a mind of its own. It chooses where its loyalties lie, but it all depends on the wielder's intentions."

"And you *always* have the best intentions at heart." With one arm wrapped around her shoulder, he used his free hand to tuck a loose curl behind her ear. "You'll be with your parents soon, and you can mourn your sister together."

"Some funeral it'll be," she said. "Her body was tossed in a pile with everyone else slain in battle. There'll be a gravestone for her, sure, but she won't rest in the way she deserves."

"I know." He pressed his lips to her forehead. "But believe she is at peace."

The truth was, she couldn't believe it, but she didn't have the strength to think about it. Grateful to have him by her side, she turned, brought both hands up to cup his cheeks, and leaned into him. Her lips met his, warm and soft at first, then moulding into a more urgent kiss. One they'd been deprived of for months.

His hands were in her hair, cradling her head as her lips parted, and his tongue flicked against hers. A light moan escaped her as his sturdy arms enveloped her. He gripped her hips and lifted her, until she straddled him.

Curls tumbled around her face as their kiss deepened. One of his hands slipped up the back of her shirt, pressing against her bare skin, pulling her closer to him.

She rested her forehead against his, and she breathed deeply against him. "As much as I want you, we can't. Not here."

"Why not?" He grinned as he carried her over to a patch of flat stones. With an arm propped either side of her face, he lay on top of her. "The tall grass shields us from Natasha."

"She may not be able to see us, but she will sure as hell *hear* us." She laughed.

"God, I've missed your laugh." His eyes burned with desire.

"I love you, Damir. So much." A fire heated in her cheeks and in her core.

She hadn't noticed her hand bunching the front of his shirt, unwilling to let go.

His mouth was on hers again, then he buried his head in her neck and kissed her there. Gasping, she tilted her chin upwards, eyes closed, encouraging him.

She weaved her hands through his hair as he worked on removing her clothes. A faint clicking sound caught her attention, and her eyes flashed open.

"Damir," she whispered. "Look."

He rolled off her, but kept an arm wrapped around her.

Fireflies. Lots of them. They cast a bright yellow glow over the stream, a vibrant contrast to the rising moon.

"Beautiful," she whispered, and a sudden lump formed in her throat. She didn't know why, but the innocence of the fireflies reminded her of her sister. "She's truly gone."

He pressed her head against his chest and smoothed her hair. "She'd be so proud of you."

She couldn't find the words to speak again. Instead, she held onto him and thought of Tihana and Yelena.

TWENTY-THREE

Unwanted Farewells

The last week of journeying passed slowly until the stone wall surrounding Aramoor came into view amongst the rolling hills of Temauten. As spring transitioned into summer, wildflowers seeded the long grass. Ample sunlight cast a warmth onto Adelina's cheeks, and a slight breeze brushed her hair.

Butterflies and dragonflies flew here and there, along with the flittering of bees from one flower to the next.

Tilting her face towards the sun, she breathed in deeply, and her body relaxed. She was so close to home and the thought of being back where she'd spent her entire life brought her immense comfort.

Birds glided overhead—the gentle flapping of their wings carried on the breeze—and disappeared into the pine trees beyond the village.

A Ballad of Severed Souls

She rode through the entrance of Aramoor with Damir and Natasha close behind. There was an eeriness hanging over the town, like a thick cloud, despite the clear sky. A heaviness perhaps. After all, the nearby town of Murtei *had* been invaded and conquered. She wondered how many locals from Aramoor were caught in the crossfire.

The streets were quiet, even though people went about their daily routines of hanging laundry, shopping at the market, working at the farm and blacksmiths. Passers-by shared nods in greeting, but little words. Her comfort from a few moments ago evaporated. Instead, her heart ached. Not just for her family, but for the entire village—the neighbours she'd known her whole life.

Dismounting, Adelina led her horse by the reins along the cobbled path. "We should take the horses to the stables before we find our parents."

Damir and Natasha followed suit, heading to the paddocks at the back of Aramoor. Once they'd handed the mounts over to the stablemaster, Adelina made way for her childhood home. The walk, which usually took ten minutes, stretched for eternity. She knew what awaited her there—her parents' grief—and she'd crumble because of it.

Falling into step beside her, Damir pressed his hand against her lower back—a small, yet reassuring gesture.

When she reached the front door, she clutched the handle and sucked in a breath. Straightening her shoulders, she opened it and walked inside.

Her mother looked up from her seated position by the stove. It seemed to take a few seconds for Velinka to register the fact her daughter stood in her doorway because her blank expression changed. Her red, puffy eyes widened, and she rose.

"Adelina." Without delay, her mother crossed the space between them and enveloped her in her arms. "My darling daughter."

In Velinka's embrace, Adelina fought not to cry. She needed to be strong for her mother.

"I'm home," is all she could manage before leaning back. "Where is Pa?"

"He's at the shop, burying himself in work." She sighed, then gestured to Damir. "Oh, I'm so glad to see you again."

Damir returned the smile and hugged her.

"And who is this?" Velinka asked, her gaze landing on Natasha.

"This is Natasha. She was my servant at the palace, and I couldn't leave her there." Adelina slid into a chair at the dinner table.

Her mother sat opposite her. "Well, come in, dears. We have a lot to catch up on."

As if they were avoiding the obvious matter of her sister's funeral, they spoke about everything *but* Tihana. The invasions of Pike and Murtei. The explosions at Kirovo Palace. Yelena's sacrifice and Filip's death. When all was spoken, a silence formed between them.

Damir held Adelina's hand the whole time and gave it a gentle squeeze. She glanced at him and shook her head. She couldn't bring the words from her mouth—ones she desperately needed to ask.

"I know this must be hard for you." Damir stroked his thumb across her hand while looking at Velinka. "And if there's anything I can do to help, please let me know. Have any preparations been made for a funeral yet?"

Velinka pressed her lips into a thin line. Drawing a handkerchief from the pocket of her skirt, she dabbed her eyes, then rose. She disappeared into the kitchen, then returned with a tray of glasses and a bottle of vodka.

"If we're going to discuss the death of my youngest child, I'll require something strong to drink." The corner of her lips curved into a sad smile.

"Whatever you need," Damir said softly.

Once she'd poured the drinks and handed one to each of them, she reclined into her chair and drank a large mouthful. "Well, seeing as we don't have her body, we cannot cremate her, as would usually be done."

Adelina grew rigid in her chair, her stomach knotted and churned. If she moved, she might vomit.

Her mother shook her head as fresh tears formed in her eyes. "My daughter will not be present in the oak boat we burn on a stack of wood. Her soul will not make the voyage across the river Smorodina on its way to the afterlife."

Although all she wanted to do was flee the house, escape the grief, Adelina moved her heavy arm, and clasped her mother's hand.

Velinka's gaze met hers.

"I'm sorry, Ma," was all Adelina could manage.

"Perhaps we should make a toast," Damir said—his tone a little lighter than theirs. "To celebrate Tihana's life."

Velinka smiled. "She would like that."

"Should I step outside?" Natasha asked.

"You're more than welcome to stay," Adelina said. "Although you didn't know her, you have been a tremendous help to me."

Natasha shook her head. "When she was in the prison cell with Damir, I should've done something—*anything*—to get her out of there. Perhaps things would've ended differently for her."

"Don't blame yourself," Adelina whispered. "It's not your fault."

She didn't voice the fact she believed it to be *her* fault. The guilt of not being able to save her sister from a fate she in no way deserved would haunt her for the rest of her life. A shame she would carry with her.

Damir stood and cleared his throat, raising his glass. "To Tihana, a wonderful sister and daughter. She was a bright young girl with so much potential, so much joy and enthusiasm for life. I know this because I have seen her grow over the years, and while my sister-in-law is no longer here to say these words, I know she is proud of her family, and she loves you very much."

His gaze met Adelina's, and her heart burst. He'd supported her when she couldn't find the words, nor the strength, and she loved him even more for it.

They clinked their glasses and finished their vodka in silence. Velinka dabbed her eyes again, then rose.

"Thank you, Damir," she said. "I'm sure you'll be wanting to visit your family."

"Yes, although I am surprised to not see them here." He frowned. "I thought they would've been with you."

"Oh, don't worry, dear." She smiled a fraction brighter than before. "Your mother and father have been here every day since Tihana's death. They've been as supportive as can be."

The house was suffocating Adelina. Her lungs constricted. She needed to get out of there.

"I should head over to the shop and see my father," Adelina said. "When we left the palace, we fled with only the clothes on our backs, so I'll want a trip to the bathhouse and the opportunity to change. Natasha, I can show you the way, and you can have some of my clothes."

"I'll come with you," Damir said. "I could do with a wash, too."

She squeezed his hand. "Stay with Ma for me, please? At least until I return."

He nodded, then pressed a kiss to her forehead.

She was out the door quickly, Natasha hot on her heels. "Are you all right, miss?"

Planting her arms on the stone wall, Adelina closed her eyes. "I just…needed some air. I'll come back for our clothes later, okay? I need to see Pa."

Adelina braced herself as she entered the restored workshop. Having not seen her father since the day her sister died, she'd no idea how badly he'd taken it. Her mother had said he'd buried himself in work, which she tried to believe would take his mind off it.

She approached the workbench and leaned over it, trying to catch a glimpse into the back room. Her father sat at a table, holding a portrait of his daughter.

"Pa?" she asked softly. "It's me."

He sniffled and cleared his throat. Setting the portrait down, he walked out to meet her. "Adelina. It's so good to see you."

Hurrying around the side of the workbench, she flung her arms around him and pressed her head to his chest. The familiar scent of excursion and paint clung to his clothes, reminding her of times before she was marked by the sun god. Before everything.

"I'm so sorry, Pa," she choked out. "If I could've done something…if I could've stopped it."

"Shh." He stroked her hair and held her close. "We'll get through this. I'm not sure how, but we are a family. We stick together, and we find a way."

She nodded, blinking rapidly to fight off the fresh tears forming in her eyes. After a deep breath, she let go.

"I'm guessing you've seen your mother?" he said.

"Yes, it was no longer safe for us to stay at the palace. There were explosions and Filip was killed. I didn't want to run anymore, and home was the safest place for us to go."

He pressed his lips into a thin line. "I'm glad you came home. I wouldn't want you out there on the run, especially not after the invasions at Murtei and Pike."

"I was there, Pa." Her voice was small. Even though she knew her father would understand, she couldn't fight the overwhelming shame and guilt flooding through her body.

"I know." His words were no louder than a whisper, but there was a gentleness in his eyes.

Silence formed between them. Unspoken words.

She ran her hand through her hair. "If it's okay, I'd like my bedroom back. Damir and I can live with you until we can secure a place of our own."

"Of course." He smiled, but his chin trembled as if he were holding in a sob. "I'd like to keep you close. For as long as possible."

"Nothing could drag me away." She embraced him again, resting her face against his chest.

"Well, I've finished up here," he said when he let go. "In all honesty, I was here for peace and quiet. My orders have been completed, and I don't start my new job until tomorrow."

"Let's go home," she said.

He nodded.

Together, they headed out of the workshop and along the cobbled path. At the end, Damir wandered towards the Orlov house, and Natasha waited outside.

When Adelina reached her, Natasha smiled—a bag in her arms. "I didn't think it was right to follow you to your father's shop, so I asked your mother for some clothes and the directions to the bathhouse."

"Thank you," Adelina said, accepting the bag. "Truly."

Later that evening, Velinka lit several candles and placed them on the dining room table. Portraits of Tihana, along with a handful of her belongings, were positioned next to them. Adelina sat beside Damir, a glass of vodka in hand. His parents arrived a little earlier with a steaming dish of stew for the family. Mirelle took it upon herself to care for the Orlovs, which Adelina appreciated endlessly.

"Thank you again for the dinner," Velinka said, clutching a blanket wrapped around her shoulders.

"Of course." Mirelle stretched her hand across the table and squeezed Velinka's. "Anything I can do to help you in this difficult time. Now Adelina and Damir are home, you can heal, as a whole family."

Velinka nodded. "I've been thinking about what we should do for Tihana's send off."

Adelina traded glances with Damir and wondered whether their conversation earlier in the morning made it any easier for her mother to come to terms with it.

"I don't want to burn an oak boat—there is no point as her body will not be in it," Velinka said. "Instead, I would like to cover the mirrors and stop the clocks. Her death was not peaceful, and she will be stuck in the living plane for a much longer time than she would've if she'd died of natural causes. Forty days until her soul reaches the afterlife, and there's no way to be sure it will apply to her but observing the traditions might bring us some comfort."

Rising, Adelina made her way around the house, draping fabric over each of the mirrors, and stopping the hands on each clock. When she was done, she returned to the table and shared a drink with her family.

"It is time to say goodbye," she said as Damir drew her close. "And pray to the gods she finds her peace."

"To Tihana." Daro raised his glass. "May she slumber eternally in the arms of gods."

A Ballad of Severed Souls

Damir and Adelina retired to her old bedroom. Several lit candles provided a warm, orange glow. She stared at the fresh bedding.

"It's so strange being here." She rubbed her arms to rid herself of the chill spreading across her, despite the warmer temperatures of the beginning of summer, and the candlelight. "It's like this place is haunted."

"I know." He drew the curtains, then turned back the sheets. "It's better than being at the palace, though. We should get some sleep."

He was right. It definitely *was* better than being in the palace. She was glad she wasn't Natasha, who'd retired to her sister's old room downstairs. The house was suffocating enough, let alone being in a space with Tihana's things.

Making her way over to the wardrobe, she plucked out a nightgown, then stripped out of her shirt and breeches.

"Beautiful," he whispered as he lifted a hand to trace a faint line along her collarbone.

She leaned into his touch, its warmth a welcome relief from the iciness the absence of her sister's presence gave her.

Lowering his head, he pressed his lips to her neck, planting kisses down the length of her throat. His arms enveloped her, holding her close against his chest. Her cheeks flamed as his mouth wandered back to her lips. She welcomed his tongue, which brushed against hers as his hands hooked under her buttocks.

He lifted her off the floor, and she wrapped her legs around him.

Carrying her to the bed, their kiss grew deeper, hungrier, desperate for the need to be joined. They'd gone without intimacy for so long, and to have it again when their hearts ached with loss—it was exactly what she needed to separate her mind from the turmoil of emotions she'd been wrapped up in.

He laid her on the bed, her naked body pressed to his. With her heart pounding, she fumbled for the hem of his shirt. Tossing it over his head, he pressed his mouth to hers, resting one arm above her head, and the other travelling across her breast to her stomach.

The sensation of his touch sent a bolt of warmth through her core, and she closed her eyes, relishing in the relief it gave her.

Slipping out of his breeches, he brought himself back up to her, his mouth finding hers. Their lips touched, and their breaths collided.

As he thrust into her, a light groan escaped his lips. Her hands trailed up his arms until they found their home on his shoulder blades.

"Gods, I love you," he whispered against her neck..

She wrapped her legs around him, holding onto him as he built up speed with each stroke. When they met their crescendo, her whole body trembled. Beads of sweat lined his head, and she was pretty sure one landed on her when he placed a gentle kiss on her cheek, but she didn't care.

As he rolled onto his side, she smiled at him lazily.

Lifting her hand, she stroked the dark hair out of his eyes. She pushed up onto her elbows and kissed him. "I love you, too."

Adelina awoke to Damir's soft, even breathing. Turning on her side, she smiled at him. Sleeping on his stomach, one arm hooked under the pillow, he seemed peaceful.

She pressed a kiss to his forehead, then slipped out of bed. She'd seen her face again—Tihana's—in her dream. It happened almost every night, and she'd grown not to mind. She'd rather see her face in her sleep than forget her altogether.

Drawing her nightgown over her head, she padded over to the windowsill. She peeled back the curtain a fraction, then sat on the ledge. She let the curtain fall back into place, allowing Damir to sleep undisturbed by the bright light of a full moon. Leaning against the wall, she glanced across the moonlit roofs and gleaming cobbled paths.

A low rumbling made her frown. Tilting her chin, she tried to place the sound but couldn't quite put her finger on what was causing it. The rumble deepened, shaking the building, rattling the vase, brushes, and bottles in the bedroom.

Yanking the curtain back, she scanned the bedroom, as if she needed visual proof of what was happening. Before she could move, the vibration sent the vase hurtling off the cabinet, where it crashed on the floorboards.

Damir jolted upright, his eyes wide and alert. "What in the—"

"Something's wrong." She was on her feet, moving over to him in quick strides.

Flinging back the covers, he got out of bed and threw his clothes on—his gaze darting from one wobbling item to the next. Downstairs, a piece of furniture fell, hitting the floor with a loud thud.

Without a knock, her mother burst into her bedroom. "Are you all right?"

"The vase." Adelina's gaze shifted from the broken china back to her mother. "I don't know what's going on."

The tremor intensified, sending Adelina hurtling into the bedframe. Damir almost lost his balance completely, toppling into the chest of drawers. Velinka fell into the door frame, her bedraggled hair flailing into her face.

When the first wave subsided, they scrambled to their feet as Daro made his way into the doorway. "We should get under furniture in case this earthquake intensifies. Adelina, Damir, get under the bed and stay there until I say it's safe to come out."

"Earthquake?" Adelina's mouth dropped open. "We don't *get* earthquakes here."

Damir grabbed her hand and urged her to the bed. He planted a kiss on her head before helping her underneath.

Adelina's hands pressed against the floorboards—her gaze remaining fixed to his bare feet as he made his way around to the other side of the bedroom.

The door slammed closed, indicating her parents were doing the same thing.

Dropping to his stomach, Damir scooted under the bed, his hand slithering between the frame and the back of her neck. "Keep your head down."

"The candles!" She gripped his wrist, unable to fight her rising panic.

"Don't worry." He rolled out and climbed to his feet.

"Damir, *hurry*," was all she could say before a second wave rippled through the house, sounding as if the quake would tear the walls off.

A loud thundering rang from outside as something collapsed—she couldn't tell what.

A few tense and dreadfully long moments later, he returned to his safe position under the frame. Her heart launched itself into her throat and stayed there.

"I've blown out the flames," he said, giving her arm a reassuring squeeze.

From her limited line of sight, she watched as dust rained onto the floor. A portrait positioned on her bedside table rattled, then fell. It landed a few inches away from her, its sudden plummet making her jump.

The roaring sound of the earthquake tearing its way through the village was deafening. She clamped her hands over her ears, squeezed her eyes shut, and focused every ounce of her attention on Damir's soft fingers on her arm.

Peeling back her fingers, she glanced at him.

"*Breathe*," he mouthed.

She nodded, swallowing the urge to scream or run. She'd been through worse, and she'd get through this. A wave of dread flooded her core despite her best efforts. Aramoor *never* experienced earthquakes. In fact, she didn't think one had *ever* been recorded in

Temauten's history. For Saintlandsther and Toichrist, she wasn't sure.

An almighty roar ripped through the air, shattering the window. Large fragments of glass hurtled. Some hit the opposite wall before falling. Her mind spiralled. Were her parents okay? She fought the urge to claw her way out from her safe position and find out for herself.

Damir wrapped her arm around her waist and held her tight against his side. Although he'd kept a relatively calm demeanour in front of her, even *she* could see the concern in his darkening eyes.

Thundering bangs rippled. The building trembled, and she feared it might cave in. She dug her nails into the hardwood floor, gripping on for dear life, as the earthquake hit its crescendo at lightning speed.

Her stomach somersaulted, fearing the surface beneath her would disappear.

"Can you use your magic to calm the earthquake?" Damir asked. "Like you did with the storm?"

She shook her head. "No. I've never seen anything in my books about quakes. Probably because they don't happen here. What if this is Veles' way of getting revenge? I thwarted his plan by killing his emissary."

"It's okay." He rested a reassuring hand on her arm. "We'll get through this. We always do."

The tremor halted. The silence was deafening. Her panting breath even louder. Ears ringing, she glanced at Damir. They listened and waited.

A Ballad of Severed Souls

After a tense and uncertain half an hour, her father hurried into the room. He dropped to the ground, dipping his head under the frame.

"Are you both all right? No injuries?" he said.

"No, we're both fine." Damir scooted out, then helped Adelina to her feet.

Adelina stared at her father, her mouth opening. "Pa, you've cut your head."

"It's only a scratch, dear. Nothing to worry about." He pulled them both into a tight embrace as her mother came skirting around the corner. She, too, embraced them.

"Oh, thank the gods you're both okay." She squeezed them tight, and when she withdrew, she gestured to the floor. "Be careful of all this glass."

Shoving her feet into a pair of shoes, Adelina dashed to the window—the cold night breeze whipping through the broken pane, thrashing her hair out. Damir was at her side in a flash, wrapping a protective arm around her shoulders.

Her hand flew to her mouth. A shriek caught in her throat, and a sickly sensation shot down her spine.

"Dear gods…" he gasped, pulling her even tighter.

Footsteps shuffled behind them as her parents drew closer. Her mother echoed Damir's gasp.

Adelina stood, frozen to the spot, as she stared out at her broken hometown. If she thought the damage the fire had caused to her father's shop was bad, it was no match for the devastation before her. Entire rows of houses were caved in. Some roofs collapsed inwards completely. Her heart fell to the floor somewhere amongst the shards of glass.

Her breath was shaky as she finally blew it out against her trembling hands. Screams rang out. Fire blazed. The village was falling—torn apart by a giant crevasse running straight through. From where she stood, it seemed like the crack was bottomless—a dark shadow emanating from its depths.

A high-pitched shriek grabbed her attention, and her instinct to help kicked in.

"We can't just stand here." She bolted for the wardrobe, grabbing clothes, throwing them on without a care whether or not her parents saw. "There are people out there—our neighbours, friends—who need us. Damir, your parents. Did anyone think to check on Natasha downstairs?"

Before she gave them the chance to answer, she flew down the staircase, climbing over the fallen furniture, and flinging the bedroom door open.

Dropping to her knees, Adelina peered under. Natasha lay under the bed, trembling. "It's all right. You can come out now."

Natasha scooted out, wobbling with fear, as Damir and her parents appeared in the doorway. "Natasha, stay with my parents. I'm going to see who needs help."

"Wait!" Her pa grabbed her by the wrist as she tried to slide past him. "It's too dangerous."

She wrapped her fingers around his hand. "Look at me. I'm strong, remember? I haven't gone through *all* I've gone through for nothing. I'm sure as hell going to do what I can if it means saving innocent people from dying."

Without meaning to use force, she barged past her parents.

Damir was hot on her heels. "I'm coming with you."

Whirling around, she'd wanted to protest, but the determined look in his eyes kept her from objecting. "Grab my sword."

With a nod, Damir dashed upstairs, and a few moments later, returned, wielding the Sword of Light.

She strapped it to her waist and was out the front door. Her gaze darted from one wreck to the next. Civilians shoved their way through the cramped streets, screaming names. She couldn't decipher any of them through the sheer volume.

Shoving into the crowd, she grabbed a hold of the first person. "Are you injured?"

The man shook his head, although his face was covered in mud and dust. "No, but I-I—my daughter." His eyes were wide and rimmed with tears. "I didn't know what to do when the earthquake started. We were already outside, and I-I thought it would be best to seek cover. I t-took her inside the tavern and the whole roof collapsed. I got out, b-but I couldn't find her."

She touched his shoulder lightly. "It's okay. We'll help her. Let's go."

The man elbowed his way through the swarming crowd, heading towards the market and the tavern beyond. He came to an abrupt halt, and she almost slammed into the back of him.

Loose stones and clumps of mud disintegrated from the edge, falling into the chasm.

Damir grabbed a hold of the man and yanked him back.

The three of them stared at the crack, too wide to jump across, and too deep to survive a fall. Endless darkness hid the bottom.

"There's got to be a way around." As she ran parallel with the chasm, someone came charging out of the crowd, freefalling into the deep void. Their screams were swallowed by the shadows.

A yell ripped through her throat. She muffled it by clamping a hand over her mouth. It was *definitely* too wide to jump across. "There are too many people out here and the streets aren't wide enough."

"You help him find his daughter." Damir grabbed her arm, pulling her to a stop. "I'll start filing people out of town. This crack is separating us from the south—only the gods know how long it is—so the only chance they've got is to travel to Saintlandsther or Toichrist."

"Just get everyone *out*," she said. "We'll find somewhere safe to go."

"I'll see you soon." He pressed an urgent kiss to her forehead, then dashed into the crowd.

Forcing herself not to worry about her family or Damir, she returned her attention to the man. "Come on."

She slid her way through the stampeding crowd, keeping a conscious distance from the chasm edge. They came to a halt outside the tavern—once a place bustling with life. The entire right-hand side of the front door had subsided, stone and glass littering the ground. The wooden door was splintered, threatening to buckle under the weight of the ceiling held up by internal beams.

A Ballad of Severed Souls

Instead of trying to open the door and risk the ceiling caving in on top of her, she rushed to the window ledge. Peering in through the broken pane, she conjured a ball of light, which floated ahead. The back end of the building was blocked off by large chunks of stone and fractured beams. Squinting through the dust, she spotted a bed post poking out of the rubble. Nearby, a chest of drawers and a shattered mirror lay, confirming her suspicions most of the upper floor had buckled from impact.

Climbing through the window, she trod across the floorboards, weaving her way between upside down tables and chairs. Half of the bar was crushed underneath the fallen ceiling..

Shadows filled the room, except for the glow of her magic. And even then, it wasn't enough to fully light her path. It was as if a black cloud hung over the whole village, thwarting the moonlight.

The man followed her, taking each step slow.

She didn't even question what exactly had happened to his daughter. If it was *her* sister trapped inside, there was no way she would've left the building without her.

"Yarmilla!" the man called. "Yarmilla! It's your pa."

"Pa!" a faint voice whimpered.

Adelina tilted her head in the direction of the sound.

"Keep talking to me, sweetie," the man encouraged. "We're going to follow your voice. You'll be safe."

"Pa," Yarmilla cried. "My leg."

He hurried forwards, but she put up her arm, blocking him. "Slow down. We'll find her."

"She is *wounded*," he said through clenched teeth—his eyes widening.

"I know." She narrowed her eyes at him. "I'm strong, I've fought in battles, and I have magic to aid me. Let me bring your daughter to you. Stay here while I focus on her."

Reluctantly, the man nodded.

Turning, she edged deeper into the tavern. "Yarmilla, my name is Adelina. I'm going to get you out of here and take you to your pa."

"Okay," the little girl said—her voice barely audible.

The ceiling groaned. Adelina flicked her gaze above her head, then back to the man. "Get out of here. The building might collapse any minute."

"I'm not leaving without my daughter." He remained rooted to the floor.

She sighed, then increased the speed of her shuffling ever so slightly. "Okay, Yarmilla. Keep talking to me. I'll follow your voice until I find you, okay?"

"Is m-my p-pa okay?" Yarmilla asked.

Adelina nodded, even though she knew the girl couldn't see, and followed the sound of her voice. "Yes, he's fine. Can you tell me how old you are?"

"I-I'm nine," she said. "My b-birthday was yesterday."

Swallowing, Adelina's heart twisted. She was the same age as her sister, Tihana.

"Okay, I think I'm close to you now," Adelina said, keeping her voice calm and steady. "What's your favourite colour, Yarmilla?"

"M-my favourite c-colour is yellow," she answered—her voice more distinct, growing closer.

"Not the b-bright y-yellow—that's nasty—but t-the w-warm yellow."

Adelina smiled. "Can you see my light? It's magic. Look up and find the sunlight."

"I can see it!" Yarmilla gasped. "Ow, I t-tried to s-sit, up but my l-leg is bleeding."

"Hold on, sweetie!" her pa called from behind.

Adelina edged through the wrecked furniture, past the caved-in stairwell. Beyond a fallen beam was a small girl—her face covered in dust and blood. A slab of stone lay across her left leg.

Yarmilla's eyes widened as her gaze landed on the golden embroidery around Adelina's wrist. "You really do have magic!"

"Yep." Adelina grinned as she knelt. "This will probably hurt a little, but I'm going to lift this stone off your leg, then use your scarf to stem the blood flow from your wound."

Her bottom lip quivered, but she nodded.

Placing both hands under the stone, she gripped the edge, ground her teeth, and forced all her strength into lifting the two-inch thick slab. Her spine and muscles screamed in protest, but there was no way she was leaving the girl to die there.

"One…" she sucked in a breath with each number, "two…three!"

Straightening her knees, she groaned, then dumped the stone aside. She wasted no time in peeling the scarf from Yarmilla's neck and wrapping it around the deep wound in her thigh and knee.

"It hurts." Fresh tears rolled down her cheeks.

"I know." Adelina shoved one arm around Yarmilla's back, and one under her knees, then hoisted her off the floor.

The ceiling groaned again, this time louder.

"We need to hurry." Adelina thrust the girl into her father's arms, then hurried towards the windowsill.

She climbed through, then held her arms out for the man to pass her his daughter.

Spinning around, she half staggered away from the tavern, Yarmilla safely stowed in her arms. An almighty rumble ripped through the air as the building collapsed.

"Pa!" Yarmilla screamed.

Adelina threw her gaze over her shoulder, scanning the wreckage for the man. Her breath lodged itself in her lungs. He was gone.

TWENTY-FOUR

Salvation

Adelina grasped Yarmilla. "Can you stand?"

Wincing, the girl nodded.

"I'm going to get you to the edge of town," Adelina said, tucking an arm around her. "You'll see my husband, Damir. He will keep you safe."

"What about Pa?" she whimpered as she hobbled along the cobbles.

"He's gone." Adelina swallowed the bile in her throat. "I'm sorry. You're injured, we need to get you out of here."

Yarmilla swatted the tears from her eyes, but she didn't look back.

Dozens of locals sprinted in all directions, fleeing the area as more buildings threatened to buckle. A deafening roar pierced the air, rumbling across the town.

Adelina's gaze darted to the sky. She'd never heard anything like it.

"What was that?" Yarmilla asked.

"I'm not sure." Adelina hurried towards the stone wall, keeping a firm grasp of the girl as they made their way out of Aramoor.

The rolling hills beyond were chaos. Civilians ran through the open. Mothers carried children. Men brought any belongings they'd salvaged.

"Adelina!" Damir called, catching her attention.

"Damir." She rushed to him, pressing a kiss on his cheek before urging the girl towards him. "This is Yarmilla. She's hurt."

"The stablemaster and a few volunteers have grabbed the horses and wagons. Not many survived the earthquake, but the injured are being prioritised. They're to travel to Saintlandsther Highlands as there's no safe route south." Damir hooked his arms under Yarmilla, holding her steady.

"Nowhere is safe." Adelina thrust a hand through her hair. "We don't know the extent of the damage this earthquake has caused. Saintlandsther could be upended too, for all we know."

"We don't have much choice, but the Highlands are the safest option," Damir said. "There are several small towns across the border."

A low-pitch rumble rippled. The ground trembled ferociously.

Adelina shot a glance over her shoulders. Screams rang from Aramoor. "Keep helping the locals. I'm going to find our parents."

Before Damir could respond, she sprinted through the entrance, shoving her way through the packed

A Ballad of Severed Souls

streets. She halted when she reached the front door of the Orlov house, then flung it open.

"Ma!" she shouted as she searched the ground floor. "Pa!"

She turned to the staircase, taking two at a time. In quick strides, she crossed the landing, barging into her parents' room. She found them frantically shoving belongings into bags.

"Adelina!" Velinka squealed. "Are you all right?"

"I'm fine. Come on. We have to get out of here. It's not safe." Adelina grabbed her mother's arm, pulling her towards the door. "And you, Pa."

Her parents were at her side. "Where's Damir?"

"He's fine—he's outside the village, aiding other civilians. It's your turn now." Adelina urged them out of the bedroom and down the stairs. In quick movements, she removed their coats from the peg and shoved them into their arms. "Put these on."

As her parents did so, Natasha flung a small bag over her shoulder.

"Where are we going?" she asked.

"Saintlandsther." Adelina threw the door open. "We need to leave."

Outside, Adelina halted, turning to face her parents and Natasha. "Head out of town. I'll come back to find you when I've gotten Damir's parents."

"We're not leaving you!" Velinka grasped her wrist. "We've already lost one daughter. We won't lose another."

Scream pierced the air as more civilians darted past the house.

"You need to go. *Now!*" Adelina pushed them onto the path. "Go."

Her parents took several steps back, keeping their gaze locked on her, before they turned. Daro held his wife's hand, and they ran to the field beyond.

Swallowing the lump in her throat, she fought to clear her mind. Her parents would be fine. Climbing over the low wall separating the terraced houses, she thumped onto the slab directly outside the Litvin house.

She heaved in the door. "Mirelle, Jasen!"

Darting through the living room, she checked the kitchen, the pantry, and the spare room on the ground floor. When she couldn't find them, she dashed upstairs and searched each bedroom.

Whizzing downstairs, she panted. Her lungs burned, and her heart ached.

Think.

Tapping her foot in a fast rhythm, she considered every possibility of where Damir's parents might be. Then she remembered they had a small basement used to store root vegetables.

In quick strides, she heaved open the door and hurried down the stone steps.

Adrenaline flooded her entire being, and heart palpitations made her chest tingle and tighten. As much as she sucked in air, she couldn't shake the sensation of being smothered.

"Mirelle!" she called. "Jasen!"

She blinked rapidly to rid herself of the spots in her vision.

Calm the hell down. Keep it together.

Her eyes adjusted to the dim lighting in the basement. Onions and potatoes and fallen to the floor, littering it like scattered glass.

"Adelina?" a quiet voice asked.

"Mirelle!" Adelina dashed to Damir's mother, who sat on the floor with her back pressed to the wall. Jasen held her tight to his chest. "Are you hurt?"

"I'm fine," Mirelle said, her eyes wild. "But Jasen—he's got a nasty cut on his arm. When the windows imploded, he threw his arm up to protect me from the glass."

"Are you okay?" Adelina dropped to her knees, quickly assessing the tightly wrapped bandage around Jasen's arm. "We need to leave. Damir and my parents are waiting for us outside Aramoor, but we can't wait any longer. There could be another wave at any moment."

"Yes." He nodded, helping his wife to her feet. "Is our son unharmed?"

"You'll see for yourself." Adelina urged them towards the stairs.

When Adelina hauled open the front door, she gasped. Raging fire licked the walls of buildings. She choked on an inhale of smoke.

"Cover your mouth with your sleeve," she yelled.

The earthquake must've disturbed lit candles, stoves…there'd be no saving Aramoor. Narrowing her gaze on the exit out of the village, she hurried along the cobbled path, keeping her sleeve pressed to her mouth. Every few seconds, she checked over her shoulder to ensure Damir's parents were following.

As they reached the stone wall surrounding the town, a strangled sob escaped Mirelle's mouth as she threw her arms around Damir.

"Oh, thank the gods you're safe," she cried.

"Here. There's enough space on this wagon for you both." Damir offered Mirelle his arm, then helped her up. He faced his father. "Your turn."

With a swift nod, Jasen scrambled into position beside his wife, tucking her against his chest.

"Adelina." Velinka's voice trembled as she reached out her hand.

"There's not enough room." Adelina shook her head. "Damir and I will take a horse."

Instinctively, Damir whirled around. All the wagons had already fled, except this one, and there were only a couple of horses left. They bucked and neighed, despite the stableman's efforts to calm them. A loud groan rumbled from the depths of Aramoor, and another burst of smoke shot into the clouds.

"Adelina." Damir grabbed her hand. "We should take one while they're still here. It's either that or risk getting trapped."

"We'll find you in the Highlands," Adelina said to her parents. "Stay together. We *will* find you. I love you."

"We love you too," her pa said. "Hurry."

Blinking back tears, Adelina rushed to the stableman, who wrestled for the horse's reins. "We'll take this one."

"He's too wild." The stableman shook his head. "The fire—he's out of control."

"Don't worry about the horse!" Damir snapped. "Get yourself *out of here*."

The man shook violently but nodded. Climbing onto the saddle of the remaining mount, he galloped away, joining the sea of fleeing wagons and poor folk on foot.

Heart pounding, Adelina watched as Damir carefully approached the trembling, distressed horse. Tail swishing, hooves pawing the ground, he looked as if he might rear up at Damir at any moment.

A Ballad of Severed Souls

"Be careful," Adelina whispered pointlessly.

"It's all right," Damir said in the gentlest of tones, displaying the palms of his hands. "I'm going to help you, okay? We'll ride away from here, where it'll be safe."

The horse snorted, lashing his neck back. Damir halted.

"You're going to be fine," he said in a soothing manner, then edged closer.

As the horse watched him tentatively, Damir raised his hand as slowly as he could until his fingers touched the reins. He kept his hand there for a few moments, perhaps until he was sure the mount wouldn't buck. "You can come now, Adelina."

Holding her breath, fingers shaking, Adelina approached the saddle. Using the stirrup, she hoisted herself up and took the reins from Damir. When he was seated behind her, she jerked the leathers hard, and they set off in a fast gallop to join the others.

Adelina brought the horse to a sharp halt. From their position in the treeline, she maintained a clear view of the devastation that had befallen her childhood home. Her heart lodged itself in her throat. The fire raged, showing no signs of letting up.

Pressure built in her chest as she struggled to breathe. Her body went numb. She brought a hand to her mouth, and a sudden weakness spread through her limbs. Her pulse quickened as the devastation of the events sunk in. Aramoor was destroyed. She'd no idea how many people survived the earthquake and the fires, and even less of an idea how many of those travelling by foot would reach Saintlandsther.

"Gods," Damir gasped from behind her. His grip around her waist tightened. "We can't stay here."

"I've lost sight of the other wagons." She shook her head as she surveyed the field ahead. "How are we to know where our families are?"

"We'll head north to the mountains. Stick to higher ground until we reach the border, then we'll make our way into the Saintlandsther Highlands," he suggested. "We'll search the villages for our parents when we get there."

"We can't travel too far," she said. "It's the middle of the night."

"Keep riding until we find somewhere to stop," he said. "We're bound to find a suitable place that's not in the open."

Nodding, she encouraged their horse towards the treeline, Aramoor disappearing behind them.

―――

When Adelina and Damir approached an old shack, they dismounted. The sky was black with night—the moon full.

Inside the shack, she paced, running a hand through her hair. Damir rummaged through the dirty sagging cabinets. "There's nothing for us here. I'll have to hunt."

She managed a nod, but her mind was elsewhere. The last thing she could think about was food. Her parents were out there somewhere, and she could think of nothing but being reunited with them. The sooner dawn broke, the better.

As Damir wandered outside, Adelina surveyed their lodgings for the remainder of the night. The ground floor was made up of one room, functioning as what she imagined was once a living space. An old, dusty stove was positioned in the centre of the room, as was tradition. Kneeling beside it, she checked the pine logs left inside. They were dry and suitable for a fire. With a wave of her hand, red and orange flames burst from the wood.

Sitting in a tattered chair, she scooted closer to the fire and prayed to any god who'd listen. Prayed for her parents—and Damir's—safety and health.

When Damir walked through the door an hour later with a rabbit in hand, she was still unsettled, tapping her fingers against her thighs. Her stomach rumbled, and she doubted she'd get much sleep.

They'd barely salvaged anything from their home, except her swords, a small bag containing her grandfather's pocket watch, and a single change of clothes for each of them.

She tried not to grimace as Damir set the rabbit on the kitchen side and used an old blade to sever the skin and fur from the flesh.

"I'm going to check what was left in the saddlebag—if anything," she said, heading for the door.

Outside, she sucked in cool, fresh air. It didn't do much to quell her unease. When she reached the horse, she ran a hand down his hide, which seemed to soothe him. She unclasped the bag and withdrew a flask, a map, and a tattered blanket. No food. No money. It would have to do.

Returning to the shack, she showed Damir what she'd found. "Something to keep us warm through the night—barely."

"You'll have me," he said, with a warmth in his eyes.

"Yes," she said, taking comfort from his words.

The following morning, Adelina and Damir were on their way to the border, leaving the shack behind them. They kept a steady pace, stopping only to hunt, water the horse, and refill their flask.

They travelled through villages, searching for any sign of their parents and the civilians who'd fled Aramoor. There were none.

Another week passed as Adelina and Damir rode farther east towards the Saintlandsther border. They kept close to the edge of the mountain range, pausing outside the perimeter of a small town nestled against the backdrop of the steep cliffside.

"We should look for a vendor," Adelina said. "I have my grandfather's pocket watch. I'll sell it."

"Are you sure?" Damir drew his bottom lip between his teeth. "I'm sorry. I know it's an heirloom."

She shrugged a shoulder and didn't tell him the thought of parting with it made her heart pang. "Needs must."

A Ballad of Severed Souls

They set off on a gentle ride through the village entrance. Smoke plumed from the blacksmiths, a stableman raked hay for the horses, and a middle-aged woman holding a basket plucked berries off bushes.

Shutters were open and windows were ajar, letting fresh air into houses and shops. Children skipped, women hung out laundry to dry in the summer sun, men tended to household maintenance. Folk filled the cobbled streets, streaming into the market ahead.

As they dismounted the horse, she kept a hold of the reins. Damir fell into step beside her, a protective hand pressed to the small of her back. She focused her gaze on the market stalls ahead, weaving between locals who strolled the cobbled path.

Coming to a stop, she rummaged in her bag and withdrew the pocket watch. She handed it to him, keeping her chin held high.

He placed a brief yet warm kiss on her temple before leading the way through the market. The wooden counter of a stall in the centre was lined with trinkets, jewellery, and leather goods. Damir approached the vendor, planting his most pleasant smile on his face.

"How much for this, sir?" Damir offered the man the pocket watch.

The man readjusted his spectacles, then accepted the item, turning it over in his hands. "Why, this is a fine timepiece indeed. Where did you find such a thing?"

"Family heirloom," Damir said.

The vendor nodded and exchanged a pouch of ruble for the timepiece.

Damir opened the pouch and checked the amount. His eyebrows rose. "A handsome price."

"A handsome price for a handsome piece," the man chimed. "Good day to you, sir."

With a nod of farewell, Damir slipped the pouch in his pocket, placed his hand on Adelina's back, and they were on their way.

When they finally reach the border of Saintlandsther, another week had gone by, and still no sightings of their parents or those who'd fled Aramoor. Filtering into the country from the north, they eventually reached the edge of the slums—the country was known for its poverty. The houses were old, weather-beaten, and appeared as if they would fall down with the faintest gust of wind.

Damir led Adelina and the horse to a crooked tavern. Its roof tiles were rusted, chipped, and some were missing altogether. The windows were dirty, and some were cracked. Outside, bags of rubbish were stacked against the fence.

Adelina tethered the horse to a damp post, then followed Damir through the creaking door. The reek of stale beer hit them like thick fog. She wrinkled her nose as he led her to a quiet table in the corner of the room.

The tavern's clientele was…interesting. Burly men with long black cloaks. Some wore masks, and she doubted it was to keep them from inhaling the stench.

Grimacing, she slid onto a chair. Damir dropped their bags by their feet.

"Can you get me a drink? Water, please," she said.

Nodding, he left the table and headed to the bar. A few moments later, he was in conversation with the barman, their mouths moving more than the few words to order a drink would require.

When he returned, she leaned forward. "Did you learn something?"

"Well, I asked him if he'd lived here a long time, and he said all his life. I told him we escaped the earthquake that devastated Aramoor, then asked if he'd seen anyone new in town recently."

"And?" Her breath hitched at the possibility of their parents being somewhere nearby.

He leaned across the table, took her hand in his, and squeezed. A reassuring smile spread across his mouth. "Three days ago, wagons were sighted entering the village. The barman said they were looking for somewhere to stay, but without enough money, they couldn't afford lodgings, and this place is already overflowing with the homeless. He said the wagons headed east, to a meadow beyond this village. And he called it the Heart of the Highlands."

"What else?" Adelina whispered, her heart soaring.

"Apparently, the governor who oversees this place has offered to provide basic necessities for them to set up a camp. Until everyone is back on their feet, of course." Damir stroked his thumb across her hand. "Wagons of tents, food, medicinal supplies, even spare bedding and clothes were taken to the meadow as a gesture of goodwill to the folk who survived the earthquake."

"We've found them." Tears formed in Adelina's eyes.

"Yes." He laughed, his own eyes glistening. "We have."

***

The next morning, Adelina and Damir rode east, towards the meadow they'd surely find. The Heart of the Highlands, the barman had called it. And she could understand why. Immeasurable beauty stretched out like a blanket draped across rolling hills. Long grass was seeded with wildflowers, sunlight drenching it, and tall trees surrounded the meadow. Leaves had turned a burned shade of orange, some drifting to the ground. Butterflies and dragonflies flew about, reminding her of springtime in Aramoor, where there was an abundance of them.

Grass swished in a gentle yet cold wind rippling across the highlands. She hunched her shoulders a fraction, raising the collar of her fur cloak to cover her neck.

"They must be somewhere close," Damir said from his position on the saddle behind her.

"I believe they are," she said in a light voice as she listened closely. Water trickled over rocks in a nearby creek—at least her family and the other survivors would have a source of freshwater—and somewhere in the distance, voices. "I can hear them."

"Keep going," Damir urged, his voice laced with anticipation.

A Ballad of Severed Souls

Shaking her reins, she encouraged her horse along the narrow trail through the tall grass. The scent of clean air and sweet flowers filled her nose as they made their way to the peak of a hill. Her mouth opened, and her heart pounded. Ahead of them, in a sweeping valley nestled between mountains, were possibly a *hundred* tents, their white tops dotting the fields.

Adrenaline pumped through her veins at the sight. Had so many people really survived the earthquake—her neighbours, people she'd known her whole life? Another wave of emotion hit her, but she held back tears. She wouldn't weep.

Riding down the slope into the valley, they made their way through smaller tents, what she could gather were residential, then passed larger ones. Giant pots were positioned on top of fires, the scent of earthy broths twirling into the air on steam. Large racks held meat up to cure, and a workbench had been set up for carving. A man was already busy with skinning and cutting up a deer, while another table nearby was covered in a dusting of flour. A woman stood over it, kneading dough.

As they navigated their way through the sea of tents and busy locals, she kept her eyes peeled for someone she might recognise. They veered past wagons stacked with blankets and what she presumed were bags of grains. Several men were unloading the goods and piling them on the ground.

"Can you see them?" Adelina glanced over her shoulder at Damir.

"Not yet," he said. "Keep going."

They weaved their way through the bustling camp until a voice called out.

"Miss Orlova!" an all too familiar voice said. "Oh, thank the gods you are okay."

Adelina turned to face Natasha, a wide smile spread across her mouth. Her apron was dirty, and her sleeves were rolled up to her elbows.

Jumping down from her saddle, Adelina threw her arms around Natasha's shoulders, bringing her into a tight embrace. "It's so good to see you."

"And you, miss." Natasha beamed.

"Do you know where my parents are?" Adelina took Natasha's hands in hers. "Can you take me to them?"

"Oh, of course!" Natasha's eyebrows skyrocketed. "You'll be glad to know they're quite fine. They are also in the company of one Mirelle Litvin and one Jasen Litvin. Damir's parents, I presume?"

Adelina spun to face her husband as he slid down from the saddle.

"Are you sure?" he said on an intake of breath.

"I'm definitely sure." Natasha gestured for them to follow as she set off at a quick pace. "They've got a little girl in their company, too."

Adelina traded glances with her husband. Holding hands, they kept up with Natasha as she rounded a corner.

"Here. Tether your horse to the post. This is where we keep them." Natasha pointed to a space of flat grass, dozens of posts poking out from the mud.

Fingers trembling with excitement, Adelina fastened the reins to the post, took their bags from the saddle, then returned her attention to Natasha.

"I found your parents not too long after arriving here," Natasha said. "Most of the tents hadn't even been erected by that point, so I managed to secure one close by."

Natasha came to a halt in front of draping canvas flaps. "Are you ready?"

Nodding, Adelina's heart lodged itself in her throat, and she held her breath as Natasha pulled back the fabric.

Inside, there wasn't much beyond the necessities: blankets, a wooden table, bags. And her mother.

A sob broke from Velinka's mouth when her eyes fell upon Adelina.

Abandoning her knitting—*knitting?*—Velinka dashed to Adelina and crushed her to her chest. "Oh, my sweet girl. It's been *weeks*. We had no idea what had happened to you, and all sorts of dreadful thoughts went through my mind, but your pa and I, we refused to believe anything bad had befallen you. We had faith you'd return to us."

"And we did." Adelina clung to her mother, breathing in the lingering scent of rosemary clinging to her skin.

"Where's Pa?" Adelina asked, finally letting go.

"Oh, don't worry, dear, he'll be along any minute." Velinka wiped the tears from her eyes. "He's been out this morning collecting logs and such for the fires. I've not long returned from a shift with the bakers—there's no way I'm allowing our famous rosemary twist to turn into a distant memory—and I've taken up knitting, can you believe it? Salma is here too—she's been teaching me the basics of garment making. We've got to do what we can here."

"You seem...happy," Adelina said rather pointlessly as she observed the mild crinkles around her mother's lips and the glint in her eyes. "Considering."

"Well." Velinka cleared her throat as she wiped her already clean hands on her skirt. "It's been a challenging few weeks, but we're fortunate to have survived. We've all come together to make the most of what we have, and the local governors have been most generous with their supply wagons."

"It's good to see you again." Damir pressed a kiss to Velinka's cheek by way of greeting. "And my parents—they're fine, too?"

"Oh, yes." Velinka beamed. "They have the tent two down from ours."

"I'll take you to them," Natasha said, beckoning him outside.

Before he left, he took Adelina's face in both of his hands and kissed her. "We're going to be okay."

She closed her eyes, resting her forehead against his. "I know."

He slipped outside, leaving her with her mother.

Moments later, Daro bundled in through the tent, his arms covered in dirt, but a grin on his face. And behind him, a little girl followed.

Adelina frowned. "*Yarmilla?*"

The girl's eyes widened. "Adelina!"

Her pa came to an abrupt halt, his gaze locking on Adelina's.

"Hey, Pa," Adelina said, her heart soaring.

Within two long strides, he had her nestled against his chest, his hand cradling the back of her head. "Oh, my daughter."

When he let go, his eyes were red and puffy. "Your mother and I were *sick* with worry. But the

A Ballad of Severed Souls

gods have been kind. And Damir! I crossed paths with him outside."

Adelina smiled, warmth enveloping her like a thick blanket. "Natasha took him to see his parents. Yarmilla, you seem to have recovered well." Adelina scanned the young girl she'd saved from the collapsing building. She had no limp, which suggested her wound had healed without infection.

"Your ma found some herbs to treat my leg," she said. "She tended to me on the way here. They've let me stay with them, since my pa didn't make it." She sniffled, dragging her sleeve across her nose.

"Of course." Adelina's voice came out quieter than she'd planned. There was something about the little girl, likely close in age to her sister, that reminded her of Tihana. Perhaps the button nose and large, round eyes.

"It's not much." Velinka gestured to the bundles of blankets. "But it's enough. Why don't you find Damir? I'll see if there's a spare tent nearby for the both of you while these two get cleaned up. This section was one of the first to be erected, but I'll see what I can do."

"Thanks, Ma," Adelina said. "Truly."

Velinka placed her hand on Adelina's cheek. "Anything for you, my darling."

She headed outside, and Adelina followed, leaving her pa and little Yarmilla to change for supper.

It didn't take Adelina long to find her husband in an embrace with both of his parents, tears streaming from their eyes. She went to them and thanked all the gods for lighting her way back to them. Back to them all. Back home.

Acknowledgements

Thank you to my editor, Jodi Christensen, for your thorough attention to detail, your kind words of encouragement, and friendship. You are so valued.

Thank you to my Street Team for being so passionate about spreading the work of this book and my other works. You're the best!

An extra special thank you to my family, for their continued support and love.

Josh, you've always been in my corner, and I'm eternally grateful for our late-night brainstorming sessions, and your genuine interest.

Abel, my little one, thank you for changing my world.

BY THIS AUTHOR

The Ancient Spells Trilogy

Crimson Kiss

Severance of Minds

Printed in Great Britain
by Amazon